THE COMPLETE

COWBOY
R E A D E R

REMEMBERING THE OPEN RANGE

THE COMPLETE

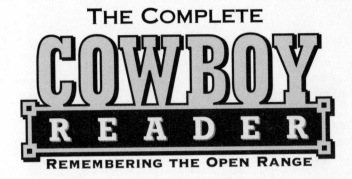

COWBOY
READER

REMEMBERING THE OPEN RANGE

EDITED BY TED STONE

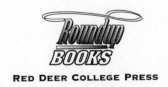

Roundup
BOOKS

RED DEER COLLEGE PRESS

The Publishers
Red Deer College Press
56 Avenue & 32 Street Box 5005
Red Deer Alberta Canada T4N 5H5

Credits
Cover art and design by Parkland Illustrators.
Text design by Dennis Johnson.
Printed and bound in Canada by Webcom Limited for Red Deer
College Press.
Special thanks to Boldface Technologies.

Acknowledgments
Financial support provided by the Alberta Foundation for the Arts, a benefi-
ciary of the Lottery Fund of the Government of Alberta, and by the Canada
Council, the Department of Canadian Heritage and Red Deer College.

COMMITTED TO THE DEVELOPMENT OF CULTURE AND THE ARTS

THE CANADA COUNCIL | LE CONSEIL DES ARTS
FOR THE ARTS | DU CANADA
SINCE 1957 | DEPUIS 1957

Canadian Cataloguing in Publication Data
The complete cowboy reader
(Roundup books)
ISBN 0-88995-169-1
 1. Cowboys. 2. Ranch life—North America—History. I. Stone,
Ted, 1947- II. Series: Roundup books (Red Deer, Alta.)
F596.C65 1997   636.2'13097   C97-910531-5

5 4 3 2 1

Contents

Introduction • *11*

Home On The Range • *13*

The Cowboy • *20*
by Emerson Hough

The Beginning of Cattle Stealing in Texas • *29*
by W.S. James

Shanghai Pierce and the Flapjacks • *37*
by J. Frank Dobie

Some Glimpses into Ranch Life • *46*
by Frank S. Hastings

The Cattle Country of the Far West • *51*
by Theodore Roosevelt

The Cattle Business • *73*
by Granville Stuart

What the Cowboy Wore • *88*
by Philip Ashton Rollins

Style on the Ranch • *102*
by W.S. James

On a Tare in Wichita, Kansas • *117*
by Charles Siringo

Old Gran'pa • *124*
by Frank S. Hastings

Roundups and Cattle Drives • *133*

A Start Up the Chisholm Trail • *140*
by Charles Siringo

The Killing of Oliver Loving • *145*
by Charles Goodnight

Abilene in 1868 • *150*
by Joseph G. McCoy

Thorns an Inch Long • *158*
by E.C. "Teddy Blue" Abbott and Helena Hunt Smith

Coming Off the Trail in '82 • *165*
by Jack Potter

A Boggy Ford • *176*
by Andy Adams

The Round-Up • *188*
by Theodore Roosevelt

The Drive • *213*
by Stewart Edward White

The End and the Myth • *231*

End of the Cattle Range • *235*
by Granville Stuart

"When You Call Me That, Smile!" • *245*
by Owen Wister

Bibliography • *261*

Acknowledgments

"Thorns an Inch Long," from *We Pointed Them North* by E.C. Abbott and Helena H. Smith is used with the permission of the University of Oklahoma Press.

"Shanghai Pierce and the Flapjacks" is taken from *Cow People.* Copyright © by J. Frank Dobie, by permission of Little Brown and Company.

"What the Cowboy Wore" is reprinted with the permission of Scribner, a division of Simon & Schuster, from *The Cowboy,* revised edition by Philip Ashton Rollins, copyright © 1922, 1936 by Charles Scribners & Sons, copyrights renewed 1950 by Philip Ashton Rollins and 1964 by Chemical Corn Exchange.

"The Cattle Business" and "The End of the Cattle Range" are from *Forty Years on the Frontier* by Granville Stuart, reprinted with the permission of the Arthur H. Clark Co.

"The Killing of Oliver Loving" by Charles Goodnight and "Coming Off the Trail in '82" by Jack Potter are from *The Trail Drivers of Texas* by Manrin Hunter, reprinted with the permission of the University of Texas Press.

THE COMPLETE
COWBOY READER

REMEMBERING THE OPEN RANGE

EDITOR'S NOTE:
To acknowledge the historical significance of writing styles reproduced in this collection, all originally published spellings, punctuation and grammar have been preserved.

Introduction

*F*OR MOST OF US, *even as we near the year 2000, images of nine-teenth-century cowboys come easily to mind: cowboys rescuing greenhorn easterners, cowboys saving beautiful young women from runaway horses and cattle stampedes, cowboys protecting home-steading families, or even whole towns, from evil and powerful des-peradoes. Somewhat paradoxically, we might even imagine a fun-loving young cowboy, fresh from the trail, drinking and dancing and perhaps shooting off his gun in a rowdy cow town saloon. No matter how we see our cowboy, however, we've seen more than enough cow-boy movies to know that he will soon ride off toward the setting sun to live a solitary life out on the range. Only occasionally will he return to town to whoop it up in a frontier saloon or bashfully court the local schoolmarm.*

Images of the stoic, super-heroic cowboy in books, movies and television shows have become so firmly established in the mythology of the American people and people around the world that the myth of the cowboy now pales the reality. The mythical cowboy on horse-back, six-shooter in hand, has become a North American knight of the round table, larger than life, more enduring than historical truth.

But accurate accounts of cowboy life also exist, many of them written by early cowboys and ranchers themselves. Histories, auto-biographies, novels and poems abound, all composed by men who helped make the cow queen of the plains. Scholars and professional writers of various stripes have contributed mightily to the literature of the cowboy, but it's hard to imagine any other working-class occu-pation where the people involved contributed so much to the telling of their own story as did cowboys and ranchers.

The cowboy, as the famed southwest historian and one-time rancher J. Frank Dobie pointed out, was essentially a hired man on horseback, a working stiff collecting a paycheck like countless oth-ers. Yet cowboys, to an extent unheard of in most other occupations, wrote copiously about their life and work. No similar amount of material came from the pens of nineteenth-century factory workers, sailors, farm hands or teamsters. But cowboys in surprising numbers put pen to paper and wrote about the life they lived.

Despite the large numbers of well-educated men from the East and even Europe who were attracted to cowboy life, the abundant supply of first-hand accounts of nineteenth-century ranching doesn't necessarily indicate cowboys were more literate than any other group of workers of that time. Instead, the cowboy's propensity to make his own literature suggests that from the beginning, he knew he was involved in something special, something grand and wonderful that had to be recorded and perhaps even celebrated.

In The Complete Cowboy Reader *you'll find some of the best of this material. The first section of the book looks at the cowboy's life and work: how the cowboy worked, what he wore, what life on an open-range ranch was like. The second section deals specifically with roundups and cattle drives, the two most heralded undertakings of the cowboy occupation. The last section of the book gives a brief account of the final days of the open range and, with a chapter from Owen Wister's* The Virginian, *a look at the development of the romanticized twentieth-century view of the cowboy.*

With the exception of Wister's selection in this last section, all the accounts found here are from the pens of men who were involved in some way—whether as rancher or cowboy—in the cattle business of the West. With the exception of J. Frank Dobie, who was born into a Texas ranch family at the tail end of the open range (and who probably learned and wrote more about the early days of Texas ranching than anyone else), all can speak first-hand about cowboying in the nineteenth-century. Their words, despite their occasionally self-serving nature, speak to today's reader with immediacy and authenticity. The selections tell of ranching in the days before barbed wire, dryland farmers and interventionist governments. They assemble a history of the open range more enduring than most because its truth speaks with the no-nonsense authority of men who were there.

HOME ON THE RANGE

*A*FTER THE CIVIL WAR, *a new type of cattle industry emerged on the North American Plains. The distinguishing feature of this new industry was that the herdsmen tended their cattle on horseback instead of on foot the way men generally raised cattle in the East. The geography of the plains, the immense size of the new ranches and the temperament of the semi-wild Texas cattle initially stocked in the West demanded this change in technique. In the early West, a man on foot was almost useless, and if anywhere near a longhorn steer, he was probably in physical danger as well.*

The new style husbandry that developed under these conditions created a new and distinct culture on the North American Plains, a culture of the rancher and cowboy. This unique society of the wide-open spaces emerged from Texas immediately after the Civil War and quickly spread across the Great Plains. But it didn't spring complete from the soil of the southern plains. Its roots spread farther back to Spain and the spread of Spanish cattle in the Americas.

The first Texas cowboys, after all, were the Mexican vaqueros, *who had been developing specialized techniques for raising cattle in North America for generations before the first Anglo-American cowboy ever branded a Texas cow. Later, when English-speaking settlers began to arrive in Texas, they learned to tend their cattle by copying the methods used by their Spanish-speaking neighbors.*

Today, the influence of the early Spanish ranchers and cowboys can still be seen in the equipment and methods of cattle ranching found throughout the North American West. Even the working language of today's cattle or horse ranch is laced with words developed from the original Spanish terms: rodeo, buckaroo, chaps, lariat, lasso, latigo, remuda, *even the word* ranch *itself, come to us as anglicized versions of the original Spanish.*

Columbus brought the first Spanish cattle to the Americas on his second voyage to the New World. Within thirty years herds had been established in Santo Domingo, Cuba and Mexico. Soon, cattle began to spread throughout the Americas as more herds were established and feral populations developed from the strays. It's hard to imagine any animal, introduced to a new continent, that could have adapted better to a new environment than these early Spanish cattle. The animals flourished here to an even greater extent than horses, which also developed feral populations after being brought to the New World by early Spanish colonizers. With no natural predators the Spanish cattle—stray and domestic—thrived in the Americas, thrived to such an extent that by the late 1500s feral cattle roamed Mexico by the thousands.

By the early 1700s, when extensive ranching operations first came to Texas on the Spanish colony's northern frontier, wild cattle could already be found north of the Rio Grande. These wild herds thrived along the southern rivers and in the latter part of the century substantially increased their numbers when Comanches drove off most of the early Spanish ranchers. Already suffering economically from lack of markets for their cattle, these early ranchers, retreating from the Indians into the Mexican heartland, simply abandoned their huge herds on the Texas plains. These animals, thriving on Texas grass, soon joined the ranks of the feral cattle already roaming the territory.

By the 1820s, when the first Anglo-American settlers arrived in Texas, great numbers of wild cattle roamed the countryside as far north as the Nueces River and in smaller numbers ranged all the way to the Red. Nobody knows how many cattle were in Texas during the early period of American settlement, but it has been reported that three million head of stock, including sheep, goats, horses and (presumably mostly wild) cattle were in the region in 1835.

Most of the new immigrants thought the Texas cattle were indigenous to North America, a breed apart from the domestic cow, as wild as the buffalo and just as ornery. These immigrants treated the wild cattle as game animals, hunting them for food as if they were deer or antelope. Reportedly, the cattle were even more elusive than the native game, and by all accounts they were more dangerous. A wounded animal usually charged the horseback hunter, and if given the chance, gored his mount, sometimes ramming a long horn all the way through the animal's body.

Not surprisingly, the disagreeable disposition of the wild cattle made them extremely hard to domesticate. According to all reports they were much harder to tame than mustang horses. With horns that averaged five feet in length wild cattle almost always charged anyone caught on foot within striking distance. Still, early ranchers began to brand and stock their ranges with the animals, along with additional cattle brought in from the East or obtained from the remaining Spanish ranches.

In the years leading up to the Civil War, Texas cows began to take on some characteristics distinct from their Mexican cousins south of the Rio Grande. Gradually, they evolved into the heavier, longer-legged and longer-horned cattle we've come to know today as Texas longhorns. By the end of the war at least five million of these cattle roamed the country from the Brazos to the Rio Grande.

In post-war Texas, cash was almost nonexistent. For cattle ranchers one of the few opportunities for earning any was to drive their cattle, along with whatever wild stock they could roundup and brand, to wherever a market could be found. Often, as pointed out in W.S. James's "The Beginning of Cattle Stealing in Texas," the cattle rounded up were not without other claims of ownership. In more than a few cases, the cattle in question were the unbranded offspring from private, already branded herds. In cash-poor, cow-rich Texas, however, the actual ownership of any cattle rounded up mattered little. For the most part, in the early years, a brand and the will to drive a steer to market was all the title needed. Some of the herds were actually rounded up and stolen from Mexican ranches south of the border and then driven north, sometimes as far as Canada.

Even before the Civil War, a few Texas cattlemen started driving herds far to the east, north and west, searching for profitable markets. As early as the 1840s, small herds had been driven through the swamps of Louisiana all the way to New Orleans. In 1846 a Texas drover named Edward Piper pushed a thousand head of cattle all the way to Ohio. After gold was discovered in California, other Texas drovers undertook to drive cattle west to the gold fields. More went to the new mining districts in Colorado. In the 1850s several Texas herds were driven north as far as Chicago.

After the Civil War several events combined to make driving Texas cattle to distant markets more profitable. In the first place, cattle, neglected and left to run wild through the long years of the war, had exploded in numbers. There were lots of them and they were cheap. Thousands upon thousands, in fact, were free for the taking. Just as many were rounded up indiscriminately and taken to northern markets with no regard given to who the legitimate owner might be.

During this time, with meat supplies depleted by the war, eastern Americans, who had until then always shown a preference for pork, suddenly started to eat more beef. The new demand for beef came just as the eastern railroads began to penetrate the land west of the Mississippi River. By 1867 the Union Pacific had completed the first transcontinental railroad, and other railroads were already nosing their way across the Mississippi, past existing frontier settlements into the Central Plains. Texas cattle, worth two to five dollars at home, if you could find a buyer, suddenly brought several times that amount at any point on a railroad where they could be safely shipped to eastern packers.

Dozens of struggling Texas cattlemen like Abel Head "Shanghai" Pierce, who J. Frank Dobie profiles in "Shanghai Pierce and the Flapjacks," soon began driving their cattle—or at least cattle they branded and claimed as their own—out of Texas, looking for northern markets. For many early drovers their efforts brought financial ruin; others, like Pierce, became more than just wealthy—they became the new barons of an emerging cattle kingdom.

Drovers of the first cattle herds moving out of Texas after the war were simply searching for a place where the animals could be marketed profitably. For the most part this meant a shipping point in Missouri or eastern Kansas, where the cattle could be transported to St. Louis. These first cattle drives however were plagued with problems, for the route required leaving the empty, grass-covered plains to cross into settled areas farther east. Here, Texas drovers were often met by angry farmers and vigilantes, intent on keeping what they thought were cattle infected with Texas fever away from their own small herds. The farmers also figured correctly that the Texas herds would drive down the value of their own stock.

The Texas drovers were also met by outright cattle thieves. Bandits practiced a rather standard method of robbery in eastern Kansas and Missouri. They would stampede a herd of cattle at night, driving them as far as possible from the drovers into some hiding spot, and then show up the next morning to offer their services in rounding up the lost animals. If the price paid was high enough, the cattle would be returned, if not; they would be left hidden and later sold to buyers farther east.

By 1868, however, Abilene, Kansas, had become firmly established as the first great shipping point for Texas longhorns and a pattern for filling the Great Plains with cattle took shape. Within fifteen more years, nearly the whole of the plains, from the Rio Grande to the Bow River would be claimed by the rancher and cowboy. Almost from the first, when cattle driven north from Texas were turned out on the prairie grass around Abilene, it was clear that northern grass was just as good and perhaps even better for raising cattle than the grass back in Texas. As the buffalo disappeared and the Indians were confined to reservations, the Texas longhorn was sent north to stock the empty ranges of Kansas, Nebraska, Wyoming, Montana and the Dakotas.

The era of the cowboy had arrived. Men on horseback, tending huge herds of cattle, made themselves masters of the Great Plains, a region larger than almost every sovereign nation in the world. Cattlemen were kings and cowboys claimed one of the most prominent and prestigious occupations in the territory. The fact that cowboying was usually monotonous and sometimes pure drudgery—as well as one of the few jobs available in the territory—mattered not at all. Cowboys literally rode proud wherever they went. As Emerson Hough, once a cowboy himself, says in this book's first selection, "There was no prouder soul on earth than the cowboy." Frank Hastings documents something of what life was like on the new ranches of the West in "Some Glimpses Into Ranch Life," taken from his book The Story of the S.M.S. Ranch. *In another selection, "Old Gran'pa" from Hastings'* A Ranchman's Recollections, *he describes how a teenage boy grew into a respected cowboy living and working on the open range.*

The cowboy's job seemed almost as natural to plains life as the Indian buffalo hunters'. A cowboy worked outdoors, living almost constantly under the prairie sky. He was an employee, but he was freer than the rancher or ranch manager who hired him. After all, if a cowboy failed to get along with the boss, he quit and rode away to take a similar job with a neighboring outfit, or if he took the notion, he rode to an outfit hundreds of miles away in another territory. The rancher was always tied to his ranch, but a cowboy, as demonstrated in Charles Siringo's account of the aftermath of a little "tare" in Wichita, could be as nomadic and free as the Indian. The cowboy held a demanding, low-paying, often dirty, mostly unglamorous and sometimes dangerous job, but—though fiercely loyal to his employer while on the payroll—he was always his own man.

The era of the free-living cowboy, however, turned out to be amazingly brief. The same economic forces that made cowboy life possible were from the beginning relentlessly bringing the days of open-range ranching to a close. Industrialization that brought the railroad and made it possible to ship cattle east soon brought barbed-wire fences and homesteaders. Business cycles that spurred the cattle boom of the early 1880s turned as naturally to the bust economy of 1887. By the fall of 1886, when Theodore Roosevelt wrote his accounts of cowboy life, the end of the open range, as Roosevelt feared, already loomed on the horizon. By the following spring, it was clear that the final days of the open-range cowboy had arrived.

The Cowboy

– by –
Emerson Hough

THE GREAT WEST, vast and rude, brought forth men also vast and rude. We pass today over parts of that matchless region, and we see the red hills and ragged mountain-fronts cut and crushed into huge indefinite shapes, to which even a small imagination may give a human or more than human form. It would almost seem that the same great hand which chiseled out these monumental forms had also laid its fingers upon the people of this region and fashioned them rude and ironlike, in harmony with the stern faces set about them.

Of all the babes of that primeval mother, the West, the cowboy was perhaps her dearest because he was her last. Some of her children lived for centuries; this one for not a triple decade before he began to be old. What was really the life of this child of the wild region of America, and what were the conditions of the experience that bore him, can never be fully known by those who have not seen the West with wide eyes—for the cowboy was simply a part of the West. He who does not understand the one can never understand the other.

If we care truly to see the cowboy as he was and seek to give our wish the dignity of a real purpose, we should study him in connection with his surroundings and in relation to his work. Then we shall see him not as a curiosity but as a product—not as an eccentric driver of horned cattle but as a man suited to his times.

Large tracts of that domain where once the cowboy reigned supreme have been turned into farms by the irrigator's ditch or by the dry-farmer's plan. The farmer in overalls is in many instances his own stockman today. On the ranges of Arizona, Wyoming, and Texas and parts of Nevada we may find the cowboy, it is true, even today: but he is no longer the Homeric figure that once dominated the plains. In what we say as to his trade, therefore, or his fashion in the practice of it, we speak in terms of thirty or forty years ago, when wire was unknown, when the round-up still was necessary, and the cowboy's life was indeed that of the open.

By the costume we may often know the man. The cowboy's costume was harmonious with its surroundings. It was planned upon lines of such stern utility as to leave no possible thing which we may call dispensable. The typical cowboy costume could hardly be said to contain a coat and waistcoat. The heavy woolen shirt, loose and open at the neck, was the common wear at all seasons of the year excepting winter, and one has often seen cowboys in the winter-time engaged in work about the yard or corral of the ranch wearing no other cover for the upper part of the body but one or more of these heavy shirts. If the cowboy wore a coat he would wear it open and loose as much as possible. If he wore a "vest" he would wear it slouchily, hanging open or partly unbuttoned most of the time. There was a reason for this slouchy habit. The cowboy would say that the vest closely buttoned about the body would cause perspiration, so that the wearer would quickly chill upon ceasing exercise. If the wind were blowing keenly when the cowboy dismounted to sit upon the ground for dinner, he would button up his waistcoat and be warm. If it were very cold he would button up his coat also.

The cowboy's boots were of fine leather and fitted tightly, with light narrow soles, extremely small and high heels. Surely a more irrational foot-covering never was invented; yet these tight, peaked cowboy boots had a great significance and may indeed be called the insignia of a calling. There was no prouder soul on earth than the cowboy. He was proud of being a horseman and had a contempt for all human beings who walked. On foot in his tight-toed boots he was lost; but he wished it to be understood that he never was on foot. If we rode beside him and watched his seat in the big cow saddle we found that his high and narrow heels prevented the slipping forward of the foot in the stirrup, into which he jammed his feet nearly full length. If there was a fall, the cowboy's foot never hung in the stirrup. In the corral roping, afoot, his heels anchored him. So he found his little boots not so unserviceable and retained them as a matter of pride. Boots made for the cowboy trade sometimes had fancy tops of bright-colored leather. The Lone Star of Texas was not infrequent in their ornamentation.

The curious pride of the horseman extended also to his gloves. The cowboy was very careful in the selection of his gloves. They were made of the finest buckskin, which could not be injured by wetting. Generally they were tanned white and cut with a deep cuff or gauntlet from which hung a little fringe to flutter in the wind when he rode at full speed on horseback.

The cowboy's hat was one of the typical and striking features of his costumes. It was a heavy, wide, white felt hat with a heavy leather band buckled about it. There has been no other head covering devised so suitable as the Stetson for the uses of the Plains, although high and heavy black hats have in part supplanted it today among stockmen. The boardlike felt was practically indestructible. The brim flapped a little and, in time, was turned up and perhaps held fast to the crown by a thong. The wearer might sometimes stiffen the brim by passing a thong through a series of holes pierced through the outer edge. He could depend upon his hat in all weathers. In the rain it was an umbrella; in the sun a shield; in the winter he could tie it down about his ears with his handkerchief.

Loosely thrown about the cowboy's shirt collar was a silk kerchief. It was tied in a hard knot in front, and though it could scarcely be said to be devoted to the uses of a neck scarf, yet it was a great comfort to the back of the neck when one was riding in a hot wind. It was sure to be of some bright color, usually red. Modern would-be cow-punchers do not willingly let this old kerchief die, and right often they overplay it. For the cowboy of the "movies," however, let us register an unqualified contempt. The real range would never have been safe for him.

A peculiar and distinctive feature of the cowboy's costume was his "chaps" *(chaparéjos)*. The chaps were two very wide and full-length trouser-legs made of heavy calfskin and connected by a narrow belt or strap. They were cut away entirely at front and back so that they covered only the thigh and lower legs and did not heat the body as a complete leather garment would. They were intended solely as a protection against branches, thorns, briers, and the like, but they were prized in cold or wet weather. Sometimes there was seen, more often on the southern range, a cowboy wearing chaps made of skins tanned with the hair on; for the cowboy of the Southwest early learned that goatskin left with the hair on would turn the cactus thorns better than any other material. Later, the chaps became a sort of affectation on the part of new men on the range; but the old-time cowboy wore them for use, not as a uniform. In hot weather he laid them off.

In the times when some men needed guns and all men carried them, no pistol of less than 44-caliber was tolerated on the range, the solid framed 45-caliber being the one almost universally used. The barrel was eight inches long, and it shot a rifle cartridge of forty grains of powder and a blunt-ended bullet that made a terrible missile. This weapon depended from a belt worn loose resting upon the left hip and hanging low down on the right hip so that none of the weight came upon the abdomen. This was typical, for the cowboy was neither fancy gunman nor army officer. The latter carries the revolver on the left, the butt pointing forward.

An essential part of the cow-puncher's outfit was his "rope." This was carried in a close coil at the side of the saddle-horn, fastened by one of the many thongs scattered over the saddle. In the Spanish country it was called *reata* and even today is sometimes seen in the Southwest made of rawhide. In the South it was called a *lariat*. The modern rope is a well-made three-quarter-inch hemp rope about thirty feet in length, with a leather or raw-hide eye. The cowboy's quirt was a short heavy whip, the stock being of wood or iron covered with braided leather and carrying a lash made of two or three heavy loose thongs. The spur in the old days had a very large rowel with blunt teeth an inch long. It was often ornamented with little bells or oblongs of metal, the tinkling of which appealed to the childlike nature of the Plains rider. Their use was to lock the rowel.

His bridle—for, since the cowboy and his mount are inseparable, we may as well speak of his horse's dress also—was noticeable for its tremendously heavy and cruel curbed bit, known as the "Spanish bit." But in the ordinary riding and even in the exciting work of the old round-up and in "cutting out," the cowboy used the bit very little, nor exerted any pressure on the reins. He laid the reins against the neck of the pony opposite to the direction in which he wished it to go, merely turning his hand in the direction and inclining his body in the same way. He rode with the pressure of the knee and the inclination of the body and the light side-shifting of both reins. The saddle was the most important part of the outfit. It was a curious thing, this saddle developed by the cattle trade, and the world has no other like it. Its great weight—from thirty to forty pounds—was readily excusable when one remembers that it was not only seat but workbench for the cowman. A light saddle would be torn to pieces at the first rush of a maddened steer, but the sturdy frame of a cow-saddle would throw the heaviest bull on the range. The high cantle would give a firmness to the cowboy's seat when he snubbed a steer with a sternness sufficient to send it rolling heels over head. The high pommel, or "horn," steel-forged and covered with cross braids of leather, served as anchor post for this same steer, a turn of the rope about it accomplishing that purpose at once. The saddle-tree forked low down over the pony's back so that the saddle sat firmly and could not readily be pulled off. The great broad cinches bound the saddle fast till horse and saddle were practically one fabric. The strong wooden house of the old heavy stirrup protected the foot from being crushed by the impact of the herd. The form of the cow-saddle has changed but little, although today one sees a shorter seat and smaller horn, a "swell front" or roll, and a stirrup of open "ox-bow" pattern.

The round-up was the harvest of the range. The time of the calf round-up was in the spring after the grass had become good and after the calves had grown large enough for the branding. The State Cattle Association divided the entire State range into a number of round-up districts. Under an elected round-up captain were all the bosses in charge of the different ranch outfits sent by men having cattle in the round-up. Let us briefly draw a picture of this scene as it was.

Each cowboy would have eight or ten horses for his own use, for he had now before him the hardest riding of the year. When the cow-puncher went into the herd to cut out calves he mounted a fresh horse, and every few hours he again changed horses, for there was no horse which could long endure the fatigue of the rapid and intense work of cutting. Before the rider stretched a sea of interwoven horns, waving and whirling as the densely packed ranks of cattle closed in or swayed apart. It was no prospect for a weakling, but into it went the cow-puncher on his determined little horse, heeding not the plunging, crushing, and thrusting of the excited cattle. Down under the bulks of the herd, half hid in the whirl of dust, he would spy a little curly calf running, dodging, and twisting, always at the heels of its mother; and he would dart in after, following the two through the thick of surging and plunging beasts. The sharp-eyed pony would see almost as soon as his rider which cow was wanted and he needed small guidance from that time on. He would follow hard at her heels, edging her constantly toward the flank of the herd, at times nipping her hide as a reminder of his own superiority. In spite of herself the cow would gradually turn out toward the edge, and at last would be swept clear of the crush, the calf following close behind her. There was a whirl of the rope and the calf was laid by the heels and dragged to the fire where the branding irons were heated and ready.

Meanwhile other cow-punchers are rushing calves to the branding. The hubbub and turmoil increase. Taut ropes cross the ground in many directions. The cutting ponies pant and sweat, rear and plunge. The garb of the cowboy is now one of white alkali which hangs gray in his eyebrows and moustache. Steers bellow as they surge to and fro. Cows charge on their persecutors. Fleet yearlings break and run for the open, pursued by men who care not how or where they ride.

We have spoken in terms of the past. There is no calf round-up of the open range today. The last of the round-ups was held in Routt County, Colorado, several years ago, so far as the writer knows, and it had only to do with shifting cattle from the summer to the winter range.

After the calf round-up came the beef round-up, the cowman's final harvest. This began in July or August. Only the mature or fatted animals were cut out from the herd. This "beef cut" was held apart and driven on ahead from place to place as the round-up progressed. It was then driven in by easy stages to the shipping point on the railroad, whence the long trainloads of cattle went to the great markets.

In the heyday of the cowboy it was natural that his chief amusements should be those of the outdoor air and those more or less in line with his employment. He was accustomed to the sight of big game, and so had the edge of his appetite for its pursuit worn off. Yet he was a hunter, just as every Western man was a hunter in the times of the Western game. His weapons were the rifle, revolver, and rope; the latter two were always with him. With the rope at times he captured the coyote, and under special conditions he has taken deer and even antelope in this way, though this was of course most unusual and only possible under chance conditions of ground and cover. Elk have been roped by cowboys many times, and it is known that even the mountain sheep has been so taken, almost incredible as that may seem. The young buffalo were easy prey for the cowboy and these he often roped and made captive. In fact the beginnings of all the herds of buffalo now in captivity in this country were the calves roped and secured by cowboys; and these few scattered individuals of a grand race of animals remain as melancholy reminders alike of a national shiftlessness and an individual skill and daring.

The grizzly was at times seen by the cowboys on the range, and if it chanced that several cowboys were together it was not unusual to give him chase. They did not always rope him, for it was rarely that the nature of the country made this possible. Sometimes they roped him and wished they could let him go, for a grizzly bear is uncommonly active and straightforward in his habits at close quarters. The extreme difficulty of such a combat, however, gave it its chief fascination for the cowboy. Of course, no one horse could hold the bear after it was roped, but, as one after another came up, the bear was caught by neck and foot and body, until at last he was tangled and tripped and haled about till he was helpless, strangled, and nearly dead. It is said that cowboys have so brought into camp a grizzly bear, forcing him to half walk and half slide at the end of the ropes. No feat better than this could show the courage of the plainsman and of the horse which he so perfectly controlled.

Of such wild and dangerous exploits were the cowboy's amusements on the range. It may be imagined what were his amusements when he visited the "settlements." The cow-punchers, reared in the free life of the open air, under circumstances of the utmost freedom of individual action, perhaps came off the drive or round-up after weeks or months of unusual restraint or hardship, and felt that the time had arrived for them to "celebrate." Merely great rude children, as wild and untamed and untaught as the herds they led, they regarded their first look at the "settlements" of the railroads as a glimpse of a wider world. They pursued to the uttermost such avenues of new experience as lay before them, almost without exception avenues of vice. It is strange that the records of those days should be chosen by the public to be held as the measure of the American cowboy. Those days were brief, and they are long since gone. The American cowboy atoned for them by a quarter of a century of faithful labor.

The amusements of the cowboy were like the features of his daily surroundings and occupation—they were intense, large, Homeric. Yet, judged at his work, no higher type of employee ever existed, nor one more dependable. He was the soul of honor in all the ways of his calling. The very blue of the sky, bending evenly over all men alike, seemed to symbolize his instinct for justice. Faithfulness and manliness were his chief traits; his standard—to be a "square man."

Not all the open range will ever be farmed, but very much that was long thought to be irreclaimable has gone under irrigation or is being more or less successfully "dry-farmed." The man who brought water upon the arid lands of the West changed the entire complexion of a vast country and with it the industries of that country. Acres redeemed from the desert and added to the realm of the American farmer were taken from the realm of the American cowboy.

The West has changed. The curtain has dropped between us and its wild and stirring scenes. The old days are gone. The house dog sits on the hill where yesterday the coyote sang. There are fenced fields and in them stand sleek round beasts, deep in crops such as their ancestors never saw. In a little town nearby is the hurry and bustle of modern life. This town is far out upon what was called the frontier, long after the frontier has really gone. Guarding its ghost here stood a little army post, once one of the pillars, now one of the monuments of the West.

Out from the tiny settlement in the dusk of evening, always facing toward where the sun is sinking, might be seen riding, not so long ago, a figure we should know. He would thread the little lane among the fences, following the guidance of hands other than his own, a thing he would once have scorned to do. He would ride as lightly and as easily as ever, sitting erect and jaunty in the saddle, his reins held high and loose in the hand whose fingers turn up gracefully, his whole body free yet firm in the saddle with the seat of the perfect horseman. At the boom of the cannon, when the flag dropped fluttering down to sleep, he would rise in his stirrups and wave his hat to the flag. Then, toward the edge, out into the evening, he would ride on. The dust of his riding would mingle with the dusk of night. We could not see which was the one or the other. We could only hear the hoof-beats passing, boldly and steadily still, but growing fainter, fainter, and more faint.

The Beginning of Cattle
Stealing in Texas

– by –
W.S. James

BEFORE THE WAR and for many years afterward, cattle stealing in Texas was virtually licensed. Don't understand by this that our honorable law-makers granted a regular license to men for so much money, to steal cattle. Not that. It was simply a finable offense to steal a cow. It was a license on the same plan that gambling and other like offenses against the peace and dignity of the State of Texas and other States, specially in the cities, have been permitted to be carried on, a kind of an understanding with the peace officers that at regular intervals they should pay their fines and run on undisturbed until the next regular grub time with the officers came round. The only difference being that a man's time for contributing to the State for stealing was not a stated one, coming only when he was caught, or some poor fellow, who couldn't steal as fast as some other fellow, put up a job on him and had him pulled.

He would then come up and either plead guilty or fight it. In either case, if he was found guilty the fine was $20, which he, easily paid and could steal enough cattle in a short time to double his investment.

Stealing cattle prior to the war was a rare thing. Perhaps one reason being they were hardly worth stealing, another, the country was so sparsely settled and the Indians were so "rolicky" it took a good part of the time to look after them. It was made a felony in 1873. As I have before stated, some old fellows who were too cowardly to go to the war and too lazy to work began the business before the war closed. Thus giving the introductory pages to the subsequent history of cattle and horse stealing in Texas which prevailed for many years to an alarming extent.

But to the credit of a reconstructed order of things be it said, the business has been waning for the past five years, and has dwindled down to such a point that there are but two classes who "monkey" with other people's cattle now. They are the natural born fool, and the fellow who has stolen a sufficient amount to make him respectable and who has it down to a science.

There has been so much written about the Mavrick that it seems useless to mention the origin of the term. Some one may wish to know however. The original Mr. Maverick located in southern Texas and being constitutionally a 'merciful man,' he had so much mercy on his animals as to refuse to mark and brand them and in the cattle-man's parlance if you should ask concerning the ownership of any animal, the answer would be according to the brand the animal bore. For illustration: Suppose we should find a cow belonging to Westmore whose brand is XW, called cross W, I ask: "Whose cow is that!" the answer would be "That is a cross double U and Mr. Maverick having no mark or brand when they came across an unmarked one it was called a Mavrick.

After the war, when the poor, half-starved, weather and war-beaten fellows returned, those who had left cattle went to work to make up for lost time, and those who had none, to get even for their four years of service. And it soon became a sort of general scramble as to who should get the greatest number, and on account of thousands of cattle having become wild and unruly because of neglect a very general license was granted, or rather taken, to kill and eat when one was hungry. Thus it was that the majority of people who lived in the West became involved in branding Mavricks, and killing strays, which at that time was not looked upon as stealing, but a kind of pull dick pull devil, the devil-take-the-hindmost sort of way of securing all the cattle one could.

This, in after years, produced a regular harvest of thieves. After it became theft the habit of taking what one could get his hands on, regardless of its origin, simply accepting it as so much found, and therefore legitimate prize, became so fixed on many that they never could quite comprehend how hard it was to quit until they were run in.

The circumstances leading to a change in the laws may be briefly stated as follows: A great many of the more active and better equipped among the scramblers began to accumulate large herds, and as there were no pasture fences then, they were compelled to turn their cattle loose on the range. The less thrifty and more extravagant classes refused to recognize the rights of the growing nabobs to have their unbranded calves left alone, while they were still keeping up their old game of branding Mavricks indiscriminately, and the little fellows thus antagonized their former associates. The consequence was the wholesale thieves, now grown powerful, had the legislature pass laws making it an offense against the peace and dignity of the State to brand and mark a calf that didn't belong to him.

Then began the battle that for years waged unceasingly until the big fish swallowed up the little ones. We had as a result the cattle king and the common cow-puncher. The real difference being that the king no longer had to do his own stealing, for he was able to hire the cow-puncher to do it for him, and if the poor cow-puncher presumed to steal a little scrub for himself once in a while, the king wouldn't kick unless some one tried to raise a fuss about it. If he could settle it without too much noise he would do it, and thus add one more link to the poor boy's chains with which to hold him in line. If there was too much noise about it, the king turned honest and sent him down East to work for Texas.

The rule above laid down has some honorable exceptions, but this is in brief what Mavricking led to. When the business first began there were men with cattle who had never stolen, that really believed they were forced to do as other men in self-defense, who began taking lessons in stealing and wound up in the penitentiary. Some became wealthy, and, thanks to true manhood, we are able to record that some men preferred to let poverty enter their home than that truth and honesty of purpose be dispossessed of their legitimate throne. One instance I recall with pleasure is the example set by my father, and, though with shame I confess it, I did not altogether follow that noble Christian object lesson. Still, I look back with pride to the living testimony left by him, and am not ashamed to be known as one of his boys where he spent the greater portion of his life. When it seemed that he and my grandfather, who were partners in cattle, would simply go to the wall if they did not, in self-defense, do as others were doing.

Grandfather said to him: "This won't do, we must protect our interests," so they fitted up an outfit and started on a round-up. They drove in perhaps five hundred range cattle, nearly all cows, calves and yearlings, among them some two hundred and fifty unbranded ones. Father and grandfather were sitting on the fence, and I, as a little "tow-head," naturally would perch myself beside them.

When the boys had marked and branded those following the JIM and the Big S cows some one threw a rope on a yearling that was following a cow of some other brand. The cow ran out of the bunch, bawling round the calf. As quick as flash father called out: "Don't put my brand on that one." The boys stopped and looked at each other and then at grandfather, evidently waiting for his decision. Very soon he said: "Don't put my brand on it either." So they put the brand of its mother on it, and thus my father and grandfather took the first step toward their financial wreckage.

But my father left to his children the legacy of an honest name, better by far, in the substantial scale of moral worth, than all the cattle that ever trod the great grass fields of the Southwest. If he had taken another course the results to his children might have been as with many others, ruin and disgrace. The wild associations and environments of the day came near wrecking some of them as it was, but the memory of his counsel with the guiding hand of One who hears and answers prayer has prevailed, coupled with the strong will of a loving mother who knew how to harness justice and love to the vehicle of parental advice and correction by means of a bridle rein or the elastic sole of an old slipper. The bunch of boys and two girls are now moving smoothly along, and bid fair to make the average citizen.

I.

When my mother called me Willie, or even simple Will,
I knew that all was smiling within the family mill;
But when she called out "William" my flesh began to crawl,
I knew I'd trampled under foot some precept great or small.

II.

When the angry passion gathered on her gently loving brow,
She stooped, withdrew her slipper, I knew there'd be a row,
She'd gently draw me forward, lay me down across her knee,
And interview my trousers twixt that slipper and poor me.

III.

You may talk of Mr. Franklin, with his bottle, kite and string,
Gathering lightning from a storm cloud while the cloud was on
    the wing;
But I tell you, now, my mother, with a slipper and a boy.
Could manufacture lighting A 1 without alloy.

IV.

As to negative, I cannot tell, but positive-ly know
My mother had the thing down fine full thirty years ago;
She couldn't light a city quite, or run a street railway,
But knew just how to raise her boys, and did it every day.

V.

She used no zinc or carbon when she charged my battery,
But played upon my trouser seat with a dogwood hickory;
But mother knew my needs quite well, it did me good—just so,
It kept the hide from growing close, and made a fellow grow.

As a rule the men who grew rich in the cattle business were the ones who were the best rustlers and who stuck the closest to business, let that be in branding mavricks or looking after the ones they had already branded. Some who started out very prosperously, just as soon as fortune began to smile upon them, lost their heads, and the consequence was they entered the field of speculation to the neglect of their cattle. Their business became wrecked upon the great sea of adventure.

The majority of men who stuck to stealing and raising, coupled with watching out for, number one, and who did not go wild over the boom in cattle of 1880 to 1885, but sold instead of buying, are the men who are now called colonel and whose names are sticking to the money end of first national banks and other money enterprises. To make this a little more palliating to some of them who are just a trifle sensitive in regard to their former connection with cattle stealing (or mavricking I should have said), I will state frankly that I believe it just possible that some cattle men who made their start after the first great tidal wave of wholesale mavricking (or stealing I should have said) were strictly honest, as much so as possible for a man to be in the business and hold his own.

It is not every man who is prominently connected with first national banks that made his start in cattle who can be accused of being a thief; in fact, they are, in a large majority, honest men, now. But, remember, I am not speaking of now, but it was then. Show me a man who began in the cattle business as early as '68 or '70 who did not go busted, who can truthfully say that he never ate stray beef, never branded cattle whose ownership was questionable, and I will show you a man too good for Texas or Chicago.

I don't mean to say that those who went busted were saints, for the great majority of the thieves went busted. I believe that those who got their money in that way will yet live to reap the whirlwind, for an all-seeing eye that never sleeps looks down upon them, and though they may be living to-day as straight as the rule of eternal truth, still the stern decree has gone forth: "Be not deceived; God is not mocked, for whatsoever a man soweth that shall he also reap."

Many good men have been and are still engaged in the cattle business, and honorable exceptions could, perhaps, be found to the rule here laid down, but they are so scarce that they have been woefully neglected. Take the man who weathered the gale and came out on top, as a rule they are big-hearted fellows, and in many instances they have not been spoiled by the milk and cider homage of a money-loving world, for they recognize the fact that it is not for themselves they are toadied to and called "captain," but for their money.

They are the same old Jim and Bob they were when they divided blankets with their less fortunate comrades. They were once cowboys, and when they meet one of the old fellows that went under, they are still on the bed ground as of old. They can get down and eat broiled beef with as good grace as twenty years ago. But, on the other hand, there are some who will set up and lie like dogs, just to tickle the fancy of greenhorns. They get so stuck up that if an old stove up cow-puncher should approach them in company and call them by the old name they would scowl at him as if he were a hungry coyote. I have seen but few of this class, however, and of all the contemptible old cow thieves on earth it is the old donker who has stolen himself into respectability and then with his thieving old carcass togged up in a $50 suit of clothes bought with his ill-gotten gains to see him stacked up on a jury to try some boy for stealing a $5 yearling is simply too much to contemplate.

It is certainly very amusing to a crowd of cow-boys to read newspaper articles sometimes written about K–E–R–N–E–L, B–, O–or D–and how he made his start by honest energy and pluck. The energy might have been honest, but the plucking part is what amuses the boys who know just how he used to pluck everything he could get off with. There is really no place for the honest part in his whole get-up. It is a wonder to me sometimes how they can stand to read such articles without choking. I suppose their swallow is like their conscience, very elastic and stretches well.

I remember once hearing my father speaking to a neighbor boy in regard to a yearling which the boy was about to brand; the calf's mother came running up—she had another man's brand on her. Father said, "Ed, I had just as soon steal a horse as that yearling." "I had rather," said the inexorable youth, "for there would be more money in it." And this is the principle upon which many men run the cattle business, the more they could steal the better pleased they were with their work.

I remember a story told on an old vinegaroon preacher, one of those old fellows who branded mavricks during the week, or hired it done, and preached on Sunday to pay for it. As some of the boys put it, he had to do something to square accounts with the Lord. He was a great stickler for water. One Sunday while preaching on the subject of baptism he related what some Methodist brother had to say about the work of John the Baptist at Jordan. He became very much exercised over it. The brother had said that maybe John had a long-handled dipper with which he dipped the water out of Jordan and poured it on the people. The old preacher called out in stentorian tones (and he had a voice like a Spanish burro), "How long was that dipper handle?" after a pause, "How long was that dipper handle?" after a longer pause in louder tones than before, he called out again, "How long was that dipper handle I say?" An old lady of the Methodist persuasion arose to her feet and pointing her fat, chubby finger at the preacher said: "About as long as your branding iron handle you branded my calves with, parson."

The old fellow stood rooted to the spot for the moment and then said: "Let us pray," He was a jolly old fellow and often told the story on himself. Whether it was true or not I can not say. I will leave it for the reader to guess.

～

Shanghai Pierce and
the Flapjacks

– by –
J. Frank Dobie

OF ALL THE OLD-TIME COWMEN of open range days Shanghai Pierce, with the possible exception of Charlie Goodnight, has come nearer becoming a legend than any other. They were opposites, Goodnight quiet, public-spirited and modest, Pierce loud, rough and vaunting, though each was "a character unto God."

How Abel Head Pierce got the nickname of Shanghai is speculative, but probably it was from his resemblance in youth to a cocky Shanghai rooster. Old Shang liked it so much that it is a wonder he did not use it instead of his initials in signing checks. He landed in Texas—from Rhode Island by way of Virginia, six foot four, nineteen years old. The published explanation of his leaving Rhode Island is that he simply had to get away from "too many doses of sanctimony." According to one of his lawyers, he said: "When I lay down in Rhode Island I'd find my head on the tits of some woman in Massachusetts and my feet tickling another woman's legs in Connecticut. I was just too fenced in." His one ambition was to get rich. As he gathered land and cattle, he seemed to be increasingly set on having his way.

When he landed at Port Lavaca, he had seventy-five cents. When he died in 1900, at the age of sixty-six, he owned over two hundred thousand acres of land besides other property. After he had acquired two hundred thousand acres he changed certain field notes to add a few more sections of land. He fenced in little men and poor widows and drove off their milch cows in his big herds—unless one of them leveled a double-barreled shotgun on him, and then he was very obliging. He'd as soon bribe a judge as tip a waiter. In fact, he was against tipping any functionary. He asserted that "if six bits won't bribe an Italian it is useless to offer more." After he had contracted a thousand steers to an Indian agency he considered it fair sport to count in 118 that he did not have past the "army greenhorns." He got his start working for $200 a year putting up a picket fence, but didn't really prosper until mavericking got on a boom following the Civil War.

Probably no mavericker of the ranges ever boomed higher than Shanghai Pierce. There were lots of cattle on the coast and lots of them unbranded. Shanghai imported four (some say only two) brothers named Lunn to maverick for him. After a while they went to mavericking for themselves, starting a brand of their own on the side. Pierce had taught them to burn his brand on any big calf—soon to be weaned—following a cow in some other man's brand. When he learned that they were stealing for themselves instead of for him alone, Pierce turned on the Lunn brothers like a tiger. He and some other ranchers surrounded them in a thicket. One vigilante persuaded them to come out and talk. The talk consisted of disarming them, putting a rope around the neck of each man while he sat on his horse under a limb to which the other end of the rope was tied, and then driving the horse away.

Before quirts were applied to a horse so that the rider would be left hanging, the youngest of the Lunn brothers was asked if he had anything to say for himself. "Yes," he replied, "I'd like to have ten minutes to tell that long-legged son-of-a-bitch," pointing to Shanghai Pierce, "what I think of a man who hired us to steal for him and then after we learned his methods wants to hang us." The hangers gave the Lunn boy's horse a lick and he was left kicking in the air. He was about eighteen years old. Joe Pickering, a cowman from way back, of Victoria, Texas, gave me this account in 1935. He said the Lunn tree was still identifiable.

After the hangings for practices that he himself had been prospering on, Shanghai Pierce found the climate too hot in Texas and, as

Joseph G. McCoy tells in his honest book *Historic Sketches of the Cattle Trade of the West and Southwest* (1874), spent a considerable time in Kansas, where he also prospered.

Most of his troubles were with big guns. "I am eternally lawing," he once wrote. Records of his lawsuits enliven Chris Emmett's biography *Shanghai Pierce: A Fair Likeness.* He lawed with George Miller, founder of the 101 Ranch, and with Dan Sullivan, a San Antonio "private" banker noted for foreclosing on cowmen. In Sullivan's declining years, two loyal-Irish, devoted-Catholic bookkeepers got away with a million dollars of his money. Once in a terrible drouth he refused to renew Jim Chittim's note. "Pay up or turn over the mortgaged stuff," he said. "I'll see what I can do," Jim Chittim left saying. Five days later he was back. "I guess you've got the money," Dan Sullivan said, exuding iron and irony, after the two had sat down in his private office. The door was closed. "I've decided to renew the note," Jim Chittim said, reaching and pulling out his private example of the Great Persuader. "Now take your choice. You're not going to get title to *my* land and cattle." Dan Sullivan chose to make out a new note.

Seated in the witness box, Shanghai Pierce shouted, "I think the best commercial record a man can make is to prove in court that he has robbed Little Dannie Sullivan. I'll be very popular for this. The people will descend upon me and pluck my locks for souvenirs and charms." As for the owner of the 101 Ranch, Shanghai Pierce, again on the witness stand, bellowed out, "Miller is known to be the biggest liar on the North American continent, and not only the biggest liar but the biggest thief and a son-of-a-bitch."

His voice, he realized, was "too loud for indoor use," and he delighted in using it. His talk was even more picturesque than loud. Once in New York he noticed a boy among strangers circled around to listen to him. "Son," he boomed, "just what do you want?" "Please, sir," came the reply, "I just want to hear you talk." Shanghai brought the boy to Texas, where he could hear runty cattle called "swamp angels" or "saddle-pocket dogies," and coastal cattle called "sea lions," they were so practiced in swimming.

Shanghai Pierce was the loudest man in the country. He would sit at one end of a day coach and in normal voice hold conversation with some man at the other end of the coach, who of course had to yell, while the train was clanking along. He knew everybody, yelled at everybody he saw. A certain cowman upon arriving in Victoria one day asked a friend if he had seen Shanghai Pierce in town. "No," the friend replied, "I haven't seen him, but I know just the same he's not here. I haven't heard him." As another old joke goes, he built the bunkhouse at Rancho Grande fully three hundred yards away from the main house—so that the hands could not hear him whispering to his wife. "Being in the most conspicuous part of a Barnum and Bailey circus parade would be no more conspicuous than being in company with Shanghai Pierce," Judge Fred Proctor, himself a very modest man, told me.

Once while Proctor was on a train going through to Houston, Shanghai, at the station outside, saw him. The train was moving out, but Shanghai yelled to the conductor to hold it. He went inside, asked Proctor how much he owed him, grumbled at the amount, and then wrote out a check for it.

Everybody knew where he stood, both physically and mentally, with respect to individuals and things. Once when he went into a hotel at Columbia, Texas, to register, his eye caught the freshly written name of R. L. Stafford. Pointing to the name, he said to the clerk—and to everybody else in the block who had ears to listen: "I know this is a comfortable hotel with ample accommodations for ordinary men, but, by God, sirs, it is entirely too small for Bob Stafford and Shanghai Pierce at the same time." He arrived at a hotel in Hot Springs, Arkansas, without a reservation, and the manager, after listening to his bluster, refused him one. "By God, sir," Shanghai bellowed out, "is this hotel for sale?" "I own a half interest, and I'll sell it for fifteen thousand dollars," the manager-owner replied. "Sold," shouted Old Shang, and he reached for his checkbook—and went up to a room he now owned. A cattle solicitor was after him to stop his herd at Dodge City, Kansas. "No, I'll not ship any more cattle to your town," Shanghai thundered. "Why, I can get a room right here in the heart of your city, with a nice clean bed, plenty of soap, water and towels, and occupy it for twenty-four hours for two bits. And your stockyards, way out past the edge of town, want to charge me twenty cents a head and let my steers stand out in the weather. No, I'll not ship any more cattle to your town."

A lawyer for his opponent in a court suit came to see him at his ranch and made what Shanghai considered a shady proposal. After being referred three or four times to Pierce's own lawyer, the visitor stood up and said, "Colonel Pierce, I don't believe you are going to commit yourself on anything." Colonel Pierce replied, "When a man owns a dog, there is no use for him to do the barking himself."

While his daughter was in school in Virginia he received a special bill for "equestrianism." He put it in his pocket until he could see his banker some weeks later. "Look at that," he said, pointing to the balance due and the word "equestrianism." "My God," he asked, "what has she done now?" It was just a charge for horsemanship, the banker explained. Shanghai Pierce waved his hand and cried out, "Horsemanship! Here I am paying out money to teach her to ride a sidesaddle in Central Park and she was raised riding straddle on a bareback Texas pony."

After a railroad built through his ranch and Pierce's Station was established near headquarters, he decided to "introduce religion in the community" and built a church. Upon seeing it, a visitor asked, "Colonel Pierce, do you belong to that church?" "Hell, no," he retorted, "the church belongs to me." The son of a cowman friend once asked him, "Mr. Pierce, do you really think there is a heaven?" "I doubt it, son," he replied. "I don't see how the good Lord would voluntarily take upon himself the immense job of cutting back so many culls out of the human race."

He was wont to identify himself as "Shanghai Pierce, Webster on cattle." "There is not a man in the United States can beat me on a ranch," he boasted, "and I have some stuff to show for it, sir."

Nobody knew him better than Fred C. Proctor, who in representing the O'Connors, Jim Chittim, Ben Q. Ward and other big cowmen came to understand the breed well. In 1932 I got him to talk about Shanghai Pierce, and immediately wrote the notes that now follow.

Ben Q. Ward had a ranch on Carankawa Bay. He and Shanghai Pierce had been neighbors for many years and at one time were partners. He went to speculating in Houston real estate at the wrong time and became so deeply involved that his whole estate was in jeopardy. About 1900 he applied to Shanghai Pierce for a loan. Shanghai instructed his counsel, Fred C. Proctor, to look into Ward's affairs and see if a loan were warranted.

Proctor looked and told Ward that his collateral would not back a loan for more than $70,000.

"But I need ninety thousand," declared Ward. "Seventy thousand won't save me. It won't do me any good."

"Well," said Proctor, "I have followed Mr. Pierce's instructions. I am his adviser, you will understand. Involved as your property is, seventy thousand is all it seems worth as collateral."

"Do you mind if I see Shanghai myself?" asked Ward. He seemed to have an idea that Proctor was acting as watchdog over Pierce.

"Why, of course not. I have nothing to do with Mr. Pierce's decisions. He makes them himself. I act only under his instructions."

Ward left. Two days later he was back in Proctor's office. "I saw Shanghai himself," he gloated. "He's going to let me have the ninety thousand. Said he would wire you."

The next day the telegram arrived. It read: "Let Uncle Ben have the $90,000. His mother used to give me flapjacks."

Proctor made out the papers and Ben Q. Ward got the $90,000. The next time Proctor saw Shanghai, he said to him, "I understand all right what you meant by saying, 'Let Uncle Ben have the ninety thousand,' but what on earth did you mean by adding, 'His mother used to give me flapjacks'?"

Shanghai laughed loud and hard. Then he told something of the story of his life.

"The first thing I did when I got to Texas was hire out to W. B. Grimes at fifty cents a day. That was in 1853, on Matagorda Bay. Directly I was put to breaking horses. It happened this way. One morning a prize buck nigger was riding a wild horse out in the pen close to the Grimes house. This horse was a terror. He was a-squalling and the nigger was a-hollering and other niggers joining in. Well, Mrs. Grimes came running out, saw what was happening, and pitched into old Bing [W. B. Grimes]. 'Don't you know,' she stormed, 'that that horse is liable to kill that nigger? He's worth a good eighteen hundred dollars. What do you mean by letting him ride pitching horses when you got a Yankee here working for four bits a day that could take the risk just as well?'

"Grimes saw the point, and from then on I took the risks. I was too poor to buy decent clothes, and the Grimes family didn't allow me to come into the polite part of the house. I ate in the kitchen and slept out in a shed. The Wards lived over on the Carankawa, where Uncle Ben still has the ranch—mortgaged to me. Once in a while I'd ride over in that country—all unfenced then, of course. Whenever I did, they'd treat me like sure enough white folks. Old Lady Ward knew I could eat more than a whole livery stable. She'd just pile the flapjacks up and keep on piling them until I was full. I can taste them yet. I'll never forget them and the good, kind woman who made them. Now you know why I let Uncle Ben have the ninety thousand against your advice."

Yet Shanghai was a businessman. When he came to write his will he asked Proctor how much he was going to charge. Proctor finally said $2500. Old Shanghai fumed, went outside, kicked a dog, and yelled at a boy. Then he came back. "All right. Agreed, is it?"

"Yes."

"Do you know how much I expected you to charge?"

"No."

"I expected you to charge five thousand."

Then he dictated the peculiar will by which his estate was to be kept intact, to be known as the A. H. Pierce Estate, until his youngest grandchild was thirty-five years old. "Nobody has any sense until he is thirty-five years old," he said, "and damned few after that." He was openly anxious to be remembered, and seemed to think that keeping the estate intact would preserve his memory. And when he later erected a monument to himself and Proctor asked him why, Shanghai answered: "If I didn't have it put up, nobody would."

Once he and Proctor went together to Galveston on business.

Upon getting off the train, Proctor got into a cab. Pierce struck out on foot. Proctor called him and asked why he would walk. "Waste of money," he said, "to ride such a little distance. Why are you riding?"

"Because," answered Proctor, "I am rich, rich as hell."

"Yes, and you will charge it to me," roared Pierce.

"Certainly I will. You walk, and when you die not long hence your son-in-law will ride."

"By God, I hadn't thought of the thing that way," Shanghai exploded. "I'll ride with you, and from now on I'm a-going to ride every time I feel like it."

A few years before he died he commissioned a San Antonio tombstone-maker to execute a statue of himself out of gray marble, "higher than any statue of any Confederate general, a fair likeness of myself, big enough to be buried under, so people can look at it and say, 'There stands old Pierce.'"

"Old Pierce" still stands in one of the pastures of the Pierce Estate, not far from Blessing. After the Galveston storm (September, 1900) he wrote, about three months before he died, a check for $80,000 to be used for the relief of Wharton County people who had been "wrecked." He could also be kind. Perhaps he thought more of old Neptune, the Negro who used to ride with him on cow-buying expeditions and carry the gold for cash payment, than of anybody else. It was old Neptune he sent to pass on the statue. "It looks like you, Mr. Shang," Neptune reported—and then Mr. Shang wrote the check.

I know what the book gives as the facts on the end of Shanghai Pierce. I know, too, from long observation that folk anecdotes about certain characters are sometimes more revealing of truth than documented facts. I know two anecdotes breathing truth about the end of old Shang. I'll tell the milder one, from Joe Pickering.

One night while he was staying with Jonathan Pierce, brother to Shanghai, a rider came with a note. After reading it Jonathan growled, "Well, I've got to go to Pierce."

"Nothing wrong, I hope," Pickering said.

"Yes, Shang's dead. I told him all along that if he didn't leave them nigger gals alone they'd sap his log."

My old friend Jim Ballard of Beeville, now dead, knew Shanghai and knew his breed. To my mind he summed him up justly in these words: "He was always bragging—and didn't have a thing to brag about but his money. He talked big but was easy tamed. He was rough even for his time, rough in ways, rough on people he rode over, and rougher in language. The day his daughter married he said, 'That feller's going to stick his pecker into a gold mine tonight.'"

Some Glimpses into Ranch Life

– by –

Frank S. Hastings

A RANCH IN ITS ENTIRETY is known as an "Outfit," and yet in a general way the word "Outfit" suggests the wagon outfit which does the cow-work and lives in the open from April 15th, when work begins, to December 1st, when it ends.

The wagon outfit consists of the "Chuck Wagon" which carries the food, bedding and tents, and from the back of which the food is prepared over an open fire. The "Hoodlum Wagon," which carries the water barrel, wood and branding irons, furnishes the Chuck Wagon with water and wood, the branding crew with wood, and attends all round-ups or branding pens with supply of drinking water.

The Remuda (cow ponies) and Horse Wrangler always travel with the "Wagon." Remuda is the Spanish word for Saddle Horses.

The wagon crew consists of the Wagon Boss, usually foreman of the ranch, Cook, Hoodlum Driver, Horse Wrangler, Straw Boss, next in authority to Wagon Boss, and eight to twelve men as the work may demand. In winter the outfit is reduced to the regular year-around men who are scattered over the different ranch camps.

In almost everything industrial the problem is reduced to "Men," but in the Ranch it is reduced to "Men and horses." One might almost say to horses: since the love of a horse explains why there are cowboys—not rough riders, or the gun-decorated hero of the moving picture, but earnest, everyday, hardworking boys who will sit twenty-four hours in a saddle and never whimper, but who "Hate your guts" if you ask them to plow an acre of land or do anything else "afoot."

Every cowboy has a mount of from eight to fourteen horses regulated by his work, and the class of horses. A line rider can get along with fewer horses than a "wagon" man, and a man with a good many young horses needs more than the man with an older or steadier mount. Every one of these men will claim they are "afoot" and that "There ain't no more good cow ponies," but woe to the "outfit" that tries to take one of the no-accounts away, or, as the saying is, "Monkey with a man's mount."

Horses are assigned and then to all intents and purposes they become the property of the man. Some foremen do not let their men trade horses among themselves, but it is quite generally permitted under supervision that avoids "sharking."

Every horse has a name and every man on the ranch knows every horse by name, and in a general way over all the S. M. S. Ranches with over 500 cow ponies in service the men know all the horses by name, and what horses are in each man's mount. A man who does not love his mount does not last long in the cow business. Very few men are cruel to their horses, and a man who does not treat his mount well is only a "bird of passage" on most ranches, and always on the S. M. S. Ranch. There is an old ranch saying that between the shoulder and the hip belongs to the rider, and the rest to the company. Beating over the head or spurring in the shoulder means "time check." Cowboys' principal topic is their horses or of men who ride, and every night about the camp fire they trade horses, run imaginary horse races, or romance about their pet ponies.

I shall speak of horses in the main as with the wagon. All the saddle horses of an outfit thrown together are called the Remuda—pronounced in Texas "Remoother"—slurring the "ther." The Remuda is in charge of a man, usually a half-grown boy known as the "Horse Wrangler," whose duty it is to have them in a band when wanted to change mounts, and to see that they are watered and grazed and kept from straying. They are always assembled early morning at noon and at night, and at such other times as the work may demand a change, as, for instance, in making a round the boys use their wildest and swiftest horses—usually their youngest—to tame them down. When the round-up is together they use their "cutting" horses, which are as a rule their oldest and best horses.

The Remuda for an ordinary outfit will number from 125 to 150 horses. The Wrangler must know every horse by sight and name, and tell at a glance if one is missing. The Remuda trails with the wagon, but is often sent to some round-up place without the wagon. A horse is a "Hoss" always in a cow camp. Horses ridden on grass may be called upon to be ridden until down and out, but are not hurt as a grain-fed horse would be, and when his turn comes again in a few days is as chipper as ever. . . . The horse breaker or "Bronc Buster" usually names horses as he breaks them; and if the horse has any flesh marks or distinct characteristics, it is apt to come out in the name, and any person familiar with the practical can often glance at a horse and guess his name. For instance, if he has peculiar black stripes toward the tail with a little white in the tail, you are pretty safe to guess "Pole Cat." If his feet are big and look clumsy, "Puddin Foot" is a good first chance. The following names occur in three mounts, and to get the full list I had to dig hard, and both men [he may mean all three] left out several horses until I asked about them, because always the suspicion that something was going to be done that would take a horse:

Red Hell, Tar Baby, Sail Away Brown, Big Henry, Streak, Brown Lina, Hammer Head, Lightning, Apron Face, Feathers, Panther, Chub, Dumbbell, Rambler, Powder, Straight Edge, Scissors, Gold Dollar, Silver City, Julius Caesar, Pop Corn, Talameslie, Louse Cage, Trinidad, Tater Slip, Cannon Ball, Big Enough, Lone Oak, Stocking, Pain, Grey Wonder, Rattler, Whiteman, Monkey Face, Snakey, Slippers, Jesse James, Buttermilk, Hop Ale, Barefoot, Tetotler, Lift Up, Pancho, Boll Weevil, Crawfish, Clabber, Few Brains, Showboy, Rat Hash, Butterbeans, Cigarette, Bull Pup. Feminine names are often used, such as Sweetheart, Baby Mine, or some girl's name.

A "Bronc" is a horse recently broken or about to be broken. The "Bronc Buster" [in some parts he is called also a peeler or a twister] rides him a few saddles. This pony is known as a Bronc the first season and as "Last Year's Bronc" the second season. Most all of the Broncs pitch some, but very few of them long or dangerously. Modern methods of breaking have reduced the percentage of bad horses— many would not pitch at all after the first few times if the rider did not deliberately make them. It is hard to get the old hands to ride anything but a pretty gentle horse, and yet there is always someone in the outfit who glories in mean horses, most of which are really fine animals, except for their "morning's morning" but the rider who likes them usually has no trouble in getting them. Every cowboy must, of course, be able to handle a mean horse if necessary.

An "Outlaw" is a horse which no amount of riding or handling will subdue. He is "turned in" and sold in the "Scalawag" bunch which goes out every year, and includes the horses no longer fit for cow use. They are bought by traders who take them into some of the older Southern States and sell them to the negro tenants for cotton horses.

A "Sunday Hoss" is one with an easy saddle gait—usually a single footer with some style. The boys go "Gallin" Sundays, and in every mount of the younger men there is apt to be such a horse, but not in any sense saved from the regular work for Sunday.

"An Individual" is the private property of a cowboy and not very much encouraged, as it is only natural that he does not get much work, and is an encouragement to go "Gallin" when the foreman holds the boys down on ranch horses more on the boys' account because it is often a long night ride and impairs the boys' capacity for a hard day's work in busy times. . . . The owner of an "Individual" may be the embodiment of general honesty, but seems to feel that oats sneaked out for "his hoss" is at worst a very small venial sin.

A cow horse is trained so that he is tied when the reins are down. He can, of course, drift off and when frightened run, but stepping on the reins seems to intimidate him into standing still as a rule. There are two reasons for this: first, the cowboy frequently has work where it is vital to leap from his horse and do something quick; second, that there is rarely anything to tie him to; though even when tying a horse a fairly even pull will loosen the reins. Cow horses are easily startled and apt to pull back and break the reins.

The regular cowboy gait for pasture riding or line work or ordinary cross-country riding is a "Jiggle"—a sort of fox trot that will make five miles per hour. For the round-up hard running is necessary part of the time and usually a stiff gallop the balance.

Cowboy life is very different from the ideas given by a Wild West Show or the "Movies." It is against Texas law to carry a pistol, and the sale is unlawful. This, however, is evaded by leasing 99 years. Occasionally a rider will carry a Winchester on his saddle for coyotes or Lobo wolves, but in the seventeen years the writer has been intimate with range life he has never seen a cowboy carry a pistol hung about him, and very few instances where one was carried concealed. There is always a gun of some sort with the outfit carried in the wagon.

Every cowboy furnishes his own saddle, bridle, saddle blanket. and spurs; also his bedding, known as "Hot Roll," a 16 to 20 oz. canvas "Tarp" about 18 feet long doubled and bedding in between, usually composed of several quilts known as "suggans" and blankets— rarely a mattress, the extra quilts serving for mattress. The top "Tarp" serves as extra covering and protects against rain.

Working outfits are composed as far as possible of unmarried men, with the exception of the Wagon Boss, who is usually the Ranch foreman. They rarely leave the wagon at night, and as the result of close association an interchange of wit, or "josh," as it is called, has sprung up. There is nothing like the chuck-wagon josh in any other phase of life, and it is almost impossible to describe, because so much of it revolves about or applies to the technical part of ranching. It is very funny, very keen, and very direct, and while the most of it is understood by an outsider, he cannot carry it away with him.

At headquarters a bunk house is always provided which is usually known as "the Dog House" or "the Dive." No gambling is permitted on the ranches, but the cowboys' great game, "Auction Pitch," or dominoes or stag dances or music fill the hours of recreation, divided with the great cowboy occupation of "Quirt" making, in which they are masters. The use of liquor is not permitted on the S. M. S. Ranches or by the men when on duty away from the ranches.

❦

The Cattle Country of the Far West

– by –
Theodore Roosevelt

THE GREAT GRAZING LANDS of the West lie in what is known as the arid belt, which stretches from British America on the north to Mexico on the south, through the middle of the United States. It includes New Mexico, part of Arizona, Colorado, Wyoming, Montana, and the western portion of Texas, Kansas, Nebraska, and Dakota. It must not be understood by this that more cattle are to be found here than elsewhere, for the contrary is true, it being a fact often lost sight of that the number of cattle raised on the small, thick-lying farms of the fertile Eastern States is actually many times greater than that of those scattered over the vast, barren ranches of the far West; for stock will always be most plentiful in districts where corn and other winter food can be grown. But in this arid belt, and in this arid belt only,— save in a few similar tracts on the Pacific slope,—stock-raising is almost the sole industry, except in the mountain districts where there is mining. The whole region is one vast stretch of grazing country, with only here and there spots of farm-land, in most places there being nothing more like agriculture than is implied in the cutting of some tons of wild hay or the planting of a garden patch for home use. This is especially true of the northern portion of the region, which comprises the basin of the Upper Missouri, and with which alone I am familiar. Here there are no fences to speak of, and all the land north of the Black Hills and the Big Horn Mountains and between the Rockies and the Dakota wheat fields might be spoken of as one gigantic, unbroken pasture, where cowboys and branding-irons take the place of fences.

The country throughout this great Upper Missouri basin has a wonderful sameness of character; and the rest of the arid belt, lying to the southward, is closely akin to it in its main features. A traveler seeing it for the first time is especially struck by its look of parched, barren desolation; he can with difficulty believe that it will support cattle at all. It is a region of light rainfall; the grass is short and comparatively scanty; there is no timber except along the beds of the streams, and in many places there are alkali deserts where nothing grows but sage-brush and cactus. Now the land stretches out into level, seemingly endless plains or into rolling prairies; again it is broken by abrupt hills and deep, winding valleys; or else it is crossed by chains of buttes, usually bare, but often clad with a dense growth of dwarfed pines or gnarled, stunted cedars. The muddy rivers run in broad, shallow beds, which after heavy rainfalls are filled to the brim by the swollen torrents, while in droughts the larger streams dwindle into sluggish trickles of clearer water, and the smaller ones dry up entirely, save in occasional deep pools.

All through the region, except on the great Indian reservations, there has been a scanty and sparse settlement, quite peculiar in its character. In the forest the woodchopper comes first; on the fertile prairies the granger is the pioneer; but on the long, stretching uplands of the far West it is the men who guard and follow the horned herds that prepare the way for the settlers who come after. The high plains of the Upper Missouri and its tributary rivers were first opened, and are still held, by the stockmen, and the whole civilization of the region has received the stamp of their marked and individual characteristics. They were from the South, not from the East, although many men from the latter region came out along the great transcontinental railway lines and joined them in their northern migration.

They were not dwellers in towns, and from the nature of their industry lived as far apart from each other as possible. In choosing new ranges, old cow-hands, who are also seasoned plainsmen, are invariably sent ahead, perhaps a year in advance, to spy out the land

and pick the best places. One of these may go by himself, or more often, especially if they have to penetrate little known or entirely unknown tracts, two or three will go together, the owner or manager of the herd himself being one of them. Perhaps their herds may already be on the border of the wild and uninhabited country: in that case they may have to take but a few days' journey before finding the stretches of sheltered, long-grass land that they seek. For instance, when I wished to move my own elkhorn steer brand on to a new ranch I had to spend barely a week in traveling north among the Little Missouri Bad Lands before finding what was then untrodden ground far outside the range of any of my neighbors' cattle. But if a large outfit is going to shift its quarters it must go much farther; and both the necessity and the chance for long wanderings were especially great when the final overthrow of the northern Horse Indians opened the whole Upper Missouri basin at one sweep to the stockmen. Then the advance-guards or explorers, each on one horse and leading another with food and bedding, were often absent months at a time, threading their way through the trackless wastes of plain, plateau, and river bottom. If possible they would choose a country that would be good for winter and summer alike; but often this could not be done, and then they would try to find a well-watered tract on which the cattle could be summered, and from which they could be driven in fall to their sheltered winter range—for the cattle in winter eat snow, and an entirely waterless region, if broken, and with good pasturage, is often the best possible winter ground, as it is sure not to have been eaten off at all during the summer; while in the bottoms the grass is always cropped down soonest. Many outfits regularly shift their herds every spring and fall; but with us in the Bad Lands all we do, when cold weather sets in, is to drive our beasts off the scantily grassed river-bottom back ten miles or more among the broken buttes and plateaus of the uplands to where the brown hay, cured on the stalk stands thick in the winding coulees.

These lookouts or foreruners having returned, the herds are set in motion as early in the spring as may be, so as to get on the ground in time to let the travel-worn beasts rest and gain flesh before winter sets in. Each herd is accompanied by a dozen, or a score, or a couple of score, of cowboys, according to its size, and beside it rumble and jolt the heavy four-horse wagons that hold the food and bedding of the men and the few implements they will need at the end of their journey. As long as possible they follow the trails made by the herds that have already traveled in the same direction, and when these end they strike out for themselves. In the Upper Missouri basin, the pioneer herds soon had to scatter out and each find its own way among the great dreary solitudes, creeping carefully along so that the cattle should not be overdriven and should have water at the halting-places. An outfit might thus be months on its lonely journey, slowly making its way over melancholy, pathless plains, or down the valleys of the lonely rivers. It was tedious, harassing work, as the weary cattle had to be driven carefully and quietly during the day and strictly guarded at night, with a perpetual watch kept for Indians or white horse-thieves. Often they would skirt the edges of the streams for days at a time, seeking for a ford or a good swimming crossing, and if the water was up and the quicksand deep the danger to the riders was serious and the risk of loss among the cattle very great.

At last, after days of excitement and danger and after months of weary, monotonous toil, the chosen ground is reached and the final camp pitched. The footsore animals are turned loose to shift for themselves, outlying camps of two or three men each being established to hem them in. Meanwhile the primitive ranch house, out buildings, and corrals are built, the unhewn cottonwood logs being chinked with moss and mud, while the roofs are of branches covered with dirt, spades and axes being the only tools needed for the work. Bunks, chairs, and tables are all home made, and as rough as the houses they are in. The supplies, of coarse, rude food are carried perhaps two or three hundred miles from the nearest town, either in the ranch-wagons or else by some regular freighting outfit, the huge canvas-topped prairie schooners of which are each drawn by several yoke of oxen, or perhaps by six or eight mules. To guard against the numerous mishaps of prairie travel, two or three of these prairie schooners usually go together, the brawny teamsters, known either as "bull-whackers" or as "mule-skinners," stalking beside their slow moving teams.

The small outlying camps are often tents, or mere dug-outs in the ground. But at the main ranch there will be a cluster of log buildings, including a separate cabin for the foreman or ranchman; often another in which to cook and eat; a long house for the men to sleep in; stables, sheds, a blacksmith's shop etc.,—the whole group forming quite a little settlement, with the corrals, the stacks of natural hay, and the patches of fenced land for gardens or horse pastures. This little settlement may be situated right out in the treeless, nearly level open, but much more often is placed in partly wooded bottom of a creek or river, sheltered by the usual background of somber brown hills.

When the northern plains began to be settled, such a ranch would at first be absolutely alone in the wilderness, but others of the same sort were sure soon to be established within twenty or thirty miles on one side or the other. The lives of the men in such places were strangely cut off from the outside world, and, indeed the same is true to a hardly less extent at the present day. Sometimes the wagons are sent for provisions, and the beef-steers are at stated times driven off for shipment. Parties of hunters and trappers call now and then. More rarely small bands of emigrants go by in search of new homes, impelled by the restless, aimless craving for change so deeply grafted in the breast of the American borderer: the white-topped wagons are loaded with domestic goods, with sallow, dispirited-looking women, and with tow-headed children; while the gaunt, moody frontiersmen slouch alongside, rifle on shoulder, lank, homely, uncouth, and yet with a curious suggestion of grim strength underlying it all. Or cowboys from neighboring ranches will ride over, looking for lost horses, or seeing if their cattle have strayed off the range. But this is all. Civilization seems as remote as if we were living in an age long past. The whole existence is patriarchal in character: it is the life of men in the open, who tend their herds on horseback; who go armed and ready to guard their lives by their own prowess, whose wants are very simple, and who call no man master. Ranching is an occupation like those of vigorous, primitive pastoral peoples, having little in common with the humdrum, workaday business world of the nineteenth century; and the free ranchman in his manner of life shows more kinship to an Arab sheik than to a sleek city merchant or tradesman.

By degrees the country becomes what in a stock-raising region passes for well settled. In addition to the great ranches smaller ones are established, with a few hundred, or even a few score, head of cattle apiece; and now and then miserable farmers straggle in to fight a losing and desperate battle with drought, cold, and grasshoppers. The wheels of the heavy wagons, driven always over the same course from one ranch to another, or to the remote frontier towns from which they get their goods, wear ruts in the soil, and roads are soon formed, perhaps originally following the deep trails made by the vanished buffalo. These roads lead down the river-bottoms or along the crests of the divides or else strike out fairly across the prairie, and a man may sometimes journey a hundred miles along one without coming to a house or a camp of any sort. If they lead to a shipping point whence the beeves are sent to market, the cattle, traveling in single file, will have worn many and deep paths on each side of the wheel-marks; and the roads between important places which are regularly used either by the United States Government, by stage-coach lines, or by freight teams become deeply worn landmarks—as, for instance, near us, the Deadwood and the old Fort Keogh trails.

Cattle-ranching can only be carried on in its present form while the population is scanty; and so in stock-raising regions, pure and simple, there are usually few towns, and these are almost always at the shipping points for cattle. But, on the other hand, wealthy cattlemen, like miners who have done well, always spend their money freely; and accordingly towns like Denver, Cheyenne, and Helena, where these two classes are the most influential in the community, are far pleasanter places of residence than cities of five times their population in the exclusively agricultural States to the eastward.

A true "cow town" is worth seeing,— such a one as Miles City, for instance, especially at the time of the annual meeting of the great Montana Stock-raisers' Association. Then the whole place is full to overflowing, the importance of the meeting and the fun of the attendant frolics, especially the horse-races, drawing from the surrounding ranch country many hundreds of men of every degree, from the rich stock-owner worth his millions to the ordinary cowboy who works for forty dollars a month. It would be impossible to imagine a more typically American assemblage, for although there are always a certain number of foreigners, usually English, Irish, or German, yet they have become completely Americanized; and on the whole it would be difficult to gather a finer body of men, in spite of their numerous shortcomings. The ranch-owners differ more from each other than do the cowboys; and the former certainly compare very favorably with similar classes of capitalists in the East. Anything more foolish than the demagogic outcry against "cattle kings" it would be difficult to imagine. Indeed, there are very few businesses so absolutely legitimate as stock-raising and so beneficial to the nation at large; and a successful stock-grower must not only be shrewd, thrifty, patient, and enterprising, but he must also possess qualities of personal bravery, hardihood, and self-reliance to a degree not demanded in the least by any mercantile occupation in a community long settled. Stockmen are in the West the pioneers of civilization, and their daring and adventurousness make the after settlement of the region possible. The whole country owes them great debt.

The most successful ranchmen are those, usually South-westerners, who have been bred to the business and have grown up with it; but many Eastern men, including not a few college graduates, have also done excellently by devoting their whole time and energy to their work,— although the Easterners who invest their money in cattle without knowing anything of the business, or who trust all to their subordinates, are naturally enough likely to incur heavy losses. Stockmen are learning more and more to act together; and certainly the meetings of their associations are conducted with a dignity and good sense that would do credit to any parliamentary body.

But the cowboys resemble one another much more and outsiders much less than is the case even with their employers, the ranchmen. A town in the cattle country, when for some cause it is thronged with men from the neighborhood, always presents a picturesque sight. On the wooden sidewalks of the broad, dusty streets the men who ply the various industries known only to frontier existence jostle one another as they saunter to and fro or lounge lazily in front of the straggling, cheap-looking board houses. Hunters come in from the plains and the mountains, clad in buckskin shirts and fur caps, greasy and unkempt, but with resolute faces and sullen, watchful eyes, that are ever on the alert. The teamsters, surly and self-contained, wear slouch hats and great cowhide boots; while the stage-drivers, their faces seamed by the hardship and exposure of their long drives with every kind of team, through every kind of country, and in every kind of weather, proud of their really wonderful skill as reinsmen and conscious of their high standing in any frontier community, look down on and sneer at the "skin hunters" and the plodding drivers of the white-topped prairie schooners. Besides these there are trappers, and wolfers, whose business is to poison wolves, with shaggy, knock-kneed ponies to carry their small bales and bundles of furs—beaver, wolf, fox, and occasionally otter; and silent sheep-herders, with cast-down faces, never able to forget the absolute solitude and monotony of their dreary lives, nor to rid their minds of the thought of the woolly idiots they pass all their days in tending. Such are the men who have come to town, either on business or else to frequent the flaunting saloons and gaudy hells of all kinds in search of the coarse, vicious excitement that in the minds of many of them does duty as pleasure—the only form of pleasure they have ever had a chance to know. Indians too, wrapped in blankets, with stolid, emotionless faces, stalk silently round among the whites, or join in the gambling and horseracing. If the town is on the borders of the mountain country, there will also be sinewy lumbermen, rough-looking miners, and packers, whose business it is to guide the long mule and pony trains that go where wagons can not and whose work in packing needs special and peculiar skill; and mingled with and drawn from all these classes are desperadoes of every grade, from the gambler up through the horse-thief to the murderous professional bully, or, as he is locally called, "bad man"—now, however, a much less conspicuous object than formerly.

But everywhere among these plainsmen and mountain-men, and more important than any, are the cowboys,—the men who follow the calling that has brought such towns into being. Singly, or in twos or threes, they gallop their wiry little horses down the street, their lithe, supple figures erect or swaying slightly as they sit loosely in the saddle; while their stirrups are so long that their knees are hardly bent, the bridles not taut enough to keep the chains from clanking. They are smaller and less muscular than the wielders of ax and pick; but they are as hardy and self-reliant as any men who ever breathed—with bronzed, set faces, and keen eyes that look all the world straight in the face without flinching as they flash out from under the broad-brimmed hats. Peril and hardship, and years of long toil broken by weeks of brutal dissipation, draw haggard lines across their eager faces, but never dim their reckless eyes nor break their bearing of defiant self-confidence. They do not walk well, partly because they so rarely do any work out of the saddle, partly because their *chaperajos* or leather overalls hamper them when on the ground; but their appearance is striking for all that, and picturesque too, with their jingling spurs, the big revolvers stuck in their belts, and bright silk handkerchiefs knotted loosely round their necks over the open collars of the flannel shirts. When drunk on the villainous whisky of the frontier towns, they cut mad antics, riding their horses into the saloons, firing their pistols right and left, from boisterous light-heartedness rather than from any viciousness, and indulging too often in deadly shooting affrays, brought on either by the accidental contact of the moment or on account of some long-standing grudge, or perhaps because of bad blood between two ranches or localities; but except while on such sprees they are quiet, rather self-contained men, perfectly frank and simple, and on their own ground treat a stranger with the most whole-souled hospitality, doing all in their power for him and scorning to take any reward in return. Although prompt to resent an injury, they are not at all apt to be rude to outsiders, treating them with what can almost be called a grave courtesy. They are much better fellows and pleasanter companions than small farmers or agricultural laborers; nor are the mechanics and workmen of a great city to be mentioned in the same breath.

The bulk of the cowboys themselves are South-westerners; but there are also many from the Eastern and the Northern States, who, if they begin young, do quite as well as the Southerners. The best hands are fairly bred to the work and follow it from their youth up. Nothing can be more foolish than for an Easterner to think he can become a cowboy in a few months' time. Many a young fellow comes out hot with enthusiasm for life on the plains, only to learn that his clumsiness is greater than he could have believed possible; that the cowboy business is like any other and has to be learned by serving a painful apprenticeship; and that this apprenticeship implies the endurance of rough fare, hard living, dirt, exposure of every kind, no little toil, and month after month of the dullest monotony. For cowboy work there is need of special traits and special training, and young Easterners should be sure of themselves before trying it; the struggle for existence is very keen in the far West, and it is no place for men who lack the ruder, coarser virtues and physical qualities, no matter how intellectual or how refined and delicate their sensibilities. Such are more likely to fail there than in older communities. Probably during the past few years more than half of the young Easterners who have come West with a little money to learn the cattle business have failed signally and lost what they had in the beginning. The West, especially the far West, needs men who have been bred on the farm or in the workshop far more than it does clerks or college graduates.

Some of the cowboys are Mexicans, who generally do the actual work well enough, but are not trustworthy; moreover, they are always regarded with extreme disfavor by the Texans in an outfit, among whom the intolerant caste spirit is very strong. Southern-born whites will never work under them, and look down upon all colored or half-caste races. One spring I had with my wagon a Pueblo Indian, an excellent rider and roper, but a drunken, worthless, lazy devil; and in the summer of 1886 there were with us a Sioux half-breed, a quiet, hard-working, faithful fellow, and a mulatto, who was one of the best cow hands in the whole round-up.

Cowboys, like most Westerners, occasionally show remarkable versatility in their tastes and pursuits. One whom I know has abandoned his regular occupation for the past nine months, during which time he has been in succession a bartender, a school-teacher, and a probate judge! Another, whom I once employed for a short while, had passed through even more varied experiences, including those of a barber, a sailor, an apothecary, and a buffalo-hunter.

As a rule the cowboys are known to each other only by their first names, with, perhaps, as a prefix, the title of the brand for which they are working. Thus I remember once overhearing a casual remark to the effect that "Bar Y Harry" had married "the Seven Open A Girl," the latter being the daughter of a neighboring ranchman. Often they receive nicknames, as, for instance, Dutch Wannigan, Windy Jack, and Kid Williams, all of whom are on the list of my personal acquaintances.

No man traveling through or living in the country need fear molestation from the cowboys unless he himself accompanies them on their drinking-bouts, or in other ways plays the fool, for they are, with us at any rate, very good fellows, and the most determined and effective foes of real law-breakers, such as horse and cattle thieves, murderers, etc. Few of the outrages quoted in Eastern papers as their handiwork are such in reality, the average Easterner apparently considering every individual who wears a broad hat and carries a six-shooter a cowboy. These outrages are, as a rule, the work of the roughs and criminals who always gather on the outskirts of civilization, and who infest every frontier town until the decent citizens become sufficiently numerous and determined to take the law into their own hands and drive them out. The old buffalo-hunters, who formed a distinct class, became powerful forces for evil once they had destroyed the vast herds of mighty beasts the pursuit of which had been their means of livelihood. They were absolutely shiftless and improvident; they had no settled habits; they were inured to peril and hardship, but entirely unaccustomed to steady work; and so they afforded just the materials from which to make the bolder and more desperate kinds of criminals. When the game was gone they hung round the settlements for some little time, and then many of them naturally took to horse-stealing, cattle-killing, and highway robbery, although others, of course, went into honest pursuits. They were men who died off rapidly, however; for it is curious to see how many of these plainsmen, in spite of their iron nerves and thews, have their constitutions completely undermined, as much by the terrible hardships they have endured as by the fits of prolonged and bestial revelry with which they have varied them.

The "bad men," or professional fighters and man-killers, are of a different stamp, quite a number of them being, according to their light, perfectly honest. These are the men who do most of the killing in frontier communities; yet it is a noteworthy fact that the men who are killed generally deserve their fate. These men are, of course, used to brawling, and are not only sure shots, but, what is equally important, able to "draw" their weapons with marvelous quickness. They think nothing whatever of murder, and are the dread and terror of their associates; yet they are very chary of taking the life of a man of good standing, and will often weaken and back down at once if confronted fearlessly. With many of them their courage arises from confidence in their own powers and knowledge of the fear in which they are held; and men of this type often show the white feather when they get in a tight place. Others, however, will face any odds without flinching; and I have known of these men fighting, when mortally wounded, with a cool, ferocious despair that was terrible. As elsewhere, so here, very quiet men are often those who in an emergency show themselves best able to hold their own. These desperadoes always try to "get the drop" on a foe—that is, to take him at a disadvantage before he can use his own weapon. I have known more men killed in this way, when the affair was wholly one-sided, than I have known to be shot in fair fight; and I have known fully as many who were shot by accident. It is wonderful, in the event of a street fight, how few bullets seem to hit the men they are aimed at.

During the last two or three years the stockmen have united to put down all these dangerous characters, often by the most summary exercise of lynch law. Notorious bullies and murderers have been taken out and hung, while the bands of horse and cattle thieves have been regularly hunted down and destroyed in pitched fights by parties of armed cowboys; and as a consequence most of our territory is now perfectly law-abiding. One such fight occurred north of me early last spring. The horse-thieves were overtaken on the banks of the Missouri; two of their number were slain, and the others were driven on the ice, which broke, and two more were drowned. A few months previously another gang, whose headquarters were near the Canadian line, were surprised in their hut; two or three were shot down by the cowboys as they tried to come out, while the rest barricaded themselves in and fought until the great log-hut was set on fire, when they broke forth in a body, and nearly all were killed at once, only one or two making their escape. A little over two years ago one committee of vigilantes in eastern Montana shot or hung nearly sixty—not, however, with the best judgment in all cases.

Out on the Range

A stranger in the North-western cattle country is especially struck by the resemblance the settlers show in their pursuits and habits to the Southern people. Nebraska and Dakota, east of the Missouri, resemble Minnesota and Iowa and the States farther east, but Montana and the Dakota cow country show more kinship with Texas; for while elsewhere in America settlement has advanced along the parallels of latitude, on the great plains it has followed the meridians of longitude and has gone northerly rather than westerly. The business is carried on as it is in the South. The rough-rider of the plains, the hero of rope and revolver, is first cousin to the backwoodsman of the southern Alleghanies, the man of the ax and the rifle; he is only a unique offshoot of the frontier stock of the South-west. The very term "round-up" is used by the cowboys in the exact sense in which it is employed by the hill people and mountaineers of Kentucky, Tennessee, and North Carolina, with whom also labor is dear and poor land cheap, and whose few cattle are consequently branded and turned loose in the woods exactly as is done with the great herds on the plains.

But the ranching industry itself was copied from the Mexicans, of whose land and herds, the South-western frontiersmen of Texas took forcible possession; and the traveler in the North-west will see at a glance that the terms and practices of our business are largely of Spanish origin. The cruel curb-bit and heavy stock-saddle, with its high horn and cantle, prove that we have adopted Spanish-American horse-gear; and the broad hat, huge blunt spurs, and leather *chaperajos* of the rider, as well as the corral in which the stock are penned, all alike show the same ancestry. Throughout the cattle country east of the Rocky Mountains, from the Rio Grande to the Saskatchewan, the same terms are in use and the same system is followed; but on the Pacific slope, in California, there are certain small differences, even in nomenclature. Thus, we of the great plains all use the double cinch saddle, with one girth behind the horse's fore legs and another farther back, while Californians prefer one with a single cinch, which seems to us much inferior for stock-work. Again, Californians use the Spanish word "lasso," which with us has been entirely dropped, no plainsman with pretensions to the title thinking of any word but "rope," either as noun or verb.

The rope, whether leather lariat or made of grass, is the one essential feature of every cowboy's equipment. Loosely coiled, it hangs from the horn or is tied to one side of the saddle in front of the thigh, and is used for every conceivable emergency, a twist being taken round the stout saddle-horn the second the noose settles over the neck or around the legs of a chased animal. In helping pull a wagon up a steep pitch, in dragging an animal by the horns out of a bog-hole, in hauling logs for the fire, and in a hundred other ways aside from its legitimate purpose, the rope is of invaluable service, and dexterity with it is prized almost or quite as highly as good horsemanship, and is much rarer. Once a cowboy is a good roper and rider, the only other accomplishment he values is skill with his great army revolver, it being taken for granted that he is already a thorough plainsman and has long mastered the details of cattlework; for the best roper and rider alive is of little use unless he is hard-working, honest, keenly alive to his employer's interest, and very careful in the management of the cattle.

All cowboys can handle the rope with more or less ease and precision, but great skill in its use is only attained after long practice, and for its highest development needs that the man should have begun in earliest youth. Mexicans literally practice from infancy; the boy can hardly toddle before he gets a string and begins to render life a burden to the hens, goats, and pigs. A really first-class roper can command his own price, and is usually fit for little but his own special work.

It is much the same with riding. The cowboy is an excellent rider in his own way, but his way differs from that of a trained school horseman or cross-country fox-hunter as much as it does from the horsemanship of an Arab or of a Sioux Indian, and, as with all these, it has its special merits and special defects—schoolman, fox-hunter, cowboy, Arab, and Indian being all alike admirable riders in their respective styles, and each cherishing the same profound and ignorant contempt for every method but his own. The flash riders, or horse-breakers, always called "bronco busters," can perform really marvelous feats, riding with ease the most vicious and unbroken beasts, that no ordinary cowboy would dare to tackle. Although sitting seemingly so loose in the saddle, such a rider cannot be jarred out of it by the wildest plunges, it being a favorite feat to sit out the antics of a bucking horse with silver half-dollars under each knee or in the stirrups under each foot. But their method of breaking is very rough, consisting only in saddling and bridling a beast by main force and then riding him, also by main force, until he is exhausted, when he is turned over as "broken." Later on the cowboy himself may train his horse to stop or wheel instantly at a touch of the reins or bit, to start at top speed at a signal, and to stand motionless when left. An intelligent pony soon picks up a good deal of knowledge about the cow business on his own account.

All cattle are branded, usually on the hip, shoulder, and side, or on any one of them, with letters, numbers, or figures in every combination, the outfit being known by its brand. Near me, for instance, are the Three Sevens, The Thistle, the Bellows, the OX, the VI., the Seventy-six Bar ($\underline{76}$), and the Quarter Circle Diamond ($\Diamond$) outfits. The dew-lap and the ears may also be cut, notched, or slit. All brands are registered, and are thus protected against imitators, any man tampering with them being punished as severely as possible. Unbranded animals are called *mavericks,* and when found on the round-up are either branded by the owner of the range on which they are, or else are sold for the benefit of the association. At every shipping point, as well as where the beef cattle are received, there are stock inspectors who jealously examine all the brands on the live animals or on the hides of the slaughtered ones, so as to detect any foul play, which is immediately reported to the association. It becomes second nature with a cowboy to inspect and note the brands of every bunch of animals he comes across.

Perhaps the thing that seems strangest to the traveler who for the first time crosses the bleak plains of this Upper Missouri grazing country is the small number of cattle seen. He can hardly believe he is in the great stock region, where for miles upon miles he will not see a single head, and will then come only upon a straggling herd of a few score. As a matter of fact, where there is no artificial food put up for winter use cattle always need a good deal of ground per head; and this is peculiarly the case with us in the North-west, where much of the ground is bare of vegetation and where what pasture there is is both short and sparse. It is a matter of absolute necessity, where beasts are left to shift for themselves in the open during the bitter winter weather, that they then should have grass that they have not cropped too far down; and to insure this it is necessary with us to allow on the average about twenty-five acres of ground to each animal. This means that a range of country ten miles square will keep between two and three thousand head of stock only, and if more are put on, it is at the risk of seeing a severe winter kill off half or three-quarters of the whole number. So a range may be in reality overstocked when to an Eastern and unpracticed eye it seems hardly to have on it a number worth taking into account.

Overstocking is the great danger threatening the stock-raising industry on the plains. This industry has only risen to be of more than local consequence during the past score of years, as before that time it was confined to Texas and California; but during these two decades of its existence the stockmen in different localities have again and again suffered the most ruinous losses, usually with overstocking as the ultimate cause. In the south the drought, and in the north the deep snows, and everywhere unusually bad winters, do immense damage; still, if the land is fitted for stock at all, they will, averaging one year with another, do very well so long as the feed is not cropped down too close.

But, of course, no amount of feed will make some countries worth anything for cattle that are not housed during the winter; and stockmen in choosing new ranges for their herds pay almost as much attention to the capacity of the land for yielding shelter as they do to the abundant and good quality of the grass. High up among the foot-hills of the mountains cattle will not live through the winter; and an open, rolling prairie land of heavy rainfall, where in consequence the snow lies deep and there is no protection from the furious cold winds, is useless for winter grazing, no matter how thick and high the feed. The three essentials for a range are grass, water, and shelter: the water is only needed in summer and the shelter in winter, while it may be doubted if drought during the hot months has ever killed off more cattle than have died of exposure on shelterless ground to the icy weather, lasting from November to April.

The finest summer range may be valueless either on account of its lack of shelter or because it is in a region of heavy snowfall—portions of territory lying in the same latitude and not very far apart often differing widely in this respect, or extraordinarily severe weather may cause a heavy death-rate utterly unconnected with overstocking. This was true of the loss that visited the few herds which spent the very hard winter of 1880 on the northern cattle plains. These were the pioneers of their kind, and the grass was all that could be desired; yet the extraordinary severity of the weather proved too much for the cattle. This was especially the case with those herds consisting of "pilgrims," as they are called—that is, of animals driven up on to the range from the south, and therefore in poor condition. One such herd of pilgrims on the Powder River suffered a loss of thirty-six hundred out of a total of four thousand, and the survivors kept alive only by browsing on the tops of cottonwoods felled for them. Even seasoned animals fared very badly. One great herd in the Yellowstone Valley lost about a fourth of its number, the loss falling mainly on the breeding cows, calves, and bulls,—always the chief sufferers, as the steers, and also the dry cows, will get through almost anything. The loss here would have been far heavier than it was had it not been for a curious trait shown by the cattle. They kept in bands of several hundred each, and during the time of the deep snows a band would make a start and travel several miles in a straight line, plowing their way through the drifts and beating out a broad track; then, when stopped by a frozen water-course or chain of buttes, they would turn back and graze over the trail thus made, the only place where they could get at the grass.

A drenching rain, followed by a severe snap of cold, is even more destructive than deep snow, for the saturated coats of the poor beasts are turned into sheets of icy mail, and the grass-blades, frozen at the roots as well as above, change into sheaves of brittle spears as uneatable as so many icicles. Entire herds have perished in consequence of such a storm. Mere cold, however, will kill only very weak animals, which is fortunate for us, as the spirit in the thermometer during winter often sinks to fifty degrees below zero, the cold being literally arctic; yet though the cattle become thin during such a snap of weather, and sometimes have their ears, tails, and even horns frozen off, they nevertheless rarely die from the cold alone. But if there is a blizzard blowing at such a time, the cattle need shelter, and if caught in the open, will travel for scores of miles before the storm, until they reach a break in the ground, or some stretch of dense woodland, which will shield them from the blasts. If cattle traveling in this manner come to some obstacle that they cannot pass, as, for instance, a wire fence or a steep railway embankment, they will not try to make their way back against the storm, but will simply stand with their tails to it until they drop dead in their tracks; and, accordingly, in some parts of the country—but luckily far to the south of us—the railways are fringed with countless skeletons of beasts that have thus perished, while many of the long wire fences make an almost equally bad showing. In some of the very open country of Kansas and Indian Territory, many of the herds during the past two years have suffered a loss of from sixty to eighty per cent., although this was from a variety of causes, including drought as well as severe winter weather. Too much rain is quite as bad as too little, especially if it falls after the 1st of August, for then, though the growth of grass is very rank and luxuriant, it yet has little strength and does not cure well on the stalk; and it is only possible to winter cattle at large at all because of the way in which the grass turns into natural hay by this curing on the stalk.

But scantiness of food, due to overstocking, is the one really great danger to us in the north, who do not have to fear the droughts that occasionally devastate portions of the southern ranges. In a fairly good country, if the feed is plenty, the natural increase of a herd is sure shortly to repair any damage that may be done by an unusually severe winter—unless, indeed, the latter should be one such as occurs but two or three times in a century. When, however, the grass becomes cropped down, then the loss in even an ordinary year is heavy among the weaker animals, and if the winter is at all severe it becomes simply appalling. The snow covers the shorter grass much quicker, and even when there is enough, the cattle, weak and unfit to travel around, have to work hard to get it; their exertions tending to enfeeble them and to render them less able to cope with the exposure and cold. The large patches of brushwood, into which the cattle crowd and which to a small number afford ample shelter and some food, become trodden down and yield neither when the beasts become too plentiful. Again, the grass is, of course, soonest eaten off where there is shelter; and, accordingly, the broken ground to which the animals cling during winter may be grazed bare of vegetation though the open plains, to which only the hardiest will at this season stray, may have plenty; and insufficiency of food, although not such as actually to starve them, weakens them so that they succumb readily to the cold or to one of the numerous accidents to which they are liable—as slipping off an icy butte or getting cast in a frozen washout. The cows in calf are those that suffer most, and so heavy is the loss among these and so light the calf crop that it is yet an open question whether our northern ranges are as a whole fitted for breeding. When the animals get weak they will huddle into some nook or corner and simply stay there till they die. An empty hut, for instance, will often in the spring be found to contain the carcasses of a dozen weak cows or poor steers that have crawled into it for protection from the cold, and once in have never moved out.

Overstocking may cause little or no harm for two or three years, but sooner or later there comes a winter which means ruin to the ranches that have too many cattle on them; and in our country, which is even now getting crowded, it is merely a question of time as to when a winter will come that will understock the ranges by the sum-mary process of killing off about half of all the cattle throughout the North-west.* The herds that have just been put on suffer most in such a case; if they have come on late and are composed of weak animals, very few indeed, perhaps not ten per cent., will survive. The cattle that have been double or single wintered do better; while a range-raised steer is almost as tough as a buffalo.

In our northern country we have "free grass"; that is, the stock-men rarely own more than small portions of the land over which their cattle range, the bulk of it being unsurveyed and still the property of the National Government—for the latter refuses to sell the soil except in small lots, acting on the wise principle of distributing it among as many owners as possible. Here and there some ranchman has acquired title to narrow strips of territory peculiarly valuable as giving water-right; but the amount of land thus occupied is small with us,—although the reverse is the case farther south,—and there is practical-ly no fencing to speak of. As a consequence, the land is one vast pas-ture, and the man who overstocks his own range damages his neigh-bors as much as himself. These huge northern pastures are too dry and the soil too poor to be used for agriculture until the rich, wet lands to the east and west are occupied; and at present we have little to fear from grangers. Of course, in the end much of the ground will be taken up for small farms, but the farmers that so far have come in

---

Written in the fall of 1886; the ensuing winter exactly fulfilled the prophecy.

have absolutely failed to make even a living, except now and then by raising a few vegetables for the use of the stockmen; and we are inclined to welcome the incoming of an occasional settler, if he is a decent man, especially as, by the laws of the Territories in which the great grazing plains lie, he is obliged to fence in his own patch of cleared ground, and we do not have to keep our cattle out of it.

At present we are far more afraid of each other. There are always plenty of men who for the sake of the chance of gain they themselves run are willing to jeopardize the interests of their neighbors by putting on more cattle than the land will support—for the loss, of course, falls as heavily on the man who has put on the right number as on him who has put on too many; and it is against these individuals that we have to guard so far as we are able. To protect ourselves completely is impossible, but the very identity of interest that renders all of us liable to suffer for the fault of a few also renders us as a whole able to take some rough measures to guard against the wrong-doing of a portion of our number; for the fact that the cattle wander intermixed over the ranges forces all the ranchmen of a locality to combine if they wish to do their work effectively. Accordingly, the stockmen of a neighborhood, when it holds as many cattle as it safely can, usually unitedly refuse to work with any one who puts in another herd. In the cow country a man is peculiarly dependent upon his neighbors, and a small outfit is wholly unable to work without their assistance when once the cattle have mingled completely with those of other brands. A large outfit is much more master of its destiny, and can do its own work quite by itself; but even such a one can be injured in countless ways if the hostility of the neighboring ranchmen is incurred.

The best days of ranching are over; and though there are many ranchmen who still make money, yet during the past two or three years the majority have certainly lost. This is especially true of the numerous Easterners who went into the business without any experience and trusted themselves entirely to their Western representatives; although, on the other hand, many of those who have made most money at it are Easterners, who, however, have happened to be naturally fitted for the work and who have deliberately settled down to learning the business as they would have learned any other, devoting their whole time and energy to it. Stock-raising, as now carried on, is characteristic of a young and wild land. As the country grows older, it will in some places die out, and in others entirely change its character; the ranches will be broken up, will be gradually modified into stock-farms, or, if on good soil, may even fall under the sway of the husbandman.

In its present form stock-raising on the plains is doomed, and can hardly outlast the century. The great free ranches, with their barbarous, picturesque, and curiously fascinating surroundings, mark a primitive stage of existence as surely as do the great tracts of primeval forests, and like the latter must pass away before the onward march of our people; and we who have felt the charm of the life, and have exulted in its abounding vigor and its bold, restless freedom, will not only regret its passing for our own sakes, but must also feel real sorrow that those who come after us are not to see, as we have seen, what is perhaps the pleasantest, healthiest, and most exciting phase of American existence.

The Cattle Business

– by –
Granville Stuart

THE WINTER OF 1882–83 was a mild one and spring came early with plenty of moisture. The grass was fine. The bounty placed on wolves and coyotes made wolfing profitable once more and the wolfers were rapidly clearing the ranges of those pests. The Canadian Indians were keeping north of the line and our own Indians were slightly less troublesome. All this promised an era of prosperity to the cattle industry but there were still some dark clouds hovering on the horizon.

The sheepmen had discovered that if Montana was not exactly "a land of milk and honey" it was a mighty good grass land and several large bands of sheep were brought on the range. Herds of from two thousand to five thousand head of cattle were being gathered in Texas and New Mexico ready to start for "the land of promise" in the early spring.

The railroads had invaded Montana destroying the Missouri river transportation and the abandoned wood yards furnished splendid rendezvous for horse thieves and cattle rustlers, who were becoming so numerous and so well organized that they threatened to destroy the cattle business.

A meeting of the Montana Stock Growers' Association was called to convene at Miles City on April 17, 1883. This meeting was a memorable one. There were two hundred seventy-nine members present. The town was gaily decorated with bunting and banners and the citizens turned out in mass to welcome the cattlemen. There was a big parade headed by the mayor of the city, and a brass band and the town was thrown wide open to the visitors. The streets were thronged with cowboys dressed in their best with picturesque paraphernalia, and riding the best horses that the country afforded.

This meeting was not all parade and social enjoyment. There were conditions facing the stock growers that called for serious consideration anyone of which if not controlled, threatened the very life of the industry. First and foremost were the "rustlers." It had come to be almost impossible to keep a team or saddle horse on a ranch unless one slept in the manger with a rifle. Our detectives pursued and brought back stolen property and caused the arrest of the thieves and we hired counsel to assist the county attorneys to prosecute them but all to no purpose. The thieves managed to evade the law and became bolder each season.

The experienced cattle men worked unceasingly at this meeting. They gathered the stock laws of our western states and territories and the rules and regulations of other associations and from these were culled and arranged, by a committee of experts, assisted by able counsel, such parts as suited our locality and circumstances, and gave the best satisfaction when in force. Everything was done to bring about better conditions for the stock interests.

With hundreds of thousands of cattle valued at $25,000,000.00 scattered over an area of fifty-eight thousand square miles of territory, it was apparent to the most casual observer that there must be the closest cooperation between the companies if we were to succeed, as what benefited one, must benefit all. From this time on the entire range business was under the direction and control of the Montana Stock Growers' Association and the business run as one large outfit.

At this meeting it was agreed to employ one man in each county as a detective whose duty it would be to track up rustlers and horse thieves and do all in his power to have them arrested and brought to trial. These detectives were to be paid by the Stock Growers' Association.

Minutes of roundup meeting held at "D-S" ranch, Fort Maginnis range May 29, 1883.

Present, Granville Stuart of Davis, Hauser and Co., A.J. Clark of Kohrs and Bielenburg, Horace Brewster for Robert Coburn, Henry Sieben, Robert Clark for N.J. Dovenspeck, Amos Snyder for Snyder and McCauley, John Milliren for Adolph Baro.

It was moved and carried that every stock owner have one vote for each rider furnished and employed by him on this range and that all persons having one thousand or less cattle on the range be required to furnish one rider, or in lieu thereof pay the roundup fund $2.00 per head for branding and marking their calves, that being the price fixed for branding and marking calves for those not attending. All owners having more than one thousand cattle on the range must furnish one rider for each one thousand head or fraction of five hundred or over.

W.C. Burnett was nominated for captain of the roundup for 1883 and was unanimously elected with pay at the rate of $2.50 per day from beginning to close of the roundup.

It was decided to send three men to the lower Musselshell to the Ryan Brothers roundup to work with them and to bring back any cattle from their range found there, with instructions to brand and mark any calves. It was also decided to send two men to Fergus's range when their roundup begins to brand and bring back any cattle from this range found there.

It was decided that one man tally all calves branded and whose duty it shall be to see that there is turned out by their respective owners seven bull calves to each one hundred heifer calves. Henry Sieben was elected to attend to same.

It was also decided to elect a committee of three to inspect the bulls at each corral and to decide upon such as are too old to be of service and order them to be castrated. The owner of each bull so disposed of is required to turn out a bull calf in its place, and said committee shall count all bulls on the range and keep a tally of each brand. Horace Brewster, Henry Sieben, and A.J. Clark were elected committee on bulls.

The spring roundup is to begin on the north side of the range May 30, 1883. It was decided to begin the fall calf roundup Sept. 1, 1883, and the beef roundup to begin Oct. 1, 1883, on the north side of the range. It was decided to pay the day and night herders and the wood haulers out of the roundup funds, and the representatives sent to other ranges were also to be paid out of that fund.

GRANVILLE STUART
SEC.

We had now increased our herd to twelve thousand head of range cattle and were buying thoroughbred bulls of short horn breed to grade them up. None of our cattle were Texas long horns all being a good grade of range stock from Idaho and Oregon.

There was now, on the Fort Maginnis range, twelve outfits, — The Davis-Hauser-Stuart, the Kohrs and Bielenburg, Robert Coburn, Henry Sieben, N.J. Dovenspeck, N.W. McCaulley, C.D. Duncan, Stuart-Anderson, W.C. and G.P. Burnett, F.E. Lawrence, Adolph Baro, and Amos Snyder.

There were also twelve outfits on the Cone butte and Moccasin range: James Fergus and Son, Robert S. Hamilton, The Judith Cattle Co., Tingley Brothers, John H. Ming, Pat Dunlevy, James Dempsey, Chas. Ranges, A. Hash, C.H. Christ, J.L. Stuart, Edward Regan. From this time on the two ranges worked together in one roundup and usually held their meeting and made the start from the "D-S" ranch.

It was a novel sight to witness the big spring roundup pull out. Early in the morning the big horse herd would be driven in and each man would catch and saddle his mount. There was a number of horses that would buck and a lot of half broken colts to ride that would cause a certain amount of excitement. The horse herder in charge of the horse wranglers would lead off in the direction of the objective corral followed by the white covered four-horse chuck wagons, and then the troop of cowboys with their gay handkerchiefs, fine saddles, and silver mounted bridles and spurs.

At the "D-S" ranch there was usually an impromptu dance the night before and there would be quite a gathering of ladies to watch the start. Often they would ride to the first corral to watch the branding and have lunch at the chuck wagon.

A roundup on the range is in charge of the captain absolutely. Every man, whether owner of the largest herd or a humble roustabout, takes his orders from the captain. There were very few orders given, every man knew what he was expected to do and did it.

Work began very early in the morning. The cook was up, breakfast ready and the horse herd in as soon as it was daylight. The riders caught up their horses and saddled them and were ready to start. The men were divided into groups. The circle riders started out two together in every direction and drove to the corral all the cattle that they could find. At the corral the cattle to be branded would be cut out of the bunches, and the ropers would catch and throw them.

There were wrestlers and the men with the branding irons in the corral to brand and mark. Occasionally an animal would get on "the fight" and make things interesting but the rope horses were as clever as the men about keeping out of danger and rarely ever did we have a serious accident. The work at the corrals was hard and fast. The dust and heat and smell of singeing hair was stifling while the bellowing of the cattle was a perfect bedlam. At the close of the day everyone was tired and ready to roll in his blankets for a night's rest.

The spring or calf roundup usually lasted from four to six weeks. As soon as it was over the hay would have to be put up at the home ranch, range cabins built or put in repair, corrals put in shape, and stray horses gathered. If the herd was being increased we tried to get the new cattle on the range not later than September first. The fall calf roundup started about October 1, and usually required four weeks. After that was the beef roundup, the most important one of all.

The fall of 1883 we shipped from Custer on the Northern Pacific and had a drive of one hundred twenty miles. Cattle must be driven slowly and allowed to graze as they go and yet they must have water regularly. They were as wild as antelope and it required eternal vigilance to keep them from stampeding and running all the fat off. The slightest unusual sight or sound would start them off pell mell.

I well remember one night on the drive. It had been storming all day, rain mixed with snow, and a cold raw wind blowing from the northeast. Our tent blew over and the cook prepared supper over a soggy smoky fire. We were camped on a branch of McDonald creek. There was a steep cut bank on one side of the herd and cut bank coulees in every direction besides prairie dog towns which are full of holes and little mounds of loose earth. The cattle were cold and restless but they were finally bedded down. We ate our supper in the cold and wet. The night herd went on duty and the rest of us unrolled our tarpaulins and turned in. I could hear the cattle moving and occasionally their horns striking together. The boys on guard kept up their monotonous singing.

About eleven o'clock something startled the herd. Instantly every animal was on its feet and the tramping of flying hoofs and rattling horns sounded like artillery. The herders were with the stampede and in an instant every man was in the saddle after them. The night was pitch dark and there was nothing to guide us but the thunder of hoofs. They must be stopped and the only way to do it was to get ahead of them and turn the leaders so that the herd would move in a circle; "milling" it is called. Through the rain and mud and pitch dark, up and down banks and over broken ground, they all went in a mad rush, but the boys succeeded in holding the herd.

Every man had risked his life and some were in the saddle twenty-four hours before they were relieved, but there was not one word of complaint and not one of them thought of his own safety or of leaving the herd so long as his services were needed.

Our beef herd this year was in charge of William C. Burnett, a young Texan, the best range foreman that I ever met. He knew the business from A to Z, and understood the psychology of range cattle and cowboys. The herd reached the Yellowstone, crossed the river, and were loaded and shipped to Chicago where they arrived in first class condition.

Here I wish to give my impression of cowboys or "cowpunchers" as they called themselves, gathered from my ten years association with them on the range. They were a class by themselves and the genuine "dyed in the wool" ones came from the southwest, most of them from Texas. Born and raised on those great open ranges, isolated from everything but cattle they came to know and understand the habits and customs of range cattle as no one else could know them. Always on the frontier beyond organized society or law, they formulated laws of their own that met their requirements, and they enforced them, if necessary, at the point of the six shooter. They were reluctant to obey any law but their own and chafed under restraint. They were loyal to their outfit and to one another. A man that was not square could not long remain with an outfit.

A herd was perfectly safe in the hands of a "boss" and his outfit. Every man would sacrifice his life to protect the herd. If personal quarrels or disputes arose while on a roundup or on a drive, the settlement of the same was left until the roundup was over and the men released from duty, and then they settled their differences man to man and without interference from their comrades. They often paid the penalty with their lives.

Cowpunchers were strictly honest as they reckoned honesty but they did not consider it stealing to take anything they could lay hands on from the government or from Indians. There was always a bitter enmity between them and soldiers.

A shooting scrape that resulted in the death of one or both of the combatants was not considered a murder but an affair between themselves. If a sheriff from Texas or Arizona arrived on one of our northern ranges to arrest a man for murder, the other cowpunchers would invariably help him make his escape.

They were chivalrous and held women in high esteem and were always gentlemen in their presence. They wore the best clothes that they could buy and took a great pride in their personal appearance and in their trapping. The men of our outfit used to pay $25.00 a pair for made-to-order riding boots when the best store boots in Helena were $10.00 a pair.

Their trappings consisted of a fine saddle, silver mounted bridle, pearl-handled six shooter, latest model cartridge belt with silver buckle, silver spurs, a fancy quirt with silver mountings, a fine riata sometimes made of rawhide, a pair of leather chaps, and a fancy hatband often made from the dressed skin of a diamond-backed rattlesnake. They wore expensive stiff-brimmed light felt hats, with brilliantly colored silk handkerchiefs knotted about their necks, light colored shirts and exquisitely fitted very high heeled riding boots.

Each cowpuncher owned one or more fine saddle horses, often a thoroughbred, on which he lavished his affections, and the highest compliments he could pay you was to allow you to ride his favorite horse. Horse racing was one of his favorite sports.

There were men among them who were lightning to draw a gun, and the best shots that I ever saw; others that could do all the fancy turns with a rope and others that could ride any horse that could be saddled or bridled; but the best and most reliable men were those who did all these things reasonably well.

On the range or the trail their work was steady, hard, and hazardous and with a good deal of responsibility. They were out from three to six months at a time, so when they did get to town it is not to be wondered at if they did do a little celebrating in their own way. Few of them drank to excess, some of them gambled, they all liked a good show and a dance and they always patronized the best restaurant or eating place in town and ice cream and fresh oysters were never omitted from their menu.

When on night herd it was necessary to sing to the cattle to keep them quiet. The sound of the boys' voices made the cattle know that their protectors were there guarding them and this gave them a sense of security. There were two songs that seemed to be favorites. The tunes were similar and all their tunes were monotonous and pitched to a certain key. I suppose they learned just the tune that was most soothing to the cattle. I know that their songs always made me drowsy and feel at peace with the world.

The first place they struck for in a town was the livery stable where they saw to it that their horses were properly cared for, and the barber shop was their next objective. The noisy fellow in exaggerated costume that rode up and down the streets whooping and shooting in the air was never a cowpuncher from any outfit. He was usually some "would be" bad man from the East decked out in paraphernalia from Montgomery, Ward's of Chicago.

As the country settled up and the range business became a thing of the past most of the old reliable cowboys engaged in other business. Their natural love of animals and an out of doors life led many of them to settle on ranches, and they are today among our most successful ranchers and cattle growers.

During the summer of 1882 Carpenter and Robertson moved three thousand stock cattle from Nebraska and located on the Rosebud. The Niobrara Cattle Company drove in ten thousand head of Oregon cattle and located them on Powder river. Scot and Hanks drove in a herd from Nevada and located on the Little Powder river.

In 1879 Robert E. Strahorn published a pamphlet called *Resources of Montana and Attractions of Yellowstone Park*, in which he gave interviews with prominent men and bankers, calling attention to the wonderful opportunities offered in Montana for range cattle business.

Following this came General Brisbin's book, *The Beef Bonanza* in which he pictured in glowing colors the wonderful possibilities of the range cattle business in Montana. The fame of Montana ranges had gone abroad. Eastern papers and magazines published all sorts of romantic tales about the ease and rapidity with which vast fortunes were being accumulated by the "cattle kings."

Profits were figured at one hundred per cent and no mention made of severe winters, storms, dry parched summer ranges, predatory animals, hostile Indians, and energetic "rustlers," or the danger of overstocking the ranges.

The business was a fascinating one and profitable so long as the ranges were not overstocked. The cattlemen found ways to control the other difficulties but the ranges were free to all and no man could say, with authority, when a range was overstocked.

In the summer of 1883 Conrad Kohrs drove in three thousand cattle and placed them on the Sun river range, and D.A.G. Floweree drove three thousand Texas cattle in and threw them on the Sun river range. The Green Mountain Cattle Company drove in twenty-two hundred and located on Emmel's creek. The Dehart Land and Cattle Company came in with two herds of three thousand each and located on the Rosebud. Griffin Brothers and Ward drove in three thousand head and located on the Yellowstone. J.M. Holt came in with three thousand head and located on Cabin creek. Tusler and Kempton brought in three herds of twenty-five hundred each and located on Tongue river. Ryan Brothers brought in three herds of three thousand each and located on the Musselshell. John T. Murphy and David Fratt drove in six thousand head and located on the Musselshell. Poindexter and Orr increased their herds in Madison county. Lepley brought in two thousand head, Green three thousand head and Conley twenty-five hundred and placed them on the range near Fort Benton. These cattle were nearly all Texas cattle and came up over the Texas trail. By the first of October there were six hundred thousand head of range cattle in the territory and these together with the horses and sheep was as much stock as the ranges could safely carry.

There was never, in Montana, any attempt on the part of the large cattle companies to keep out small owners, homesteaders, or permanent settlers. On the contrary every possible assistance was given to the settlers by the larger companies.

It was customary to allow settlers to milk range cows, provided they let the calves have a share of the milk and we frequently purchased the butter from the homesteader, paying him fifty cents a pound for it. The company would lend horses and farm machinery, employ the men and recover stolen horses and cattle at times when it would have been utterly impossible for a lone rancher to do so. One instance to illustrate. A settler on our range had the misfortune to break his leg and while he lay helpless in his cabin thieves drove off his span of fine mares. Cowboys immediately started in pursuit, recovered the mares and kept them at the ranch until the owner was able to look after them himself. Had they not done so the thieves would have crossed the British line and been safely in Canada before the authorities could have been notified and the team would have been irretrievably lost.

The large companies encouraged schools and their taxes largely supported them. On our range whenever as many as six children could be assembled I provided a good log school house and a six months' term of school each year. The cowboys on the range saw to it that the teacher, if a young woman, was provided with a good saddle horse and not allowed to become lonely.

At the ranch I had a library of three thousand volumes and we subscribed for the leading newspapers and magazines. At the James Fergus' ranch on Armell's creek, there was another splendid library and the leading periodicals. These books were at the disposal of everybody.

Few of the cattle outfits had any money invested in land nor did they attempt to fence or control large bodies of land. The land on the ranges was unsurveyed and titles could not be had. The cattleman did not want to see fences on the range as during severe storms the cattle drifted for miles and if they should strike a fence they were likely to drift against it and perish with the cold.

In the days of the big ranges there was never any serious trouble between the cattlemen and the sheepmen and there was never a "range war" between them in Montana. Many of the cattlemen also had bands of sheep.

It would be impossible to make persons not present on the Montana cattle ranges realize the rapid change that took place on those ranges in two years. In 1880 the country was practically uninhabited. One could travel for miles without seeing so much as a trapper's bivouac. Thousands of buffalo darkened the rolling plains. There were deer, antelope, elk, wolves, and coyotes on every hill and in every ravine and thicket. In the whole territory of Montana there were but two hundred and fifty thousand head of cattle, including dairy cattle and work oxen.

In the fall of 1883 there was not one buffalo remaining on the range and the antelope, elk, and deer were indeed scarce. In 1880 no one had heard tell of a cowboy in "this niche of the woods" and Charlie Russell had made no pictures of them; but in the fall of 1883 there were six hundred thousand head of cattle on the range. The cowboy, with leather chaps, wide hats, gay handkerchiefs, clanking silver spurs, and skin fitting high heeled boots was no longer a novelty but had become an institution. Small ranches were being taken by squatters along all the streams and there were neat and comfortable log school houses in all the settlements.

The story of the Montana cattle ranges would not be complete without a brief description of the Texas trail, as more than one half of the Montana range cattle were driven over that trail and almost every cowboy that worked on the ranges made one or more drives up the trail.

The trail started at the Rio Grande, crossing the Colorado river at San Angelo, then across the Llanos Estacado, or Staked Plains to the Red river about where Amarillo now is. From there it ran due north to the Canadian river and on to Dodge City where it crossed the Arkansas river and then on to Ogalalla, crossing the North Platte at

Camp Clark. From Ogalalla it followed the Sidney and Black hills stage road north to Cottonwood creek, then to Hat creek and across to Belle Fourche, then over to Little Powder river and down that stream to its mouth where it crossed Tongue river to the Yellowstone, crossing that stream just above Fort Keogh. From here it ran up Sunday creek across the Little Dry, following up the Big Dry to the divide, then down Lodge Pole creek to the Musselshell river which was the end of the trail. Texas cattle were sometimes driven clear up into Canada but never in any considerable numbers. Ogalalla was a great trading center in the range days. Many herds were driven up from Texas, sold, and turned over to northern buyers, at that place.

There were usually from two to three thousand cattle in a trail herd, and the outfit consisted of a trail boss, eight cowpunchers, a cook, a horse wrangler, about sixty-five cow horses, and a four-horse chuck wagon that carried provisions and the men's blankets. The food provided was corn meal, sorghum molasses, beans, salt, sugar, and coffee.

The cattle were as wild as buffalo and difficult to handle for the first week or ten days, until they had gained confidence in the cowpunchers and accustomed themselves to the daily routine. By that time some old range steer had established himself leader of the herd and everything settled down to a regular system.

The daily program was breakfast at daylight and allow the herd to graze awhile. The horse herd and mess wagon pulled out and then the herd started, with two cowpunchers in the lead or "point." The man on the left point was next, in command, to the "trail boss," two on the swing, two on the flank, and two drag drivers whose business it was to look after the calves that played out, the footsore and the laggards. In this order they grazed along until noon. The mess wagon would camp; one-half the crew would go in, eat dinner, change horses and go back to the herd as quickly as possible and the other half would eat, change horses and the herd would be started forward again. It would be kept moving until the sun was low and sufficient water for the cattle would be found. Camp would then be made, one half the men would go in to supper, catch up night horses and return to the herd when the remaining half would do the same. The herd would be grazing on bed ground and by dark would all be down.

The nights were divided into four periods. The first watch stood until 10 o'clock, the second until 12 o'clock, the third until 2 A. M. and the fourth until morning. In case of storms or a stampede, the entire crew was on duty and remained with the herd until it was back on the trail again, no matter how long that might be. It was no unusual thing for cowpunchers to remain in the saddle thirty-six hours at a stretch but they never complained and not one of them ever left a herd until relieved. Of all the thousands of herds driven over the Texas trail, there was never one lost or abandoned by the cowpunchers.

When the first herds started north, Indians and Mexican outlaws tried the experiment of slipping up to the herd on a dark night popping a blanket to stampede it, with the hope of cutting off some of the lead cattle and driving them east to a market. The practice did not last long. The dead bodies of a few Indians and Mexicans found on the plains, told the story and was sufficient warning to others similarly minded. The cowpunchers were loyal to their outfit and would fight for it quicker than they would for themselves.

One of the worst things that they had to contend with on the trail was the terrific electrical storms so prevalent on the plains, and along the Arkansas and Platte rivers during the summer months. They came on suddenly with a high wind that blew the tent over and the chuck wagon too, if it was not staked to the ground. Zigzag streaks of lightning tore through the inky blackness of the sky, followed by deafening claps of thunder that fairly made the ground tremble. Over and around the herd the lightning was always worst. Every man in the outfit is out in the darkness and pouring rain, riding around the cattle, singing their weird cowboy songs in an effort to keep the herd quiet. Two of their favorites were "We go North in the Spring but will return in the Fall," and "We are bound to follow the Lone Star Trail." All at once comes a flash and a crash and a bolt strikes in the midst of them. It is too much. The cattle spring to their feet as one animal. There is a rattling of horns and thunder of hoofs as the maddened herd dashes off across the slippery broken ground and the men riding at breakneck speed to keep ahead of and turn them; for the only way to stop them is to throw them in a circle and "mill" them. If a horse should fall it was certain death to horse and rider and not a few lost their lives in that way.

In the morning the herd might be fifteen or twenty miles from camp and it would take all day or longer to get them on the trail again and all the cowpunchers would be kept in the saddle without rest or food until all were moving along again. If a cowboy was killed in a stampede his comrades dug a shallow grave, wrapped the trampled form in his blankets and laid him to rest.

The greatest responsibility rested on the trail boss. He had to know where water was a day ahead and the drive made according. There was one dry drive forty miles long. When there was a long dry drive the cattle would be watered and then pushed on away into the night. Cattle can smell water for a very long distance and if the wind was from the north next morning, the herd would travel along all right, but if there was no wind they would travel slow. If the wind blew up from behind late in the afternoon when they were suffering for water, there was trouble. They would "bull," that is try to turn and go back to water and it required all the skill and best efforts of every cowpuncher in the outfit to keep the herd moving forward and then it could not always be done.

I have seen a herd traveling along only a few miles from where they were going in to water, when the wind would suddenly blow from a river behind them. The cattle would turn as one cow, start for that water, possibly ten miles distant, and nothing could stop them.

A herd cannot be made to swim a large river if the sunshine on the water reflects in their eyes; nor will they go into a river if the wind is blowing and the water ripples. In 1885 John Lea, one of the experienced trail bosses, struck the Yellowstone river with a herd. The wind blew hard for three days and kept the water rippled, and nothing would induce those cattle to cross the river until the water was smooth.

A day's drive on the trail is from ten to fifteen miles, but it is always governed by water. A herd of steers make much better time than a mixed herd. There was never any such thing as "resting up" or "laying over;" the herd was kept moving forward all the time.

A company or an individual stocking range, would go south, buy the cattle and notify his foreman to send an outfit to some point south to receive a herd of cattle and to trail them to somewhere in Montana, and give him the brands and money for expenses. There was a fortune in that herd of cattle but he was not worried. He knew the cattle would arrive on time and in the best possible condition. While in St. Louis in 1884, a friend of mine told me that he had just bought three thousand two-year old steers in Texas for his range on the Musselshell. I asked him if he was going south to come up with the drive.

"H—l, no!" was the reply. "I am going to Miles City and play poker and be comfortable until those steers arrive." And that is just what he did and the herd was on the Musselshell in August and the steers were fat enough for beef.

Trailing cattle came to be a profession and the trail men a distinct class. They came north with a herd in the spring and returned south in the fall, worked in the chaparral, gathering another herd during the winter and then drove north again in the spring. They took a great pride in their work and were never so happy as when turning a fine herd on the range at the end of the trail.

It was a pleasing sight to see a herd strung out on the trail. The horses and the white-covered mess wagon in the lead, followed by a mass of sleek cattle a half mile long; the sun flashing on their bright horns and on the silver conchos, bridles, spurs, and pearl-handled six shooters of the cowpunchers. The brilliant handkerchiefs knotted about their necks furnished the needed touch of color to the picture.

What the Cowboy Wore

– by –

Philip Ashton Rollins

THE CLOTHING WORN by members of the trade was distinctive. Although picturesque, it was worn not for the production of this effect, but solely because it was the dress best suited to the work in hand. Inasmuch as it was selected with view only to comfort and convenience, it knew nothing of variable fashion and suffered from no change in style.

It, however, was subject, as were many of the cowboys' customs, to differences in form according as the locality involved was the Northwest or the Southwest. The line of demarcation between these sections, though never very clearly defined, was in effect an imaginary westward extension of Mason and Dixon's Line, this extension zigzagging a bit in some places.

The hat was, in material, of smooth, soft felt; and, in color, dove-gray, less often light brown, occasionally black. It had a cylindrical crown seven inches or more in height, and a flat brim so wide as to overtop its wearer's shoulders. The brim might or might not be edged with braid, which, if it appeared, was silken and was of the same color as the felt. In the Southwest, the crown was left at its full height, but its circumference above the summit of the wearer's head was contracted by three or, more commonly, four, vertical, equidistant dents, the whole resembling a mountain from whose sharp peak descended three or four deep gullies. In the Northwest, the crown was left flat on top, but was so far telescoped by a pleat as to remain but approximately two and a half inches high.

Few men of either section creased their hats in the manner of the other. A denizen of the Northwest appearing in a high-crowned hat was supposed to be putting on airs, and was subject openly to be accused of "chucking the Rio," vernacular for affecting the manners of the Southwesterners, whose dominant river was the Rio Grande. Present-day Northwesterners, faithless to this tradition, have foresworn the low crown and assumed the peak. The United States War Department recently has flown into the face of history by formally designating the dented high peak as the Montana poke.

Around the crown, just above the brim and for the purpose of regulating the fit of the hat, ran a belt, which was adjustable as to length. The belt was made usually of leather, but, particularly in the Southwest, occasionally of woven silver or gold wire. The belt, if of leather, commonly was studded with ornamental nails, or, did the owner's purse permit, with "conchas," which were flat metal plates, usually circular, generally of silver, in rare instances of gold, in much rarer instances set with jewels. Rattlesnake's rattles, gold nuggets, or other showy curiosities not infrequently adorned the leather. For leather, some men substituted the skin of a rattlesnake.

From either side of the brim at its inner edge, depended a buckskin thong; these two thongs, sometimes known as "bonnet strings," being tied together and so forming a guard, which, during rapid riding or in windy weather, was pushed under the base of the skull, but which at other times was thrust inside the hat.

Did the brim sag through age or unduly flop, it could be rectified by cutting, near its outer edge, a row of slits and threading through them a strip of buckskin.

The wide brim of the hat was not for appearance's sake. It was for use. It defended from a burning sun and shaded the eyes under any conditions, particularly when clearness of vision was vital to a man awake or shelter was desirable for one asleep. In rainy weather it served as an umbrella. The brim, when grasped between the thumb and fingers and bent into a trough, was on its upper surface the only drinking-cup of the outdoors; when pulled down and tied over the ears, it gave complete protection from frost-bite. It fanned into activity every camp-fire started in the open, and enlarged the carrying capacity of the hat when used as a pail to transport water for extinguishing embers. The broad hat swung to right or left of the body or overhead provided conspicuous means of signalling; and, when shoved between one's hip or shoulder and the hard ground, it sometimes hastened the arrival of a nap. Folded, it made a comfortable pillow. No narrow-brimmed creation could have had so many functions.

A Philadelphian manufacturer virtually monopolized the making of at least the better grades; and, from his name, every broad-brimmed head covering was apt everywhere slangily to be designated as a "Stetson," instead of by either one of its two legitimate and interchangeable titles of "hat" and "sombrero." While these two legitimate titles were interchangeable, throughout the West, the Northwest leaned toward "hat," the Southwest toward "sombrero."

There were slang names other than the one just mentioned, but none that had more than infrequent usage. These other names included "lid," "war-bonnet," "conk cover," "hair case," and a list of like inventions.

Southwesterners often wore, in lieu of the hat already described, the real sombrero of Mexico, with its high crown either conical or cylindrical, its brim saucer-shaped, and its shaggy surface of plush, frequently embroidered with gold or silver thread. No Northwesterner ventured, while in his home country, to "chuck the Rio" to the extent of such a head-gear.

Most of these sombreros, though reaching the American wearer by the route of importation from Mexico, had been made in Philadelphia by the very manufacturer who is mentioned above.

Along the Mexican border, some men, principally "Greasers," wore the huge straw hats of Mexico; but these head coverings were not often assumed by Americans, for there was a suggestion of peonage in the straw.

Many punchers had such vanity as to their hats that the makers gave, in the so-called "feather-weight" quality, a felt far better than that used in the shapes offered to city folk, and so fine as to roll up almost as would a handkerchief, a felt so costly that only ranchmen would pay its price, and thus they alone made use of it. Not infrequently a puncher spent from two to six months' wages for his hat or sombrero and its ornamental belt.

Those hats and sombreros, while by Western classification "soft hats," should not be confused with the unstiffened, cheap felt hats worn by city-dwellers; for these latter head coverings, though admittedly "soft," were subject to the contemptuous accusation of being mere "wool hats." Furthermore the Range knew that the city-dwellers wore also "hard" or "hard-boiled" hats, subdivided into the two classes of, first, "derby" or "pot" and, second, "plug" or "stovepipe"; but no "hard hat" attempted, unless accompanied by a tenderfoot, to appear within the Cattle Country.

The handkerchief which encircled every cowboy's neck was intended as a mask for occasional use, and not as an article of dress.

This handkerchief, diagonally folded and with its two thus most widely separated corners fastened together by a square knot, ordinarily hung loosely about the base of the wearer's neck; but, as the wearer rode in behind a bunch of moving live stock, the still knotted handkerchief's broadest part was pulled up over the wearer's mouth and nose. The mask thus formed eliminated the otherwise suffocating dust and made breathing possible. It offered relatively like protection against stinging sleet and freezing wind.

The cowboy did not dare risk being without this vitally necessary mask when need for it should come, and so he ever kept it on the safest peg he knew; under his chin.

In color and material the handkerchief, though sometimes of silk, usually was of red bandanna cotton; of red, not because the puncher affirmatively demanded it, but because ordinarily that was the only color other than white obtainable from the local shopkeepers. The shopping cowboy was very tolerant save in his selection of hats, chaps, spurs, guns, ropes, and saddles.

The handkerchief-selling shopkeeper in his own turn had followed the line of least resistance; and, being subject to no special demand for green, blue, or whatever, had forborne to make among the manufacturers a hunt for varied colors, and had stocked himself with an article which he readily could obtain, the red bandanna.

Thanks to the requirements of the Southern negro, this article constantly was manufactured. Thus the "Aunt Dinahs" of the Southern kitchens unwittingly dictated as to what the cowboy of the West should hang about his neck.

A relatively similar reason foisted the Texan heraldic star upon the saddles, bridles, chaps, and boots of many of the Northwesterners. The Texans, with their intense State pride, asked for this adornment, and the manufacturers, putting it on the Texans' accoutrements, standardized output, and starred the equipment of almost everybody who did not object.

White handkerchiefs were eschewed by many punchers, because these handkerchiefs, when clean, reflected light; and thus sometimes, upon the Range, called attention to their wearers when the latter wished to avoid notice by other people or by animals. Moreover white soon so suffered from dust as to appear unpleasantly soiled.

There was nothing peculiar about the shirt beyond that it was always of cotton or wool, always was collarless and starchless (not "boiled," "biled," or "bald-faced"); and, though of any checked or striped design or solid color, almost never was red. That latter tone was reputed to go badly among the cattle, and, in any event, belonged to the miners. Furthermore, the puncher's taste in colors was in the main quite subdued.

Collars were unknown. A white one starched would have wrecked its wearer's social position. This denying the ranchman a white collar did not withhold it from such of the professional gamblers as cared to wear it. A "turndown" collar of celluloid (of paper in the early years), provided the wearer's handkerchief and salivary glands occasionally functioned in unison, would make the gambler showily immaculate, and so would advertise apparent prosperity.

Each of the cowboy's shirt-sleeves customarily was drawn in above the elbow by a garter, which was of either twisted wire or of elastic webbing, and frequently, and as an exception to the general demureness of sartorial tone, was brightly colored, crude shades of pink or blue being much in favor.

Nor was there anything distinctive about the coat and trousers, which were woollen and, in cut, of the sack-suit variety; then, as now, the usual garb of American men, unless one regards as distinctive the fact that almost universally these garments were sombre in hue.

Possibly this predilection for black and darkest shades found its source in Texas and Missouri, where the frock coat, string tie, and slouch hat of the Southern "colonel" had ever been of black.

However, the cowboy sometimes substituted for his woollen coat one of similar cut, but made of either brown canvas or black or brown leather.

Denim overalls were considered beneath the dignity of riders, and were left to wearing by the farmers, the townsfolk, and the subordinate employees of the ranches.

The puncher's trousers, universally called "pants," stayed in place largely through luck, because the puncher both avoided "galluses," the suspenders of the tenderfoot, as tending to bind the shoulders, and also was wary of supporting belts, as the latter, if drawn at all tightly, were conducive to hernia when one's horse was pitching. However, if the puncher were of Mexican blood, he would gird himself with a sash of red or green silk.

In the mending of rents the safety-pin or a strip of buckskin often functioned in lieu of thread and needle.

The pistol's belt, wide and looped for extra cartridges, ever loosely sagged, and so threw the weapon's weight upon the thigh instead of placing strain upon the abdomen.

When possible the cowboy went coatless, but he always wore a vest. The coat was arrestive to ease of motion. Also it somewhat invited perspiration, and perspiration for a man condemned to remain out of doors day and night in a country of cold winds was uncomfortable, if not dangerous.

In every-day life the vest was of ordinary, civilian type, and usually was left unbuttoned. It was worn, not as a piece of clothing, but solely because its outside pockets gave handy storage not only to matches but also to "makings," which last-mentioned articles were cigarette papers and a bag of "Bull Durham" tobacco.

Mixed in with these necessaries were, in all probability, a gold nugget, an Indian arrow-head, or an "elk tush" or two. These "tush-es," the canine teeth from the wapiti's upper jaw, now widely known as insignia of a great secret order, were in the West of years ago equal-ly well known as the most treasured jewels of the Indian squaw. Every cowboy acquired all the "tushes" he conveniently could, doing so usually with no purpose of ultimate trade with the Indians, but only because of a vague, boylike idea that somehow, some day, they might be useful. In reality, as he got them he gave them to Eastern souvenir hunters, as he also gave the nuggets and the arrow-heads.

This naive predilection for so-called "natural curiosities" went hand in hand with desire to benefit either science or the federal gov-ernment; was shared, in this public-spirited form, with the scouts and hunters, and worked for the inconvenience of the receiving clerks at the Smithsonian Institution. There flowed, for years, to the door of the latter's museum and from out of the West a steady stream of use-less bones, horns, skins, crystals, pieces of wood, and other things, all enthusiastically started on their journeys and most of them ultimately and properly landing on the scrapheap at Washington.

Men would undergo great personal risks to obtain "fine speci-mens."

The prevalent desire to patronize "The Smithsonian" was exem-plified in the experience of two Northwestern scouts who had the same beneficent attitude toward science as had the punchers.

The Crow Indians had "jumped" their reservation and were on the war-path. They were being trailed by Taxe-well Woody and James Dewing, Woody riding a horse, Dewing a mule.

These scouts discovered an enormous bald eagle, which feeding at a carcass, was so gorged as to be helpless. The tremendous size of the bird suggested immediately that Washington was in great need of this fine specimen, so a heavy stick was brought down on the nation-al emblem's neck, and the latter's immediate owner was then pro-nounced to be dead. The eagle's legs were lashed to the back of Dew-ing's saddle, while a thong held in place the folded wings of the hang-ing bird.

The men mounted, and forthwith a war party broke from cover

and attacked them. The scouts spurred their mounts into a retreat, but were rapidly being overhauled by the Indians, whose ponies were fleeter than Dewing's mule. Meanwhile shots were flying.

Just as it began to look hopeless for the two whites, there happened simultaneously three things: First, a bullet struck the ground in front of the galloping mule, raised a flurry of dust, and caused the brute to spin around and to hurry toward the foe. Second, a bullet cut the thong which had bound the eagle's wings. Third, the eagle came to life, and, though with legs still fastened to the saddle, stood erect.

Then the charge completely reversed its direction and appearance. It had been to both whites and Reds a hundred armed warriors chasing two helpless victims. Now it seemed to the Reds a pursuing demon hastening to destroy a fleeing Indian tribe. What Woody witnessed was a screaming eagle with talons imbedded in the rump of a crazed mule, with wings outspread and beating the air, and with beak digging, amid the screams, into uncomfortable Dewing's back, while the mule rushed after the Indians, intermittently pausing to buck and bray, Dewing himself meanwhile shouting, cursing, and shooting.

The matches in the cowboy's pocket, like all matches on the Range, were in thin sheets like coarsely toothed combs. They had small brown or blue heads that were slow to start a blaze, and, for some time after striking, merely bubbled and emitted strong fumes of sulphur. To obtain a light, the West tightened its trousers by raising its right knee, and then drew the match across the trouser's seat.

There has been described the vest of every day, but there were occasional days which were not like every day, the occasional days when the puncher went in state either to town or to call upon his lady-love. On these infrequent and important errands, he was fain to put on a waistcoat which was specially manufactured for the Western trade, and which, though normal in size and shape, was monumental in appearance. Plush or shaggy woollen material was prey to the dyer's brutality, and on the cowboy's manly but innocent front the Aurora Borealis, and the artist's paint-box met their chromatic rival. A man of modest taste, and such were the majority of the punchers, was content with brown plush edged with wide, black braid. But what was such passive pleasure as compared with the bouncing gladness which another and more primitive being derived from a still well-remembered vest of brilliant purple checker-boarded in pink and green?

The overcoat was of canvas, light brown in color, with skirts to the knee, was blanket-lined, and, to make it wholly wind-proof, commonly received an exterior coat of paint, which latter process often successfully invited the sketching of the owner's brand upon the freshly covered surface.

All men donned gloves in cold weather; this, of course, to keep the hands warm. In warm weather most men wore gloves when roping, this to prevent burns or blisters from the hurrying lariat, and wore them also when riding bucking horses, this to avoid manual injury. But some men, regardless of temperature or the nature of their work, wore gloves all the waking hours. This latter habit, while an affectation, did not necessarily indicate effeminacy. It rather was an expression of vanity, and permitted the wearer tacitly but conspicuously to advertise that his riding and roping were so excellent as to excuse him from all other tasks. The hands of such men frequently were as white and soft as those of a young girl.

The ungloved fraternity, being without excuse for absence from the wood-pile, resented the fragile hands, though not their owners, and to visitors gruntingly descanted on the theme that it was "cheaper to grow skin than to buy it."

The gloves were sometimes of horse-hide or smooth-surfaced leather, but usually were of buckskin of the best quality. Whatever the material, they customarily were in color yellow, gray, or a greenish or creamy white, though brown was not infrequent.

They had to be of good quality, lest they stiffen after a wetting; for an unduly stiff glove well might misdirect a lariat throw, or even cause a man to miss hold upon the saddle horn when he essayed to mount a plunging horse.

Practically all gloves had flaring gantlets of generous size, five inches or so in both depth and maximum width, the gantlets commonly being embroidered with silken thread or with thin wire of silver or brass, and being edged with a deep leathern or buckskin fringe along the little-finger side. The designs for such embroidery followed principally geometrical forms, and very often included a spread eagle or the Texan heraldic star.

Conchas not infrequently augmented the decoration.

When the thermometer was very low, either gloves or mittens of knitted wool or of fur made their appearance.

Almost always in the absence of gloves, and frequently when gloves were present, men wore tightly fitting brown or black, stiff, leathern cuffs, which extended backward for four or five inches from the wearer's wrist joint, were adjustable by buckled straps, protected the wrists, and held the sleeves in pound.

Although upon the Range any one not professing to be a puncher incased his feet in whatever form of leather covering he preferred, all cowboys wore the black, high-topped high-heeled boots typical of the craft.

These boots had vamps of the best quality of pliable, thin leather, and legs of either like material or finest kid. The vamps fitted tightly around the instep, and thus gave to the boot its principal hold, for there were no lacings, and the legs were quite loose about the wearer's entrousered calf. The boots' legs, coming well up toward the wearer's knees, usually ended in a horizontal line, but sometimes were so cut as to rise an inch or so higher at the front than at the back. The legs were prone to show much fancy stitching. This was of the quilting pattern, when, as was often the case, thin padding was inserted for protective purposes.

A concha or an inlay of a bit of colored leather might appear at the front of each boot-leg at its top.

These tall legs shielded against rain, and supplemented the protection which was furnished by the leathern overalls or "chaparejos."

The boots' heels, two inches in height, were vertical at the front, and were in length and breadth much smaller at the bottom than at the top.

The tall heel, highly arching the wearer's instep, insured, as did the elimination of all projections, outstanding nails, and square corners from the sole, against the wearer's foot slipping through the stirrup or being entangled in it. The tall heel also so moulded the shod foot that the latter automatically took in the stirrup such position as brought the leg above it into proper fitting with the saddle's numerous curves. The heel's height and peg-like shape together gave effective anchorage to the wearer when he threw his lariat afoot, instead of from his horse's back.

The sole usually was quite thin, this to grant to the wearer a semi-prehensile "feel of the stirrup." To these necessary attributes, the vanity of many a rider added another and uncomfortable one, tight fit; and throughout the Range unduly cramped toes appeared in conjunction with the enforced, highly arched insteps.

The conventions of Range society permitted to the buckaroo at any formal function no foot-gear other than this riding-boot. It was as obligatory for him at a dance as it was useful to him when ahorse.

The puncher with vanity for his tight, thin boots, and with contempt for the heavily soled foot coverings of Easterners, "put his feet into decent boots, and not into entire cows."

In very cold weather, this boot sometimes gave way to one of felt or to the ordinary Eastern "arctic" overshoe worn over a "German sock," this last a knee-high stocking of thick shoddy. Save under such frigid conditions and save also when the puncher was in bed, his feet were ever in his leathern boots.

Spurs were a necessary implement when upon the horse, and a social requirement when off its back. One, when in public, would as readily omit his trousers as his spurs.

The spurs were of a build far heavier than those of more effete sections of the country. Their rowels were very blunt, since they were intended as much for a means of clinging to a bucking horse as for an instrument of punishment. This assistance to clinging was augmented in many spurs by adding, to the frame of the spur, a blunt-nosed, up-curved piece, the "buck hook," which rose behind the rider's heel, and which it was reassuring to engage or "lock" in the cinch or in the side of a plunging horse. A rider, intending to lock his spurs, usually first wired or jammed their wheels so as to prevent their revolving. Ordinarily, the rowels were half an inch in length, the wheel of which they formed the spokes being slightly larger in diameter than an American, present-day, twenty-five-cent piece; but spurs imported from Mexico, and having two-and-a-half-inch wheels with rowels of corresponding length, frequently were used in the Southwest as a matter of course, in the Northwest as an advertisement of distant travel.

Each spur, or "grappling-iron," as slang often dubbed it, was kept in place both by two chains passing under the wearer's instep and also by a "spur-leather," which last-mentioned object was a broad, crescentic shield of leather laid over the instep. This spur-leather tended as well to protect the ankle from chafing, and incidentally was usually decorated by a concha and stamped with intricate designs.

The shank of almost every spur turned downward, thus allowing the buck hook, if there were one, to catch without interference by the rowels, and also permitting the wheel, when the rider was afoot, to roll noisily along the ground. This noise frequently was increased by disconnecting from the spur one of the two chains at one of its end and allowing it to drag, and also by the addition of "danglers." Danglers were inch-long, pear-shaped pendants loosely hanging from the end of the wheel's axle.

A cowboy moving across a board floor suggested the transit of a knight in armor. This purposely created jangle fought loneliness when one was completely isolated, and was not abhorrent in public, even thought it might announce the presence of a noted man.

Not more specialized than the spurs but more conspicuous were the "chaparejos," universally called "chaps." They were skeleton overalls worn primarily as armor to protect a rider's legs from injury when he was thrown or when his horse fell upon him, carried him through sage-brush, cactus, or chaparral, pushed him against either a fence or another animal, or attempted to bite; but also they were proof against both rain and cold wind.

Take a pair of long trousers of the city, cut away the seat, sever the seam between the legs, and fasten to a broad belt buckled at the wearer's back as much of the two legs as is thus left. Then you have a pattern for a pair of chaps. Reproduce your pattern in either dehaired, heavy leather, preferably brown, but black if you must, or else in a shaggy skin of a bear, wolf, dog, goat, or sheep, and you have the real article. You must, of course, make your pattern very loosely fitting, have on the length of each leg but a single seam, and that at the rear, and do a bit of shaping at the knee. Should you employ dehaired leather, so cut it that long fringe will hang from the leg seam, and you might well cover this seam with a wide strip of white buckskin. You will hurt nobody's feelings should you stamp the leather here and there with frontier animals or with women's heads, or all over in tiny checker-board, or should you stud the belt with conchas. In so doing you will be no inventor, but merely a follower of custom.

The long hair or wool upon a pair of shaggy chaps represented not so much artistic preference as it did judgment that thereby protection would be increased. Naked leather was not oversoft under a prone horse, and could not be relied upon to withstand the stab of either the yucca's pointed leaves or the spines of the tall cacti.

The cowboy wore chaps when riding and also when either within the confines of a settlement or in the presence of womankind. Chaps and his fancy vest, if he had the latter, were, in combination with his gun and spurs, his "best Sunday-go-to-meeting clothes," or what he called his "full warpaint." When there was no riding to be done, no social convention to fulfil, or there were neither jealousies to excite nor hearts to conquer, the chaps, unless their owner was either a slave to habit or very vain, often hung from a nail. They were heavy and, for a pedestrian, quite uncomfortable.

"Hung from a nail," to be truthful, is poetic license for "thrown on the floor." The Cattle Country, thoroughly masculine, "hung its clothes on the floor, so they couldn't fall down and get lost." Only saddles, bridles, lariats, and firearms received considerate care.

Fur coat and cap for winter use, of buffalo skin in earlier days or wolf pelt in later times, were regularly worn in cold climates, but were distinguishing not of the vocation but of the temperature. Generally they were not owned by the cowboy, but were loaned to him by his employer.

The conditions which called forth the furs often compelled a cowboy, as a preventative of snow blindness, to "wear war-paint on his face," that is, to daub below his eyes and upon his cheek bones a mixture of soot and grease. This made him look, as Ed Johnson, said, like a "grief-stricken Venus."

Lastly and affectionately is recalled the horsehair chain, which was laboriously and often most excellently woven from the hairs of horses' tails. These chains usually were of length sufficient to surround the neck and to reach to the bottom pocket of the vest, and, at the lower end, had a small loop and a "crown knot" wherewith to engage the watch. They were a factor in the courting on the Range, for among cowboys it was as axiomatic that the female doted on horsehair chains as it now is among the cowboys' descendants that she has no aversion to pearl necklaces. The puncher, disdaining to shoot Cupid's arrows at his inamorata, essayed to lasso her with a tiny lariat made from the discards of his favorite pony's tail.

Ranch owners and such of their employees as were not cowboys dressed as did the cowboy; save that, having no dignity of position to maintain, they felt less compelled to wear fine quality of raiment and, as already stated, reserved the right to use foot-gear other than the conventional, high-topped boot.

A few of the ranch owners, either Englishmen or such Easterners as had been much in Europe, laid aside from time to time long trousers and appeared in shorts. These latter abbreviated garments, then still a novelty upon the Atlantic coast, were to the cowboy an enigma, a cause of irritation and an object of surprise and contempt. In the words of Kansas Evans, "Bill, what' je think? Yesterday, up to that English outfit's ranch, I seen a grown man walkin' around in boy's knee pants. And they say he's second cousin to a dook. Gosh! Wonder what the dook wears." "Knee pants" were resented as being un-American, and they cost their wearers no small loss of caste upon the Range. None save a ranch owner would dare appear in them.

❦

Style on the Ranch

– by –
W.S. James

IF THERE IS ANY ONE THING that has engaged the mind of the majority of the human family more than another in the past, it is the question of their personal appearance and style or fashion has been as changeable as Texas weather, and I dare say the locality and peculiar people that never change style are the exception. If one should wish to know anything about the rural districts of Old Mexico, they would have to go back four or five thousand years and read in Genesis, but only give them time and they too will change.

In the mountains of eastern Tennessee and the swamps of Louisiana and Arkansas, as well as the piney woods of eastern Texas, they have changed from the old flint-lock to the cap and ball gun, and some of them have quit making their own clothing and wear store clothes, because it is stylish now to wear brown duck instead of "jeans." The cow-boy is no exception to the rule. He has his flights of fancy as clearly defined as the most fashionable French belle.

In 1867, I remember distinctly the style that prevailed, flowing toefenders, narrow stirrup, and the rider stood on his toe. The saddle at that time was almost anything that could be had, but preferably the broad horn standing at an angle of forty-five degrees, pointing heavenward. The bridle was hardly to be called a creation of fancy, as it was all they had, and was made from the hide of a cow, rubbed and grained until it was pliable.

Some men broke the monotony by adopting the Mexican plan of

making them of hair, which was a very popular article of which to make ropes. Some made their bridles of rawhide by platting, which made quite an artistic one, some would plait the quirt on the end of the rein. The rope used for catching and handling horses and cattle was a platted one and was one of the best ropes for the purpose I ever used. I have seen a few ropes that were very good, made of rawhide, of three strands twisted and run together. In fact, during, and for several years after the war, long after reconstruction days in Texas, it was said—and not without some foundation—that a Texan could take a butcher knife and rawhide and make a steamboat, of course he could not have made the boiler, but when it came to the top part he would have been at home. One thing certain, if the thing had broken to pieces, he could have tied it up.

During the war his clothing was made from homespun cloth, he had no other, home-made shoes or boots, even his hat was home-made, the favorite hat material being straw. Rye straw was the best. Sometimes a fellow would get hold of a Mexican hat, and then he was sailing.

The popular way for protecting the clothing, was to make a leather cap for the knee and seat of the pants, the more enterprising would make leggins of calf-skin, hair out, and sometimes buckskin with fringe down the side.

By 1872 most everything on the ranch had undergone a change, even some of the boys had changed their range headquarters for sunnier climes, because they had to, some had sold out to a lawyer and had taken a contract from the State; others had changed their spurs and leggins for a crown, harp and wings, and gone to pastures green, perhaps. But especially had style changed, the wool hat, the leather leggins, leather bridle and the broad stirrup; the invention of an old fellow who lived on the Llano river had become so popular that one who was not provided with them was not in the style.

The stirrup was from six to eight inches broad, and the rider drew his leathers so as to ride with legs crooked up considerably. The saddle used was one with a broad flat horn, much higher in front than behind, adorned with saddle pockets, covered with either goat or bear skin. The spur too was another article that changed, the long shank with bells had taken the place of the little straight shank and sharp rowel, the long ones making a curve downward and having long teeth rowel. In this age of the cow-man they wore buckskin gloves with long gauntlets.

The style changed again by '77. The John B. Stetson hat with a deeper crown and not so broad a rim, and the ten-ounce hat took the cake. Up to this date, the high-heeled boots were the rage, and when it was possible to have them, the heel was made to stand under the foot, for what reason I never knew, unless it was the same motive that prompts the girls to wear the opera heel in order to make a small track, thus leaving the impression that a number ten was only a six, this I am guessing at and will leave it open for the reader to draw to. By the last named date, '77 or '78, the cow-man had in many places adopted the box-toed boot with sensible heels, and the California saddle was taking the place of all others. This was an extremely heavy saddle, with a small horn but very strong and the most comfortable saddle to be found for steady use, and as a rule, the easiest one on a horse.

There was another saddle, a Texas production, closely allied to the Bucharia, but not so heavy, that was, and is to this day, a very popular saddle. The slicker and tarpaulin were two of the most valuable accessions to the cow-man's outfit that ever came into the business. They were made of good cotton stuff, and a preparation of linseed oil filled every pore so completely that they were as thoroughly waterproof as a shingle roof, and became the cow-boy's right bower.

A cow-boy's outfit is never complete except he has a good supply of hopples on hand. After sea-grass ropes became so plentiful and cheap, the good old rawhide hopples and platted lariettes were relegated to the rear, and if the cow-pony could talk, unless he was a good, religious pony, he would curse the day when sea-grass hopples were introduced. His feelings toward the inventor of that article would be something like those of the native toward the barbed-wire manufacturer, for the poor little fellows sometimes wore a very sore pair of legs by the use of the strand of a rope for a hopple.

There has been much said about pack-ponies, and that method of working a range, by taking the grub on a pack. Some very amusing things will occur with the pack. I remember once, while driving through Waco, the pack-pony became a little unruly, and was running up and down street after street, when the pack slipped and turned under. This put the little gentlemen to kicking. The result was that flour, bacon, beans, tincups and plates, coffee-pot, sugar, onions and bedding were strewn over about five acres of ground. Some of the boys suggested that we hire the ground broke and harrowed before it rained and thus secure a good crop of grub.

The pack-pony was very handy, but the greatest trouble of any one thing in the outfit, and it was the most cruel thing imaginable to fasten the pack on so as to make it secure, even with a saddle, and fasten it well, let the pony or donkey, as the case might be, run into a pond of water and get the ropes wet; it was terrible on him. When an outfit had to resort to a pack, they usually hired their bread made, or made it sometimes, when they couldn't find a woman, not infrequently making it up in the mouth of the sack, and if they had no skillet would either fry it or cook it hoe-cake fashion, but I have seen it cooked by rolling the dough round a stick and holding it over the fire, turning it until cooked.

The change in the styles of saddles brought the change, also, in the stirrup. Since '78, and the introduction of the California saddle, the narrow stirrup has been used, and has been found to be the most comfortable. The change in position of the legs, too, accompanied this change in the fashion. The foot is thrust through the stirrup until the stirrup rests in the hollow of the foot, or the foot rests thus in the stirrup, just as you like, and when the rider sits in his saddle the straps are lengthened so as to let him rest his weight just comfortably in the stirrup, while at the same time he is not removed from the saddle-seat.

It has been fully demonstrated that the man who rides thus, and sits straight on his horse, is capable of riding farther, and with less fatigue to himself and horse, than one who is all the time changing.

The methods of handling cattle change as well as the paraphernalia. I remember it was a rare thing ever to see a man branding cattle on horseback. If they did, they usually threw the rope on the animal's head, and then tied them to a tree and heeled them, or threw the rope round their hind legs and simply stretched them out. In branding yearlings or calves on the range, they would make a run, toss the tug on the animal; one man would hold while another would dismount, catch it by the tail, jerk it down, draw its tail between its hind legs, place his knee against its back while it would be lying on its side, and thus hold it while the first man would brand and mark it. In the way described above, one man could hold the largest animal on the range, if he understood his business. Range-branding was a very popular method of branding mavericks. The necessary outfit usually was a sharp knife, a straight bar and half circle; the ring end of a wagon-rod, or common iron rings, were good. In the case of using rings, one needed a pair of pincers. However, one used to such work, could very successfully run a brand with them by using a couple of sticks, with which to hold them.

For many years, however, the custom was to drive the cattle to some pen, many of which were located over each range, and then brand up all those that belonged to any one in the outfit, or those they knew and sometimes a miracle would be performed by branding all those left in the brand of the cows they followed, and if any were left whose owner was not known, and was too old to claim a mother, they were—well, I can't exactly say, as I was not always by, but usually those whose mothers were strays were turned out and left to run until they were too old to be known. In after years they were usually dealt with differently.

The style changed to catching cattle as well as horses by the front feet or fore feet, as we called them, which was a much better method of throwing them.

The horse when roped by the head if wild, will choke himself down and the best method of holding him when once down is to take him by the ear with one hand, nose with the other. To illustrate, if the horse falls on his left side you want to take hold of his ear with your right hand and nose with the left hand, raising it until his mouth is at an angle of forty five degrees, placing one knee on his neck near his head. In this way a small man can hold a large horse on the ground.

The difference in holding a horse and cow down is that you must hold the horse's front legs or head on the ground because he never gets up behind first but throws his front feet out and then gets up: the cow on the contrary gets up directly the reverse, gets up on her hind feet first, therefore you must hold her down by the tail. The horse is easily choked down but it is almost an impossibility to choke a cow down. It is a noted fact that a colt that is handled when sucking, being staked and becoming used to a rope between the time he is two months and a year old, is never very wild. He may be hard to drive when allowed to run with wild horses but when once in hand is easily managed. The cow on the other hand may be raised perfectly gentle and if allowed to run out and become wild, may become the most vicious of any other.

Speaking of the method of holding cattle and horses down calls to mind a little incident that came under my observation. A cattleman employed a Swede who was a very stout fellow, he was as willing as he was green, and was green enough to make up for all his other virtues. This cattleman was not over-sensitive about what another had to perform. One day they roped a wild horse of good size and when they choked him until he fell to the ground, the cow-man called to the Swede "Jump on his head," meaning, of course, for him to catch the horse as before described but instead of that the ignorant fellow jumped right astride the horse's head and the rope being slacked the horse made a lunge and threw the poor fellow his length on the ground and ran over him. It seemed a miracle if he came out alive but he only received a few bruises.

At another time when handling a bad cow, the same parties being engaged, the cow made a run at the Swede when his boss called him to catch her by the horns which he did and the cow simply lifted him a double somersault over her back. He eventually got tired and quit the cattle business, went to farming and as a good story book would say, "did well and lived happy ever afterward."

Those who think the cow-boy is not stylish simply let them hunt him up, study his character, note his fancy and while it is true that like poor Yorick of old he is "a fellow of infinite jest, of most peculiar fancy," still he is stylish after a fashion of his own.

To say that any law of fashion does or could wield an influence over him, I think, would be a mistake. I don't think one could be induced to wear a plug hat. If he did at all it would be for the novelty of the thing. If you see him in New York or Chicago you see him wearing the same sort of hat and boots he wears at home.

He is looked upon by some as a law breaker. It is true in some cases, but is it not equally true of all classes? I maintain that it is not more universal with this than any other class of men in any one vocation of life. It may be a little more out-breaking but of the same kind. His wild free range and constant association with nature and natural things makes him more sensitive to restraint than he otherwise would be. Under the influences of a free wild life he has grown to be self-reliant and like Davie Crocket, "he asks no favors and shuns no responsibilities;" he, however, measures his responsibilities by rule of his own construction which is oftener the outgrowth of personal inclination than a well balanced consciousness of moral responsibility, like his brother of more favorable surroundings who is prone to reject the moral teaching of God's word and fall back for a refuge to the unreliable guidance of conscience; when this moral guide has been so educated as to be like the material of which he makes his hopples which, by a little dampening and working becomes pliable, has a tendency to stretch and thus meet the demands of its environments.

The cow-boy's outfit of clothing, as a rule, is of the very best from hat to boots, he may not have a dollar in the world, but he will wear good, substantial clothing, even if he has to buy it on a credit, and he usually has plenty of that, that is good. I once heard a minister in a little Northern town, in using the cow-boy as an illustration, say "The cow-boy with an eighteen dollar hat and a two dollar suit of clothing is as happy as a king on his throne," or words to that effect.

With those who knew no better the illustration perhaps held good, but to a crowd of the boys it would have been very ridiculous and amusing. In fact extravagance is one of the cow-boy's failing. The

inventory of his wardrobe could be very correctly summed up as follows: Hat, five to ten dollars; pants, five to ten dollars; coat and vest,
from eight to twenty dollars; overshirt, from three to five dollars, and
everything else to match. They may be cheated in buying, but are
never beat by the same man the second time, they at least think they
are getting the best, and always make the best of their bargain.

The days of free grass are gone. If you wish to arouse recollections
of by-gones that will make the old timer in the cattle business heave a
sigh of regret, just mention the good old days of free range when the
grass was as free as the air they breathed and when the "Wo hau
come" of the horny handed son of the granger was never heard in the
sacred precincts of the land of free grass and water.

The man who came to Texas when the wild cayote and the lion of
the tribe of Mexico were his most intimate neighbors, when the hiss of
the rattle-snake and the unearthly yell of the panther were by far the
most familiar sounds to his ear, and after years of toil and scratching
shins, breaking the briers mixed with fighting the blood-thirsty savage
thief, the red child of the desert, is it strange that he should think it an
infringement on his natural rights for people to come in and begin to
plow up the land, thus limiting his cattle range? He had enjoyed this
unalloyed bliss of living "monarch of all he surveyed" so long that he
felt almost as though it was his by the statute of limitation.

There was never any contention worth naming among the cattle
men. It is true they didn't wish to be crowded. In illustration of their
ideas of what that meant I recite a little incident in connection with
one of the old residenters. He lived out perhaps a hundred miles from
our little country town and seventy-five miles from the nearest trading point except the government post. While down in the settlement
with his teams after bread my grandfather asked him how he was getting on. "Very well, very well, thank you, Bill. I've got to move,
though." "Why?" said grandfather. "O, because they are crowding me
out there, the nesters are settling all 'round me and I will not be
crowded. One of the impudent varmints has settled right down in my
back yard."

Upon close inquiry we found the location of the obnoxious nester referred to, to be twenty-eight miles below him on the opposite side of the river. Of course, it was more of a jest than earnest; the real fact, however, is there were none who enjoyed the presence of the nester, he was held in somewhat the same contempt that a physician of the old school looks upon patent medicine men, or a sheep-man would a wolf.

The cattlemen looked upon the country as being fit for nothing but pasture and the man that presumed to squat down and attempt to dig his living out of the ground by the sweat of his brow as being in very small business. In fact they went on the principle that they had put no grubs in the ground and didn't propose to take any out and, as I once heard a cow man say, that "God had discriminated in favor of the stock man when he had respect unto Abel in his offering and despised the offering of Cain, consequently the cattleman had a right to his range." This gentleman reminds one very much of the theologians of today who simply construe God's word to mean that which meets the demands of their own inclination. This is clearly proven by their antagonism of the sheep-man a few years later. Of all the despicable characters to the cattlemen it was the sheep-man. They then quoted the passage portraying the churlishness of Nabal, the son of folly, and fain would assume the character of an insulted and outraged David and further would have wiped him off the face of the earth with all his coolies but for the reconciling influences of "Abigal," though not so graciously polite as the Abigal of old, yet quite as effective, the great strong arm of the law.

One discrimination this modern Abigal made, however, and that was the sheep-man must keep his stock on his own land while the "King of the Kow" was allowed to turn his cattle loose to roam at will. As there is not an event in history without its forerunner or prophecy so the coming of the sheep-man and the attending results was a prophecy of the eventual downfall of the reign of free grass, and if one will stop and think for a moment, as some men did think, it was an inevitable result, the discrimination against the sheep-man in favor of the cow-puncher was enough to bring it about.

The snoozer was not allowed to herd or turn his sheep loose on the range that he didn't own. The cow-man could with impunity locate on the line of the sheep-man's range, though the snoozer owned his miles of range, the cattle of a dozen ranches were allowed to roam at will on his land. This would naturally drive him to fence. Other sheep-men seeing the prosperity of one would come in and buy up large tracts of land and say to Mr. cow-puncher "move your ranch;" then he "had to" and in order to protect himself he was forced to buy or lease and fence. So the ball began to roll and accumulate until the trouble precipitated between the pasture men and the free grass fellows.

The weather class, of course, could buy up larger tracts and lease more land than the little fellow, and when it once began to be a fixed rule for each man to get all he could and keep all he had, the demon of avarice that goes to make up the leaven of so many of our lives, stepped in as the initiator of schemes for swindling and prompted many men to buy up and lease land on all sides of large bodies of individual property that was not likely for years to be molested, fence all together and thus utilize thousands of acres of land that they had no right to.

This had the natural tendency to bring out all the rough points of antagonism in the little fellow, who was thus cheated out of what he conceived to be his legitimate heritage, and the consequence was that he bought a pair of nippers and went to cutting or hired some enterprising fellow to do it for him.

There was at one time a law passed in favor of the cattleman, allowing one man to take up seven sections of State school land on certain conditions, giving a certain time in which to pay it out. A cattleman of means would take up seven sections and then have as many of his hands as he wished to take seven sections each, and thus enable one man to control whole counties. This brought about a state of affairs that culminated in the repeal of that law and the passage of a new one allowing but one section to each man and opening all land to actual settlers, not leased or legitimately held by former claimants; this resulted in a more relentless war between the big pasture men and the squatter, or the man with the hoe, than had ever been waged between any two classes in the state, making litigation almost endless and causing the larger cattle owners to combine, forming cattle companies and syndicates sufficiently powerful to crush out of existence the smaller frey.

The advent of barbed wire into Texas brought with it a reign of lawlessness and terror, such as has no parallel in the State's eventful history.

Then there were decidedly two classes, free grass and pasture men, and never in any land has there been greater bitterness and eternal hatred than existed between those two factions. It was to be heard on the range, at home 'round the fireside, in the courts, in the legislative halls, every election was carried or lost on this issue, the best men of the country were on one or the other side of this question. If a man was a pasture man, he was favoring the wealthy, when in reality neither charge was necessarily true. It is useless for me to enter into the arguments on the two sides of the question as it has been thoroughly "cussed and discussed" by writers better qualified than I am to do the subject justice, besides it is not my object to deal in theory but facts, and this I shall do as far as in me lies.

From my knowledge of the true state of affairs wire-cutting was merely another or new form of mob law; the beginning of such work was, to some who never stopped to reason, a justifiable act of self-defense, but to a thinking man lawlessness is never justifiable.

An outraged community unable to bring to justice a known criminal, takes the law into its own hands and meets out to the offender summary punishment; they argue that "this is the only way to deal with him" never looking to their own crime. If a man is hanged without a trial, the perpetrators in the eyes of the law are murderers and instead of lessening crime they have increased the criminal class. A man fenced up land he had no legal right to, he was criminal; his neighbors band together and cut his fence and there are more criminals.

The first thing that especially aroused the indignation of the stockman relative to barbed wire was the terrible destruction to stock caused from being torn first on the wire, and the screw worm doing the rest—this was especially the case with horses. When the first fences were made, the cattle never having had experience with it, would run full till right into it and many of them got badly hurt, and when one got a scratch sufficient to draw the blood, the worms would take hold of it. Some man would come into a range, where the stock had regular rounds or beaten way, and fence up several hundred acres right across the range and thus endanger thousands of cattle and horses. After the first three years of wire fences, I have seen horses and cattle that could hardly drive between two posts, and if there was a line of posts running across the prairie, I have seen a bunch of range horses follow the line out to the end and then turn, but in a few years the old tough hided cow found a way to crawl through into a cornfield if the wire was not well stretched and the posts close together. The man who had horses cut up and killed by the wire, often felt like cutting it down all of it, and in many instances did; but like every other class of lawlessness it ran to extremes and before it had gotten very far, was taken up by the more vicious, and such a time one would hardly dream of, who has never had the misfortune to witness it. It became so common that whole pastures would fall in one night and it made no difference who owned them, the presence of the dread enemy was sufficient evidence, and down she came. The men who cut the wire with a very few exceptions were men who owned but few if any horses or cattle; many of them owned nothing at all, they came out to find room and grass and that class was the most rabid of all others.

I once met one of those fellows, who was working a little East Texas dogy stag and a little bull to an old human wagon (wood axle). He had seven dogs, nine children, a wife, a cob pipe and a roll of home-spun tobacco stuck down in his hip pocket. I mean the tobacco was in his pocket—not the family. I asked him where he was from: "I am from Arkansaw, Whoa Bully." "Where are you going?" "Going West to find grass and room. Ike-lep." He was a regular copperas-breeches and one-gallus sort of a character; had just as soon live as to die; fight one man as two, and would spend more time twisting a rabbit out of a hollow tree than he would to secure a shelter for his family in time of a storm. He could afford to have one or two children blown away, but rabbits were too scarce to take the chances on losing one.

There would seem to be some excuse for the man who had stock injured by the wire, but for the man who had nothing on earth to lose or gain, who just did it from pure unadulterated cussedness there can be no mitigation of his crime. Doubtless many good men for the lack of better judgment on the impulse of the moment, when they came face to face with the evidence of their loss were led to cut fences, but the cutting of fences made them no better citizens, but had the direct tendency to lead them into other evils. "Evil communications corrupt good manners." One starts out down the stream of wrongdoing, and soon he finds its water growing deeper, the cause being that every little rivulet of evil wends it way on downward to the River of Crime and the man who once allows himself launched upon this dangerous stream is too apt to drift with the tide of evil, until at last he is disrobed of his power to battle with the awful current, and is helplessly swept out into the whirlpool of ruin, irretrievably sinking at last into the ocean of eternity, where he receives his wages for "The wages of sin is death."

The legislature eventually made it a felony to cut a fence, with punishment at "State Contract." Many men, both good and bad, lost their lives in the conflict and a bitterness engendered of neighbor against neighbor that will tend to chill the blood of good citizenship for years to come. Free grass has gone and nothing to show for its usefulness but the fact that the country was opened and the way made possible for our present development and growth, by men who had iron nerve and will to brave the difficulties of a frontier life, all for the benefits offered by free range, and that, that was good.

Suffice to say that the old fellows who came, saw and conquered, were not the wire cutters, and, to their credit be it said, almost to a man they condemned it. I mean the older settlers, those men who came in the early days and carved out of the wilderness a home for themselves. Many of the dear old "diamonds in the rough" have gone to answer the summons of the great pioneer of the universe and those who are still with us and witnessing the advancement of civilization as a rule are not appropriating to themselves the credit due them for the patient toil and hardships that have given to many a poor man a home in the land of milk and honey, and very few of those who are enjoying the fruits of their labors properly appreciate their real worth, plodding along as they do their chief occupation gone, often looking as they do with an eye of longing toward the setting sun that so often in early life marked the course of their journey, taking delight in nothing now so much as the privilege of recounting their experiences of more exciting times.

But some day the eye that was so keen to discover the presence of his inveterate foe, the red man, and draw so fine a bead along the barrel of an old "Human rifle" as to make it extremely unhealthy for the varmint or game that came within the range of his trusty piece, that eye will look for the last time upon the accoutrements that were once his trusty companions in the times that tried men's hearts, and then the soul will take its place in the phantom bark that will bear it across the River of Death to the "better shores of the spiritland," where there will be no more heartaches, no more Indians to encounter in deadly strife, no more wild beasts to trouble the peacefulness of that home of delight, no more struggles between free grass advocates and pasture men.

Nearly all of the old frontiersmen of my knowledge are soldiers of King Emanuel, many of those who took part in the struggles recorded in this chapter have since laid down the sword and taken up the cross, many of the thoughtless youths who were led into lawlessness are now living in a way that bids fair to render them useful. Let us hope that the gospel of peace will yet reach many more who are yet on the "broad trail," may be as a pointer to the herd, may be as a common hustler keeping up the drags fet on the "broad trail" that leads to eternal condemnation, for "Wide is the gate and broad the way that leads to destruction and many there be which go in thereat."

Yes, the great free grass struggles are over, the people have as a rule buried the tomahawk. Barbed wire, like the Johnson grass, came to stay, and the people of Texas have decided to make it a blessing instead of wrestling with it. It is bad medicine when a fellow fools with it, and no sadder plight can be imagined than one in which a man is described as being between a mad Texas steer and a good wire fence the only thing possible for him to do is to drop to the ground and roll under, leaving the steer to interview the fence.

The experience of the free grass men wrestling with barbed wire reminds me of a story told on an old frontiersman which occurred in an early day. He lived out on the Colorado river not far from the mouth of the Concho. While out hunting one day with one or two of his boys, they became separated and were on opposite sides of the creek, the water hole, unfortunately, was swimming for some distance up and down from where they were, the old gentleman discovered a young wildcat, and it being small, he decided to take it prisoner, so he caught it, but it was large enough to make him regret the rash act, so he decided to turn the thing loose, but when he pulled its fore feet loose, it would catch him with its hind feet, it was simply making sausage meat of him, when he called for help. His boy ran down to the bank opposite to where he was and being unable to reach him called out to know what the trouble was. "I have caught a wildcat and it is tearing me all to pieces," said the father. "Turn it loose," said the boy. "Turn it loose that is just what I have been trying to do," said the father, "but I can't turn it loose." So with the wire cutter, he caught a wildcat and could not turn it loose.

I shall never forget the first wire fence I ever saw. I took a trip to Fannin county with my grandfather to buy some cow horses. While passing through Tarrant county we stopped near his old ranch on Deer Creek to see about some stock horses of his that ranged near the old place. While there, I saw a horse that had been cut across the knee, and we were told that the wire fence we had just passed was the cause. When I saw a barbed-wire machine at work manufacturing it and was told that there were thousands of them at the same work, I went home and told the boys they might just as well put up their cutters and quit splitting rails and use barbed-wire instead. I was as confident than as I am to-day that wire would win and just as confident when we landed the first train-load of cattle at Forth Worth, Texas, that between wire and railroads the cow-boy's days were numbered, as I am that he is now almost a thing of the past.

On a Tare in Wichita, Kansas

– by –

Charles Siringo

ON THE FOURTH DAY OF JULY, after being on the trail just three months, we landed on the "Ninnasquaw" river, thirty miles west of Wichita, Kansas.

Nearly all the boys, the boss included, struck out for Wichita right away to take the train for Houston, Texas, the nearest railroad point to their respective homes. Mr. Grimes paid their railroad fares according to custom in those days. I concluded I would remain until fall.

Mr. Grimes had come around by rail, consequently he was on hand to receive us. He already had several thousand steers—besides our herd—on hand; some that he drove up the year before and others he bought around there. He had them divided up into several different herds—about eight hundred to the herd—and scattered out into different places, that is each camp off by itself, from five to ten miles from any other. With each herd or bunch would be a cook and "chuck" wagon, four riders, a "boss" included—and five horses to the rider. During the day two men would "herd" or watch the cattle until noon and the other two until time to "bed" them, which would be about dark. By "bedding" we mean take them to camp, to a certain high piece of ground suitable for a "bed ground" where they would all lie down until morning, unless disturbed by a storm or otherwise. The nights would be divided up into four equal parts—one man "on" at a time, unless storming, tormented with mosquitos or something of the kind, when every one except the cook would have to be "out" singing to them.

The herd I came up the trail with was split into three bunches and I was put with one of them under a man by the name of Phillups, but shortly afterwards changed and put with a Mr. Taylor.

I spent all my extra time when not on duty, visiting a couple of New York damsels, who lived with their parents five miles east of our camp. They were the only young ladies in the neighborhood, the country being very thinly settled then, therefore the boys thought I was very "cheeky"—getting on courting terms with them so quick. One of them finally "put a head on me"—or in grammatical words, gave me a black eye—which chopped my visits short off; she didn't understand the Texas way of proposing for one's hand in marriage, was what caused the fracas. She was cleaning roasting-ears for dinner when I asked her how she would like to jump into double harness and trot through life with me? The air was full of flying roasting-ears for a few seconds—one of them striking me over the left eye—and shortly afterwards a young Cow Puncher rode into camp with one eye in a sling. You can imagine the boys giving it to me about monkeying with civilized girls, etc.

After that I became very lonesome; had nothing to think of but my little Texas girl—the only one on earth I loved. While sitting "on herd" in the hot sun, or lounging around camp in the shade of the wagon—there being no trees in that country to supply us with shade—my mind would be on nothing but her. I finally concluded to write to her and find out just how I stood. As often as I had been with her I had never let her know my thoughts. She being only fourteen years of age, I thought there was plenty time. I wrote a long letter explaining everything and then waited patiently for an answer. I felt sure she would give me encouragement, if nothing more.

A month passed by and still no answer. Can it be possible that she don't think enough of me to answer my letter? thought I. "No," I would finally decide, "she is too much of an angel to be guilty of such."

At last the supply wagon arrived from Wichita and among the mail was a letter for me. I was on herd that forenoon and when the other boys came out to relieve Collier and I, they told me about there being a letter in camp for me, written by a female, judging from the fine hand-writing on the envelope.

I was happy until I opened the letter and read a few lines. It then dropped from my fingers and I turned deathly pale. Mr. Collier wanted to know if some of my relations wasn't dead? Suffice it to say that the object of my heart was married to my old playmate Billy Williams. The letter went on to state that she had given her love to another and that she never thought I loved her only as a friend, etc. She furthermore went on advising me to grin and bear it, as there were just as good fish in the sea as ever was caught etc.

I wanted some one to kill me, so concluded to go to the Black hills—as everyone was flocking there then. Mr. Collier, the same man I traded the crippled horse to—agreed to go with me. So we both struck out for Wichita to settle up with daddy Grimes. Mr. Collier had a good horse of his own and so did I; mine was a California pony that I had given fifty-five dollars for quite awhile before. My intention was to take him home and make a race horse of him; he was only three years old and according to my views a "lightning striker."

After settling up, we, like other "locoed" Cow Punchers proceeded to take in the town, and the result was, after two or three days carousing around, we left there "busted" with the exception of a few dollars.

As we didn't have money enough to take us to the Black hills, we concluded to pull for the Medicine river, one hundred miles west.

We arrived in Kiowa, a little one-horse town on the Medicine, about dark one cold and disagreeable evening.

We put up at the Davis House, which was kept by a man named Davis—by the way one of the whitest men that ever wore shoes. Collier made arrangements that night with Mr. Davis to board us on "tick" until we could get work. But I wouldn't agree to that.

The next morning after paying my night's lodging I had just one dollar left and I gave that to Mr. Collier as I bade him adieu. I then headed southwest across the hills, not having any destination in view; I wanted to go somewhere but didn't care where. To tell the truth I was still somewhat rattled over my recent bad luck.

That night I lay out in the brush by myself and next morning changed my course to southeast, down a creek called Driftwood. About noon I accidentally landed in Gus Johnson's Cow camp at the forks of Driftwood and "Little Mule" creeks.

I remained there all night and next morning when I was fixing to pull out—God only knows where, the boss, Bill Hudson, asked me if I wouldn't stay and work in his place until he went to Hutchison, Kansas and back? I agreed to do so finally if he would furnish "Whisky-peat," my pony, all the corn he could eat—over and above my wages, which were to be twenty-five dollars a month. The outfit consisted of only about twenty-five hundred Texas steers, a chuck wagon, cook and five riders besides the boss.

A few days after Mr. Hudson left we experienced a terrible severe snow storm. We had to stay with the drifting herd night and day, therefore it went rough with us—myself especially, being from a warm climate and only clad in common garments, while the other boys were fixed for winter.

When Mr. Hudson came back from Hutchison he pulled up stakes and drifted south down into the Indian territory—our camp was then on the territory and Kansas line—in search of good winter quarters.

We located on the "Eagle Chief" river, a place where cattle had never been held before. Cattlemen in that section of country considered it better policy to hug the Kansas line on account of indians.

About the time we became settled in our new quarters, my month was up and Mr. Hudson paid me twenty-five dollars, telling me to make that my home all winter if I wished.

My "pile" now amounted to forty-five dollars, having won twenty dollars from one of the boys, Ike Berry, on a horse race. They had a race horse in camp called "Gray-dog," who had never been beaten, so they said, but I and Whisky-peat done him up, to the extent of twenty dollars, in fine shape.

I made up my mind that I would build me a "dugout" somewhere close to the Johnson camp and put in the winter hunting and trapping. Therefore as Hudson was going to Kiowa, with the wagon, after a load of provisions, etc., I went along to lay me in a supply also.

On arriving at Kiowa I found that my old "pard" Mr. Collier had struck a job with a cattleman whose ranch was close to town. But before spring he left for good "Hold Hengland" where a large pile of money was awaiting him; one of his rich relations had died and willed him everything he had. We suppose he is now putting on lots of "agony," if not dead, and telling his green countrymen of his hair-breadth escapes on the wild Texas plains.

We often wonder if he forgets to tell of his experience with "old gray," the pony I traded to him for the boat.

After sending mother twenty dollars by registered mail and laying in a supply of corn, provisions, ammunition, etc., I pulled back to Eagle Chief, to make war with wild animals—especially those that their hides would bring me in some money, such as gray wolves, coyotes, wild oats, buffaloes and bears. I left Kiowa with just three dollars in money.

The next morning after arriving in camp I took my stuff and moved down the river about a mile to where I had already selected a spot for my winter quarters.

I worked like a turk all day long building me a house out of dry poles—covered with grass. In the north end I built a "sod" chimney and in the south end, left an opening for a door. When finished it lacked about two feet of being high enough for me to stand up straight.

It was almost dark and snowing terribly when I got it finished and a fire burning in the low, Jim Crow fire-place. I then fed Whiskey-peat some corn and stepped out a few yards after an armful of good solid wood for morning. On getting about half an armful of wood gathered I heard something crackling and looking over my shoulder discovered my mansion in flames. I got there in time to save nearly everything in the shape of bedding, etc. Some of the grub, being next to the fire-place, was lost. I slept at Johnson's camp that night.

The next morning I went about two miles down the river and located another camp. This time I built a dug-out right on the bank of the stream, in a thick bunch of timber.

I made the dug-out in a curious shape; started in at the edge of the steep bank and dug a place six feet long, three deep and three wide, leaving the end next to the creek open for a door. I then commenced at the further end and dug another place same size in an opposite direction, which formed an "L." I then dug still another place, same size, straight out from the river which made the whole concern almost in the shape of a "Z." In the end furthest from the stream I made a fire-place by digging the earth away—in the shape of a regular fire-place. And then to make a chimney I dug a round hole, with the aid of a butcher knife, straight up as far as I could reach; then commencing at the top and connecting the two holes. The next thing was to make it "draw," and I did that by cutting and piling sods of dirt around the hole, until about two feet above the level.

I then proceeded to build a roof over my 3 x 18 mansion. To do that I cut green poles four feet long and laid them across the top, two or three inches apart. Then a layer of grass and finally, to finish it off, a foot of solid earth. She was then ready for business. My idea in making it so crooked was, to keep the indians, should any happen along at night, from seeing my fire. After getting established in my new quarters I put out quite a number of wolf baits and next morning in going to look at them found several dead wolves besides scores of skunks, etc. But they were frozen too stiff to skin, therefore I left them until a warmer day.

The next morning on crawling out to feed my horse I discovered it snowing terribly, accompanied with a piercing cold norther. I crawled back into my hole after making Whisky-peat as comfortable as possible and remained there until late in the evening, when suddenly disturbed by a horny visitor.

It was three or four o'clock in the evening, while humped up before a blazing fire, thinking of days gone by, that all at once, before I had time to think, a large red steer came tumbling down head first, just missing me by a few inches. In traveling ahead of the storm the whole Johnson herd had passed right over me, but luckily only one broke through.

Talk about your ticklish places! That was truly one of them; a steer jammed in between me and daylight, and a hot fire roasting me by inches.

I tried to get up through the roof—it being only a foot above my head—but failed. Finally the old steer made a terrible struggle, just about the time I was fixing to turn my wicked soul over to the Lord, and I got a glimpse of daylight under his flanks. I made a dive for it and by tight squeezing I saved my life.

After getting out and shaking myself I made a vow that I would leave that God-forsaken country in less than twenty-four hours; and I did so.

Old Gran'pa

– by –
Frank S. Hastings

IT WAS EARLY IN JUNE, 1906. Those were the days of Hynes Ranch buggies and "broom tails." Throckmorton Ranch was a full day's drive away. An unexpected turn in events made it necessary for me to make the drive by night. I stopped at headquarters and asked Mage, the foreman, to meet me in Stamford at 7:00 P. M. I told him we would drive Beauty and Black Dolly, two spanking mares he had bought for me. They could take their ten miles an hour steadily for hours, and I threw them in as a special bait to tempt Mage against any local duty he might urge.

Mage stood six feet five inches in his socks, every inch of it cowman and horseman. He came to the ranches at thirteen years of age—a much misunderstood kid. But he had grown into a manhood of sweetness and strength, which had surrounded him with the love and respect of every man, woman, and child in the country. Mage was a dead-game sport, a rider whose skill and daring are still traditions in the big-pasture country. His stories and personal reminiscences, told with rare humor and dramatic force, made a journey with him a real entertainment. I always sparred for an opening to get him going when we made drives together.

At seven o'clock he was on hand to the minute, talking to the mares as though they were human. We were off—"heads up and tails over the dashboard." As we swung into the main thoroughfare, the people on the street turned round to watch Mage handle the mares.

They were having their little fun before settling to the steady, distance-killing gait, and they were a pair to look at. Beauty a deep chestnut, both wilful and beautiful, and Black Dolly, with her sleek sable coat, still at the giddy age. Mage had the stage driver's trick of coming into town or going out in style. The mares knew his voice and hand, and the light that shone in his eyes told where his heart was. For two hours we chatted or were silent by spells, as is the habit on long drives.

The moon came up in soft fullness—one of those southern moons like the ripeness of love, a perfect heart full. The cool night air was stirring caressingly, and we were both under the spell. The mares had steadied down to normal. We were crossing a prairie near Rice Springs, once a famous round-up ground in the open range days. Mage raised his six-feet-five in the buggy, looked all around, and as he sat down, said: "This here's the place. Here's where me and Old Gran'pa won our first ditty."

The moon had risen high enough to flood a great flat until we could see for a mile or more. I saw just a beautiful expanse of curly mesquite grass, blending its vivid green with the soft silver moonlight, but Mage saw great crowds lined on either side of a straight half-mile track; two riders; the one on a midnight black and the other on a speed-mad sorrel, in deadly contest for supremacy. The stillness of the night—which to me was the calm benediction of peace and rest—was broken for him by wild cheers as a boy and a sorrel horse crossed the line, victors. His face was tense, his eyes shone with the fire of strain and excitement, and then slowly he came back to the stillness and to the moonlight, and to me.

I waited a minute, and asked, "What was it, Mage?"

He did not answer until we had crossed the flat. Then, with a little short laugh, peculiar to him before telling a story, he began: "As fur as thet's consarn, it was this away—."

But here let me tell some true things I knew about Old Gran'pa. He was a famous cow pony, originally known as Sorrel Stud. Mage broke him as a three-year-old, and had ridden him some eighteen years. The last few years of that time Stud had come to be known as Old Gran'pa. He was still alive, but had been turned out under good keep, winter and summer, to end his days in peace. He was very fast, and was considered among the top cutting horses of his time. Mage's worship of this horse is only typical of every cowboy's love for his pet horse. But to his story:

"It was this away. We hed fenced some, but allus hed lots o' strays on the open range, an' Shorty Owen [who, by the way, stood six feet six inches] tole me early in the spring he would send me out to gather strays when the big round-ups begun, an' 'lowed I best be gettin' my plunder rounded up. That was 'fore you come, but you know he was the SMS range boss, an' mighty nigh raised me. He tuk to me the day I hit the ranch. 'Kid,' he says, 'you ain't never hed no chanct? an' I'm a-goin' to giv' you one.'

"Shorty taught me to ride—hobbled my feet under a three-year-ole steer onct, an' turned him a-loose. We hed it roun' an' roun' with the whole outfit hollerin', 'Stay with 'im, kid!' I stayed all right, but when he pitched into a bunch o' mesquites, I sure would 'a' left 'im if these here preachers is right 'bout 'free moral agency,' but them hobbles helt me back, and I stayed fer the benediction. Since thet time I never seed a hoss I was scairt to climb on.

"Shorty cut Sorrel Stud out to me when he was a bronc, an' said, 'Break him right, kid; I think you got a cow hoss if he ain't spoilt in the breakin'. An' I done it without ever hittin' him a lick. As fur as thet's consarn, I never hit him but onct, an' thet was the time him an' me both failed, only Shorty said we didn't fail; we jes' went to the las' ditch. But thet's another story.

"I wisht you could a-seed Sorrel Stud in his prime. He was a hoss! I thought 'bout it today when you hed yore arms roun' his neck an' was a-talkin' to him 'bout me, an' I wondered if anybody 'cept me could understan' thet Sorrel Stud an' Ole Gran'pa was the same hoss. But when I got up an' thumbed him an' made him pitch me off jest to show you what a twenty-year-old hoss could do, did you see the fire come back into them eyes, an' them ears lay back? Hones' to God, Frank, he was a hoss!

"I know I was jest a tough kid when I come, but a-tween Shorty Owen an' maybe a little doin' right fer right's sake, I tried to live an hones' life. But they's two things me an' St. Peter may hev to chew 'bout a little at the gate. You know what a fool I am 'bout tomatoes? Well, onct I stole a dozen cans from the chuck wagon and hid 'em out in the cedar brakes. But the boys at the wagon hed me so plum scart 'bout Injuns thet I never did git to them tomatoes. Well, Ole Gran'pa is jest as plum a fool 'bout oats as I be 'bout tomatoes. I'll admit I stole this here outfit's oats fer him ten years, till the high boss was out onct from New York and seed Ole Gran'pa go to a prairie fire. Of course I was up, an' he sed he guessed he could pay fer Gran'pa's oats the rest o' his days. Joe was mighty perticular 'bout company oats. We hed to haul 'em sixty miles, but I think he slipped a mess to White Pet onct in a while hisself. I used to wait 'til the boys hed hit their hot rolls, then I'd slip out to the corner o' the hoss pasture, an' Ole Gran'pa was allus waitin' fur me an' he'd never leave a stray oat to give us away.

"They called me 'the S M S Kid.' I was 'bout sixteen. I could ride some an' I allus hed a little money back from my wages. So when Shorty Owen tole me I was a-goin', I used thet an' all I made up to the goin' time fer an outfit. I hed a good season saddle, a Gallup; but I bought a bridle with plenty o' doo-dads on it. Then you know my Injun likin' fer color. I bought a yaller swet blanket, an' a top red Navajo blanket fer Gran'pa. He kinda leaned to color too. I set up all night with Swartz an' made him finish a pair o' top- stitched boots, an' I hed enuff left fer new duckin' pants, red flannel shirt, an' a plaid fer change, shop-made bit an' spurs, both inlaid, a yaller silk handkerchief, a new hot roll, an' a twelve-dollar beaver John B. Then Shorty Owen cut out my mount. In course I hed Sorrel Stud; he was six years old, right in his prime, an' I kep' him shinin'. Then there war nine more, all good ones—Blutcher, Alma, Polecat, Tatterslip, Bead Eye, Louscage, Possum, Silver Dollar, an' Badger, three of 'em from Shorty's own mount.

"'Kid,' says Shorty, 'you got as good as the best o' 'em. I wants fer you to mind thet on this here work you're representin' this here outfit. Keep yore head, an' come back with it up. But I'd bet my life on you, an' this here outfit is trailin' you to the las' ditch.'"

Mage's voice was getting low here, and he swallowed on the last words, paused for a moment, then with that laugh of his continued: "Well, I'm stringin' 'em out a mile here, when I ought to have 'em bunched. Thet was a great summer. I worked in the big outfit with men an' hosses thet knowed how to turn a cow, an' the captain o' the round-up got to puttin' me an' Stud into the thick o' it purty reg'ler.

"It allus seemed thet when I rode Stud, Split Miller rode a little hoss called Midnight, an' he sure was a hoss; black as midnight, 'cept fer a white star in the forehead, short-coupled an' quicker then forked lightnin'. He would cut with the bridle off, an' fast? He was a cyclone. Every night 'roun' the camp-fire Split kep' pitchin' a load into me 'bout the Stud. Onct it was, 'Well, Kid, I seed you hed the little scrub out watchin' Midnight work.' Or, 'Say, Kid, I believe if you hed somethin' to ride you'd be a hand.' I swelled up some, but I remembered what Shorty Owens sed, 'Keep yore head an' come back with it up.' An' Split wusn't mean. He jest loved to josh. Two or three times the captain said, 'Split, let the Kid alone.' But he'd shoot one at me as he rode by in the work, and was allus badgerin' me fer a race.

"Then I kinda fell into watchin' Midnight run somethin'; an' I'd start Stud in the same direction to pace him. An' I come alive; the Stud was full as fast. I jest naturally supposed thet Midnight could beat anything, but I kep' a-tryin' an' my eyes kep' a-openin'. One night Split got mighty raw, an' finally says, 'Kid, I'll jest give you twenty dollars to run a half-mile race, standin' start, saddle agin' saddle.' An' then I fergot Shorty's instructions an' los' my head.

"'Split,' I ses, 'you been pickin' on me ever sinct I come to this here work. Me an' Stud don't need no twenty dollars to run you. An even break's good enuff fer us, saddle fer saddle, bridle fer bridle, blanket fer blanket, spur fer spur.'

"'Good enuf, Kid,' sez Split. 'Got enything else—eny money?'

"'No,' I sez, 'ain't got no money, but I got sum damned good rags and a new hot roll.'

"Then the captain o' the round-up tuk a hand. But my blood wus up, an' they put cash allowance on all my plunder, an' I bet it 'gainst money. They give me twelve dollars fer my Swartz boots, eight dollars fer my John B., five dollars fer my cordaroy coat, four dollars fer my shirts, an' two dollars fer my duckin's. It war Wednesday, an' the race was to be pulled off Saturday evenin', straight half-mile, standin' start at the pop o' a gun. The captain tuk the thing in charge an' sed he'd lick eny damned puncher thet tried to run a sandy on the kid.

"It was all settled, but by the time I hed crawled into my hot roll thet night I 'membered the talk Shorty Owen give me. Stud was kinda mine, but he war a company hoss, arter all, to work on an' not fer racin', an' I sure was in a jackpot fer losin' my head. Well, the nex' day I tuk Stud off to practice fer a standin' start. You know how I say 'Now!' when I'm workin' on a hoss and jest as I want him to do somethin'. Well, Stud he'd been trained thet away, with jest a little touch o' the spur, an' I figured to say 'Now!' as the gun popped an' touch him thet away, an' he got the idee.

"Thet night I tuk him to the track an' put him over it four or five times. An' onct when we was restin' a-tween heats I says to him, 'Stud, if me an' you loses this here race, looks like we'd hev to steal off home in the night an' both o' us mighty nigh naked.' Everybody knocked off work Saturday. You know how even in them days word gits 'bout by the grape-vine. Well, by noon they was ridin' an' drivin' in from all directions. The wimin' folks brought pies and cakes. The cusey cooked up two sacks o' flour an' we hed to kill two beeves. Everybody et at the chuck wagon an' it was some picnic.

"I tol' the fellers not to bet on me an' Stud, but they was plenty o' money on both sides. An' a girl with black eyes an' hair jest as purty as a bran' new red wagon, sez, 'Kid, if you win I'm a-goin' to knit you some hot-roll socks.' An' Ole Pop Sellers sez, 'Better look at them feet an' begin figgurin' on yarn, 'cause the Kid's a-goin' to win.' But Split hed a girl, too, an' she up an' sez, 'If the Kid's depending on them there socks to keep warm, he's mighty apt to git frost-bit this winter.' Well, you know the josh thet goes 'round when a big bunch o' cow people git together. An' they was a plenty, until I was plumb flustrated. When the time cum, a starter on a good hoss was to see thet we got off fair an' then ride with us as sort o' pace-maker an' try an' see the finish. But his hoss wasn't in Midnight's an' Stud's class.

"Split he seemed to figure thet Midnight didn't need no trainin',

he hed run so meny races an' never been beat. So all Split did was saddle Midnight an' stan' 'round an' josh. But me an' Stud was addled,
an' I warmed him up a bit, talkin' to him all the time. I was worrited
'bout urgin' him in a tight place. I hed played with my spurs on him,
but he never hed been spurred in his life 'cept a signal touch to turn
or jump. I allus carried a quirt on the horn o' my saddle, but 'cept to
tap him in a frenly way or in work he hed never knowed its use. What
was I a-goin' to do in a pinch? I knowed he would use his limit under
my word, but what if he didn't? Did I hev to hit him? If I owned this
here ranch I'd hev give it all to be out o' the race an' not look like a
quitter.

"Well, the time was cum. Stud he'd been frettin' an' I was stewin,'
but when we toed the line sumthin' funny happened: We both
seemed to settle down an' was as cam as this here night. I jest hed
time to give him one pat an' say, 'God A'mighty, Stud, I'm glad I got
you,' when the starter hollered, 'Git ready!' An' the gun popped! I
yelled, 'Now!' at the same time, an' we was off.

"Midnight was a mite the quickest, but Stud caught his neck in the
third jump, an' I helt him there. I wanted Midnight to lead, but kep'
pushin' him. We didn't change a yard in the fust quarter, en' Split
yelled, 'Kid, yer holdin' out well, but I got to tell you farewell.' An' he
hit Midnight a crack with his quirt. Stud heard it singin' through the
air an' jumped like he was hit hisself. In thirty yards we was nose an'
nose; ten more, a nose ahead. Then I knowed we hed to go fer it. I
was ridin' high over his neck, spurs ready, my quirt heft high, an I kep'
talkin' to him an' saying, 'Good boy, Stud!' The crowd was a-yellin'
like demons. We was in the last eighth, nose an' nose, an' I let out one
o' them Injun yells, an', 'Now, Stud! Now!'

"It seemed like he'd been waitin' fer it. I could feel his heart beat-
in' faster. There was a quiver wint through him like a man nervin' hisself fer some big shock. An' I could see him gainin'—slow, but gainin.'
The crowd hed stopt yellin'. It come sudden. They was so still you
could hear 'em breathe. I I guess we must a-been three feet ahead,
with a hundred yards to go. Split was a-cussin' an' spurrin', an' whip-
pin'. I didn't hev no mind to yell in all thet stillness. I was ready to

spur, ready to whip, an' my heart was a-bleedin'. I don't think now thet I could a-done it to win, an' I jest whispered, 'Now, Stud! Now! Now!'

"I thought he was a-runnin' a-fore, but he shot out like a cry o' joy when a los' child is foun'; an' we crossed the line a length an' a half ahead. I seed the black-eyed girl with her arms 'round Pop Sellers' neck an' a-jumpin up an' down. Pop was jumpin' too, like a yearlin', an' the crowd was doin' an Injun dance generally. Stud didn't seem to sense the race was over, an' was still hittin' the breeze. I checked him in slow, pattin' him on the neck, an' talkin' to him like a crazy man, 'til he stood still, all a-quiver, his nostrils red as fire an' eyes still blazin'. Then I clum down an' throwed my arms 'roun' his neck and sez, 'God A'mighty, Stud, I didn't hev to hit you.' Stud's eyes seemed to softin, an' he laid his head down over my shoulder. I was cryin' like a baby, huggin' him hard. The boys was ridin' to us an' Stud raised his head an' whinnied. I guess it was jest the other hosses comin', but I thought he sed, 'Didn't we raise hell with em?' An' I sez, 'You bet we did, Stud, but it was you done it.'

"News travels fast, an' long 'fore I got in with my strays, they knowed all 'bout it at headquarters. I kep' thinkin' 'bout what Shorty sed, 'Come back with your hed up,' but I hed mine down when he met me at the corral. I knowed we hadn't no hosses to race fer money. He looked kinda hard at my extra saddled hoss an' roll o'plunder an sez, 'Kid, this ain't no racin' stable. This here is a cow outfit, an' our best hosses is fer cuttin', not racin'.' I didn't say a word, jest unsaddled, an' started fer the dog-house, when I heard him comin'.

"He caught up with me, grabbed me by both shoulders an' turned me 'roun'. I saw a great big tear stealin' down his cheek, an' he sez, 'God A'mighty, Kid, I wisht you was my boy!' Then he turned away quick an' was gone, while I set down on the groun' an' blubbered in my ole fool way thet I hev never got over. When pay day come, Shorty handed me my wage check, which had growed some, an' sed, 'Kid, when a boy does a man's work he gits a man's pay. You begin doin' a man's work when you went to gather them strays, and you come back the same way.'

"Then he started to go on, but turned an' sed, 'Say, Kid, if I owned this here S M S Ranch, hosses an' cattle, I'd a-give the whole damned outfit to a-seed you an' Stud come over thet line.'"

ROUNDUPS AND CATTLE DRIVES

*F*OR COWBOYS, *work in the nineteenth-century was as diverse as the ranges he rode and the cows he tended. He could leave the bunkhouse in the morning, intending to ride out and check conditions in a far pasture and end up spending his day doctoring cows for blowflies or pulling bogged steers from a creek bed—all the while never getting within five miles of the pasture he meant to check. The cowboy's job could be dangerous, but his work was just as apt to be dirty and monotonous.*

Of all the jobs of the cowboy, though, none have come to symbolize the profession more than those the historian Walter Prescott Webb characterized as the "twin spectacles of the range": roundups and cattle drives. The long cattle drives up the trail from Texas and the gathering, cutting out and branding of cattle on the great roundups of the nineteenth-century were by any standards remarkable undertakings. The roundups, held in the spring and fall, were the most important jobs in the cowboy's year. A cattle drive, on the other hand, was often the most memorable job of a cowboy's career.

The cattle drives were unparalleled events in American history. At first, they seemed to be almost desperate attempts by Texas cattlemen to find markets for their herds. However, once Abilene, Kansas, the first genuine cow town, was established as a shipping point in 1867, relatively secure markets for Texas cattle were established. New ranches also began to appear all across the northern plains. Cowboys began driving cattle north, not just to sell them to eastern buyers, but to stock the new ranges.

Abilene was essentially the offspring of one man, an Illinois cattle trader and livestock shipper named Joe McCoy. In the following selection, he describes the town of Abilene in 1868, as the first to come up with the idea of establishing a safe strategic shipping point for Texas cattle on one of the new railroad lines then inching deeper into the Great Plains. After examining maps of the new railroad routes then under construction, McCoy traveled to Kansas City in the spring of 1867 to present his plan to the competing railroads.

The Kansas Pacific initially showed only mild interest in McCoy's idea. The president of the Missouri Pacific actually had McCoy thrown out of his office for taking up his time with what to him seemed a hairbrained scheme. It wasn't until McCoy reached the offices of the Hannibal and St. Joe Railroad that he found sufficient interest in his plan. Officials there liked the idea enough to guarantee McCoy favorable rates for shipping cattle from the Missouri River to Chicago. This one event, McCoy would later claim, became the deciding factor in making Chicago the transportation and meatpacking center of the country instead of St. Louis.

After his visit with railroad officials in Kansas City, McCoy headed for the plains of Kansas to search for a suitable place to build his stockyards. In several towns where homesteaders had already settled, or were about to settle, officials were inhospitable to McCoy's plan. They wanted nothing to do with bringing huge herds of Texas cattle to their towns. Junction City seemed more receptive, but land to build stockyards there turned out to be too expensive.

Abilene, however, had what McCoy was looking for. It was in most ways a typical frontier railroad town when he arrived in the summer of 1867. That is to say, it wasn't much of a town at all. Only one shingle-covered roof could be found among the scattered sod-roofed shanties. But good grass grew in the country around Abilene. The land was well-watered, and homesteaders had not yet arrived in large numbers. At least initially, Texas cowboys could drive their great cattle herds into the area without encountering conflict with the homesteaders.

As soon as McCoy settled on Abilene as the sight of his new shipping point, he sent a rider south into Indian territory to intercept Texas cattle drovers already heading for cattle markets farther east. He then set to work building stockyards on the edge of Abilene. Although it was late in the season, McCoy managed to attract enough Texas drovers to bring thirty-five thousand head of cattle to the town. A thousand cattle cars of Texas beef were shipped east before winter. The following year, in 1868, Abilene was the destination for most of the herds starting north from Texas. While the seventy-five thousand head of cattle that reached the new cow town that year were a relatively modest increase, word of the money made from the drives quickly filtered back to Texas. In 1869 the number of cattle arriving in Abilene skyrocketed with 350,000 head going through McCoy's stockyards.

The years that followed became the golden age of the cowboy on the Great Plains. Several million head of cattle were eventually driven from Texas, first to Abilene and then, as homesteaders settled Kansas, to new cow towns like Ellsworth and Dodge City farther west. Other herds continued north, past the railroads, to stock new ranges or fulfill contracts with the federal government to deliver beef to Indian reservations as far away as Montana. A few herds went from south Texas all the way to Canada.

A typical trail herd contained about 2,500 head of cattle and employed fourteen to sixteen cowboys. Some herds were much larger. Others, especially in the early years, were smaller. The trail boss generally worked at the head of the drive, with two point men on either side at the front of the herd. Farther back were the swing riders, then the flank with drag riders—usually the least experienced cowboys—bringing up the rear. Trail crews also included a cook and at least one teenage wrangler to look after the horses. Several descriptions of life on the trail follow in this section, including a selection from Charles Siringo, whose 1885 book A Texas Cowboy *was the first serious account of cowboy life ever published.*

In another selection Charles Goodnight tells of a Comanche attack that killed Oliver Loving, who was on a trail drive over what became the Goodnight–Loving Trail in 1867. Goodnight and Loving had been the first to open the trail when they drove cattle west up the Brazos and then north on the Pecos to New Mexico and Colorado in 1866. While trying to repeat their feat in the summer of 1867 Loving left Goodnight and the herd to ride ahead and arrange the sale of some cattle at Fort Sumner, New Mexico. Along the way he and a companion were attacked by several hundred Comanches. The two men took cover in some brush along the riverbank where Loving, though mortally wounded, helped his companion escape. This is the point in the tale at which Goodnight's account of Loving's death ends, but Loving somehow made it to Fort Sumner on his own before he finally died from his wounds.

In other selections Andy Adams and E.C. "Teddy Blue" Abbott offer their rich accounts of trail life. In a piece from his book Log of A Cowboy, *Adams tells of the dangers and troubles encountered trying to get a herd across a boggy river. Abbott, in a selection from* We Pointed Them North *(co-authored by Helena Hunt Smith), tells of fulfilling his ambition as a cowboy when he hired on to an outfit driving cattle from south Texas to Montana in the 1880s. In contrast to Adams and Abbott, Jack Potter, who helped drive a herd north in 1882, found his greatest adventure not in the rigors of the drive, which included a stampede, but in taking his first train ride to get home to Texas after the drive was over.*

By 1880 five million cattle had been trailed north to Kansas rail towns to be shipped to eastern markets, and almost as many had gone to stock the northern ranges as well. Cattle had first been pastured near Abilene, Kansas, right after it became a shipping point. At first only the herds that reached the railroad in poor condition, or perhaps herds that reached Abilene during a downturn in the market were turned out to fatten on Kansas grass. Soon, though, it became apparent that Texas cattle did as well on northern grass as southern. In the following years, as the buffalo were killed off and the aboriginal people confined to reservations, Texas cattle were driven north to stock new ranges in Nebraska and Colorado, the Dakotas and Montana. Eventually, almost the entire area from the Red River of the South to the Saskatchewan River on the Canadian prairies became one vast cattle range.

Huge ranches were established, almost all of them claimed on the first-come-first-choice system known as range rights. These ranches, with titles claimed by custom only, were usually located along creeks or rivers. Neighboring ranches were built across the divide of land or far enough up- or downstream so that in theory they would not crowd a neighbor. In truth, once cattle were turned out they went where they pleased. By law, the land was owned by no one, so there was no legal way to keep ranchers fron overgrazing the area with large herds of cattle.

Ranchers survived for a time under this haphazard system by cooperation, organizing huge roundups in the spring and fall to sort and claim cattle. At the spring roundups in the north, cattle and calves from each ranch were separated calves branded, and all driven back to their own ranges. In the fall the same kind of roundups were designed to brand any animals missed in the spring and sort cattle from neighboring ranches in preparation for driving market-ready animals to the nearest shipping point.

After a slump in 1873 cattle prices began to rise, and stocking the northern ranges increased sharply. All over the West, breeding programs began to improve the character of cattle herds, gradually replacing the longhorn Texas cattle with beefier foreign breeds. Demand for cattle increased steadily through the late 1870s, culminating in 1880 when two million Western cattle were shipped to market. For the next four years demand for cattle boomed as wealthy eastern Americans and Canadians, as well as English, Scotish and European investors, were lured west to take part in what was being touted as a sure way to make money.

Future President Theodore Roosevelt, heir to a wealthy eastern family's fortune, was typical in many ways. The main difference was that, following the death of his mother and first wife, Roosevelt turned to the West more for adventure and a new life than for making huge returns on his money. Of course, Roosevelt expected to make money, but unlike most of the wealthy new ranch owners from the east, the twenty-five year old Roosevelt threw himself into his new life completely, much to the amusement of the cowboys he employed.

Just the sight of the young easterner in his expensive and ostentatious cowboy getup, glasses and perpetual grin could bring a smile to a cowboy's face. When Roosevelt talked it was sometimes hard for his men to stifle their laughter. Reportedly, he once gave the order "Sally forth there, fellows," when he wanted his men to ride off in pursuit of escaping cattle. His eastern accent and constant use of the word bully *also proved hilarious to his men. Even more delightful, from the cowboys' point of view, was the inexperienced Roosevelt's inept attempts at the work itself.*

Eventually, Roosevelt settled somewhat comfortably into his new life, but like other inexperienced eastern and European owners who came late to the cow business the brutal climate of the northwest and the unforgiving economy of cattle markets soon drove him from ranching. Before Roosevelt departed, though, he was able to write an observant and detailed, though somewhat inflated, account of the life he found on the open range reflected in this section of The Complete Cowboy Reader.

The section's final entry comes from Stewart Edward White, a well-educated—though not so wealthy—easterner. White was born in Michigan but cowboyed in the southwest as a young man before he went on to become a professional writer. His story, "The Drive," is of an Arizona roundup and was first published in his book Arizona Nights. *In it White recreates the magnificent spirit of life and work on the range, a spirit that could be found all over the cattle country of the West.*

A Start Up the Chisholm Trail

– by –
Charles Siringo

I PUT IN THE FOLLOWING WINTER branding Mavricks, skinning cattle and making regular trips to Matagorda; I still remained in partnership with Horace Yeamans in the skinning business. I made considerable money that winter as I sold a greater number of Mavricks than ever before. But the money did me no good as I spent it freely.

That coming spring, it being 1874, I hired to Leander Ward of Jackson county to help gather a herd of steers for the Muckleroy Bros., who were going to drive them to Kansas. I had also made a contract with Muckleroy's boss, Tom Merril, to go up the trail with him, therefore I bid my friends good-bye, not expecting to see them again until the coming fall. My wages were thirty-five dollars per month and all expenses, including railroad fare back home.

After a month's hard work we had the eleven hundred head of wild and woolly steers ready to turn over to the Muckleroy outfit at Thirteen mile point on the Mustang, where they were camped, ready to receive them. Their outfit consisted mostly of Kansas "short horns" which they had brought back with them the year before.

It was a cold, rainy evening when the cattle were counted and turned over to Tom Merril. Henry Coats, Geo. Gifford and myself were the only boys who were turned over with the herd—that is kept right on. We were almost worn out standing night guard half of every night for the past month and then starting in with a fresh outfit made it appear tough to us.

That night it began to storm terribly. The herd began to drift early and by midnight we were five or six miles from camp. The steers showed a disposition to stampede but we handled them easy and sang melodious songs which kept them quieted. But about one o'clock they stampeded in grand shape. One of the "short horns," a long legged fellow by the name of Saint Clair got lost from the herd and finally when he heard the singing came dashing through the herd at full speed yelling "let 'em slide, we'll stay with 'em!" at every jump.

They did slide sure enough, but he failed to "stay with 'em." For towards morning one of the boys came across him lying in the grass sound asleep. When he came dashing through the herd a stampede followed; the herd split up into a dozen different bunches—each bunch going in a different direction. I found myself all alone with about three hundred of the frightened steers. Of course all I could do was to keep in front or in the lead and try to check them up. I finally about three o'clock got them stopped and after singing a few "lulla-by" songs they all lay down and went to snoring.

After the last steer dropped down I concluded I would take a little nap too, so locking both legs around the saddle-horn and lying over on the tired pony's rump, with my left arm for a pillow, while the other still held the bridle-reins, I fell asleep. I hadn't slept long though when, from some unaccountable reason, every steer jumped to his feet at the same instant and was off like a flash. My pony which was sound asleep too, I suppose, became frightened and dashed off at full speed in the opposite direction. Of course I was also frightened and hung to the saddle with a death grip. I was unable to raise myself up as the pony was going so fast, therefore had to remain as I was, until after about a mile's run I got him checked up.

Just as soon as I got over my scare I struck out in a gallop in the direction I thought the cattle had gone, but failed to overtake them. I landed in camp almost peetered out about nine o'clock next morning. The rest of the boys were all there, just eating their breakfast. Tom Merril and Henry Coats had managed to hold about half of the herd, while the balance were scattered and mixed up with "range" cattle for twenty miles around.

After eating our breakfast and mounting fresh horses we struck out to gather up the lost steers. We could tell them from the range cattle by the fresh "road" brand—a brand that had been put on a few days before—therefore, by four o'clock that evening we had all but about one hundred head back to camp and those Leander Ward bought back at half price—that is he just bought the road brand or all cattle that happened to be left behind.

On arriving at camp, we all caught fresh horses before stopping to eat dinner or supper, whichever you like to call it, it being then nearly night. The pony I caught was a wild one and after riding up to camp and dismounting to eat dinner, he jerked loose from me and went a flying with my star-spangled saddle.

I mounted a pony belonging to one of the other boys and went in hot pursuit. I got near enough once to throw my rope over his rump and that was all. After a run of fifteen miles I gave it up as a bad job and left him still headed for the Rio Grande.

I got back to camp just at dark and caught a fresh horse before stopping to eat my supper. It was still raining and had kept it up all day long. Mr. "Jim" Muckleroy had an extra saddle along therefore I borrowed it until I could get a chance to buy me another one.

After eating a cold supper, the rain having put the fire out, I mounted and went on "guard," the first part of the night, until one o'clock, being my regular time to stay with the herd, while the last "guard" remained in camp and slept.

About ten o'clock it began to thunder and lightning, which caused the herd to become unruly. Every time a keen clash of thunder would come the herd would stampede and run for a mile or two before we could get them to stop. It continued in that way all night so that we lost another night's rest; but we managed to "stay with 'em" this time; didn't even lose a steer.

That morning we struck out on the trail for Kansas. Everything went on smoothly with the exception of a stampede now and then and a fuss with Jim Muckleroy, who was a regular old sore-head. Charlie, his brother was a white man. Where the trouble began, he wanted Coats and I, we being the only ones in the crowd who could ride wild horses—or at least who were willing to do so, to do the wild horse riding for nothing. We finally bolted and told him that we wouldn't ride another wild horse except our regular "mount," unless he gave us extra pay. You see he expected us to ride a horse a few times until he began to get docile and then turn him over to one of his muley pets while we caught up a fresh one.

At High Hill in Fayette county I got the bounce from old Jim and a little further on Coats got the same kind of a dose; while nearing the northern state-line Geo. Gifford and Tom Merril, the boss, were fired; so that left old Jim in full charge. He hired other men in our places. He arrived in Wichita, Kansas with eight hundred steers, out of the eleven hundred we started with.

After leaving the outfit I rode to the Sunset railroad at Shusenburg and boarded a train for Columbus on the Colorado river. "Pat" Muckleroy, Charlie's son, who was about eighteen years old, quit and went with me. His home was in Columbus and he persuaded me to accompany him and have a good time.

On arriving in Columbus I went with Pat to his home where I remained during my stay in that place. I found Mrs. M., Pat's mother, to be a kind-hearted old lady, and I never shall forget the big, fat apple cobblers she used to make; she could beat the world making them. There were also two young Misses in the family, Nannie and Mary, who made time pass off pleasantly with me.

It being seventy-five miles to Tresspalacious and there being no railroad nearer than that, I had to wait for a chance to get home. I could have bought a horse and saddle when I first struck town but after remaining there a week I began to get light in the pocket, for it required quite a lot of money to keep up my end with the crowd that Pat associated with.

At last after about a three weeks stay, I struck Asa Dawdy, an old friend from Tresspalacious. He was there with a load of stock and was just fixing to load them on the cars to ship them to Galveston when I ran afoul of him. He had sold his saddle and was going to put his pet pony, one that he wouldn't sell, into a pasture until some other time when he happend up there. So you see I was in luck, he turned the pony over to me to ride home on.

After buying and rigging up a saddle I left town flat broke. I spent my last dime for a glass of lemonade just before leaving. Thus ended my first experience on the "trail."

The Killing of Oliver Loving

– by –

Charles Goodnight

OLIVER LOVING, SENIOR, is undoubtedly the first man who ever trailed cattle from Texas. His earliest effort was in 1858 when he took a herd across the frontier of the Indian Nation or "No Mans Land," through eastern Kansas and north western Missouri into Illinois. His second attempt was in 1859; he left the frontier on the upper Brazos and took a northwest course until he struck the Arkansas River, somewhere about the mouth of the Walnut, and followed it to just about Pueblo, where he wintered.

In 1866 he joined me on the Upper Brazos. With a large herd we struck southwest until we reached the Pecos River, which we followed up to Mexico and thence, to Denver, the herd being closed out to various posts and Indian reservations.

In 1867 we started another herd west over the same trail and struck the Pecos the latter part of June. After we had gone up this river about one hundred miles it was decided that Mr. Loving should go ahead on horseback in order to reach New Mexico and Colorado in time to bid on the contracts which were to be let in July, to use the cattle we then had on trail, for we knew that there were no other cattle in the west to take their place.

Loving was a man of religious instincts and one of the coolest and bravest men I have ever known, but devoid of caution. Since the journey was to be made with a one-man escort I selected Bill Wilson, the clearest headed man in the outfit, as his companion.

Knowing the dangers of traveling through an Indian infested country I endeavored to impress on these men the fact that only by traveling by night could they hope to make the trip in safety.

The first two nights after the journey was begun they followed my instructions. But Loving, who detested night riding, persuaded Wilson that I had been over-cautious and one fine morning they changed their tactics and proceeded by daylight. Nothing happened until 2 o'clock that afternoon, when Wilson who had been keeping a look-out, sighted the Comanches heading toward them from the south-west. Apparently they were five or six hundred strong. The men left the trail and made for the Pecos River which was about four miles to the northwest and was the nearest place they could hope to find shelter. They were then on the plain which lies between the Pecos and Rio Sule, or Blue River. One hundred and fifty feet from the bank of the Pecos this bank drops abruptly some one hundred feet. The men scrambled down this bluff and dismounted. They hitched their horses (which the Indians captured at once) and crossed the river where they hid themselves among the sand dunes and brakes of the river. Meantime the Indians were hot on their tracks, some of them halted on the bluff and others crossed the river and surrounded the men. A brake of carrea, or Spanish cane, which grew in the bend of the river a short distance from the dunes was soon filled with them. Since this cane was from five to six feet tall these Indians were easily concealed from view of the men; they dared not advance on the men as they knew them to be armed. The Indian on the bluff speaking in Spanish begged the men to come out for a consultation. Wilson instructed Loving to watch the rear so they could not shoot him in the back, and he stepped out to see what he could do with them. Loving attempting to guard the rear was fired on from the cane. He sustained a broken arm and bad wound in the side. The men then retreated to the shelter of the river bank and had much to do to keep the Indians off.

Toward dawn of the next day Loving deciding that he was going to die from the wound in his side, begged Wilson to leave him and go to me, so that if I made the trip home his family would know what had become of him. He had no desire to die and leave them in ignorance of his fate. He wished his family to know that rather than be captured and tortured by the Indians, he would kill himself. But in case he survived and was able to stand them off we would find him two miles down the river. He gave him his Henry rifle which had metallic or water proof cartridges, since in swimming the river any other kind would be useless. Wilson turned over to Loving all of the pistols—five—and his six-shooting rifle, and taking the Henry rifle departed. How he expected to cross the river with the gun I have never comprehended for Wilson was a one armed man. But it shows what lengths a person will attempt in extreme emergencies.

It happened that some one hundred feet from their place of concealment down the river there was a shoal, the only one I know of within 100 miles of the place. On this shoal an Indian sentinel on horseback was on guard and Wilson knew this. The water was about four feet deep. When Wilson decided to start he divested himself of clothing except underwear and hat. He hid his trousers in one place, his boots in another and his knife in another all under water. Then taking his gun he attempted to cross the river. This he found to be impossible, so he floated down stream about seventy-five feet, where he struck bottom. He stuck down the muzzle of the gun in the sand until the breech came under water and then floated noiselessly down the river. Though the Indians were all around him he fearlessly began his "get-a-way." He climbed up a bank and crawled out through a cane brake which fringed the bank, and started out to find me, barefooted and over ground that was covered with prickly pear, mesquite and other thorny plants. Of course he was obliged to travel by night at first, but fearing starvation used the day some, when he was out of sight of the Indians.

Now Loving and Wilson had ridden ahead of the herd for two nights and the greater part of one day, and since herd had lain over one day the gap between us must have been something like one hundred miles.

The Pecos River passes down a country that might be termed a plain, and from one to two hundred miles there is not a tributary or break of any kind to mark its course until it reaches the mouth of the

Concho, which comes up from the west, where the foot hills begin to jut in toward the river. Our trail passed just around one of these hills. In the first of these hills there is a cave which Wilson had located on a prior trip. This cave extended back into the hill some fifteen or twenty feet and in this cave Wilson took refuge from the scorching sun to rest. Then he came out of the cave and looked for the herd and saw it coming up the valley. His brother, who was "pointing" the herd with me, and I saw him at the same time. At sight both of us thought it was an Indian as we didn't suppose that any white man could be in that part of the country. I ordered Wilson to shape the herd for a fight, while I rode toward the man to reconnoiter, believing the Indians to be hidden behind the hills and planing to surprise us. I left the trail and jogged toward the hills as though I did not suspect anything. I figured I could run to the top of the hill to look things over before they would have time to cut me off the herd. When I came within a quarter of the mile of the cave Wilson gave me the frontier sign to come to him. He was between me and the declining sun and since his underwear was saturated with red sediment from the river he made a queer looking object. But even when some distance away I recognized him. How I did it, under his changed appearance I do not know. When I reached him I asked him man questions, too many in fact, for he was so broken and starved and shocked by knowing he was saved, I could get nothing satisfactory from him. I put him on the horse and took him to the herd at once. We immediately wrapped his feet in wet blankets. They were swollen out of all reason, and how he could walk on them is more than I can comprehend. Since he had starved for three days and nights I could give him nothing but gruel. After he had rested and gotten himself together I said:

"Now tell me all about this matter."

"I think Mr. Loving has died from his wounds, he sent me to deliver a message to you. It was to the effect that he had received a mortal wound, but before he would allow the Indians to take him and torture him he would kill himself, but in case he lived he would go two miles down the river from where we were and there we would find him."

"Now tell me where I may find this place," I said. Then he proceeded to relate the story I have just given, of how they left the Rio Sule or Blue Rive, cutting across to the Pecos, how the Indians discovered them and how they sought shelter from them by hiding in the sand dunes on the Pecos banks; how Loving was shot and begged Wilson to save himself and to tell his (Loving's) family of his end; how Wilson took the Henry rifle and attempted to swim but gave it up, as the splashing he made would attract the Indian sentinel stationed on the shoal.

Then Wilson instructed me how to find his things. He told me to go down where the bank is perpendicular and the water appeared to be swimming but was not. "Your legs will strike the rifle" he said. I searched for his things as he directed and found them every one, even to the pocket knife. His remarkable coolness in deliberately hiding these things, when the loss of a moment might mean his life, is to me the most wonderful occurrence I have ever known, and I have experienced many unusual phases of frontier life.

This is as I get it from memory and I think I am correct, for though it all happened fifty years ago, it is printed idelibly in my mind.

❧

Abilene in 1868

– by –
Joseph G. McCoy

NO SOONER HAD IT BECOME a conceded fact that Abilene, as a cattle depot, was a success, than trades' people from all points came to the village and, after putting up temporary houses, went into business. Of course the saloon, the billiard table, the ten-pin alley, the gambling table—in short, every possible device for obtaining money in both an honest and dishonest manner, were abundant.

Fully seventy-five thousand cattle arrived at Abilene during the summer of 1868, and at the opening of the market in the spring fine prices were realized and snug fortunes were made by such drovers as were able to effect a sale of their herds. It was the custom to locate herds as near the village as good water and plenty of grass could be found. As soon as the herd is located upon its summer grounds a part of the help is discharged, as it requires less labor to hold than to travel. The camp was usually located near some living water or spring where sufficient wood for camp purposes could be easily obtained. After selecting the spot for the camp, the wagon would be drawn up. Then a hole dug in the ground in which to build a fire of limbs of trees or drift wood gathered to the spot, and a permanent camp instituted by unloading the contents of the wagon upon the ground. And such a motley lot of assets as come out of one of those camp carts would astonish one, and beggar minute description: a lot of saddles and horse-blankets, a camp-kettle, coffee-pot, bread pan, battered tin cups, a greasy mess chest, dirty soiled blankets, an ox yoke, a log chain, spurs and quirts, a coffee-mill, a broken-helved ax, bridles, picket-ropes, and last, but not least, a side or two of fat mast-fed bacon; to which add divers pieces of raw-hide in various stages of dryness. A score of other articles not to be thought of will come out of that exhaustless camp cart. But one naturally inquires what use would a drover have for a raw-hide, dry or fresh? Uses infinite; nothing breaks about a drover's outfit that he cannot mend with strips or thongs of raw-hide. He mends his bridle or saddle or picket-rope, or sews his ripping pants or shirt, or lashes a broken wagon tongue, or binds on a loose tire, with raw-hide. In short, a raw-hide is a concentrated and combined carpenter and blacksmith shop, not to say saddler's and tailor's shop, to the drover. Indeed, it is said that what a Texan cannot make or mend with a rawhide is not worth having, or is irretrievably broken into undistinguishable fragments. It is asserted that the agricultural classes of that State fasten their plow points on with raw-hide, but we do not claim to be authority on Texan agriculture, therefore cannot vouch for this statement.

The herd is brought upon its herd ground and carefully watched during the day, but allowed to scatter out over sufficient territory to feed. At nightfall it is gathered to a spot selected near the tent, and there rounded up and held during the night. One or more cow-boys are on duty all the while, being relieved at regular hours by relays fresh aroused from slumber, and mounted on rested ponies, and for a given number of hours they ride slowly and quietly around the herd, which, soon as it is dusk, lies down to rest and ruminate. About midnight every animal will arise, turn about for a few moments, and then lie down again near where it arose, only changing sides so as to rest. But if no one should be watching to prevent straggling, it would be but a short time before the entire herd would be up and following off the leader, or some uneasy one that would rather travel than sleep or rest. All this is easily checked by the cow-boy on duty. But when storm is imminent, every man is required to have his horse saddled ready for an emergency. The ponies desired for use are picketed out, which is done by tying one end of a half inch rope, sixty or seventy feet long, around the neck of the pony and fastening the other end to a pointed iron or wooden stake, twelve or more inches long, which is driven in the firm ground. As all the strain is laterally and none upward, the picket pin will hold the strongest horse. The length of the rope is such as to permit the animal to graze over considerable space, and when he has all the grass eat off within his reach, it is only necessary to move the picket pin to give him fresh and abundant pasture. Such surplus ponies as are not in immediate use, are permitted to run with the cattle or herded to themselves, and when one becomes jaded by hard usage, he is turned loose and a rested one caught with the lasso and put to service. Nearly all cow-boys can throw the lasso well enough to capture a pony or a beef when they desire so to do. Day after day the cattle are held under herd and cared for by the cow-boys, whilst the drover is looking out for a purchaser for his herd, or a part thereof, especially if it be a mixed herd—which is a drove composed of beeves, three, two and one year old steers, heifers and cows. To those desiring any one or more classes of such stock as he may have, the drover seeks to sell, and if successful, has the herd rounded up and cuts out the class sold; and after counting carefully until all parties are satisfied, straightway delivers them to the purchaser. The counting of the cattle, like the separating or cutting out, is invariably done on horseback. Those who do the counting, take positions a score of paces apart, whilst the cow-boys cut off small detachments of cattle and force them between those counting, and when the bunch or cut is counted satisfactorily, the operation is repeated until all are counted. Another method is to start the herd off, and when it is well drawn out, to begin at the head and count back until the last are numbered. As a rule, stock cattle are sold by the herd, and often beeves are sold in the same manner, but in many instances sale is made by the pound, gross weight. The latter manner is much the safest for the inexperienced, for he then pays only for what he gets; but the Texan prefers to sell just as he buys at home, always by the head. However, in late years, it is becoming nearly the universal custom to weigh all beeves sold in Northern markets.

Whilst the herd is being held upon the same grazing grounds, often one or more of the cow-boys, not on duty, will mount their ponies and go to the village nearest camp and spend a few hours; learn all the items of news or gossip concerning other herds and the cow-boys belonging thereto. Besides seeing the sights, he gets such little articles as may be wanted by himself and comrades at camp; of these a supply of tobacco, both chewing and smoking, forms one of the principal, and often recurring wants. The cow-boy almost invariably smokes or chews tobacco—generally both, for the time drags dull at camp or herd ground. There is nothing new or exciting occurring to break the monotony of daily routine events. Sometimes the cow-boys off duty will go to town late in the evening and there join with some party of cow-boys—whose herd is sold and they preparing to start home—in having a jolly time. Often one or more of them will imbibe too much poison whisky and straightway go on the "war path." Then mounting his pony he is ready to shoot anybody or anything; or rather than not shoot at all, would fire up into the air, all the while yelling as only a semi-civilized being can. At such times it is not safe to be on the streets, or for that matter within a house, for the drunk cow-boy would as soon shoot into a house as at anything else.

The life of the cow-boy in camp is routine and dull. His food is largely of the "regulation" order, but a feast of vegetables he wants and must have, or scurvy would ensue. Onions and potatoes are his favorites, but any kind of vegetables will disappear in haste when put within his reach. In camp, on the trail, on the ranch in Texas, with their countless thousands of cattle, milk and butter are almost unknown, not even milk or cream for the coffee is had. Pure shiftlessness and the lack of energy are the only reasons for this privation, and to the same reasons can be assigned much of the privations and hardships incident to ranching.

It would cost but little effort or expense to add a hundred comforts, not to say luxuries, to the life of a drover and his cow-boys. They sleep on the ground, with a pair of blankets for bed and cover. No tent is used, scarcely any cooking utensils, and such a thing as a camp cook-stove is unknown. The warm water of the branch or the standing pool is drank; often it is yellow with alkali and other poisons. No wonder the cow-boy gets sallow and unhealthy, and deteriorates in manhood until often he becomes capable of any contemptible thing; no wonder he should become half-civilized only, and take to whisky with a love excelled scarcely by the barbarous Indian.

When the herd is sold and delivered to the purchaser, a day of rejoicing to the cow-boy has come, for then he can go free and have a jolly time; and it is a jolly time they have. Straightway after settling with their employers the barber shop is visited, and three to six months' growth of hair is shorn off, their long-grown, sunburnt beard "set" in due shape, and properly blacked; next a clothing store of the Israelitish style is "gone through," and the cow-boy emerges a new man, in outward appearance, everything being new, not excepting the hat and boots, with star decorations about the tops, also a new— — —, well, in short everything new. Then for fun and frolic. The bar-room, the theatre, the gambling-room, the bawdy house, the dance house, each and all come in for their full share of attention. In any of these places an affront, or a slight, real or imaginary, is cause sufficient for him to unlimber one or more "mountain howitzers," invariably found strapped to his person, and proceed to deal out death in unbroken doses to such as may be in range of his pistols, whether real friends or enemies, no matter, his anger and bad whisky urge him on to deeds of blood and death.

At frontier towns where are centered many cattle and, as a natural result, considerable business is transacted, and many strangers congregate, there are always to be found a number of bad characters, both male and female; of the very worst class in the universe, such as have fallen below the level of the lowest type of the brute creation. Men who live a soulless, aimless life, dependent upon the turn of a card for the means of living. They wear out a purposeless life, ever looking bleareyed and dissipated; to whom life, from various causes, has long since become worse than a total blank; beings in the form of man whose outward appearance would betoken gentlemen, but whose heart-strings are but a wisp of base sounding chords, upon which the touch of the higher and purer life have long since ceased to be felt. Beings without whom the world would be better, richer and more desirable. And with them are always found their counterparts in the opposite sex; those who have fallen low, alas! how low! They, too, are found in the frontier cattle town; and that institution known in the West as a dance house, is there found also. When the darkness of the night is come to shroud their orgies from public gaze, these miserable beings gather into the halls of the dance house, and "trip the fantastic toe" to wretched music, ground out of dilapidated instruments, by beings fully as degraded as the most vile. In this vortex of dissipation the average cow-boy plunges with great delight. Few more wild, reckless scenes of abandoned debauchery can be seen on the civilized earth, than a dance house in full blast in one of the many frontier towns. To say they dance wildly or in an abandoned manner is putting it mild. Their manner of practising the terpsichorean art would put the French "Can-Can" to shame.

The cow-boy enters the dance with a peculiar zest, not stopping to divest himself of his sombrero, spurs or pistols, but just as he dismounts off of his cow-pony, so he goes into the dance. A more odd, not to say comical sight, is not often seen than the dancing cow-boy; with the front of his sombrero lifted at an angle of fully forty-five degrees; his huge spurs jingling at every step or motion; his revolvers flapping up and down like a retreating sheep's tail; his eyes lit up with excitement, liquor and lust; he plunges in and "hoes it down" at a terrible rate, in the most approved yet awkward country style; often swinging "his partner" clear off of the floor for an entire circle, then "balance all" with an occasional demoniacal yell, near akin to the war whoop of the savage Indian. All this he does, entirely oblivious to the whole world "and the balance of mankind." After dancing furiously, the entire "set" is called to "waltz to the bar," where the boy is required to treat his partner, and, of course, himself also, which he does not hesitate to do time and again, although it costs him fifty cents each time. Yet if it cost ten times that amount he would not hesitate, but the more he dances and drinks, the less common sense he will have, and the more completely his animal passions will control him. Such is the manner in which the cow-boy spends his hard earned dollars. And such is the entertainment that many young men—from the North and the South, of superior parentage and youthful advantages in life—give themselves up to, and often more, their lives are made to pay the forfeit of their sinful foolishness.

After a few days of frolic and debauchery, the cow-boy is ready, in company with his comrades, to start back to Texas, often not having one dollar left of his summer's wages. To this rather hard drawn picture of the cow-boy, there are many creditable exceptions—young men who respect themselves and save their money, and are worthy young gentlemen—but it is idle to deny the fact that the wild, reckless conduct of the cow-boys while drunk, in connection with that of the worthless Northern renegades, have brought the *personnel* of the Texan cattle trade into great disrepute, and filled many graves with victims, bad men and good men, at Abilene, Newton, Wichita, and Ellsworth. But by far the larger portion of those killed are of that class that can be spared without detriment to the good morals and respectability of humanity.

It often occurs when the cow-boys fail to get up a melee and kill each other by the half dozen, that the keepers of those "hell's half acres" find some pretext arising from "business jealousies" or other causes, to suddenly become belligerent, and stop not to declare war, but begin hostilities at once. It is generally effective work they do with their revolvers and shot guns, for they are the most desperate men on earth. Either some of the principals or their subordinates are generally "done for" in a thorough manner, or wounded so as to be miserable cripples for life. On such occasions there are few tears shed, or even inquiries made, by the respectable people, but an expression of sorrow is common that, active hostilities did not continue until every rough was stone dead.

In concluding we offer a few reflections on the general character of Southwestern cattle men. In doing so we are not animated by other motives than a desire to convey a correct impression of that numerous class as a whole; reflections and impressions based upon close observation and a varied experience of seven or eight years spent in business contact and relation with them.

They are, as a class, not public spirited in matters pertaining to the general good, but may justly be called selfish, or at least indifferent to the public welfare. They are prodigal to a fault with their money, when opportunity offers to gratify their appetites or passions, but it is extremely difficult to induce them to expend even a small sum in forwarding a project or enterprise that has other than a purely selfish end in view. In general they entertain strong suspicions of Northern men, and do not have the profoundest confidence in each other. They are disposed to measure every man's action and prompting motives by the rule of selfishness, and they are slow indeed to believe that other than purely selfish motives could or ever do prompt a man to do an act or develop an enterprise. If anything happens to a man, especially a Northern man, so that he cannot do or perform all that they expect or require of him, no explanation or reasons are sufficient to dispel the deep and instant conviction formed in their breasts, that he is deliberately trying to swindle them, and they can suddenly see a thousand evidences of his villainy, in short, instantly vote such an one a double dyed villain.

Their reputation is wide spread for honorably abiding their verbal contracts. For the very nature of their business, and the circumstances under which it is conducted, renders an honorable course imperative; and, as a rule, where agreements or contracts are put into writing, they will stand to them unflinchingly, no matter how great the sacrifice; but when the contract or understanding is verbal only, and not of the most definite nature, their consciences are full as pliant as are those of any other section. A promise made as to some future transaction is kept or broken, as their future interests may dictate.

Thorns an Inch Long

– by –

E.C. "Teddy Blue" Abbott and Helena Hunt Smith

I STAYED ON THE PLATTE all the summer of '82 with different outfits and made several trips to the railroad with beef herds. In the fall I got paid off and went home to see about my own cattle. I ain't a damn bit proud of that winter, too much wine, women, and song. So in the spring I sold my cattle and drifted south once more.

I hired out in Texas to the F U F outfit, that was run by some people from New England, to take another herd up the trail. And that was the time I went all the way up to the Yellowstone River in Montana, which was the goal of every cowpuncher's ambition in the eighties. They all wanted to get to the Yellowstone.

We started out the tenth day of April, 1883, and we turned them loose on Armell's Creek, near Forsyth, Montana, in October. We put up that herd near San Antone. The trail outfit was hired there, and the different ranches was bringing the cattle in to us in little bunches, and we received them and road-branded them. The country south of San Antone is brush country, South Texas brush, mesquite and cactus and thorn and I don't know what else, but I know everything that grows has thorns on it except the willows, and some of them are an inch long.

One night at sundown, after we had been working the cattle in the brush all day, we came to a little open prairie just about big enough to bed down the herd. I tied my night horse to the wagon, took off my chaps and laid down on them, pulled my slicker over me, and went to sleep. About nine o'clock a clap of thunder woke me up, and some-body hollered: "They're running." I grabbed my hat and jumped for my horse, forgetting to put on my chaps, and I spent half the night chasing the cattle through that thorny brush. When daylight come and we got them all together, we hadn't lost a head. But I was a bloody sight, I had a big hole in my forehead, and my face was all over blood, my hands was cut to pieces—because I'd left my gloves in my chaps pocket—and my knees was the worst of all. I was picking thorns out of them all the way to Kansas. That morning I said to the boss: "If God Almighty ever lets me out of this brush, I'm never going back into it." And I never have.

On the other hand there was fellows brought up in the brush that like it and never could feel at home in any other kind of country. Another outfit that came up the trail that year had a little Texas cowboy with them who had never gotten out of the brush. He would start up the trail, but as soon as they got out of the Cross Timbers in the Nations, which was the last piece of timbered country on the trail, this little fellow would stampede back to Texas. He had run away like this three times—leaving the outfit short a hand—and the bunch he was with this time had made up their minds he wouldn't do it to them. So they jumped him one day at noon and hog-tied him and put him in the wagon until after dark, and then they let him out on herd. Next day it was too far to run away, so he stayed and went up the trail. But he said: "You know, when I get out on that big prairie I feel kind of naked."

It was open country all the way up, until he got to Squaw Creek on the Missouri. There is lots of brush and bull pines on Squaw Creek, so when he got there he felt at home, and I heard that in the end he took up land there.

In the eighties, conditions on the trail were a whole lot better than they were in the seventies. Someone had invented mess boxes to set up in the hind end of the wagon; they had four-horse teams to pull it, lots of grub, and from six to eight horses for each man to ride; and the saddles had improved. When I was on the trail in '83, we didn't have hardly a sore-backed horse all the way up to Montana, and the trail bosses had got the handling of a herd down to a science.

After some experience in the business, they found that about 2,000 head on an average was the best number in a herd. After you crossed Red River and got out on the open plains, it was sure a pretty sight to see them strung out for almost a mile, the sun flashing on their horns. At noon you would see the men throw them off the trail, and half the crew would go to dinner while the other half would graze them onto water. No orders were given; every man knew his place and what to do. The left point, right swing, left flank, and right drag would go in to dinner together. The first men off would eat in a hurry, catch up fresh horses, and go out on a lope to the herd. It sure looks good, when you are on herd and hungry, to see the relief come out on a lope.

Eleven men made the average crew with a trail herd. The two men in the lead were called the point men, and then as the herd strung out there would be two men behind them on the swing, two on the flank, and the two drag drivers in the rear. With the cook and horse wrangler and boss, that made eleven. The poorest men always worked with the drags, because a good hand wouldn't stand for it. I have seen them come off herd with the dust half an inch deep on their hats and thick as fur in their eyebrows and mustaches, and if they shook their head or you tapped their cheek, it would fall off them in showers. That dust was the reason a good man wouldn't work back there, and if they hired out to a trail outfit and were put with the drags, they would go to the boss and ask for their time. But the rest of them were pretty nearly as bad off when they were on the side away from the wind. They would go to the water barrel at the end of the day and rinse their mouths and cough and spit and bring up that black stuff out of their throats. But you couldn't get it up out of your lungs.

Going into a new country, the trail boss had to ride his tail off hunting for water. But he would come back to the wagon at night. Lots of times he would ride up on a little knoll and signal to the point—water this way, or water that way. And that is when you will see some trail work, when they are going to turn the herd. If they're going to turn to the right the man on the right point will drop back, and the man on left point will go ahead and start pushing them over, and the men behind can tell from their movements what they want to do. By watching and cutting the curve, you can save the drags two or three hundred yards. It's the drags you have to protect—they are the weak and sore-footed cattle—and that's what counts in the management of a herd.

There is quite an art, too, to watering a herd. You bring them up and spread them out along the bank, with the lead cattle headed downstream. The leads get there first, and of course they drink clear water, and as the drags keep coming in they get clear water, too, because they are upstream.

Oh, those trail bosses know their business, and their business was to get their herd through in good shape; that was all they thought about. Coming up to the mouth of the Musselshell in '84—I had been in Montana a year by that time, but I was going further north with the N Bar herd—we watered one day on a little muddy creek, and they sure roiled it up. That day at dinner my pal Harry Rutter told Burgess, the boss: "Say, you go ahead and water the wagon and horses, and then you water the herd, and then we get a drink. I ain't kicking, but I had to chew that water before I could swallow it."

1883 and 1884 were the biggest years there ever was on the Texas trail. John Blocker says that 500,000 cattle passed through Ogallala alone in those two years, and that was just one point. A lot of the herds going north went to the west of there, while others never got into Nebraska at all, but were shipped east from Dodge City, Kansas. After 1884 the cattle drives began to fall off. In the winter of 1884–85 Kansas passed a quarantine law against Texas cattle on account of Texas fever, and next season the trail had to move west to Trail City, Colorado. In '86 there was a big drive of stock cattle to northern Wyoming and Montana, and a 90 per cent loss that winter, which took the heart out of the business as far as the northern ranges were concerned. From then on the drives got smaller and smaller, till in '95 the X I T Ranch in the Texas Panhandle brought up three herds. And that was the last of the Texas trail.

But in 1883 all the cattle in the world seemed to be coming up from Texas. On the trail we were hardly ever out of sight of a herd, and when we got to that big flat country along the North Platte we could see the dust of the others for twenty miles. One afternoon I was out hunting some of our horses—because we had brought a lot of wild range horses up from Texas with us, and bought more at North Platte, and they were always getting away. And I rode up on a little hill to look for the horses, and from the top of the hill I could see seven herds behind us; I knew there were eight herds ahead of us, and I could see the dust from thirteen more of them on the other side of the river.

On another hill on the north side of the North Platte, near Cold Water, was where I left the herd and lay down in the shade. That was counted a disgrace, but I had been in the saddle two nights and three days.

The first night after we crossed the river with the F U F herd I was on night guard, ten to twelve, and it came up an awful hailstorm. I told my partner, a kid from Boston, to ride to one side and take the saddle off and hold it over his head. And pretty soon I had to quit, too, and hold my saddle over my head, and there were still dents in that saddle when I traded it off in Buffalo, Wyoming, a year later. Nobody knows now what those storms were like, because nobody has to stay out in them any more, but believe me, they were awful. If you had to take that drumming on your head, it would drive you crazy.

I lost my horse that night, because a big hailstone hit my hand, and it hurt so bad I let go the reins as he plunged. The rest of the night I was afoot and helpless. Nobody came out from camp to relieve us, because camp was on the other side of a big coulee—arroyo, they call it down there—and it was swimming water and they couldn't get across. So all that night my partner and I were out there with the herd alone.

The next night another storm came up and, by God, it was my relief again. The second night nobody in the outfit got any sleep, but the rest of them only had one night of it, and my partner and I had two. Five herds was camped close together when that storm struck, and next day 10,000 range cattle was all mixed up. We rounded up and cut our cattle out; it was hot as hell, and in that country along the Platte there wasn't a tree nor even any brush for fifty or sixty miles.

About three in the afternoon, on Cold Water Creek, I saw a sod house that some cow outfit had built there for a line camp, and I saw where this little bit of a house made a patch of shade. So I rode over to it, and got off my horse and I took my rope down and laid on it, so the horse couldn't leave me. And I just died.

When I woke up, it was dark. I could see our campfire away up the flat. I rode out there and asked the boss to figure out what he owed me, because I thought I would get fired for quitting the herd and I wanted to beat him to it.

But all he said was: "Hell, Ted, I thought you was going to do that yesterday."

They used to have some terrible storms on the North and South Platte. The year before this, in '82, I was in one that killed fourteen head of cattle and six or seven horses and two men, on the different herds. One man was so scared he threw his six-shooter away, for fear it would draw the lightning; and I remember old Matt Winter, with the rain apouring down and the lightning flashing, taking off his hat and yelling at God Almighty: "All right, you old bald-headed son of a bitch up there, if you want to kill me, come on do it!" It scared the daylights out of the rest of us.

Lots of cowpunchers were killed by lightning, and that is history. I was knocked off my horse by it twice. The first time I saw a ball of fire coming toward me and felt something strike me on the head. When I came to, I was lying under old Pete and the rain was pouring down on my face. The second time I was trying to get under a railroad bridge when it hit me, and I came to in the ditch. The cattle were always restless when there was a storm at night, even if it was a long way off, and that was when any little thing would start a run. Lots of times I have ridden around the herd, with lightning playing and thunder muttering in the distance, when the air was so full of electricity that I would see it flashing on the horns of the cattle, and there would be balls of it on the horse's ears and even on my mustache, little balls about the size of a pea. I suppose it was static electricity, the same as when you shake a blanket on a winter night in a dark room.

But when you add it all up, I believe the worst hardship we had on the trail was loss of sleep. There was never enough sleep. Our day wouldn't end till about nine o'clock, when we grazed the herd onto the bed ground. And after that every man in the outfit except the boss and horse wrangler and cook would have to stand two hours' night guard. Suppose my guard was twelve to two. I would stake my night horse, unroll my bed, pull off my boots, and crawl in at nine, get about three hours' sleep, and then ride two hours. Then I would come off guard and get to sleep another hour and a half, till the cook yelled, "Roll out," at half past three. So I would get maybe five hours' sleep when the weather was nice and everything smooth and pretty, with cowboys singing under the stars. If it wasn't so nice, you'd be lucky to sleep an hour. But the wagon rolled on in the morning just the same.

That night guard got to be part of our lives. They never had to call me. I would hear the fellow coming off herd—because laying with your ear to the ground you could hear that horse trotting a mile off— and I would jump up and put my hat and boots on and go out to meet him. We were all just the same. I remember when we got up to the mouth of the Musselshell in '84 we turned them loose, and Johnny Burgess, the trail boss, said: "We won't stand no guard tonight, boys," and it sounded good, But every man in that outfit woke when his time to go on guard came, and looked around and wanted to know why they didn't call him.

Sometimes we would run tobacco juice in our eyes to keep awake. It was rubbing them with fire. I have done that a few times, and I have often sat in my saddle sound asleep for just a few minutes. In '79, when we hit the Platte River with that Olive herd, a strong north wind was blowing waves two feet high in their faces, and they bulled on us, which means they won't do nothing, only stand and look at you. So since they wouldn't take the water we had to hold them, and we had one of those bad electric storms and they run near-ly all night. We got them across the river the next day, and that night on guard my partner, Joe Buckner, says: "Teddy, I am going to Green-land where the nights are six months long, and I ain't agoing to get up until ten o'clock next day."

But if you said anything to the boss, he would only say: "What the hell are you kicking about? You can sleep all winter when you get to Montana."

Coming Off the Trail
in '82

– by –
Jack Potter

IN THE SPRING OF 1882, the New England Livestock Co. bought three thousand short horns in Southwest Texas, cut them into four herds and started them on the trail to Colorado, with King Hennant of Corpus Christi in charge of the first herd, Asa Clark of Legarta the second herd, Billie Burke the third herd, and John Smith of San Antonio in charge of the fourth. When they reached a point near San Antonio Smith asked me to go with the herd at $30 a month and transportation back. Now, friends, it will not take long to tell my experiences going up the trail, but it will require several pages to recount what I had to endure coming back home.

There was no excitement whatever on this drive. It was to me very much like a summer's outing in the Rocky Mountains. We went out by way of Fredericksburg, Mason and Brady City, and entered the Western trail at Cow Gap, going through Albany near Fort Griffin, where we left the Western trail and selected a route through to Trinidad, Colorado, via Double Mountain Fork of the Brazos, Wichita and Pease Rivers to the Charles Goodnight ranch on the Staked Plains. We had several stampedes while crossing the plains.

En route we saw thousands of antelope crossing the trail in front of the herd. We crossed the Canadian at Tuscosa. This was a typical cowboy town, and at this time a general roundup was in progress, and l believe there were a hundred and fifty cow-punchers in the place. They had taken a day off to celebrate, and as there were only seven saloons in Tuscosa they were all doing a flourishing business. We had trouble in crossing the river with our herd, as those fellows were riding up and down the streets yelling and shooting.

Our next point was over the Dim Trail and freight road to Trindad, Colorado, where we arrived the tenth of July. Here the manager met us and relieved two of the outfits, saying the country up to the South Platte was easy driving and that they would drift the horses along with two outfits instead of four. The manager and King Hennant made some medicine and called for the entire crews of John Smith and Asa Clark, and told Billie Burke to turn his crew over to Hennant, who was to take charge of the whole drive. I was disappointed, for I did not want to spoil the summer with a two months' drive. They called the men up one at a time and gave them their checks. However, King Hennant arranged with the manager for me to remain with them, and then it was agreed to send me with some of the cow ponies to the company's cattle ranch in the Big Horn Basin later on.

The drive up the South Platte was fine. We traveled for three hundred miles along the foothills of the Rockies, where we were never out of sight of the snowy ranges. We went out by way of La Junta, Colorado, on the Santa Fe, and then to Deer Trail. We would throw our two herds together at night and the next morning again cut them into two herds for the trail. We arrived at the South Platte River near Greeley, Colorado, about the tenth of August.

The itch or ronia had broken out on the trail and in those days people did not know how to treat it successfully. Our manager sent us a wagon load of kerosene and sulphur with which to fight the disease.

When we reached Cow Creek we turned the herds loose and began building what is known as the Crow Ranch. I worked here thirty days and it seemed like thirty years. One day the manager came out and gave instructions to shape up a herd of one hundred and fifty select cow ponies to be taken to the Big Horn Ranch, and I was chosen to go with the outfit. This was the first time I had seen an outfit fixed up in the North. I supposed we would get a pack horse and fit up a little outfit and two of us hike out with them. It required two days to get started. The outfit consisted of a wagon loaded with chuck, a big wall tent, cots to sleep on, a stove, and a number one cook. We hit the trail, and it was another outing for me, for this time we were traveling in new fields.

After leaving Cheyenne we pulled out for Powder River and then up to Sheridan. The weather was getting cold and I began to get homesick. When we reached the Indian country I was told that it was only one day's drive to Custer's battleground. I was agreeably surprised the next morning as we came down a long slope into the Little Big Horn Valley to the battleground. I was under the impression that Sitting Bull had hemmed Custer up in a box canyon and came up from behind and massacred his entire army. But that was a mistake, as Sitting Bull with his warriors was camped in the beautiful valley when Custer attacked him in the open. It seems that the Indians retreated slowly up a gradual slope to the east and Custer's men followed. The main fight took place at the top of the rise, as there is a headstone where every soldier fell, and a monument where Custer was killed.

The balance of that day we passed thousands of Indians who were going the same direction we were traveling. When they go to the agency to get their monthly allowance they take along everything with them, each family driving their horses in a separate bunch. When we arrived at the Crow Agency the boss received a letter from the manager instructing him to send me back to Texas, as the company were contracting for cattle for spring delivery, and I would be needed in the trail drives. The next morning I roped my favorite horse and said to the boys: "Good-bye, fellows, I am drifting south where the climate suits my clothes." That day I overtook an outfit on the way to Ogallala, and traveled with them several days, and then cut out from them and hiked across the prairie one hundred and fifty miles to the Crow ranch, where I sold my two horses and hired a party to take me and my saddle to Greeley, where I expected to set out for home.

Now, reader, here I was, a boy not yet seventeen years old, two thousand miles from home. I had never been on a railroad train, had never slept in a hotel, never taken a bath in a bath house, and from babyhood I had heard terrible stories about ticket thieves, money-changers, pickpockets, three-card monte, and other robbing schemes, and I had horrors about this, my first railroad trip. The first thing I did was to make my money safe by tying it up in my shirt tail. I had a draft for $150 and some currency. I purchased a second-hand trunk and about two hundred feet of rope with which to tie it. The contents of the trunk were one apple-horn saddle, a pair of chaps, a Colt's 45, one sugan, a hen-skin blanket, and a change of dirty clothes. You will see later that this trunk and its contents caused me no end of trouble.

My cowboy friends kindly assisted me in getting ready for the journey. The company had agreed to provide me with transportation, and they purchased a local ticket to Denver for me and gave me a letter to deliver to the general ticket agent at this point, instructing him to sell me a reduced ticket to Dodge City, Kansas, and enable me to secure a cowboy ticket from there to San Antonio for twenty-five dollars. Dodge City was the largest delivering point in the Northwest, and by the combined efforts of several prominent stockmen a cheap rate to San Antonio had been perfected for the convenience of the hundreds of cowboys returning home after the drives.

About four p.m. the Union Pacific train came pulling into Greeley. Then it was a hasty handshake with the boys. One of them handed me my trunk check, saying, "Your baggage is loaded. Good-bye, write me when you get home," and the train pulled out. It took several minutes for me to collect myself, and then the conductor came through and called for the tickets. When I handed him my ticket he punched a hole in it, and then pulled out a red slip, punched it, too, and slipped it into my hatband. I jumped to my feet and said, "You can't come that on me. Give me back my ticket," but he passed out of hearing, and as I had not yet learned how to walk on a moving train, I could not follow him. When I had become fairly settled in my seat again the train crossed a bridge, and as it went by I thought the thing was going to hit me on the head. I dodged those bridges all the way up to Denver. When I reached there I got off at the Union Station and walked down to the baggage car, and saw them unloading my trunk. I stepped up and said: "I will take my trunk." A man said, "No; we are handling this baggage." "But," said I, "that is my trunk, and has my saddle and gun in it." They paid no attention to me and wheeled the trunk off to the baggage room, but I followed right along, determined that they were not going to put anything over me. Seeing that I was so insistent one of the men asked me for the check. It was wrapped up in my shirt tail, and I went after it, and produced the draft I had been given as wages. He looked at it and said, "This is not your trunk check. Where is your metal check with numbers on it?" Then it began to dawn on me what the darn thing was, and when I produced it and handed it to him he asked me where I was going. I told him to San Antonio, Texas, if I could get there. I then showed him my letter to the general ticket agent, and he said: "Now, boy, you leave this trunk right here and we will recheck it and yon need not bother about it." That sounded bully to me.

I followed the crowd down Sixteenth and Curtiss Streets and rambled around looking for a quiet place to stop. I found the St. Charles Hotel and made arrangements to stay all night. Then I went off to a barber shop to get my hair cut and clean up a bit. When the barber finished with me he asked if I wanted a bath, and when I said yes, a negro porter took me down the hallway and into a side room. He turned on the water, tossed me a couple of towels and disappeared. I commenced undressing hurriedly, fearing the tub would fill up before I could get ready. The water was within a few inches of the top of the tub when I plunged in. Then I gave a yell like a Comanche Indian, for the water was boiling hot! I came out of the tub on all fours, but when I landed on the marble floor it was so slick that I slipped and fell backwards with my head down. I scrambled around promiscuously, and finally got my footing with a chair for a brace. I thought: "Jack Potter, you are scalded after the fashion of a hog." I caught a lock of my hair to see if it would "slip," at the same time fanning myself with my big Stetson hat. I next examined my toe nails, for they had received a little more dipping than my hair, but I found them in fairly good shape, turning a bit dark, but still hanging on.

That night I went to the Tabor Opera House and saw a fine play. There I found a cowboy chum, and we took in the sights until midnight, when I returned to the St. Charles. The porter showed me up to my room and turned on the gas. When he had gone I undressed to go to bed, and stepped up to blow out the light. I blew and blew until I was out of breath, and then tried to fan the flame out with my hat, but I had to go to bed and leave the gas burning. It was fortunate that I did not succeed, for at that time the papers were full of accounts of people gassed just that way.

The next morning I started out to find the Santa Fe ticket office, where I presented my letter to the head man there. He was a nice appearing gentleman, and when he had looked over the letter he said, "So you are a genuine cowboy? Where is your gun and how many notches have you on its handle? I suppose you carry plenty of salt with you on the trail for emergency? I was just reading in a magazine a few days ago about a large herd which stampeded and one of the punchers mounted a swift horse and ran up in front of the leaders and began throwing out salt, and stopped the herd just in time to keep them from running off a high precipice." I laughed heartily when he told me this and said, "My friend, you can't learn the cow business out of books. That yarn was hatched in the brain of some fiction writer who probably never saw a cow in his life. But I am pleased to find a railroad man who will talk, for I always heard that a railroad man only used two words, Yes and No." Then we had quite a pleasant conversation. He asked me if I was ever in Albert's Buckhorn saloon in San Antonio and saw the collection of fine horns there. Then he gave me an emigrant cowboy ticket to Dodge City and a letter to the agent at that place stating that I was eligible for a cowboy ticket to San Antonio.

As it was near train time I hunted up the baggage crew and told them I was ready to make another start. I showed them my ticket and asked them about my trunk. They examined it, put on a new check, and gave me one with several numbers on it. I wanted to take the trunk out and put it on the train, but they told me to rest easy and they would put it on. I stood right there until I saw them put it on the train, then I climbed aboard.

This being my second day out, I thought my troubles should be over, but not so, for I couldn't face those bridges. They kept me dodging and fighting my head. An old gentleman who sat near me said, "Young man, I see by your dress that you are a typical cowboy, and no doubt you can master the worst bronco or rope and tie a steer in less than a minute, but in riding on a railway train you seem to be a novice. Sit down on this seat with your back to the front and those bridges will not bother you." And sure enough it was just as he said.

We arrived at Coolidge, Kansas, one of the old landmarks of the Santa Fe Trail days, about dark. That night at twelve o'clock we reached Dodge City, where I had to lay over for twenty-four hours. I thought everything would be quiet in the town at that hour of the night, but I soon found out that they never slept in Dodge. They had a big dance hall there which was to Dodge City what Jack Harris' Theater was to San Antonio. I arrived at the hall in time to see a gambler and a cowboy mix up in a six-shooter duel. Lots of smoke, a stampede, but no one killed. I secured a room and retired. When morning came I arose and fared forth to see Dodge City by daylight. It seemed to me that the town was full of cowboys and cattle owners. The first acquaintance I met here was George W. Saunders, now the president and chief remudero of the Old Trail Drivers. I also found Jesse Pressnall and Slim Johnson there, as well as several others whom I knew down in Texas. Pressnall said to me: "Jack, you will have lots of company on your way home. Old 'Dog Face' Smith is up here from Cotulla and he and his whole bunch are going back tonight. Old 'Dog Face' is one of the best trail men that ever drove a cow, but he is all worked up about having to go back on a train. I wish you would help them along down the line in changing cars." That afternoon I saw a couple of chuck wagons coming in loaded with punchers, who had on the same clothing they wore on the trail, their pants stuck in their boots and their spurs on. They were bound for San Antonio. Old "Dog Face" Smith was a typical Texan, about thirty years of age, with long hair and three months' growth of whiskers. He wore a blue shirt and a red cotton handkerchief around his neck. He had a bright, intelligent face that bore the appearance of a good trail hound, which no doubt was the cause of people calling him "Dog Face."

It seemed a long time that night to wait for the train and we put in time visiting every saloon in the town. There was a big stud poker game going on in one place, and I saw one Texas fellow, whose name I will not mention, lose a herd of cattle at the game. But he might have won the herd back before daylight.

I will never forget seeing that train come into Dodge City that night. Old "Dog Face" and his bunch were pretty badly frightened and we had considerable difficulty in getting them aboard. It was about 12:30 when the train pulled out. The conductor came around and I gave him my cowboy ticket. It was almost as long as your arm, and as he tore off a chunk of it I said: "What authority have you to tear up a man's ticket?" He laughed and said, "You are on my division. I simply tore off one coupon and each conductor between here and San Antonio will tear off one for each division." That sounded all right, but I wondered if that ticket would hold out all the way down.

Everyone seemed to be tired and worn out and the bunch began bedding down. Old "Dog Face" was out of humor, and was the last one to bed down. At about three o'clock our train was sidetracked to let the west-bound train pass. This little stop caused the boys to sleep the sounder. Just then the westbound train sped by traveling at the rate of about forty miles an hour, and just as it passed our coach the engineer blew the whistle. Talk about your stampedes! That bunch of sleeping cowboys arose as one man, and started on the run with old "Dog Face" Smith in the lead. I was a little slow in getting off, but fell in with the drags. I had not yet woke up, but thinking I was in a genuine cattle stampede, yelled out, "Circle your leaders and keep up the drags." Just then the leaders circled and ran into the drags, knocking some of us down. They circled again and the news butcher crawled out from under foot and jumped through the window like a frog. Before they could circle back the next time, the train crew pushed in the door and caught old "Dog Face" and soon the bunch quieted down. The conductor was pretty angry and threatened to have us transferred to the freight department and loaded into a stock car.

We had breakfast at Hutchinson, and after eating and were again on our way, speeding through the beautiful farms and thriving towns of Kansas, we organized a kangaroo court and tried the engineer of that westbound train for disturbing the peace of passengers on the eastbound train. We heard testimony all morning, and called in some of the train crew to testify. One of the brakemen said it was an old trick for that engineer to blow the whistle at that particular siding and that he was undoubtedly the cause of a great many stampedes. The jury brought in a verdict of guilty and assessed the death penalty. It was ordered that he be captured, taken to some place on the western trail, there to be hog-tied like a steer, and then have the road brand applied with a good hot iron and a herd of not less than five thousand long-horn Texas steers made to stampede and trample him to death.

We had several hours lay-over at Emporia, Kansas, where we took the M., K. & T. for Parsons, getting on the main line through Indian Territory to Denison, Texas. There was a large crowd of punchers on the through train who were returning from Ogallala by way of Kansas City and Omaha.

As we were traveling through the Territory old "Dog Face" said to me: "Potter, I expect it was me that started that stampede up there in Kansas, but I just couldn' help it. You see, I took on a scare once and since that time I have been on the hair trigger when suddenly awakened. In the year 1875 me and Wild Horse Jerry were camped at a water hole out west of the Nueces River, where we were snaring mustangs. One evening a couple of peloncias pitched camp nearby, and the next morning our remuda was missing, all except our night horses. I told Wild Horse Jerry to hold down the camp and watch the snares, and I hit the trail of those peloncias which headed for the Rio Grande. I followed it for about forty miles and then lost all signs. It was nightfall, so I made camp, prepared supper and rolled up in my blanket and went to sleep. I don't know how long I slept, but I was awakened by a low voice saying: "Dejarle desconsar bien por que en un rato el va a comenzar su viaje por el otro mundo." (Let him rest well, as he will soon start on his journey to the other world.) It was the two Mexican horse thieves huddled around my campfire smoking their cigarettes and taking it easy, as they thought they had the drop on me. As I came out of my bed two bullets whizzed near my head, but about that time my old Colt's forty-five began talking, and the janitor down in Hades had two more peloncias on his hands. Ever since that night, if I am awakened suddenly I generally come out on my all fours roaring like a buffalo bull. I never sleep on a bedstead, for it would not be safe for me, as I might break my darn neck, so I always spread down on the floor."

It was a long ride through the Territory, and we spent the balance of the day singing songs and making merry. I kept thinking about my trunk, and felt grateful that the railroad people had sent along a messenger to look out for it. At Denison we met up with some emigrant families going to Uvalde, and soon became acquainted with some fine girls in the party. They entertained us all the way down to Taylor, where we changed cars. As we told them good-bye one asked me to write a line in her autograph album. Now I was sure enough "up a tree." I had been in some pretty tight places, and had had to solve some pretty hard problems, but this was a new one for me. You see, the American people go crazy over some new fad about once a year, and in 1882 it was the autograph fad. I begged the young lady to excuse me, but she insisted, so I took the album and began writing down all the road brands that I was familiar with. But she told me to write a verse of some kind. I happened to think of a recitation I had learned at school when I was a little boy, so I wrote as follows: "It's tiresome work says lazy Ned, to climb the hill in my new sled, and beat the other boys. Signed, Your Bulliest Friend, JACK POTTER."

We then boarded the I. & G. N. for San Antonio, and at Austin a lively bunch joined us, including Hal Gosling, United States Marshal, Captain Joe Sheeley and Sheriff Quigley of Castroville. Pretty soon the porter called out "San Antonio, Santonnie-o," and that was music to my ears. My first move on getting off the train was to look for my trunk and found it had arrived. I said to myself, "Jack Potter, you're a lucky dog. Ticket held out all right, toe nails all healed up, and trunk came through in good shape." After registering at the Central Hotel, I wrote to that general ticket agent at Denver as follows:

San Antonio, Texas, Oct. 5th, 1882.

Gen. Ticket Agt. A. T. & S. F.,

    1415 Lamar St., Denver, Colo.:

Dear Sir—I landed in San Antonio this afternoon all O. K. My trunk also came through without a scratch. I want to thank you very much for the man you sent along to look after my trunk. He was very accommodating, and would not allow me to assist him in loading it on at Denver. No doubt he will want to see some of the sights of San Antonio, for it is a great place, and noted for its chili con carne. When he takes a fill of this food, as every visitor does, you can expect him back in Denver on very short notice, as he will be seeking a cooler climate. Did you ever eat any chili con carne? I will send you a dozen cans soon, but tell your wife to keep it in the refrigerator as it might set the house on fire. Thank you again for past favors.

        Your Bulliest Friend,

            JACK POTTER.

~

A Boggy Ford

– by –

Andy Adams

THAT NIGHT WE LEARNED from Straw our location on the trail. We were far above the Indian reservation, and instead of having been astray our foreman had held a due northward course, and we were probably as far on the trail as if we had followed the regular route. So in spite of all our good maxims, we had been borrowing trouble; we were never over thirty miles to the westward of what was then the new Western Cattle Trail. We concluded that the "Running W" herd had turned back, as Straw brought the report that same herd had recrossed Red River the day before his arrival, giving for reasons the wet season and the danger of getting waterbound.

About noon of the second day after leaving the North Fork of Red River, we crossed the Washita, a deep stream, the slippery banks of which gave every indication of a recent rise. We had no trouble in crossing either wagon or herd, it being hardly a check in our onward course. The abandonment of the regular trail the past ten days had been a noticeable benefit to our herd, for the cattle had had an abundance of fresh country to graze over as well as plenty of rest. But now that we were back on the trail, we gave them their freedom and frequently covered twenty miles a day, until we reached the South Canadian, which proved to be the most delusive stream we had yet encountered. It also showed, like the Washita, every evidence of having been on a recent rampage. On our arrival there was no volume of water to interfere, but it had a quicksand bottom that would bog a saddle blanket. Our foreman had been on ahead and examined the regular crossing, and when he returned, freely expressed his opinion that we would be unable to trail the herd across, but might hope to effect it by cutting it into small bunches. When we came, therefore, within three miles of the river, we turned off the trail to a nearby creek and thoroughly watered the herd. This was contrary to our practice, for we usually wanted the herd thirsty when reaching a large river. But any cow brute that halted in fording the Canadian that day was doomed to sink into quicksand from which escape was doubtful.

We held the wagon and saddle horses in the rear, and when we were half a mile away from the trail ford, cut off about two hundred head of the leaders and started for the crossing, leaving only the horse wrangler and one man with the herd. On reaching the river we gave them an extra push, and the cattle plunged into the muddy water. Before the cattle had advanced fifty feet, instinct warned them of the treacherous footing, and the leaders tried to turn back; but by that time we had the entire bunch in the water and were urging them forward. They had halted but a moment and begun milling, when several heavy steers sank; then we gave way and allowed the rest to come back. We did not realize fully the treachery of this river until we saw that twenty cattle were caught in the merciless grasp of the quicksand. They sank slowly to the level of their bodies, which gave sufficient resistance to support their weight, but they were hopelessly bogged. We allowed the free cattle to return to the herd, and immediately turned our attention to those that were bogged, some of whom were nearly submerged by water. We dispatched some of the boys to the wagon for our heavy corral ropes and a bundle of horse-hobbles; and the remainder of us, stripped to the belt, waded out and surveyed the situation at close quarters. We were all experienced in handling bogged cattle, though this quicksand was the most deceptive that I, at least, had ever witnessed. The bottom of the river as we waded through it was solid under our feet, and as long as we kept moving it felt so, but the moment we stopped we sank as in a quagmire. The "pull" of this quicksand was so strong that four of us were unable to lift a steer's tail out, once it was imbedded in the sand. And when we had released a tail by burrowing around it to arm's length and freed it, it would sink of its own weight in a minute's time until it would have to be burrowed out again. To avoid this we had to coil up the tails and tie them with a soft rope hobble.

Fortunately none of the cattle were over forty feet from the bank, and when our heavy rope arrived we divided into two gangs and began the work of rescue. We first took a heavy rope from the animal's horns to solid footing on the river bank, and tied to this five or six of our lariats. Meanwhile others rolled a steer over as far as possible and began burrowing with their hands down alongside a fore and hind leg simultaneously until they could pass a small rope around the pastern above the cloof, or better yet through the cloven in the hoof, when the leg could be readily lifted by two men. We could not stop burrowing, however, for a moment, or the space would fill and solidify. Once a leg was freed, we doubled it back short and securely tied it with a hobble, and when the fore and hind leg were thus secured, we turned the animal over on that side and released the other legs in a similar manner. Then we hastened out of the water and into our saddles, and wrapped the loose end of our ropes to the pommels, having already tied the lariats to the heavy corral rope from the animal's horns. When the word was given, we took a good swinging start, and unless something gave way there was one steer less in the bog. After we had landed the animal high and dry on the bank, it was but a minute's work to free the rope and untie the hobbles. Then it was advisable to get into the saddle with little loss of time and give him a wide berth, for he generally arose angry and sullen.

It was dark before we got the last of the bogged cattle out and retraced our way to camp from the first river on the trip that had turned us. But we were not the least discouraged, for we felt certain there was a ford that had a bottom somewhere within a few miles, and we could hunt it up on the morrow. The next one, however, we would try before we put the cattle in. There was no question that the treacherous condition of the river was due to the recent freshet, which had brought down new deposits of sediment and had agitated the old, even to changing the channel of the river, so that it had not as yet had sufficient time to settle and solidify.

The next morning after breakfast, Flood and two or three of the boys set out up the river, while an equal number of us started, under the leadership of The Rebel, down the river on a similar errand,—to prospect for a crossing. Our party scouted for about five miles, and the only safe footing we could find was a swift, narrow channel between the bank and an island in the river, while beyond the island was a much wider channel with water deep enough in several places to swim our saddle horses. The footing seemed quite secure to our horses, but the cattle were much heavier; and if an animal ever bogged in the river, there was water enough to drown him before help could be rendered. We stopped our horses a number of times, however, to try the footing, and in none of our experiments was there any indication of quicksand, so we counted the crossing safe. On our return we found the herd already in motion, headed up the river where our foreman had located a crossing. As it was then useless to make any mention of the island crossing which we had located, at least until a trial had been given to the upper ford, we said nothing. When we came within half a mile of the new ford, we held up the herd and allowed them to graze, and brought up the *remuda* and crossed and recrossed them without bogging a single horse. Encouraged at this, we cut off about a hundred head of heavy, lead cattle and started for the ford. We had a good push on them when we struck the water, for there were ten riders around them and Flood was in the lead. We called to him several times that the cattle were bogging, but he never halted until he pulled out on the opposite bank, leaving twelve of the heaviest steers in the quicksand.

"Well, in all my experience in trailwork," said Flood, as he gazed back at the dozen animals struggling in the quicksand, "I never saw as deceptive a bottom in any river. We used to fear the Cimarron and Platte, but the old South Canadian is the girl that can lay it over them both. Still, there ain't any use crying over spilt milk, and we haven't got men enough to hold two herds, so surround them, boys, and we'll recross them if we leave twenty-four more in the river. Take them back a good quarter, fellows, and bring them up on a run, and I'll take the lead when they strike the water; and give them no show to halt until they get across."

As the little bunch of cattle had already grazed out nearly a quarter, we rounded them into a compact body and started for the river to recross them. The nearer we came to the river, the faster we went, till we struck the water. In several places where there were channels, we could neither force the cattle nor ride ourselves faster than a walk on account of the depth of the water, but when we struck the shallows, which were the really dangerous places, we forced the cattle with horse and quirt. Near the middle of the river, in shoal water, Rod Wheat was quirting up the cattle, when a big dun steer, trying to get out of his reach, sank in the quicksand, and Rod's horse stumbled across the animal and was thrown. He floundered in attempting to rise, and his hind feet sank to the haunches. His ineffectual struggles caused him to sink farther to the flanks in the loblolly which the tramping of the cattle had caused, and there horse and steer lay, side by side, like two in a bed. Wheat loosened the cinches of the saddle on either side, and stripping the bridle off, brought up the rear, carrying saddle, bridle, and blankets on his back. The river was at least three hundred yards wide, and when we got to the farther bank, our horses were so exhausted that we dismounted and let them blow. A survey showed we had left a total of fifteen cattle and the horse in the quicksand. But we congratulated ourselves that we had bogged down only three head in recrossing. Getting these cattle out was a much harder task than the twenty head gave us the day before, for many of these were bogged more than a hundred yards from the bank. But no time was to be lost; the wagon was brought up in a hurry, fresh horses were caught, and we stripped for the fray. While McCann got dinner we got out the horse, even saving the cinches that were abandoned in freeing him of the saddle.

During the afternoon we were compelled to adopt a new mode of procedure, for with the limited amount of rope at hand, we could only use one rope for drawing the cattle out to solid footing, after they were freed from the quagmire. But we had four good mules to our chuck wagon, and instead of dragging the cattle ashore from the pommels of saddles, we tied one end of the rope to the hind axle and used the mules in snaking the cattle out. This worked splendidly, but every time we freed a steer we had to drive the wagon well out of reach, for fear he might charge the wagon and team. But with three crews working in the water, tying up tails and legs, the work progressed more rapidly than it had done the day before, and two hours before sunset the last animal had been freed. We had several exciting incidents during the operation, for several steers showed fight, and when released went on the prod for the first thing in sight. The herd was grazing nearly a mile away during the afternoon, and as fast as a steer was pulled out, some one would take a horse and give the freed animal a start for the herd. One big black steer turned on Flood, who generally attended to this, and gave him a spirited chase. In getting out of the angry steer's way, he passed near the wagon, when the maddened beef turned from Flood and charged the commissary. McCann was riding the nigh wheel mule, and when he saw the steer coming, he poured the whip into the mules and circled around like a battery in field practice, trying to get out of the way. Flood made several attempts to cut off the steer from the wagon, but he followed it like a mover's dog, until a number of us, fearing our mules would be gored, ran out of the water, mounted our horses, and joined in the chase. When we came up with the circus, our foreman called to us to rope the beef, and Fox Quarternight, getting in the first cast, caught him by the two front feet and threw him heavily. Before he could rise, several of us had dismounted and were sitting on him like buzzards on carrion. McCann then drove the team around behind a sand dune, out of sight; we released the beef, and he was glad to return to the herd, quite sobered by the throwing.

Another incident occurred near the middle of the afternoon. From some cause or other, the hind leg of a steer, after having been tied up, became loosened. No one noticed this; but when, after several successive trials, during which Barney McCann exhausted a large vocabulary of profanity, the mule team was unable to move the steer, six of us fastened our lariats to the main rope, and dragged the beef ashore with great éclat. But when one of the boys dismounted to unloose the hobbles and rope, a sight met our eyes that sent a sickening sensation through us, for the steer had left one hind leg in the river, neatly disjointed at the knee. Then we knew why the mules had failed to move him, having previously supposed his size was the difficulty, for he was one of the largest steers in the herd. No doubt the steer's leg had been unjointed in swinging him around, but it had taken six extra horses to sever the ligaments and skin, while the merciless quicksands of the Canadian held the limb. A friendly shot ended the steer's sufferings, and before we finished our work for the day, a flight of buzzards were circling around in anticipation of the coming feast.

Another day had been lost, and still the South Canadian defied us. We drifted the cattle back to the previous night camp, using the same bed ground for our herd. It was then that The Rebel broached the subject of a crossing at the island which we had examined that morning, and offered to show it to our foreman by daybreak. We put two extra horses on picket that night, and the next morning, before the sun was half an hour high, the foreman and The Rebel had returned from the island down the river with word that we were to give the ford a trial, though we could not cross the wagon there. Accordingly we grazed the herd down the river and came opposite the island near the middle of the forenoon. As usual, we cut off about one hundred of the lead cattle, the leaders naturally being the heaviest, and started them into the water. We reached the island and scaled the farther bank without a single animal losing his footing. We brought up a second bunch of double, and a third of triple the number of the first, and crossed them with safety, but as yet the Canadian was dallying with us. As we crossed each successive bunch, the tramping of the cattle increasingly agitated the sands, and when we had the herd about half over, we bogged our first steer on the farther landing. As the water was so shallow that drowning was out of the question, we went back and trailed in the remainder of the herd, knowing the bogged steer would be there when we were ready for him.

The island was about two hundred yards long by twenty wide, lying up and down the river, and in leaving it for the farther bank, we always pushed off at the upper end. But now, in trailing the remainder of the cattle over, we attempted to force them into the water at the lower end, as the footing at that point of this middle ground had not, as yet, been trampled up as had the upper end. Everything worked nicely until the rear guard of the last five or six hundred congested on the island, the outfit being scattered on both sides of the river as well as in the middle, leaving a scarcity of men at all points. When the final rear guard had reached the river the cattle were striking out for the farther shore from every quarter of the island at their own sweet will, stopping to drink and loitering on the farther side, for there was no one to hustle them out.

All were over at last, and we were on the point of congratulating ourselves,—for, although the herd had scattered badly, we had less than a dozen bogged cattle, and those near the shore,—when suddenly up the river over a mile, there began a rapid shooting. Satisfied that it was by our own men, we separated, and, circling right and left, began to throw the herd together. Some of us rode up the river bank and soon located the trouble. We had not ridden a quarter of a mile before we passed a number of our herd bogged, these having reëntered the river for their noonday drink, and on coming up with the men who had done the shooting, we found them throwing the herd out from the water. They reported that a large number of cattle were bogged farther up the river. All hands rounded in the herd, and drifting them out nearly a mile from the river, left them under two herders, when the remainder of us returned to the bogged cattle. There were by actual count, including those down at the crossing, over eighty bogged cattle that required our attention, extending over a space of a mile or more above the island ford.

The outlook was anything but pleasing. Flood was almost speechless over the situation, for it might have been guarded against. But realizing the task before us, we recrossed the river for dinner, well knowing the inner man needed fortifying for the work before us. No sooner had we disposed of the meal and secured a change of mounts all round, than we sent two men to relieve the men on herd. When they were off, Flood divided up our forces for the afternoon work.

"It will never do," said he, "to get separated from our commissary. So, Priest, you take the wagon and *remuda* and go back up to the regular crossing and get our wagon over somehow. There will be the cook and wrangler besides yourself, and you may have two other men. You will have to lighten your load; and don't attempt to cross those mules hitched to the wagon; rely on your saddle horses for getting the wagon over. Forrest, you and Bull, with the two men on herd, take the cattle to the nearest creek and water them well. After watering, drift them back, so they will be within a mile of these bogged cattle. Then leave two men with them and return to the river. I'll take the remainder of the outfit and begin at the ford and work up the river. Get the ropes and hobbles, boys, and come on."

John Officer and I were left with The Rebel to get the wagon across, and while waiting for the men on herd to get in, we hooked up the mules. Honeyman had the *remuda* in hand to start the minute our herders returned, their change of mounts being already tied to the wagon wheels. The need of haste was very imperative, for the river might rise without an hour's notice, and a two-foot rise would drown every hoof in the river as well as cut us off from our wagon. The South Canadian has its source in the Staked Plains and the mountains of New Mexico, and freshets there would cause a rise here, local conditions never affecting a river of such width. Several of us had seen these Plains rivers,—when the mountain was sportive and dallying with the plain,—under a clear sky and without any warning of falling weather, rise with a rush of water like a tidal wave or the stream from a broken dam. So when our men from herd galloped in, we stripped their saddles from tired horses and cinched them to fresh ones, while they, that there might be no loss of time, bolted their dinners. It took us less than an hour to reach the ford, where we unloaded the wagon of everything but the chuck-box, which was ironed fast. We had an extra saddle in the wagon, and McCann was mounted on a good horse, for he could ride as well as cook. Priest and I rode the river, selecting a route; and on our return, all five of us tied our lariats to the tongue and sides of the wagon. We took a running start, and until we struck the farther bank we gave the wagon no time to sink, but pulled it out of the river with a shout, our horses' flanks heaving. Then recrossing the river, we lashed all the bedding to four gentle saddle horses and led them over. But to get our provisions across was no easy matter, for we were heavily loaded, having taken on a supply at Doan's sufficient to last us until we reached Dodge, a good month's journey. Yet over it must go, and we kept a string of horsemen crossing and recrossing for an hour, carrying everything from pots and pans to axle grease, as well as the staples of life. When we had got the contents of the wagon finally over and reloaded, there remained nothing but crossing the saddle stock.

The wagon mules had been turned loose, harnessed, while we were crossing the wagon and other effects; and when we drove the *remuda* into the river, one of the wheel mules turned back, and in spite of every man, reached the bank again. Part of the boys hurried the others across, but McCann and I turned back after our wheeler. We caught him without any trouble, but our attempt to lead him across failed. In spite of all the profanity addressed personally to him, he proved a credit to his sire, and we lost ground in trying to force him into the river. The boys across the river watched a few minutes, when all recrossed to our assistance.

"Time's too valuable to monkey with a mule to-day," said Priest, as he rode up; "skin off that harness."

It was off at once, and we blindfolded and backed him up to the river bank; then taking a rope around his forelegs, we threw him, hog-tied him, and rolled him into the water. With a rope around his forelegs and through the ring in the bridle bit, we asked no further favors, but snaked him ignominiously over to the farther side and reharnessed him into the team.

The afternoon was more than half spent when we reached the first bogged cattle, and by the time the wagon overtook us we had several tied up and ready for the mule team to give us a lift. The herd had been watered in the mean time and was grazing about in sight of the river, and as we occasionally drifted a freed animal out to the herd, we saw others being turned in down the river. About an hour before sunset, Flood rode up to us and reported having cleared the island ford, while a middle outfit under Forrest was working down towards it. During the twilight hours of evening, the wagon and saddle horses moved out to the herd and made ready to camp, but we remained until dark, and with but three horses released a number of light cows. We were the last outfit to reach the wagon, and as Honeyman had tied up our night horses, there was nothing for us to do but eat and go to bed, to which we required no coaxing, for we all knew that early morning would find us once more working with bogged cattle.

The night passed without incident, and the next morning in the division of the forces, Priest was again allowed the wagon to do the snaking out with, but only four men, counting McCann. The remainder of the outfit was divided into several gangs, working near enough each other to lend a hand in case an extra horse was needed on a pull. The third animal we struck in the river that morning was the black steer that had showed fight the day before. Knowing his temper would not be improved by soaking in the quicksand overnight, we changed our tactics. While we were tying up the steer's tail and legs, McCann secreted his team at a safe distance. Then he took a lariat, lashed the tongue of the wagon to a cottonwood tree, and jacking up a hind wheel, used it as a windlass. When all was ready, we tied the loose end of our cable rope to a spoke, and allowing the rope to coil on the hub, manned the windlass and drew him ashore. When the steer was freed, McCann, having no horse at hand, climbed into the wagon, while the rest of us sought safety in our saddles, and gave him a wide berth. When he came to his feet he was sullen with rage and refused to move out of his tracks. Priest rode out and baited him at a distance, and McCann, from his safe position, attempted to give him a scare, when he savagely charged the wagon. McCann reached down, and securing a handful of flour, dashed it into his eyes, which made him back away; and, kneeling, he fell to cutting the sand with his horns. Rising, he charged the wagon a second time, and catching the wagon sheet with his horns, tore two slits in it like slashes of a razor. By this time The Rebel ventured a little nearer, and attracted the steer's attention. He started for Priest, who gave the quirt to his horse, and for the first quarter mile had a close race. The steer, however, weakened by the severe treatment he had been subjected to, soon fell to the rear, and gave up the chase and continued on his way to the herd.

After this incident we worked down the river until the outfits met. We finished the work before noon, having lost three full days by the quicksands of the Canadian. As we pulled into the trail that afternoon near the first divide and looked back to take a parting glance at the river, we saw a dust cloud across the Canadian which we knew must be the Ellison herd under Nat Straw. Quince Forrest, noticing it at the same time as I did, rode forward and said to me, "Well, old Nat will get it in the neck this time, if that old girl dallies with him as she did with us. I don't wish him any bad luck, but I do hope he'll bog enough cattle to keep his hand in practice. It will be just about his luck, though, to find it settled and solid enough to cross."

And the next morning we saw his signal in the sky about the same distance behind us, and knew he had forded without any serious trouble.

The Round-Up

– by –
Theodore Roosevelt

URING THE WINTER-TIME there is ordinarily but little work done among the cattle. There is some line riding, and a continual lookout is kept for the very weak animals,— usually cows and calves, who have to be driven in, fed, and housed; but most of the stock are left to shift for themselves, undisturbed. Almost every stock-growers' association forbids branding any calves before the spring round-up. If great bands of cattle wander off the range, parties may be fitted out to go after them and bring them back; but this is only done when absolutely necessary, as when the drift of the cattle has been towards an Indian reservation or a settled granger country, for the weather is very severe, and the horses are so poor that their food must be carried along.

The bulk of the work is done during the summer, including the late spring and early fall, and consists mainly in a succession of round-ups, beginning, with us, in May and ending towards the last of October.

But a good deal may be done in the intervals by riding over one's range. Frequently, too, herding will be practiced on a large scale.

Still more important is the "trail" work: cattle, while driven from one range to another, or to a shipping point for beef, being said to be "on the trail." For years, the over-supply from the vast breeding ranches to the south, especially in Texas, has been driven northward in large herds, either to the shipping towns along the great railroads, or else to the fattening ranges of the North-west; it having been found, so far, that while the calf crop is larger in the South, beeves become much heavier in the North. Such cattle, for the most part, went along tolerably well-marked routes or trails, which became for the time being of great importance, flourishing—and extremely lawless—towns growing up along them; but with the growth of the railroad system, and above all with the filling-up of the northern ranges, these trails have steadily become of less and less consequence, though many herds still travel them on their way to the already crowded ranges of western Dakota and Montana, or to the Canadian regions beyond. The trail work is something by itself. The herds may be on the trail several months, averaging fifteen miles or less a day. The cowboys accompanying each have to undergo much hard toil, of a peculiarly same and wearisome kind, on account of the extreme slowness with which everything must be done, as trail cattle should never be hurried. The foreman of a trail outfit must be not only a veteran cowhand, but also a miracle of patience and resolution.

Round-up work is far less irksome, there being an immense amount of dash and excitement connected with it; and when once the cattle are on the range, the important work is done during the round-up. On cow ranches, or wherever there is breeding stock, the spring round-up is the great event of the season, as it is then that the bulk of the calves are branded. It usually lasts six weeks, or thereabouts; but its end by no means implies rest for the stockman. On the contrary, as soon as it is over, wagons are sent to work out-of-the-way parts of the country that have been passed over, but where cattle are supposed to have drifted; and by the time these have come back the first beef round-up has begun, and thereafter beeves are steadily gathered and shipped, at least from among the larger herds, until cold weather sets in; and in the fall there is another round-up, to brand the late calves and see that the stock is got back on the range. As all of these round-ups are of one character, a description of the most important, taking place in the spring, will be enough.

In April we begin to get up the horses. Throughout the winter very few have been kept for use, as they are then poor and weak, and must be given grain and hay if they are to be worked. The men in the line camps need two or three apiece, and each man at the home ranch has a couple more; but the rest are left out to shift for themselves, which the tough, hardy little fellows are well able to do. Ponies can pick up a living where cattle die; though the scanty feed, which they may have to uncover by pawing off the snow, and the bitter weather often make them look very gaunt by spring-time. But the first warm rains bring up the green grass, and then all the live-stock gain flesh with wonderful rapidity. When the spring round-up begins the horses should be as fat and sleek as possible. After running all winter free, even the most sober pony is apt to betray an inclination to buck; and, if possible, we like to ride every animal once or twice before we begin to do real work with him. Animals that have escaped for any length of time are almost as bad to handle as if they had never been broken. One of the two horses mentioned in a former chapter as having been gone eighteen months has, since his return, been suggestively dubbed "Dynamite Jimmy," on account of the incessant and eruptive energy with which he bucks. Many of our horses, by the way, are thus named from some feat or peculiarity. Wire Fence, when being broken, ran into one of the abominations after which he is now called; Hackamore once got away and remained out for three weeks with a hackamore, or breaking-halter, on him; Macaulay contracted the habit of regularly getting rid of the huge Scotchman to whom he was intrusted; Bulberry Johnny spent the hour or two after he was first mounted in a large patch of thorny bulberry bushes, his distracted rider unable to get him to do anything but move round sidewise in a circle; Fall Back would never get to the front; Water Skip always jumps mud-puddles; and there are a dozen others with names as purely descriptive.

The stock-growers of Montana, of the western part of Dakota, and even of portions of extreme northern Wyoming,—that is, of all the grazing lands lying in the basin of the Upper Missouri,—have united, and formed themselves into the great Montana Stockgrowers' Association. Among the countless benefits they have derived from this course, not the least has been the way in which the various round-ups work in with and supplement one another. At the spring meeting of the association, the entire territory mentioned above, including perhaps a hundred thousand square miles, is mapped out into round-up districts, which generally are changed but slightly from year to year, and the times and places for the round-ups to begin refixed so that those of adjacent districts may be run with a view to the best interests of all. Thus the stockmen along the Yellowstone have one round-up; we along the Little Missouri have another; and the country lying between, through which the Big Beaver flows, is almost equally important to both. Accordingly, one spring, the Little Missouri round-up, beginning May 25, and working down-stream, was timed so as to reach the mouth of the Big Beaver about June 1, the Yellowstone round-up beginning at that date and place. Both then worked up the Beaver together to its head, when the Yellowstone men turned to the west and we bent back to our own river; thus the bulk of the strayed cattle of each were brought back to their respective ranges. Our own round-up district covers the Big and Little Beaver creeks, which rise near each other, but empty into the Little Missouri nearly a hundred and fifty miles apart, and so much of the latter river as lies between their mouths.

The captain or foreman of the round-up, upon whom very much of its efficiency and success depends, is chosen beforehand. He is, of course, an expert cowman, thoroughly acquainted with the country; and he must also be able to command and to keep control of the wild rough-riders he has under him—a feat needing both tact and firmness.

At the appointed day all meet at the place from which the round-up is to start. Each ranch, of course, has most work to be done in its own round-up district, but it is also necessary to have representatives in all those surrounding it. A large outfit may employ a dozen cowboys, or over, in the home district, and yet have nearly as many more representing its interest in the various ones adjoining. Smaller outfits generally club together to run a wagon and send outside representatives, or else go along with their stronger neighbors, they paying part of the expenses. A large outfit, with a herd of twenty thousand cattle or more, can, if necessary, run a round-up entirely by itself, and is able to act independently of outside help; it is therefore at a great advantage compared with those that can take no step effectively without their neighbors' consent and assistance.

If the starting-point is some distance off, it may be necessary to leave home three or four days in advance. Before this we have got everything in readiness; have overhauled the wagons, shod any horse whose forefeet are tender,—as a rule, all our ponies go barefooted,— and left things in order at the ranch. Our outfit may be taken as a sample of every one else's. We have a stout four-horse wagon to carry the bedding and the food; in its rear a mess-chest is rigged to hold the knives, forks, cans, etc. All our four team-horses are strong, willing animals, though of no great size, being originally just "broncos," or unbroken native horses, like the others. The teamster is also cook: a man who is a really first-hand at both driving and cooking—and our present teamster is both—can always command his price. Besides our own men, some cowboys from neighboring ranches and two or three representatives from other round-up districts are always along, and we generally have at least a dozen "riders," as they are termed,—that is, cowboys, or "cowpunchers," who do the actual cattle-work,—with the wagon. Each of these has a string of eight or ten ponies; and to take charge of the saddle-band, thus consisting of a hundred odd head, there are two herders, always known as "horse-wranglers"—one for the day and one for the night. Occasionally there will be two wagons, one to carry the bedding and one the food, known, respectively, as the bed and the mess wagon; but this is not usual.

While traveling to the meeting point the pace is always slow, as it is an object to bring the horses on the ground as fresh as possible. Accordingly we keep at a walk almost all day, and the riders, having nothing else to do, assist the wranglers in driving the saddle-band, three or four going in front, and others on the side, so that the horses shall keep on a walk. There is always some trouble with the animals at the starting out, as they are very fresh and are restive under the saddle. The herd is likely to stampede, and any beast that is frisky or vicious is sure to show its worst side. To do really effective cowwork a pony should be well broken; but many even of the old ones have vicious traits, and almost every man will have in his string one or two young horses, or broncos, hardly broken at all. Thanks to the rough methods of breaking in vogue on the plains many even of the so called broken animals retain always certain bad habits, the most common being that of bucking. Of the sixty odd horses on my ranch all but half a dozen were broken by ourselves; and though my men are all good riders, yet a good rider is not necessarily a good horse-breaker, and indeed it was an absolute impossibility properly to break so many animals in the short time at our command—for we had to use them almost immediately after they were bought. In consequence, very many of my horses have to this day traits not likely to set a timid or a clumsy rider at his ease. One or two run away and cannot be held by even the strongest bit; others can hardly be bridled or saddled until they have been thrown; two or three have a tendency to fall over backward; and half of them buck more or less, some so hard that only an expert can sit them; several I never ride myself, save from dire necessity.

In riding these wild, vicious horses, and in careering over such very bad ground, especially at night, accidents are always occurring. A man who is merely an ordinary rider is certain to have a pretty hard time. On my first round-up I had a string of nine horses, four of them broncos, only broken to the extent of having each been saddled once or twice. One of them it was an impossibility to bridle or to saddle single-handed; it was very difficult to get on or off him, and he was exceedingly nervous if a man moved his hands or feet; but he had no bad tricks. The second soon became perfectly quiet. The third turned out to be one of the worst buckers on the ranch: once, when he bucked me off, I managed to fall on a stone and broke a rib. The fourth had a still worse habit, for he would balk and then throw himself over backward: once, when I was not quick enough, he caught me and broke something in the point of my shoulder, so that it was some weeks before I could raise the arm freely. My hurts were far from serious, and did not interfere with my riding and working as usual through the round-up; but I was heartily glad when it ended, and ever since have religiously done my best to get none but gentle horses in my own string. However, every one gets falls from or with his horse now and then in the cow country; and even my men, good riders though they are, are sometimes injured. One of them once broke his ankle; another a rib; another was on one occasion stunned, remaining unconscious for some hours; and yet another had certain of his horses buck under him so hard and long as finally to hurt his lungs and make him cough blood. Fatal accidents occur annually in almost every district, especially if there is much work to be done among stampeded cattle at night; but on my own ranch none of my men have ever been seriously hurt, though on one occasion a cowboy from another ranch, who was with my wagon, was killed, his horse falling and pitching him heavily on his head.

For bedding, each man has two or three pairs of blankets, and a tarpaulin or small wagon-sheet. Usually, two or three sleep together. Even in June the nights are generally cool and pleasant, and it is chilly in the early mornings; although this is not always so, and when the weather stays hot and mosquitoes are plenty, the hours of darkness, even in midsummer, seem painfully long. In the Bad Lands proper we are not often bothered very seriously by these winged pests; but in the low bottoms of the big Missouri, and beside many of the reedy ponds and great sloughs out on the prairie, they are a perfect scourge. During the very hot nights, when they are especially active, the bed-clothes make a man feel absolutely smothered, and yet his only chance for sleep is to wrap himself tightly up, head and all; and even then some of the pests will usually force their way in. At sunset I have seen the mosquitoes rise up from the land like a dense cloud, to make the hot, stifling night one long torture; the horses would neither lie down nor graze, traveling restlessly to and fro till daybreak, their bodies streaked and bloody, and the insects settling on them so as to make them all one color, a uniform gray; while the men, after a few hours' tossing about in the vain attempt to sleep, rose, built a little fire of damp sage brush, and thus endured the misery as best they could until it was light enough to work.

But if the weather is fine, a man will never sleep better nor more pleasantly than in the open air after a hard day's work on the round-up; nor will an ordinary shower or gust of wind disturb him in the least, for he simply draws the tarpaulin over his head and goes on sleeping. But now and then we have a wind-storm that might better be called a whirlwind and has to be met very differently; and two or three days or nights of rain insure the wetting of the blankets, and therefore shivering discomfort on the part of the would-be sleeper. For two or three hours all goes well; and it is rather soothing to listen to the steady patter of the great raindrops on the canvas. But then it will be found that a corner has been left open through which the water can get in, or else the tarpaulin will begin to leak somewhere; or perhaps the water will have collected in a hollow underneath and have begun to soak through. Soon a little stream trickles in, and every effort to remedy matters merely results in a change for the worse. To move out of the way insures getting wet in a fresh spot; and the best course is to lie still and accept the evils that have come with what fortitude one can. Even thus, the first night a man can sleep pretty well; but if the rain continues, the second night, when the blankets are already damp, and when the water comes through more easily, is apt to be most unpleasant.

Of course, a man can take little spare clothing on a round-up; at the very outside two or three clean handkerchiefs, a pair of socks, a change of underclothes, and the most primitive kind of washing-apparatus, all wrapped up in a stout jacket which is to be worn when night-herding. The inevitable "slicker," or oil-skin coat, which gives complete protection from the wet, is always carried behind the saddle.

At the meeting-place there is usually a delay of a day or two to let every one come in; and the plain on which the encampment is made becomes a scene of great bustle and turmoil. The heavy four-horse wagons jolt in from different quarters, the horse-wranglers rushing madly to and fro in the endeavor to keep the different saddle-bands from mingling, while the "riders," or cowboys, with each wagon jog along in a body. The representatives from outside districts ride in singly or by twos and threes, every man driving before him his own horses, one of them loaded with his bedding. Each wagon wheels out of the way into some camping-place not too near the others, the bedding is tossed out on the ground, and then every one is left to do what he wishes, while the different wagon bosses, or foremen, seek out the captain of the round-up to learn what his plans are.

There is a good deal of rough but effective discipline and method in the way in which a round-up is carried on. The captain of the whole has as lieutenants the various wagon foremen, and in making demands for men to do some special service he will usually merely designate some foreman to take charge of the work and let him parcel it out among his men to suit himself. The captain of the round-up or the foreman of a wagon may himself be a ranchman; if such is not the case, and the ranchman nevertheless comes along, he works and fares precisely as do the other cowboys.

While the head men are gathered in a little knot, planning out the work, the others are dispersed over the plain in every direction, racing, breaking rough horses, or simply larking with one another. If a man has an especially bad horse, he usually takes such an opportunity, when he has plenty of time, to ride him; and while saddling he is surrounded by a crowd of most unsympathetic associates who greet with uproarious mirth any misadventure. A man on a bucking horse is always considered fair game, every squeal and jump of the bronco being hailed with cheers of delighted irony for the rider and shouts to "stay with him." The antics of a vicious bronco show infinite variety of detail, but are all modeled on one general plan. When the rope settles round his neck the fight begins, and it is only after much plunging and snorting that a twist is taken over his nose, or else a hackamore—a species of severe halter, usually made of plaited hair—slipped on his head. While being bridled he strikes viciously with his fore feet, and perhaps has to be blindfolded or thrown down; and to get the saddle on him is quite as difficult. When saddled, he may get rid of his exuberant spirits by bucking under the saddle, or may reserve all his energies for the rider. In the last case, the man keeping tight hold with his left hand of the cheek-strap, so as to prevent the horse from getting his head down until he is fairly seated, swings himself quickly into the saddle. Up rises the bronco's back into an arch; his head, the ears laid straight back, goes down between his forefeet, and, squealing savagely, he makes a succession of rapid, stiff-legged, jarring bounds. Sometimes he is a "plunging" bucker, who runs forward all the time while bucking; or he may buck steadily in one place, or "sun-fish,"—that is, bring first one shoulder down almost to the ground and then the other,—or else he may change ends while in the air. A first-class rider will sit throughout it all without moving from the saddle, quirting* his horse all the time, though his hat may be jarred off his head and his revolver out of its sheath. After a few jumps, however, the average man grasps hold of the horn of the saddle—the delighted onlookers meanwhile earnestly advising him not to "go to leather"—and is contented to get through the affair in any shape provided he can escape without being thrown off. An accident is of necessity borne with a broad grin, as any attempt to resent the raillery of the bystanders—which is perfectly good-humored—would be apt to result disastrously. Cowboys are certainly extremely good riders. As a class they have no superiors. Of course, they would at first be at a disadvantage in steeple-chasing or fox-hunting, but their average of horsemanship is without doubt higher than that of the men who take part in these latter amusements. A cowboy would learn to ride across country in a quarter of the time it would take a cross-country rider to learn to handle a vicious bronco or to do good cow-work round and in a herd.

On such a day, when there is no regular work, there will often also be horse-races, as each outfit is pretty sure to have some running pony which it believes can outpace any other. These contests are always short-distance dashes, for but a few hundred yards. Horse-racing is a mania with most plainsmen, white or red. A man with a good racing pony will travel all about with it, often winning large sums, visiting alike cow ranches, frontier towns, and Indian encampments. Sometimes the race is "pony against pony," the victor taking both steeds. In racing the men ride bareback, as there are hardly any light saddles in the cow country. There will be intense excitement and very heavy betting over a race between two well-known horses, together with a good chance of blood being shed in the attendance quarrels.

Quirt is the name of the short flexible riding-whip used throughout cowboy land. The term is a Spanish one.

Indians and whites often race against each other as well as among themselves. I have seen several such contests, and in every case but one the white man happened to win. A race is usually run between two thick rows of spectators, on foot and on horseback, and as the racers pass, these rows close in behind them, every man yelling and shouting with all the strength of his lungs, and all waving their hats and cloaks to encourage the contestants, or firing off their revolvers and saddle guns. The little horses are fairly maddened, as is natural enough, and run as if they were crazy: were the distances longer some would be sure to drop in their tracks.

Besides the horse-races, which are, of course, the main attraction, the men at a round-up will often get up wrestling matches or foot-races. In fact, every one feels that he is off for a holiday; for after the monotony of a long winter, the cowboys look forward eagerly to the round-up, where the work is hard, it is true, but exciting and varied, and treated a good deal as a frolic. There is no eight-hour law in cow-boy land: during round-up time we often count ourselves lucky if we get off with much less than sixteen hours; but the work is done in the saddle, and the men are spurred on all the time by the desire to out do one another in feats of daring and skillful horsemanship. There is very little quarreling or fighting; and though the fun often takes the form of rather rough horse-play, yet the practice of carrying danger-ous weapons makes cowboys show far more rough courtesy to each other and far less rudeness to strangers than is the case among, for instance, Eastern miners, or even lumbermen. When a quarrel may very probably result fatally, a man thinks twice before going into it: warlike people or classes always treat one another with a certain amount of consideration and politeness. The moral tone of a cow-camp, indeed, is rather high: than otherwise. Meanness, cowardice, and dishonesty are not tolerated. There is a high regard for truthful-ness and keeping one's word, intense contempt for any kind of hypocrisy, and a hearty dislike for a man who shirks his work. Many of the men gamble and drink, but many do neither; and the conver-sation is not worse than in most bodies composed wholly of male human beings. A cowboy will not submit tamely to an insult, and is ever ready to avenge his own wrongs; nor has he an overwrought fear of shedding blood. He possesses, in fact, few of the emasculated, milk-and-water moralities admired by the pseudo-philanthropists; but he does possess, to a very high degree, the stern, manly qualities that are invaluable to a nation.

The method of work is simple. The mess-wagons and loose horses, after breaking camp in the morning, move on in a straight line for some few miles, going into camp again before midday; and the day herd, consisting of all the cattle that have been found far off their range, and which are to be brought back there, and of any others that it is necessary to gather, follows on afterwards. Meanwhile the cowboys scatter out and drive in all the cattle from the country round about, going perhaps ten or fifteen miles back from the line of march, and meeting at the place where camp has already been pitched. The wagons always keep some little distance from one another, and the saddle-bands do the same, so that the horses may not get mixed. It is rather picturesque to see the four-horse teams filing down at a trot through a pass among the buttes—the saddle-bands being driven along at a smart pace to one side or behind, the teamsters cracking their whips, and the horse-wranglers calling and shouting as they ride rapidly from side to side behind the horses, urging on the stragglers by dexterous touches with the knotted ends of their long lariats that are left trailing from the saddle. The country driven over is very rough, and it is often necessary to double up teams and put on eight horses to each wagon in going up an unusually steep pitch, or hauling through a deep mud-hole, or over a river crossing where there is quicksand.

The speed and thoroughness with which a country can be worked depends, of course, very largely upon the number of riders. Ours is probably about an average roundup as regards size. The last spring I was out, there were half a dozen wagons along; the saddle-bands numbered about a hundred each; and the morning we started, sixty men in the saddle splashed across the shallow ford of the river that divided the plain where we had camped from the valley of the long winding creek up which we were first to work.

In the morning the cook is preparing breakfast long before the first glimmer of dawn. As soon as it is ready, probably about 3 o'clock, he utters a long-drawn shout, and all the sleepers feel it is time to be up on the instant, for they know there can be no such thing as delay on the round-up, under penalty of being set afoot. Accordingly they bundle out, rubbing their eyes and yawning, draw on their boots and trousers,—if they have taken the latter off,—roll up and cord their bedding, and usually without any attempt at washing crowd over to the little smoldering fire, which is placed in a hole dug in the ground, so that there may be no risk of its spreading. The men are rarely very hungry at breakfast, and it is a meal that has to be eaten in shortest order, so it is perhaps the least important. Each man, as he comes up, grasps a tin cup and plate from the mess-box, pours out his tea or coffee, with sugar, but, of course, no milk, helps himself to one or two of the biscuits that have been baked in a Dutch oven, and perhaps also to a slice of the fat pork swimming in the grease of the frying-pan, ladles himself out some beans, if there are any, and squats down on the ground to eat his breakfast. The meal is not an elaborate one; nevertheless a man will have to hurry if he wishes to eat it before hearing the foreman sing out, "Come, boys, catch your horses"; when he must drop everything and run out to the wagon with his lariat. The night wrangler is now bringing in the saddle-band, which he has been up all night guarding. A rope corral is rigged up by stretching a rope from each wheel of one side of the wagon, making a V-shaped space, into which the saddle-horses are driven. Certain men stand around to keep them inside, while the others catch the horses: many outfits have one man to do all the roping. As soon as each has caught his horse—usually a strong, tough animal, the small, quick ponies being reserved for the work round the herd in the afternoon—the band, now in charge of the day wrangler, is turned loose, and every one saddles up as fast as possible. It still lacks some time of being sunrise, and the air has in it the peculiar chill of the early morning. When all are saddled, many of the horses bucking and dancing about, the riders from the different wagons all assemble at the one where the captain is sitting, already mounted. He waits a very short time—for laggards receive but scant mercy—before announcing the proposed camping-place and parceling out the work among those present. If, as is usually the case, the line of march is along a river or creek, he appoints some man to take a dozen others and drive down (or up) it ahead of the day herd, so that the latter will not have to travel through other cattle; the day herd itself being driven and guarded by a dozen men detached for that purpose. The rest of the riders are divided into two bands, placed under men who know the country, and start out, one on each side, to bring in every head for fifteen miles back. The captain then himself rides down to the new camping-place, so as to be there as soon as any cattle are brought in.

Meanwhile the two bands, a score of riders in each, separate and make their way in opposite directions. The leader of each tries to get such a "scatter" on his men that they will cover completely all the land gone over. This morning work is called circle riding, and is peculiarly hard in the Bad Lands on account of the remarkably broken, rugged nature of the country. The men come in on lines that tend to a common center—as if the sticks of a fan were curved. As the band goes out, the leader from time to time detaches one or two men to ride down through certain sections of the country, making the shorter, or what was called inside, circles, while he keeps on; and finally, retaining as companions the two or three whose horses are toughest, makes the longest or outside circle himself, going clear back to the divide, or whatever the point may be that marks the limit of the round-up work, and then turning and working straight to the meeting-place. Each man, of course, brings in every head of cattle he can see.

These long, swift rides in the glorious spring mornings are not soon to be forgotten. The sweet, fresh air, with a touch of sharpness thus early in the day, and the rapid motion of the fiery little horse combine to make a man's blood thrill and leap with sheer buoyant light-heartedness and eager, exultant pleasure in the boldness and freedom of the life he is leading. As we climb the steep sides of the first range of buttes, wisps of wavering mist still cling in the hollows of the valley; when we come out on the top of the first great plateau, the sun flames up over its edge, and in the level, red beams the galloping horsemen throw long fantastic shadows. Black care rarely sits behind a rider whose pace is fast enough; at any rate, not when he first feels the horse move under him.

Sometimes we trot or pace, and again we lope or gallop; the few who are to take the outside circle must needs ride both hard and fast. Although only grass-fed, the horses are tough and wiry; and, moreover, are each used but once in four days, or thereabouts, so they stand the work well. The course out lies across great grassy plateaus, along knife-like ridge crests, among winding valleys and ravines, and over acres of barren, sun-scorched buttes, that look grimly grotesque and forbidding, while in the Bad Lands the riders unhesitatingly go down and over places where it seems impossible that a horse should even stand. The line of horsemen will quarter down the side of a butte, where every pony has to drop from ledge to ledge like a goat, and will go over the shoulder of a soapstone cliff, when wet and slippery, with a series of plunges and scrambles which if unsuccessful would land horses and riders in the bottom on the cañon-like washout below. In descending a clay butte after a rain, the pony will put all four feet together and slide down to the bottom almost or quite on his haunches. In very wet weather the Bad Lands are absolutely impassable; but if the ground is not slippery, it is a remarkable place that can shake the matter-of-course confidence felt by the rider in the capacity of his steed to go anywhere.

When the men on the outside circle have reached the bound set them,—whether it is a low divide, a group of jagged hills, the edge of the rolling, limitless prairie, or the long, waste reaches of alkali and sage brush,—they turn their horses' heads and begin to work down the branches of the creeks, one or two riding down the bottom, while the others keep off to the right and the left, a little ahead and fairly high up on the side hills, so as to command as much of a view as possible. On the level or rolling prairies the cattle can be seen a long way off, and it is an easy matter to gather and drive them; but in the Bad Lands every little pocket, basin, and coulée has to be searched, every gorge or ravine entered, and the dense patches of brushwood and spindling, wind-beaten trees closely examined. All the cattle are carried on ahead down the creek; and it is curious to watch the different behavior of the different breeds. A cowboy riding off to one side of the creek, and seeing a number of long-horned Texans grazing in the branches of a set of coulées, has merely to ride across the upper ends of these, uttering the drawn-out "ei-koh-h-h," so familiar to the cattlemen, and the long-horns will stop grazing, stare fixedly at him, and then, wheeling, strike off down the coulées at a trot, tails in air, to be carried along by the center riders when they reach the main creek into which the coulées lead. Our own range cattle are not so wild, but nevertheless are easy to drive; while Eastern-raised beasts have little fear of a horseman, and merely stare stupidly at him until he rides directly towards them. Every little bunch of stock is thus collected, and all are driven along together. At the place where some large fork joins the main creek another band may be met, driven by some of the men who have left earlier in the day to take one of the shorter circles; and thus, before coming down to the bottom where the wagons are camped and where the actual "round-up" itself is to take place, this one herd may include a couple of thousand head; or, on the other hand, the longest ride may not result in the finding of a dozen animals. As soon as the riders are in, they disperse to their respective wagons to get dinner and change horses, leaving the cattle to be held by one or two of their number. If only a small number of cattle have been gathered, they will all be run into one herd; if there are many of them, however, the different herds will be held separate.

A plain where a round-up is taking place offers a picturesque sight. I well remember one such. It was on a level bottom in a bend of the river, which here made an almost semicircular sweep. The bottom was in shape a long oval, hemmed in by an unbroken line of steep bluffs so that it looked like an amphitheater. Across the faces of the dazzling white cliffs there were sharp bands of black and red, drawn by the coal seams and the layers of burned clay: the leaves of the trees and the grass had the vivid green of spring-time. The wagons were camped among the cottonwood trees fringing the river, a thin column of smoke rising up from beside each. The horses were grazing round the outskirts, those of each wagon by themselves and kept from going too near the others by their watchful guard. In the greater circular corral, towards one end, the men were already branding calves, while the whole middle of the bottom was covered with lowing herds of cattle and shouting, galloping cowboys. Apparently there was nothing but dust, noise, and confusion; but in reality the work was proceeding all the while with the utmost rapidity and certainty.

As soon as, or even before, the last circle riders have come in and have snatched a few hasty mouthfuls to serve as their midday meal, we begin to work the herd—or herds, if the one herd would be of too unwieldy size. The animals are held in a compact bunch, most of the riders forming a ring outside, while a couple from each ranch successively look the herds through and cut out those marked with their own brand. It is difficult, in such a mass of moving beasts,—for they do not stay still, but keep weaving in and out among each other,—to find all of one's own animals: a man must have natural gifts, as well as great experience, before he becomes a good brand-reader and is able really to "clean up a herd"—that is, be sure he has left nothing of his own in it.

To do good work in cutting out from a herd, not only should the rider be a good horseman, but he should also have a skillful, thoroughly trained horse. A good cutting pony is not common, and is generally too valuable to be used anywhere but in the herd. Such an one enters thoroughly into the spirit of the thing, and finds out immediately the animal his master is after; he will then follow it closely of his own accord through every wheel and double at top speed. When looking through the herd, it is necessary to move slowly; and when any animal is found it is taken to the outskirts at a walk, so as not to alarm the others. Once at the outside, however, the cowboy has to ride like lightning; for as soon as the beast he is after finds itself separated from its companions it endeavors to break back among them, and a young, range-raised steer or heifer runs like a deer. In cuffing out a cow and a calf two men have to work together. As the animals of a brand are cut out they are received and held apart by some rider detailed for the purpose, who is said to be "holding the cut."

All this time the men holding the herd have their hands full, for some animal is continually trying to break out, when the nearest man flies at it at once and after a smart chase brings it back to its fellows. As soon as all the cows, calves, and whatever else is being gathered have been cut out, the rest are driven clear off the ground and turned loose, being headed in the direction contrary to that in which we travel the following day. Then the riders surround the next herd, the men holding cuts move them up near it, and the work is begun anew.

If it is necessary to throw an animal, either to examine a brand or for any other reason, half a dozen men will have their ropes down at once; and then it is spur and quirt in the rivalry to see which can outdo the other until the beast is roped and thrown. A first-class hand will, unaided, rope, throw, and tie down a cow or steer in wonderfully short time; one of the favorite tests of competitive skill among the cowboys is the speed with which this feat can be accomplished. Usually, however, one man ropes the animal by the head and another at the same time gets the loop of his lariat over one or both its hind legs, when it is twisted over and stretched out in a second. In following an animal on horseback the man keeps steadily swinging the rope round his head, by a dexterous motion of the wrist only, until he gets a chance to throw it; when on foot, especially if catching horses in a corral, the loop is allowed to drag loosely on the ground. A good roper will hurl out the coil with marvelous accuracy and force; it fairly whistles through the air, and settles round the object with almost infallible certainty. Mexicans make the best ropers; but some Texans are very little behind them. A good horse takes as much interest in the work as does his rider, and the instant the noose settles over the victim wheels and braces himself to meet the shock, standing with his legs firmly planted, the steer or cow being thrown with a jerk. An unskillful rider and untrained horse will often themselves be thrown when the strain comes.

Sometimes an animal—usually a cow or steer, but, strangely enough, very rarely a bull—will get fighting mad, and turn on the men. If on the drive, such a beast usually is simply dropped out; but if they have time, nothing delights the cowboys more than an encounter of this sort, and the charging brute is roped and tied down in short order. Often such an one will make a very vicious fight, and is most dangerous. Once a fighting cow kept several of us busy for nearly an hour; she gored two ponies, one of them, which was luckily, hurt but slightly, being my own pet cutting horse. If a steer is hauled out of a mud-hole, its first act is usually to charge the rescuer.

As soon as all the brands of cattle are worked, and the animals that are to be driven along have been put in the day herd, attention is turned to the cows and calves, which are already gathered in different bands, consisting each of all the cows of a certain brand and all the calves that are following them. If there is a corral, each band is in turn driven into it; if there is none, a ring of riders does duty in its place. A fire is built, the irons heated, and a dozen men dismount to, as it is called, "wrestle" the calves. The best two ropers go in on their horses to catch the latter; one man keeps tally, a couple put on the brands, and the others seize, throw, and hold the little unfortunates. A first-class roper invariably catches the calf by both hind feet, and then, having taken a twist with his lariat round the horn of the saddle, drags the bawling little creature, extended at full-length, up to the fire, where it is held before it can make a struggle. A less skillful roper catches round the neck, and then, if the calf is a large one, the one who seizes it has his hands full, as the bleating, bucking animal develops astonishing strength, cuts the wildest capers, and resists frantically and with all its power. If there are seventy or eighty calves in a corral, the scene is one of the greatest confusion. The ropers, spurring and checking the fierce little horses, drag the calves up so quickly that a dozen men can hardly hold them; the men with the irons, blackened with soot, run to and fro; the calf-wrestlers, grimy with blood, dust, and sweat, work like beavers; while with the voice of a stentor the tallyman shouts out the number and sex of each calf. The dust rises in clouds, and the shouts, cheers, curses, and laughter of the men unite with the lowing of the cows and the frantic bleating of the roped calves to make a perfect babel. Now and then an old cow turns vicious and puts every one out of the corral. Or a *maverick* bull,—that is, an unbranded bull,—a yearling or a two-years-old, is caught, thrown, and branded; when he is let up there is sure to be a fine scatter. Down goes his head, and he bolts at the nearest man, who makes out of the way at top speed, amidst roars of laughter from all of his companions; while the men holding down calves swear savagely as they dodge charging mavericks, trampling horses, and taut lariats with frantic, plunging little beasts at the farther ends.

Every morning certain riders are detached to drive and to guard the day herd, which is most monotonous work, the men being on from 4 in the morning till 8 in the evening, the only rest coming at dinner-time, when they change horses. When the herd has reached the camping ground there is nothing to do but to loll listlessly over the saddle-bow in the blazing sun watching the cattle feed and sleep, and seeing that they do not spread out too much. Plodding slowly along on the trail through the columns of dust stirred up by the hoofs is not much better. Cattle travel best and fastest strung out in long lines; the swiftest taking the lead in single file, while the weak and the lazy, the young calves and the poor cows, crowd together in the rear. Two men travel along with the leaders, one on each side, to point them in the right direction; one or two others keep by the flanks, and the rest are in the rear to act as "drag-drivers" and hurry up the phalanx of reluctant weaklings. If the foremost of the string travels too fast, one rider will go along on the trail a few rods ahead, and thus keep them back so that those in the rear will not be left behind.

Generally all this is very tame and irksome; but by fits and starts there will be little flurries of excitement. Two or three of the circle riders may unexpectedly come over a butte near by with a bunch of cattle, which at once start for the day herd, and then there will be a few minutes' furious riding hither and thither to keep them out. Or the cattle may begin to run, and then get "milling"—that is, all crowd together into a mass like a ball, wherein they move round and round, trying to keep their heads towards the center, and refusing to leave it. The only way to start them is to force one's horse in among them and cut out some of their number, which then begin to travel off by themselves, when the others will probably follow. But in spite of occasional incidents of this kind, day-herding has a dreary sameness about it that makes the men dislike and seek to avoid it.

From 8 in the evening till 4 in the morning the day herd becomes a night herd. Each wagon in succession undertakes to guard it for a night, dividing the time into watches of two hours apiece, a couple of riders taking each watch. This is generally chilly and tedious; but at times it is accompanied by intense excitement and danger, when the cattle become stampeded, whether by storm or otherwise. The first and the last watches are those chosen by preference; the others are disagreeable, the men having to turn out cold and sleepy, in the pitchy darkness, the two hours of chilly wakefulness completely breaking the night's rest. The first guards have to bed the cattle down, though the day-herders often do this themselves; it simply consists in hemming them into as small a space as possible, and then riding round them until they lie down and fall asleep. Often, especially at first, this takes some time—the beasts will keep rising and lying down again. When at last most become quiet, some perverse brute of a steer will deliberately hook them all up; they keep moving in and out among one another, and long strings of animals suddenly start out from the herd at a stretching walk, and are turned back by the nearest cowboy only to break forth at a new spot. When finally they have lain down and are chewing their cud or slumbering, the two night guards begin riding round them in opposite ways, often, on very dark nights, calling or singing to them, as the sound of the human voice on such occasions seems to have a tendency to quiet them. In inky black weather, especially when rainy, it is both difficult and unpleasant work; the main trust must be placed in the horse, which, if old at the business, will of its own accord keep pacing steadily round the herd, and head off any animals that, unseen by the rider's eyes in the darkness, are trying to break out. Usually the watch passes off without incident, but on rare occasions the cattle become restless and prone to stampede. Anything may then start them—the plunge of a horse, the sudden approach of a coyote, or the arrival of some outside steers or cows that have smelt them and come up. Every animal in the herd will be on its feet in an instant, as if by an electric shock, and off with a rush, horns and tail up. Then, no matter how rough the ground nor how pitchy black the night, the cowboys must ride for all there is in them and spare neither their own nor their horses' necks. Perhaps their charges break away and are lost altogether; perhaps, by desperate galloping, they may head them off, get them running in a circle, and finally stop them. Once stopped, they may break again, and possibly divide up, one cowboy, perhaps, following each band. I have known six such stops and renewed stampedes to take place in one night, the cowboy staying with his ever-diminishing herd of steers until daybreak, when he managed to get them under control again, and, by careful humoring of his jaded, staggering horse, finally brought those there were left back to the camp, several miles distant. The riding in these night stampedes is wild and dangerous to a degree, especially if the man gets caught in the rush of the beasts. It also frequently necessitates an immense amount of work in collecting the scattered animals. On one such occasion a small party of us were thirty-six hours in the saddle, dismounting only to change horses or to eat. We were almost worn out at the end of the time; but it must be kept in mind that for a long spell of such work a stock-saddle is far less tiring then the ordinary Eastern or English one, and in every way superior to it.

By very hard riding, such a stampede may sometimes be prevented. Once we were bringing a thousand head of young cattle down to my lower ranch, and as the river was high were obliged to take the inland trail. The third night we were forced to make a dry camp, the cattle having had no water since the morning. Nevertheless, we got them bedded down without difficulty, and one of the cowboys and myself stood first guard. But very soon after nightfall, when the darkness had become complete, the thirsty brutes of one accord got on their feet and tried to break out. The only salvation was to keep them close together, as, if they once got scattered, we knew they could never be gathered; so I kept on one side, and the cowboy on the other, and never in my life did I ride so hard. In the darkness I could but dimly see the shadowy outlines of the herd, as with whip and spurs I ran the pony along its edge, turning back the beasts at one point barely in time to wheel and keep them in at another. The ground was cut up by numerous little gullies, and each of us got several falls, horses and riders turning complete somersaults. We were dripping with sweat, and our ponies quivering and trembling like quaking aspens when, after more than an hour of the most violent exertion, we finally got the herd quieted again.

On another occasion while with the round-up we were spared an excessively unpleasant night only because there happened to be two or three great corrals not more than a mile or so away. All day long it had been raining heavily, and we were well drenched; but towards evening it lulled a little, and the day herd, a very large one, of some two thousand head, was gathered on an open bottom. We had turned the horses loose, and in our oilskin slickers cowered, soaked and comfortless, under the lee of the wagon, to take a meal of damp bread and lukewarm tea, the sizzling embers of the fire having about given up the ghost after a fruitless struggle with the steady downpour. Suddenly the wind began to come in quick, sharp gusts, and soon a regular blizzard was blowing, driving the rain in stinging level sheets before it. Just as we were preparing to turn into bed, with the certainty of a night of more or less chilly misery ahead of us, one of my men, an iron-faced personage, whom no one would ever have dreamed had a weakness for poetry, looked towards the plain where the cattle were, and remarked, "I guess there's 'racing and chasing on Cannobie Lea' now, sure." Following his gaze, I saw that the cattle had begun to drift before the storm, the night guards being evidently unable to cope with them, while at the other wagons riders were saddling in hot haste and spurring off to their help through the blinding rain. Some of us at once ran out to our own saddle-band. All of the ponies were standing huddled together, with their heads down and their tails to the wind. They were wild and restive enough usually; but the storm had cowed them, and we were able to catch them without either rope or halter. We made quick work of saddling; and the second each man was ready, away he loped through the dusk, splashing and slipping in the pools of water that studded the muddy plain. Most of the riders were already out when we arrived. The cattle were gathered in a compact, wedge-shaped, or rather fan-shaped mass, with their tails to the wind—that is, towards the thin end of the wedge or fan. In front of this fan-shaped mass of frightened, maddened beats was a long line of cowboys, each muffled in his slicker and with his broad hat pulled down over his eyes, to shield him from the pelting rain. When the cattle were quiet for a moment every horseman at once turned round with his back to the wind, and the whole line stood as motionless as so many sentries. Then, if the cattle began to spread out and overlap at the ends, or made a rush and broke through at one part of the lines, there would be a change into wild activity. The men, shouting and swaying in their saddles, darted to and fro with reckless speed, utterly heedless of danger—now racing to the threatened point, now checking and wheeling their horses so sharply as to bring them square on their haunches, or even throw them flat down, while the hoofs plowed long furrows in the slippery soil, until, after some minutes of this mad galloping hither and thither, the herd, having drifted a hundred yards or so, would be once more brought up standing. We always had to let them drift a little to prevent their spreading out too much. The din of the thunder was terrific, peal following peal until they mingled in one continuous, rumbling roar; and at every thunder-clap louder than its fellows the cattle would try to break away. Darkness had set in, but each flash of lightning showed us a dense array of tossing horns and staring eyes. It grew always harder to hold in the herd; but the drift took us along to the corrals already spoken of, whose entrances were luckily to windward. As soon as we reached the first we cut off part of the herd, and turned it within; and after again doing this with the second, we were able to put all the remaining animals into the third. The instant the cattle were housed five-sixth of the horsemen started back at full speed for the wagons; the rest of us barely waited to put up the bars and make the corrals secure before galloping after them. We had to ride right in the teeth of the driving storm; and once at the wagons we made small delay in crawling under our blankets, damp though the latter were, for we were ourselves far too wet, stiff, and cold not to hail with grateful welcome any kind of shelter from the wind and the rain.

All animals were benumbed by the violence of this gale of cold rain: a prairie chicken rose from under my horse's feet so heavily that, thoughtlessly striking at it, I cut it down with my whip; while when a jack rabbit got up ahead of us, it was barely able to limp clumsily out of our way.

But though there is much work and hardship, rough fare, monotony, and exposure connected with the round-up, yet there are few men who do not look forward to it and back to it with pleasure. The only fault to be found is that the hours of work are so long that one does not usually have enough time to sleep. The food, if rough, is good; beef, bread, pork, beans, coffee or tea, always canned tomatoes, and often rice, canned corn, or sauce made from dried apples. The men are good-humored, bold and thoroughly interested in their business, continually vying with one another in the effort to see which can do the work best. It is superbly health-giving, and is full of excitement and adventure, calling for the exhibition of pluck, self-reliance, hardihood, and dashing horsemanship; and of all forms of physical labor the earliest and pleasantest is to sit in the saddle.

The Drive

– by –
Stewart Edward White

A CRY AWAKENED ME. It was still deep night. The moon sailed overhead, the stars shone unwavering like candles, and a chill breeze wandered in from the open spaces of the desert. I raised myself on my elbow, throwing aside the blankets and the canvas tarpaulin. Forty other indistinct, formless bundles on the ground all about me were sluggishly astir. Four figures passed and repassed between me and a red fire. I knew them for the two cooks and the horse wranglers. One of the latter was grumbling.

"Didn't git in till moon-up last night," he growled. "Might as well trade my bed for a lantern and be done with it."

Even as I stretched my arms and shivered a little, the two wranglers threw down their tin plates with a clatter, mounted horses and rode away in the direction of the thousand acres or so known as the pasture.

I pulled on my clothes hastily, buckled in my buckskin shirt, and dove for the fire. A dozen others were before me. It was bitterly cold. In the east the sky had paled the least bit in the world, but the moon and stars shone on bravely and undiminished. A band of coyotes was shrieking desperate blasphemies against the new day, and the stray herd, awakening, was beginning to bawl and bellow.

Two crater-like dutch ovens, filled with pieces of fried beef, stood near the fire; two galvanised water buckets, brimming with soda biscuits, flanked them; two tremendous coffee pots stood guard at either end. We picked us each a tin cup and a tin plate from the box at the rear of the chuck wagon; helped ourselves from a dutch oven, a pail, and a coffee pot, and squatted on our heels as close to the fire as possible. Men who came too late borrowed the shovel, scooped up some coals, and so started little fires of their own about which new groups formed.

While we ate, the eastern sky lightened. The mountains under the dawn looked like silhouettes cut from slate-coloured paper; those in the west showed faintly luminous. Objects about us became dimly visible. We could make out the windmill, and the adobe of the ranch houses, and the corrals. The cowboys arose one by one, dropped their plates into the dishpan, and began to hunt out their ropes. Everything was obscure and mysterious in the faint grey light. I watched Windy Bill near his tarpaulin. He stooped to throw over the canvas. When he bent, it was before daylight; when he straightened his back, daylight had come. It was just like that, as though someone had reached out his hand to turn on the illumination of the world.

The eastern mountains were fragile, the plain was ethereal, like a sea of liquid gases. From the pasture we heard the shoutings of the wranglers, and made out a cloud of dust. In a moment the first of the remuda came into view, trotting forward with the free grace of the unburdened horse. Others followed in procession: those near sharp and well defined, those in the background more or less obscured by the dust, now appearing plainly, now fading like ghosts. The leader turned unhesitatingly into the corral. After him poured the stream of the remuda—two hundred and fifty saddle horses—with an unceasing thunder of hoofs.

Immediately the cook-camp was deserted. The cowboys entered the corral. The horses began to circle around the edge of the enclosure as around the circumference of a circus ring. The men, grouped at the centre, watched keenly, looking for the mounts they had already decided on. In no time each had recognised his choice, and, his loop trailing, was walking toward that part of the revolving circumference where his pony dodged. Some few whirled the loop, but most cast it with a quick flip. It was really marvellous to observe the accuracy with which the noose would fly, past a dozen tossing heads, and over a dozen backs, to settle firmly about the neck of an animal perhaps in the very centre of the group. But again, if the first throw failed, it was interesting to see how the selected pony would dodge, double back, twist, turn, and hide to escape a second cast. And it was equally interesting to observe how his companions would help him. They seemed to realise that they were not wanted, and would push themselves between the cowboy and his intended mount with the utmost boldness. In the thick dust that instantly arose, and with the bewildering thunder of galloping, the flashing change of grouping, the rush of the charging animals, recognition alone would seem almost impossible, yet in an incredibly short time each had his mount, and the others, under convoy of the wranglers, were meekly wending their way out over the plain. There, until time for a change of horses, they would graze in a loose and scattered band, requiring scarcely any supervision. Escape? Bless you, no, that thought was the last in their minds.

In the meantime the saddles and bridles were adjusted. Always in a cowboy's "string" of from six to ten animals the boss assigns him two or three broncos to break in to the cow business. Therefore, each morning we could observe a half dozen or so men gingerly leading wicked looking little animals out to the sand "to take the pitch out of them." One small black, belonging to a cowboy called the Judge, used more than to fulfil expectations of a good time.

"Go to him, Judge!" someone would always remark.

"If he ain't goin' to pitch, I ain't goin' to make him," the Judge would grin, as he swung aboard.

The black would trot off quite calmly and in a most matter of fact way, as though to shame all slanderers of his lamb-like character. Then, as the bystanders would turn away, he would utter a squeal, throw down his head, and go at it. He was a very hard bucker, and made some really spectacular jumps, but the trick on which he based his claims to originality consisted in standing on his hind legs at so perilous an approach to the perpendicular that his rider would conclude he was about to fall backwards, and then suddenly springing forward in a series of stifflegged bucks. The first manoeuvre induced the rider to loosen his seat in order to be ready to jump from under, and the second threw him before he could regain his grip.

"And they say a horse don't think!" exclaimed an admirer.

But as these were broken horses—save the mark! —the show was all over after each had had his little fling. We mounted and rode away, just as the mountain peaks to the west caught the rays of a sun we should not enjoy for a good half hour yet.

I had five horses in my string, and this morning rode "that C S horse Brown Jug." Brown Jug was a powerful and well-built animal, about fourteen two in height, and possessed of a vast enthusiasm for cow-work. As the morning was frosty, he felt good.

At the gate of the water corral we separated into two groups. The smaller, under the direction of Jed Parker, was to drive the mesquite in the wide flats; the rest of us, under the command of Homer, the round-up captain, were to sweep the country even as far as the base of the foothills near Mount Graham. Accordingly we put our horses to the full gallop.

Mile after mile we thundered along at a brisk rate of speed. Sometimes we dodged in and out among the mesquite bushes, alternately separating and coming together again; sometimes we swept over grassy plains apparently of illimitable extent; sometimes we skipped and hopped and buck-jumped through and over little gullies, barrancas, and other sorts of malpais—but always without drawing rein. The men rode easily, with no thought to the way nor care for the footing. The air came back sharp against our faces. The warm blood stirred by the rush flowed more rapidly. We experienced a delightful glow. Of the morning cold only the very tips of our fingers and the ends of our noses retained a remnant. Already the sun was shining low and level across the plains. The shadows of the cañons modelled the hitherto flat surfaces of the mountains.

After a time we came to some low hills helmeted with the outcrop of a rock escarpment. Hitherto they had seemed a termination of Mount Graham, but now, when we rode around them, we discovered them to be separated from the range by a good five miles of sloping plain. Later we looked back and would have sworn them part of the Dos Cabesas system, did we not know them to be at least eight miles' distant from that rocky rampart. It is always that way in Arizona. Spaces develop of whose existence you had not the slightest intimation. Hidden in apparently plane surfaces are valleys and prairies. At one sweep of the eye you embrace the entire area of an eastern State; but nevertheless the reality as you explore it foot by foot proves to be infinitely more than the vision has promised.

Beyond the hill we stopped. Here our party divided again, half to the right and half to the left. We had ridden, up to this time, directly away from camp, now we rode a circumference of which headquarters was the centre. The country was pleasantly rolling and covered with grass. Here and there were clumps of soapweed. Far in a remote distance lay a slender dark line across the plain. This we knew to be mesquite; and once entered, we knew it, too, would seem to spread out vastly. And then this grassy slope, on which we now rode, would show merely as an insignificant streak of yellow. It is also like that in Arizona. I have ridden in succession through grass land, brush land, flower land, desert. Each in turn seemed entirely to fill the space of the plains between the mountains.

From time to time Homer halted us and detached a man. The business of the latter was then to ride directly back to camp, driving all cattle before him. Each was in eight of his right- and left-hand neighbour. Thus was constructed a drag-net whose meshes contracted as home was neared.

I was detached, when of our party only the Cattleman and Homer remained. They would take the outside. This was the post of honour, and required the hardest riding, for as soon as the cattle should realise the fact of their pursuit, they would attempt to "break" past the end and up the valley. Brown Jug and I congratulated ourselves on an exciting morning in prospect.

Now, wild cattle know perfectly well what a drive means, and they do not intend to get into a round-up if they can help it. Were it not for the two facts, that they are afraid of a mounted man, and cannot run quite so fast as a horse, I do not know how the cattle business would be conducted. As soon as a band of them caught sight of any one of us, they curled their tails and away they went at a long, easy lope that a domestic cow would stare at in wonder. This was all very well; in fact we yelled and shrieked and otherwise uttered cow-calls to keep them going, to "get the cattle started," as they say. But pretty soon a little band of the many scurrying away before our thin line, began to bear farther and farther to the east. When in their judgment they should have gained an opening, they would turn directly back and make a dash for liberty. Accordingly the nearest cowboy, clapped spurs to his horse and pursued them.

It was a pretty race. The cattle ran easily enough, with long, springy jumps that carried them over the ground faster than appearances would lead one to believe. The cow-pony, his nose stretched out, his ears slanted, his eyes snapping with joy of the chase, flew fairly "belly to earth." The rider sat slightly forward, with the cowboy's loose seat. A whirl of dust, strangely insignificant against the immensity of a desert morning, rose from the flying group. Now they disappeared in a ravine only to scramble out again the next instant, pace undiminished. The rider merely rose slightly and threw up his elbows to relieve the jar of the rough gully. At first the cattle seemed to hold their own, but soon the horse began to gain. In a short time he had come abreast of the leading animal. The latter stopped short with a snort, dodged back, and set out at right angles to his former course. From a dead run the pony came to a stand in two fierce plunges, doubled like a shot, and was off on the other tack. An unaccustomed rider would here have lost his seat. The second dash was short. With a final shake of the head, the steers turned to the proper course in the direction of the ranch. The pony dropped unconcernedly to the shuffling jog of habitual progression.

Far away stretched the arc of our cordon. The most distant rider was a speck, and the cattle ahead of him were like maggots endowed with a smooth, swift onward motion. As yet the herd had not taken form; it was still too widely scattered. Its units, in the shape of small bunches, momently grew in numbers. The distant plains were crawling and alive with minute creatures making toward a common tiny centre.

Immediately in our front the cattle at first behaved very well. Then far down the long gentle slope I saw a break for the upper valley. The manikin that represented Homer at once became even smaller as it departed in pursuit. The Cattleman moved down to cover Homer's territory until he should return, and I in turn edged farther to the right. Then another break from another bunch. The Cattleman rode at top speed to head it. Before long he disappeared in the distant mesquite. I found myself in sole charge of a front three miles long.

The nearest cattle were some distance ahead, and trotting along at a good gait. As they had not yet discovered the chance left open by unforeseen circumstance, I descended and took in on my cinch while yet there was time. Even as I mounted, an impatient movement on the part of experienced Brown Jug told me that the cattle had seen their opportunity.

I gathered the reins and spoke to the horse. He needed no further direction, but set off at a wide angle, nicely calculated, to intercept the truants. Brown Jug was a powerful beast. The spring of his leap was as whalebone. The yellow earth began to stream past like water. Always the pace increased with a growing thunder of hoofs. It seemed that nothing could turn us from the straight line, nothing check the headlong momentum of our rush. My eyes filled with tears from the wind of our going. Saddle strings streamed behind. Brown Jug's mane whipped my bridle hand. Dimly I was conscious of soapweed, saca-tone, mesquite, as we passed them. They were abreast and gone before I could think of them or how they were to be dodged. Two antelope bounded away to the left; birds rose hastily from the grass-es. A sudden *chirk, chirk, chirk,* rose all about me. We were in the very centre of a prairie-dog town, but before I could formulate in my mind the probabilities of holes and broken legs, the *chirk, chirk, chirk*ing had fallen astern. Brown Jug had skipped and dodged suc-cessfully.

We were approaching the cattle. They ran stubbornly and well, evidently unwilling to be turned until the latest possible moment. A great rage at their obstinacy took possession of us both. A broad shal-low wash crossed our way, but we plunged through its rocks and boulders recklessly, angered at even the slight delay they necessitated. The hard land on the other side we greeted with joy. Brown Jug extended himself with a snort.

Suddenly a jar seemed to shake my very head loose. I found myself staring over the horse's head directly down into a deep and precipitous gully, the edge of which was so cunningly concealed by the grasses as to have remained invisible to my blurred vision. Brown Jug, however, had caught sight of it at the last instant, and had executed one of the wonderful stops possible only to a cow-pony.

But already the cattle had discovered a passage above, and were scrambling down and across. Brown Jug and I, at more sober pace, slid off the almost perpendicular bank, and out the other side.

A moment later we had headed them. They whirled, and without the necessity of any suggestion on my part Brown Jug turned after them, and so quickly that my stirrup actually brushed the ground. After that we were masters. We chased the cattle far enough to start them well in the proper direction, and then pulled down to a walk in order to get a breath of air.

But now we noticed another band, back on the ground over which we had just come, doubling through in the direction of Mount Graham. A hard run set them to rights. We turned. More had poured out from the hills. Bands were crossing everywhere, ahead and behind. Brown Jug and I set to work.

Being an indivisible unit, we could chase only one bunch at a time; and, while we were after one, a half dozen others would be taking advantage of our preoccupation. We could not hold our own. Each run after an escaping bunch had to be on a longer diagonal. Gradually we were forced back, and back, and back; but still we managed to hold the line unbroken. Never shall I forget the dash and clatter of that morning. Neither Brown Jug nor I thought for a moment of sparing horseflesh, nor of picking a route. We made the shortest line, and paid little attention to anything that stood in the way. A very fever of resistance possessed us. It was like beating against a head wind, or fighting fire, or combating in any other way any of the great forces of nature. We were quite alone. The Cattleman and Homer had vanished. To our left the men were fully occupied in marshalling the compact brown herds that had gradually massed—for these antagonists of mine were merely the outlying remnants.

I suppose Brown Jug must have run nearly twenty miles with only one check. Then we chased a cow some distance and into the dry bed of a stream, where she whirled on us savagely. By luck her horn hit only the leather of my saddle skirts, so we left her; for when a cow has sense enough to "get on the peck," there is no driving her farther. We gained nothing, and had to give ground, but we succeeded in holding a semblance of order, so that the cattle did not break and scatter far and wide. The sun had by now well risen, and was beginning to shine hot. Brown Jug still ran gamely and displayed as much interest as ever, but he was evidently tiring. We were both glad to see Homer's grey showing in the fringe of mesquite.

Together we soon succeeded in throwing the cows into the main herd. And, strangely enough, as soon as they had joined a compact band of their fellows, their wildness left them and, convoyed by outsiders, they set themselves to plodding energetically toward the home ranch.

As my horse was somewhat winded, I joined the "drag" at the rear. Here by course of natural sifting soon accumulated all the lazy, gentle, and sickly cows, and the small calves. The difficulty now was to prevent them from lagging and dropping out. To that end we indulged in a great variety of the picturesque cow-calls peculiar to the cowboy. One found an old tin can which by the aid of a few pebbles he converted into a very effective rattle.

The dust rose in clouds and eddied in the sun. We slouched easily in our saddles. The cowboys compared notes as to the brands they had seen. Our ponies shuffled along, resting, but always ready for a dash in chase of an occasional bull calf or yearling with independent ideas of its own.

Thus we passed over the country, down the long gentle slope to the "sink" of the valley, whence another long gentle slope ran to the base of the other ranges. At greater or lesser distances we caught the dust, and made out dimly the masses of the other herds collected by our companions, and by the party under Jed Parker. They went forward toward the common centre, with a slow ruminative movement, and the dust they raised went with them.

Little by little they grew plainer to us, and the home ranch, hitherto merely a brown shimmer in the distance, began to take on definition as the group of buildings, windmills, and corrals we knew. Miniature horsemen could be seen galloping forward to the open white plain where the herd would be held. Then the mesquite enveloped us; and we knew little more, save the anxiety lest we overlook laggards in the brush, until we came out on the edge of that same white plain.

Here were more cattle, thousands of them, and billows of dust, and a great bellowing, and dim, mounted figures riding and shouting ahead of the herd. Soon they succeeded in turning the leaders back. These threw into confusion those that followed. In a few moments the cattle had stopped. A cordon of horsemen sat at equal distances holding them in.

"Pretty good haul," said the man next to me; a good five thousand head."

It was somewhere near noon by the time we had bunched and held the herd of some four or five thousand head in the smooth, wide flat, free from bushes and dog holes. Each sat at ease on his horse facing the cattle, watching lazily the clouds of dust and the shifting beasts, but ready at any instant to turn back the restless or independent individuals that might break for liberty.

Out of the haze came Homer, the round-up captain, on an easy lope. As he passed successively the sentries he delivered to each a low command, but without slacking pace. Some of those spoken to wheeled their horses and rode away. The others settled themselves in their saddles and began to roll cigarettes.

"Change horses; get something to eat," said he to me; so I swung after the file trailing at a canter over the low swells beyond the plain.

The remuda had been driven by its leaders to a corner of the pasture's wire fence and there held. As each man arrived he dismounted, threw off his saddle, and turned his animal loose. Then he flipped a loop in his rope and disappeared in the eddying herd. The discarded horse, with many grunts, indulged in a satisfying roll, shook himself vigorously, and walked slowly away. His labour was over for the day, and he knew it, and took not the slightest trouble to get out of the way of the men with the swinging ropes.

Not so the fresh horses, however. They had no intention of being caught, if they could help it, but dodged and twisted, hid and doubled behind the moving screen of their friends. The latter, seeming as usual to know they were not wanted, made no effort to avoid the men, which probably accounted in great measure for the fact that the herd as a body remained compact, in spite of the cowboys threading it, and in spite of the lack of an enclosure.

Our horses caught, we saddled as hastily as possible; and then at the top speed of our fresh and eager ponies we swept down on the chuck wagon. There we fell off our saddles and descended on the meat and bread like ravenous locusts on a cornfield. The ponies stood where we left them, "tied to the ground" in the cattle-country fashion.

As soon as a man had stoked up for the afternoon he rode away. Some finished before others, so across the plain formed an endless procession of men returning to the herd, and of those whom they replaced coming for their turn at the grub.

We found the herd quiet. Some were even lying down, chewing their cuds as peacefully as any barnyard cows. Most, however, stood ruminative, or walked slowly to and fro in the confines allotted by the horsemen, so that the herd looked from a distance like a brown carpet whose pattern was constantly changing—a dusty brown carpet in the process of being beaten. I relieved one of the watchers, and settled myself for a wait.

At this close inspection the different sorts of cattle showed more distinctly their characteristics. The cows and calves generally rested peacefully enough, the calf often lying down while the mother stood guard over it. Steers, however, were more restless. They walked ceaselessly, threading their way in and out among the standing cattle, pausing in brutish amazement at the edge of the herd, and turning back immediately to endless journeyings. The bulls, excited by so much company forced on their accustomed solitary habit, roared defiance at each other until the air fairly trembled. Occasionally two would clash foreheads. Then the powerful animals would push and wrestle, trying for a chance to gore. The decision of supremacy was a question of but a few minutes, and a bloody topknot the worst damage. The defeated one side-stepped hastily and clumsily out of reach, and then walked away.

Most of the time all we had to do was to sit our horses and watch these things, to enjoy, the warm bath of the Arizona sun, and to converse with our next neighbours. Once in a while some enterprising cow, observing the opening between the men, would start to walk out. Others would fall in behind her until the movement would become general. Then one of us would swing his leg off the pommel and jog his pony over to head them off. They would return peacefully enough.

But one black muley cow, with a calf as black and muley as herself, was more persistent. Time after time, with infinite patience, she tried it again the moment my back was turned. I tried driving her far into the herd. No use; she always returned. Quirtings and stones had no effect on her mild and steady persistence.

"She's a San Simon cow," drawled my neighbour. "Everybody knows her. She's at every round-up, just naturally raisin' hell."

When the last man had returned from chuck, Homer made the dispositions for the cut. There were present probably thirty men from the home ranches round about, and twenty representing owners at a distance, here to pick up the strays inevitable to the season's drift. The round-up captain appointed two men to hold the cow-and-calf cut, and two more to hold the steer cut. Several of us rode into the herd, while the remainder retained their positions as sentinels to hold the main body of cattle in shape.

Little G and I rode slowly among the cattle looking everywhere. The animals moved sluggishly aside to give us passage, and closed in as sluggishly behind us, so that we were always closely hemmed in wherever we went. Over the shifting sleek backs, through the eddying clouds of dust, I could make out the figures of my companions moving slowly, apparently aimlessly, here and there.

Our task for the moment was to search out the unbranded J H calves. Since in ranks so closely crowded it would be physically impossible actually to see an animal's branded flank, we depended entirely on the ear-marks.

Did you ever notice how any animal, tame or wild, always points his ears inquiringly in the direction of whatever interests or alarms him? Those ears are for the moment his most prominent feature. So when a brand is quite indistinguishable because, as now, of press of numbers, or, as in winter, from extreme length of hair, the cropped ears tell plainly the tale of ownership. As every animal is so marked when branded, it follows that an uncut pair of ears means that its owner has never felt the iron.

So, now we had to look first of all for calves with uncut ears. After discovering one, we had to ascertain his ownership by examining the ear-marks of his mother, by whose side he was sure, in this alarming multitude, to be clinging faithfully.

Calves were numerous, and J H cows everywhere to be seen, so in somewhat less than ten seconds I had my eye on a mother and son. Immediately I turned Little G in their direction. At the slap of my quirt against the stirrup, all the cows immediately about me shrank suspiciously aside. Little G stepped forward daintily, his nostrils expanding, his ears working back and forth, trying to the best of his ability to understand which animals I had selected. The cow and her calf turned in toward the centre of the herd. A touch of the reins guided the pony. At once he comprehended. From that time on he needed no further directions. Cautiously, patiently, with great skill, he forced the cow through the press toward the edge of the herd. It had to be done very quietly, at a foot pace, so as to alarm neither the objects of pursuit nor those surrounding them. When the cow turned back, Little G somehow happened always in her way. Before she knew it she was at the outer edge of the herd. There she found herself, with a group of three or four companions, facing the open plain. Instinctively she sought shelter. I felt Little G's muscles tighten beneath me. The moment for action had come. Before the cow had a chance to dodge among her companions the pony was upon her like a thunderbolt. She broke in alarm, trying desperately to avoid the rush. There ensued an exciting contest of dodgings, turnings, and doublings. Wherever she turned Little G was before her. Some of his evolutions were marvellous. All I had to do was to sit my saddle, and apply just that final touch of judgment denied even the wisest of the lower animals. Time and again the turn was so quick that the stirrup swept the ground. At last the cow, convinced of the uselessness of further effort to return, broke away on a long lumbering run to the open plain. She was stopped and held by the men detailed, and so formed the nucleus of the new cut-herd. Immediately Little G, his ears working in conscious virtue, jog-trotted back into the herd, ready for another.

After a dozen cows had been sent across to the cut-herd, the work simplified. Once a cow caught sight of this new band, she generally made directly for it, head and tail up. After the first short struggle to force her from the herd, all I had to do was to start her in the proper direction and keep her at it until her decision was fixed. If she was too soon left to her own devices, however, she was likely to return. An old cowman knows to a second just the proper moment to abandon her.

Sometimes in spite of our best efforts a cow succeeded in circling us and plunging into the main herd. The temptation was then strong to plunge in also, and to drive her out by main force; but the temptation had to be resisted. A dash into the thick of it might break the whole band. At once, of his own accord, Little G dropped to his fast, shuffling walk, and again we addressed ourselves to the task of pushing her gently to the edge.

This was all comparatively simple—almost any pony is fast enough for the calf cut—but now Homer gave orders for the steer cut to begin, and steers are rapid and resourceful and full of natural cussedness. Little G and I were relieved by Windy Bill, and betook ourselves to the outside of the herd.

Here we had leisure to observe the effects that up to this moment we had ourselves been producing. The herd, restless by reason of the horsemen threading it, shifted, gave ground, expanded, and contracted, so that its shape and size were always changing in the constant area guarded by the sentinel cowboys. Dust arose from these movements, clouds of it, to eddy and swirl, thicken and dissipate in the currents of air. Now it concealed all but the nearest dimly-out lined animals; again it parted in rifts through which mistily we discerned the riders moving in and out of the fog; again it lifted high and thin, so that we saw in clarity the whole herd and the outriders and the mesas far away. As the afternoon waned, long shafts of sun slanted through this dust. It played on men and beasts magically, expanding them to the dimensions of strange genii, appearing and effacing themselves in the billows of vapour from some enchanted bottle.

We on the outside found our sinecure of hot noontide filched from us by the cooler hours. The cattle, wearied of standing, and perhaps somewhat hungry and thirsty, grew more and more impatient. We rode continually back and forth, turning the slow movement in on itself. Occasionally some particularly enterprising cow would conclude that one or another of the cut-herds would suit her better than this mill of turmoil. She would start confidently out, head and tail up, find herself chased back, get stubborn on the question, and lead her pursuer a long, hard run before she would return to her companions. Once in a while one would even have to be roped and dragged back. For know, before something happens to you, that you can chase a cow safely only until she gets hot and winded. Then she stands her ground and gets emphatically "on the peck."

I remember very well when I first discovered this. It was after I had had considerable cow work, too. I thought of cows as I had always seen them—afraid of a horseman, easy to turn with the pony, and willing to be chased as far as necessary to the work. Nobody told me anything different. One day we were making a drive in an exceedingly broken country. I was bringing in a small bunch I had discovered in a pocket of the hills, but was excessively annoyed by one old cow that insisted on breaking back. In the wisdom of further experience, I now conclude that she probably had a calf in the brush Finally she got away entirely. After starting the bunch well ahead, I went after her.

Well, the cow and I ran nearly side by side for as much as half a mile at top speed. She declined to be headed. Finally she fell down and was so entirely winded that she could not get up.

"Now, old girl, I've got you!" said I, and set myself to urging her to her feet.

The pony, acted somewhat astonished, and suspicious of the job. Therein he knew a lot more than I did. But I insisted, and, like a good pony, he obeyed. I yelled at the cow, and slapped my hat, and used my quirt. When she had quite recovered her wind, she got slowly to her feet—and charged me in a most determined manner.

Now, a bull, or a steer, is not difficult to dodge. He lowers his head, shuts his eyes, and comes in on one straight rush. But a cow looks to see what she is doing; her eyes are open every minute, and it overjoys her to take a side hook at you even when you succeed in eluding her direct charge.

The pony I was riding did his best, but even then could not avoid a sharp prod that would have ripped him up had not my leather bastos intervened. Then we retired to a distance in order to plan further, but we did not succeed in inducing that cow to revise her ideas, so at last we left her. When, in some chagrin, I mentioned to the round-up captain the fact that I had skipped one animal, he merely laughed.

"Why, kid," said he, "you can't do nothin' with a cow that gets on the prod that away 'thout you ropes her; and what could you do with her out there if you *did* rope her?"

So I learned one thing more about cows.

After the steer cut had been finished, the men representing the neighbouring ranges looked through the herd for strays of their brands. These were thrown into the stray-herd, which had been brought up from the bottom lands to receive the new accessions. Work was pushed rapidly, as the afternoon was nearly gone.

In fact, so absorbed were we that until it was almost upon us we did not notice a heavy thunder-shower that arose in the region of the Dragoon Mountains, and swept rapidly across the zenith. Before we knew it the rain had begun. In ten seconds it had increased to a deluge, and in twenty we were all to leeward of the herd striving desperately to stop the drift of the cattle down wind.

We did everything in our power to stop them, but in vain. Slickers waved, quirts slapped against leather, six-shooters flashed, but still the cattle, heads lowered, advanced with a slow and sullen persistence that would not be stemmed. If we held our ground, they divided around us. Step by step we were forced to give way—the thin line of nervously plunging horses sprayed before the dense mass of the cattle.

"No, they won't stampede, "shouted Charley to my question. "There's cows and calves in them. If they was just steers or grown critters, they might."

The sensations of those few moments were very vivid—the blinding beat of the storm in my face, the unbroken front of horned heads bearing down on me, resistless as fate, the long slant of rain with the sun shining in the distance beyond it.

Abruptly the downpour ceased. We shook our hats free of water, and drove the herd back to the cutting grounds again.

But now the surface of the ground was slippery, and the rapid manoeuvring of horses had become a matter precarious in the extreme. Time and again the ponies fairly sat on their haunches and slid when negotiating a sudden stop, while quick turns meant the rapid scramblings that only a cow-horse could accomplish. Nevertheless the work went forward unchecked. The men of the other outfits cut their cattle into the stray-herd. The latter was by now of considerable size, for this was the third week of the round-up.

Finally everyone expressed himself as satisfied. The largely diminished main herd was now started forward by means of shrill cowboy cries and beating of quirts. The cattle were only too eager to go. From my position on a little rise above the stray-herd I could see the leaders breaking into a run, their heads thrown forward as they snuffed their freedom. On the mesa side the sentinel riders quietly withdrew. From the rear and flanks the horsemen closed in. The cattle poured out in a steady stream through the opening thus left on the mesa side. The fringe of cowboys followed, urging them on. Abruptly the cavalcade turned and came loping back. The cattle continued ahead on a trot, gradually spreading abroad over the landscape, losing their integrity as a herd. Some of the slower or hungrier dropped out and began to graze. Certain of the more wary disappeared to right or left.

Now, after the day's work was practically over, we had our first accident. The horse ridden by a young fellow from Dos Cabesas slipped, fell, and rolled quite over his rider. At once the animal lunged to his feet, only to be immediately seized by the nearest rider. But the Dos Cabesas man lay still, his arms and legs spread abroad, his head doubled sideways in a horribly suggestive manner. We hopped off. Two men straightened him out, while two more looked carefully over the indications on the ground.

"All right," sang out one of these, "the horn didn't catch him."

He pointed to the indentation left by the pommel. Indeed five minutes brought the man to his senses. He complained of a very twisted back. Homer sent one of the men in after the bed-wagon, by means of which the sufferer was shortly transported to camp. By the end of the week he was again in the saddle. How men escape from this common accident with injuries so slight has always puzzled me. The horse rolls completely over his rider, and yet it seems to be the rarest thing in the world for the latter to be either killed or permanently injured.

Now each man had the privilege of looking through the J H cuts to see if by chance strays of his own had been included in them. When all had expressed themselves as satisfied, the various bands were started to the corrals.

From a slight eminence where I had paused to enjoy the evening I looked down on the scene. The three herds, separated by generous distances one from the other, crawled leisurely along; the riders, their hats thrust back, lolled in their saddles, shouting conversation to each other, relaxing after the day's work; through the clouds strong shafts of light belittled the living creatures, threw into proportion the vastness of the desert.

THE END AND THE MYTH

*T*HE COWBOY OF WESTERN LEGEND *rode the open range for a surprisingly brief period. Hardly more than a generation passed after the Civil War before cattle ranching on the open range came to an end. The halcyon days of the cowboy, in fact, glowed brightest in the boom years of the early 1880s, when cattle prices were at their highest.*

The price boom was fueled by eastern and European syndicates as well as wealthy men like Theodore Roosevelt who invested heavily in the ranching business of the West. Books and newspaper stories at the time boasted of huge fortunes made in cattle ranching. Although some of the reports were relatively balanced, many were sensationalized accounts written by journalists who knew nothing of the cattle business or the West. One reporter described how the purchase of even one hundred head of cattle would multiply every year until after just a decade the purchaser would own a herd of several thousand head. A careful reading of the reporter's story reveals only two miscalculations. The obviously city-bred writer had assumed that all calves born in the herd would be heifers and all of these would begin giving birth to calves of their own as two-year-olds.

Inaccuracies aside, the sensational headlines still managed to fan the flames burning in the excited hearts of would-be ranchers from all over the world. So-called range rights to land that, in law, belonged to the government were often sold at staggering prices to newcomers lacking a realistic understanding of their purchases. Prices for cattle rose too. Range stock that sold by the herd for nine dollars a head in 1880 brought twelve dollars in 1881 and thirty-five dollars in 1882, the year the fever for Western cattle ranching peaked. Prices in Chicago for market animals reached seventy dollars and more. By this time, most of the northern ranges were already overstocked from both additional ranches and the increased cattle populations held on the older claims. Experienced cattlemen knew that a serious drought or winter blizzard would spell death for great numbers of animals and possible financial ruin for ranchers.

The time of reckoning had arrived. Prices began to weaken substantially in 1884. In the summer of 1885 they fell further and a drought that had begun in Texas two years earlier began to extend into the northern ranges. In 1886 the drought worsened. Prices remained weak. Many cattlemen held their animals from market, waiting for an upturn. Then came the terrible winter of 1886–87. Across the northern ranges cattle, many in poor condition because of drought and overgrazed ranges, were driven by fierce blizzards into coulees and creek beds, where they piled up and died by the thousands.

Granville Stuart, who wrote "End of the Cattle Range," lost half his cattle in one storm. By spring, two-thirds of the herd were dead and Stuart, one of Montana's earliest ranchers, quit the business in disgust. Easterners who had come West only a few years before sold what stock they had left for any price they could get and quit the country.

After the winter of 1886–87 the only winners. if you could call them that, were the smaller cattlemen who had been able to put up enough hay to see their animals through the season. In the depressed cattle market and in the rush of many big ranchers and syndicates to get out of the business, cattle could be purchased in the spring of 1887 for a song. From then on ranchers knew they had to put up hay to see cattle through the worst winters. Fences would have to be built to contain the grazing herds with their pure-bred bulls. Windmills and cattle tanks would be needed to provide water. Even the influx of homesteaders from the east had to be accommodated. The days of the old-time cowboy and ranchman were over. Only the memory of the open range would remain.

Like the fish that got away, the legends of the cattle country grew larger with time. The days of the open range would be remembered nostalgically by the participants, but as the newly arrived twentieth-century progressed, popular notions of the cowboy stretched to mythological proportions. Even during the 1880s and 1890s newspapers and magazine accounts romanticized the life of the cowboy. Then in 1902 Owen Wister, a Philadelphia lawyer infatuated with the West, wrote a novel he called The Virginian. *The novel became an almost instant bestseller and created a romanticized version of the cowboy that has stayed with us to this day.*

The character Wister called the Virginian was remade into countless other cowboy heroes by writers hoping to duplicate Wister's popularity. None did it more successfully than Zane Gray. Before the century was a decade old, Gray had begun modeling his own protagonists from Wister's hero. Though Gray's stories suffer from incredibly manipulated plots and two-dimensional characters, his success and prolific output soon saw his tales forming the templates for the thousands of formula Westerns that followed. Whether emanating from the pulp presses or the movies, Gray's and Wister's spectacularly inflated version of the cowboy came to dominate the popular view of this nineteenth-century range worker. The cowboy—strong and taciturn, hater of violence, upholder of all that is good—would be forever killing the bad guys.

Something in the nature of these good–versus–evil accounts of the open range sound an appealing chord for most of us. In this section of The Complete Cowboy Reader, we admire the Virginian's cool response to Trampas's ugly slur in "When You Call Me That, Smile!" Placing a six-gun in the open, within his reach, the Virginian merely stares at the devil Trampas and says, Trampas, proving beyond doubt his cowardice, smiles, and thus postpones the showdown the reader knows will eventually come. When the totally evil Trampas is finally shot to death by the Virginian we applaud.

Well-worn stories like these will never be thought great literature, but the real tragedy of the cowboy of popular myth is that the myth has displaced a far more remarkable and genuinely heroic figure, the real cowboy of the open range. Cowboys who drove cattle up the trails from Texas and tended the herds of the great ranches of the nineteenth-century were far from the demigods of pulp fiction. They were men with all of the frailties, misguided notions and absurdities common to us all. But they took part in one of the most remarkable episodes in American and Canadian history. For the most part they met the challenges with dignity and fortitude, and as the accounts written here demonstrate, the real cowboy of the open range was far more interesting and admirable than the cardboard characters of B-movies and pulp fiction will ever be.

End of the Cattle Range

– by –

Granville Stuart

DURING THE SUMMER OF 1885 more than one hundred thousand head of cattle were brought into Montana, most of them trailed up from the South. There were also many bands of sheep driven in and these together with the natural rapid increase (under the most favorable conditions) trebled the number of sheep in the territory and by the fall of 1885 the Montana ranges were crowded. A hard winter or a dry summer would certainly bring disaster. There was no way of preventing the over-stocking of the ranges as they were free to all and men felt disposed to take big chances for the hope of large returns. The range business was no longer a reasonably safe business; it was from this time on a "gamble" with the trump cards in the hands of the elements.

During the summer we kept our beef cattle in the grassy cañons and along the rolling foothills at the base of the mountains. In these favored places the grass was good and water plentiful and the cattle did not lose flesh traveling long distances to water as they did when left down in the plains.

These cañons were very beautiful and there were many lovely wild flowers growing here that I had not found anywhere else in Montana. There were tiger lillies, Maraposa lillies, white purple clematis, laurel, several varieties of the orchid family, wild primroses, the Scotch bluebells, several varieties of larkspurs and lobelia, and the most fragrant and beautiful wild roses that I had ever seen. There were also choke-cherries, huckleberries, wild raspberries, and goose-berries.

The autumn foliage was beautiful; groves of golden quaking aspen, orange cottonwood, scarlet thornbushes, crimson rose briers, and the trailing clematis with its white cotton balls intermingling with the evergreen of the pines, fir, and spruce.

In the fall we had two thousand head of beef cattle ready for shipment when a great rush of half fat range stuff from Texas, Indian Territory, and New Mexico flooded the markets and the price of beef cattle fell to a low water-mark. We cut out all of our three year old steers and turned them back on the range and only shipped nine hundred and eighty-two head. This left us eighteen thousand eight hundred and eighty head of stock on the range after the fall shipment.

This year the National Cattle Growers' Association met in Chicago on November 17-18. The Montana delegation devoted their time and energies to two subjects, namely:

To have the government perfect and take charge of a system of quarantine against diseases of animals in all the states and territories; and to have the Indians allotted their lands in severalty and the rest of their immense reservations thrown open to actual settlers. We succeeded in having our resolutions adopted and a delegation appointed to take them to Washington and have them presented before Congress.

There was a big fight led by the delegations from Texas and Indian territory, to set aside a wide strip of country from Texas to the British line for a cattle trail and to allow the leasing from the government of the public domain. These measures did not pass.

I returned from Chicago to the range late in December accompanied by the Marquis De Mores and we stopped off at Glendive and hunted for a week. The country was dry and dusty with only an occasional snow drift in the coulees and in deep ravines. The Marquis was anxious to visit Butte, our then flourishing mining town, and as I was going there on business he continued on with me to Helena and then to Butte.

In 1885, Butte was a hustling, bustling, mining town and everything ran wide open. We arrived at seven o'clock in the evening on a little local stub from Garrison. Volumes of yellowish sulphuric smoke rolled up from the heaps of copper ore that was roasting on the flat east of Meaderville and spread over the town like a pall enveloping everything in midnight darkness and almost suffocating one. The depot was little better than a box car and the light from the windows did not penetrate the darkness. We could not see and we could scarcely breathe.

The Marquis grabbed my arm and between sneezes gasped— "What is this to which you have brought me?"

As the cab slowly crawled along the street, music from the saloons and dance halls floated out to us but we could not even see the lights in the windows. Next day it was no better and I began to feel that our visit to Butte was destined to be a disappointment in so far as seeing the town was concerned. About ten o'clock a stiff breeze blew up from the south and scattered the smoke and we were able to visit our friends, transact business, and then view the novel sights of a big mining camp.

At the meeting of the Stock Growers' Association at Miles City, Dr. Azel Ames, F.C. Robertson, Marquis De Mores and myself were appointed a committee to confer with the people of St. Paul for the purpose of inducing them to establish stockyards and a cattle market at that city so as to relieve us from the monopoly held over us by Chicago. We succeeded in our mission and the following autumn the St. Paul yards were ready to receive shipments of cattle.

This spring we lost quite a number of cattle from their eating poisonous plants. It was the first trouble of the kind that we had encountered. These poisonous plants made their appearance after the drouths and when the grass was eaten out. Being drouth resisting they come up early, grow luxuriantly and are the first green things to appear in the spring and the cattle will eat them.

The spring roundup did not start until May 25, because with the continued drouth the green grass would not start. The cattle were in fine condition and the "calf crop" unusually large. Our outfit branded thirty-eight hundred and eighty-one calves on this roundup.

At this time a group of eastern capitalists offered to purchase our entire herd. Negotiations reached the point where we were to turn the outfit over to them, when Mr. Elkins, the man who represented the eastern company, died suddenly and the sale was not consummated.

The drouth continued and in July the short grass was dry and parched, streams and water holes drying up; but in spite of the drouth and short grass, cattle were being brought in from Washington and Oregon and the herds from the south were coming in undiminishing numbers and they were all thrown on the already over-stocked ranges of Montana.

Added to the drouth was unprecedented heat. The thermometer stood at one hundred to one hundred and ten degrees in the shade for days at a time and then would come hot winds that licked up every drop of moisture and shriveled the grass. There was nothing to be done but move at least a part of the herd.

In July I started out to look for better range and after going through the lower Judith basin, Shonkin, Highwoods, Belt creek, Sun river, and Teton ranges, finally decided to drive some of the cattle north of the Missouri river, along the foot of the Little Rockies. There was more water over there and some good grass.

In spite of every precaution range fires would start and as it was so hot and dry it was very hard to put them out when they did start. Big fires along the foot of the Judith range and on the Musselshell filled the air with smoke and cinders. Crews of fire fighters were kept busy all summer.

On arriving home, I found a telegram from Conrad Kohrs stating that he had leased range in Canada and to prepare to move. He failed to state where the leased range was located. I was not in favor of taking the herd north of the British line because of the severe blizzards that swept the open treeless plains that afforded no shelter for stock and was too far north to get the warm chinook winds. It was too late in the season to move the cattle a great distance. It always injures range cattle more or less to move them and it would never do to throw them on a strange range too late in the season.

A meeting of the stockholders of the Pioneer Cattle Company decided that we would reduce the herd as much as possible by shipping to market all the cattle fit for beef, gather the bulls and feed them at the home ranches and move five thousand head across the Missouri river to the foot of the Little Rockies. To G.P. Burnett was given the difficult task of gathering and moving the herd.

The beef could not be shipped until fall so the fat steers must not be disturbed and it was very hard to drive out the others and not disturb them, for all were as wild as antelope. Extreme care had to be used so that the herd would reach the new range in as good condition as possible.

August 10 we began gathering the cattle that were to be moved. Ordinarily one could see for miles across the range in our clear atmosphere, but not so at this time. Dense smoke obscured everything and this together with the cinders and the clouds of hot dry alkali dust almost choked and blinded us, causing much suffering to men and horses.

Moving a mixed herd is always hard. The young cattle travel fast and the old cows and young calves go slowly, so the whole herd has to be driven to suit the pace of the slowest animal in it. The drive to the new range was not a long one but under the existing circumstances it was a hard one and taxed to the fullest the ingenuity of the plucky young Texan in charge of the herd.

The weather continued extremely hot, and creeks, water-holes, and small lakes, never before dry, were completely so now. The water in all the flowing streams was very low and strongly alkaline, so much so, that in places the tired and thirsty horses refused to drink. It was so bitter that one could not drink the coffee made with it. Nearly every man with the drive was ill from drinking it. For days the herd moved forward through the smoke and stifling dust across the dry parched country.

At last we were nearing the Missouri river, intending to cross at Rocky Point. The wind was from the north and the cattle smelled the water and broke for it. No power on earth could stop the poor thirsty beasts; bellowing and lowing they ran pell-mell for the water, with the cowboys in hot pursuit. There was a point of quicksand in the river just above the ford and before the men could prevent it the cattle had plunged into it and were miring down. A small steamboat tied at the landing used their donkey engine to help drag out some of them, but we lost seventy head in spite of our best efforts.

After this mishap we crossed the herd without further trouble and from here on there was more water and better grass. The herd reached its destination in splendid condition. This fall we branded two thousand and seventy-four calves.

Seven thousand head of cattle belonging to the Powder River Cattle Company crossed the Missouri river at Great Falls and were driven through the Judith basin destined for our range, but when they saw the condition of the range and found that we were moving cattle out, they continued on north across the British line and threw their herds on the range near Fort McLeod.

John H. Conrad also had two thousand seven hundred head that he intended to bring in, but later drove them north of the line to the Cypress hills.

These changes, together with the very heavy shipments of beef to the markets relieved the over-stocked condition of the range and could we have had copious rains early in the fall to start the grass and a reasonably easy winter, all would have gone well.

We did not get the fall rains. There was quite a severe storm in November. On the sixteenth the thermometer fell to two degrees below zero, with a cutting northeast wind and on the seventeenth and eighteenth six inches of snow fell, but blew into drifts. The cattle north of the Missouri being unaccustomed to the range drifted badly and kept working back to the river.

This year we noticed that the wild animals moved south. The wild geese and ducks and song birds started south early and many that were accustomed to stay with us all winter disappeared: even the range cattle seemed to take on a heavier, shaggier coat of hair. For the first time since I had come to the range, the white Arctic owls came on the range and into the Judith basin. The old Indians pointed to them and drawing their blankets more closely about them, gave a shrug and "Ugh! Heap Cold!" expressive of some terrible experience in the long past that still lingered in their memory. One old Gros Ventre warrior assured me that not since he was a small boy had he seen the owls on their reservation. Everything pointed to a severe winter and we made what preparations we could to meet it with as little suffering to the stock and loss to ourselves as possible.

December 5, there was another storm, with the thermometer twelve degrees below and four inches of snow. I returned home from Chicago December 14 and rode from Custer station to the ranch, distant one hundred and twenty miles, in a blizzard, the thermometer down to zero and high east wind that pierced to the marrow of my bones.

Between the Musselshell and Flat Willow the snow blew in our faces so that the driver could not keep the road. There were two other passengers on the stage besides myself and we took turns walking ahead of the horses with a lantern to guide them. This storm lasted three days and then cleared up warm and bright and remained so until January 9, 1887. On that day a cold wind blew from the north. It began to snow and snowed steadily for sixteen hours, in which sixteen inches of snow fell on a level. The thermometer dropped to twenty-two degrees below zero, then twenty-seven degrees, then thirty degrees, and on the night of January 15 stood at forty-six degrees below zero, and there were sixteen inches of snow on the level. It was as though the Arctic regions had pushed down and enveloped us. Everything was white. Not a point of bare ground was visible in any direction. This storm lasted ten days without abating. The cattle drifted before the storm and fat young steers froze to death along their trails.

Conditions were so changed from what they were in 1880–81. The thick brush and tall rye-grass along the streams that afforded them excellent shelter at that time was now all fenced in and the poor animals drifted against those fences and perished.

Our herd was one of the first large herds brought into northeastern Montana, consequently had been on the range longer than others. They were all northern grown range stock and occupied the best range in the northwest. We kept plenty of men on the range to look after them as best they could, keeping them back from the rivers, and out of air holes and open channels in the ice, helping them out of drifts and keeping them in what shelter the cut banks and ravines offered. The herd could be said to be a favored one, yet we lost fifty per cent of them in this storm.

There was a series of storms in February and while not so severe yet they came at a time when the cattle were least able to withstand them and there were heavy losses then. The cows were all thin and the losses in spring calves was about thirty per cent.

The herds that were driven up from the south and placed on the range late in the summer, perished outright. Others lost from seventy-five to eighty per cent of their cattle.

It was impossible to tell just what the losses were for a long time as the cattle drifted so badly in the big January storm. We did not get some of ours back for a year. Our entire losses for the year were sixty-six per cent of the herd. In the fall of 1886 there were more than one million head of cattle on the Montana ranges and the losses in the "big storm" amounted to twenty million dollars. This was the death knell to the range cattle business on anything like the scale it had been run on before.

Charles Russell, "The Cow Boy Artist" told the story of the "snuffing out of the big ranges" most graphically in his charcoal sketch, "The Last of 5000." Charlie was in charge of a herd in the Judith basin, when the owner, who lived in Helena, wrote and asked how his cattle was getting along? For answer Charlie sent him the sketch.

The large outfits were the heaviest losers as they could not feed or shelter their immense herds. Most of the big outfits had borrowed large sums of money at a high rate of interest and the cattle that they had left would hardly pay their indebtedness. They had to stay in the business and begin all over again. Eastern men who had large sums of money invested, closed out the remnant of their herds and quit.

The rancher with a good body of hay land and from one hundred to two hundred head of cattle was the man that profited. He had hay enough to feed through storms and could gather his cattle around the ranch and partially shelter them, and in the spring he was enabled to buy cattle cheap. Here again I wish to say a word in defense of the "cattle barons" whom our leading newspapers abused so unmercifully at the time, accusing them of driving settlers from their homes and of "hogging" all the land. There were a good many settlers who had milch cows and a few "dogies" and did not have hay enough to feed them. The big ranches all had more or less hay and could have saved a few cattle by feeding, but instead they let the man with a family and a few cows have the hay to save their domestic animals; and they did not sell it to them at ruinous prices either but let them have it at cost of production.

In the spring of 1887 the ranges presented a tragic aspect. Along the streams and in the coulees everywhere were strewn the carcasses of dead cattle. Those that were left alive were poor and ragged in appearance, weak and easily mired in the mud holes.

A business that had been fascinating to me before, suddenly became distasteful. I wanted no more of it. I never wanted to own again an animal that I could not feed and shelter.

The spring was very wet, one heavy rain followed another in succession and the grass came on luxuriantly. We moved the remainder of the herd over on the Milk river range. I did not like the country and did not move over there. Conrad Kohrs took the management of the herd.

Much has been said and written about the extravagant mismanagement of the big cow outfits, of the selfish arrogance of the cattlemen, of the wild and reckless irresponsible cow boy.

I began at the beginning and was with it to the end and I want to say that there was never a great business that was systematized and worked more economically than the range cattle business. Some of the big outfits were owned by eastern capitalists who invested for their sons, boys who were fascinated with the free untrammeled life of the west, others were owned by men who, like myself, had been more or less in cattle in Montana for years and these small herds became the nucleus for the big outfits. Then there were men like Conrad Kohrs who had never done anything but raise cattle, and there were cattle breeders (range men) from the southwest.

It was apparent from the first that to be successful the entire range business must be run as one outfit, hence the two strong organizations, The Montana Stock Growers' Association and the Board of Stock Commissioners. These two organizations acted as Boards of Directors and they ran the cattle business absolutely. Their administration was just, honest, and economical, so much so that they have been in operation for thirty-five years and are still in operation.

The young men, scions of wealthy and influential families, loved the business and were anxious to learn, and under the leadership of older and more experienced heads, developed into splendid business men, many of them still in the state and numbered among our best citizens.

The handling of the herds on the range was entrusted to the cow boys from the southwest. These men were bred and born on the range and knew how to handle range cattle. It is impossible for me to describe one of them and do him justice. Their understanding of cattle was almost supernatural, their patience, ingenuity, faithfulness, and loyalty to their outfit cannot be described. They were to their outfit what a good mother is to her family and their way of handling herds has never been improved upon.

The idea of lavish expenditure was an erroneous one. I have described the headquarters ranch of a big outfit; few rude log cabins, comprising a bunk house, a cook house, a blacksmith shop, stable and corral, with hay land enough fenced to cut a hundred tons of hay. The food provided was beans, bacon, coffee, syrup, bread and beef. A can of tomatoes or oysters was a luxury.

The big outfits never imposed on the smaller ones or on the ranchers or squatters, but helped them in every way. In fact it was the big outfits that protected the little ones and made it possible for them to settle in the uninhabited country.

The big outfits brought millions of capital into a sparsely settled country and their herds converted the millions of tons of grass that had for thousands of years gone to waste into millions of dollars worth of beef. Their heavy taxes built roads and schools and did much for the advancement of civilization.

"When You Call Me
That, Smile!"

– by –
Owen Wister

W E CANNOT SEE OURSELVES as others see us, or I should know what appearance I cut at hearing this from the tall man. I said nothing, feeling uncertain.

"I reckon I am looking for you, seh," he repeated politely.

"I am looking for Judge Henry," I now replied.

He walked toward me, and I saw that in inches he was not a giant. He was not more than six feet. It was Uncle Hughey that had made him seem to tower. But in his eye, in his face, in his step, in the whole man, there dominated a something potent to be felt, I should think, by man or woman.

"The Judge sent me afteh you, seh," he now explained, in his civil Southern voice; and he handed me a letter from my host. Had I not witnessed his facetious performances with Uncle Hughey, I should have judged him wholly ungifted with such powers. There was nothing external about him but what seemed the signs of a nature as grave as you could meet. But I had witnessed; and therefore supposing that I knew him in spite of his appearance, that I was, so to speak, in his secret and could give him a sort of wink, I adopted at once a method of easiness. It was so pleasant to be easy with a large stranger who instead of shooting at your heels had very civilly handed you a letter.

"You're from old Virginia, I take it?" I began.

He answered slowly, "Then you have taken it correct, seh."

A slight chill passed over my easiness, but I went cheerily on with a further inquiry, "Find many oddities out here like Uncle Hughey?"

"Yes, seh, there is a right smart of oddities around. They come in on every train."

At this point I dropped my method of easiness.

"I wish that trunks came on the train," said I. And I told him my predicament.

It was not to be expected that he would be greatly moved at my loss; but he took it with no comment whatever. "We'll wait in town for it," said he, always perfectly civil.

Now, what I had seen of "town" was, to my newly arrived eyes, altogether horrible. If I could possibly sleep at the Judge's ranch, I preferred to do so.

"Is it too far to drive there to-night?" I inquired.

He looked at me in a puzzled manner.

"For this valise," I explained, "contains all that I immediately need; in fact, I could do without my trunk for a day or two, if it is not convenient to send. So if we could arrive there not too late by start-ing at once—" I paused.

"It's two hundred and sixty-three miles," said the Virginian.

To my loud ejaculation he made no answer, but surveyed me a moment longer, and then said, "Supper will be about ready now." He took my valise, and I followed his steps toward the eating-house in silence. I was dazed.

As we went, I read my host's letter—a brief, hospitable message. He was very sorry not to meet me himself. He had been getting ready to drive over, when the surveyor appeared and detained him. There-fore in his stead he was sending a trustworthy man to town, who would look after me and drive me over. They were looking forward to my visit with much pleasure. This was all.

Yes, I was dazed. How did they count distance in this country? You spoke in a neighborly fashion about driving over to town, and it meant—I did not know yet how many days. And what would be meant by the term "dropping in," I wondered. And how many miles would be considered really far? I abstained from further questioning the "trustworthy man." My questions had not fared excessively well. He did not purpose making me dance, to be sure: that would scarcely be trustworthy. But neither did he purpose to have me familiar with him. Why was this? What had I done to elicit that veiled and skilful sarcasm about oddities coming in on every train? Having been sent to look after me, he would do so, would even carry my valise; but I could not be jocular with him. This handsome, ungrammatical son of the soil had set between us the bar of his cold and perfect civility. No polished person could have done it better. What was the matter? I looked at him, and suddenly it came to me. If he had tried familiarity with me the first two minutes of our acquaintance, I should have resented it; by what right, then, had I tried it with him? It smacked of patronizing: on this occasion he had come off the better gentleman of the two. Here in flesh and blood was a truth which I had long believed in words, but never met before. The creature we call a *gentleman* lies deep in the hearts of thousands that are born without chance to master the outward graces of the type.

Between the station and the eating-house I did a deal of straight thinking. But my thoughts were destined presently to be drowned in amazement at the rare personage into whose society fate had thrown me.

Town, as they called it, pleased me the less, the longer I saw it. But until our language stretches itself and takes in a new word of closer fit, town will have to do for the name of such a place as was Medicine Bow. I have seen and slept in many like it since. Scattered wide, they littered the frontier from the Columbia to the Rio Grande, from the Missouri to the Sierras. They lay stark, dotted over a planet of treeless dust, like soiled packs of cards. Each was similar to the next, as one old five-spot of clubs resembles another. Houses, empty bottles, and garbage, they were forever of the same shapeless pattern. More forlorn they were than stale bones. They seemed to have been strewn there by the wind and to be waiting till the wind should come again and blow them away. Yet serene above their foulness swam a pure and quiet light, such as the East never sees; they might be bathing in the air of creation's first morning. Beneath sun and stars their days and nights were immaculate and wonderful.

Medicine Bow was my first, and I took its dimensions, twenty-nine buildings in all,—one coal chute, one water tank, the station, one store, two eating-houses, one billiard hall, two tool-houses, one feed stable, and twelve others that for one reason and another I shall not name. Yet this wretched husk of squalor spent thought upon appearances; many houses in it wore a false front to seem as if they were two stories high. There they stood, rearing their pitiful masquerade amid a fringe of old tin cans, while at their very doors began a world of crystal light, a land without end, a space across which Noah and Adam might come straight from Genesis. Into that space went wandering a road, over a hill and down out of sight, and up again smaller in the distance, and down once more, and up once more, straining the eyes, and so away.

Then I heard a fellow greet my Virginian. He came rollicking out of a door, and made a pass with his hand at the Virginian's hat. The Southerner dodged it, and I saw once more the tiger undulation of body, and knew my escort was he of the rope and the corral.

"How are yu', Steve?" he said to the rollicking man. And in his tone I heard instantly old friendship speaking. With Steve he would take and give familiarity.

Steve looked at me, and looked away—and that was all. But it was enough. In no company had I ever felt so much an outsider. Yet I liked the company, and wished that it would like me.

"Just come to town?" inquired Steve of the Virginian.

"Been here since noon. Been waiting for the train."

"Going out to-night?"

"I reckon I'll put out to-morro'."

"Beds are all took," said Steve. This was for my benefit.

"Dear me!" said I.

"But I guess one of them drummers will let yu' double up with him." Steve was enjoying himself, I think. He had his saddle and blankets, and beds were nothing to him.

"Drummers, are they?" asked the Virginian.

"Two drummers handling cigars, one medicine-man with consumption killer, and another drummer with jew'lry."

The Virginian set down my valise, and seemed to meditate. "I did want a bed to-night," he murmured gently.

"Well," Steve suggested, "the medicine-man looks like he washed the oftenest."

"That's of no consequence to me," observed the Southerner.

"Guess it'll be when yu' see 'em."

"Oh, I'm meaning something different. I wanted a bed to myself."

"Then you'll have to build one."

"Bet yu' I have the jewelry drummer's."

"Take a man that won't scare. Bet yu' drinks yu' can't have the medicine-man's."

"Go yu'," said the Virginian. "I'll have his bed without any fuss. Drinks for the crowd."

"I suppose you have me beat," said Steve, grinning at him affectionately. "You're such a son-of-a—when you get down to work. Well, so-long! I got to fix my horse's hoofs."

I had expected that the man would be struck down. He had used to the Virginian a term of heaviest insult, I thought. I had marvelled to hear it come so unheralded from Steve's friendly lips. And now I marvelled still more. Evidently he had meant no harm by it, and evidently no offence had been taken. Used thus, this language was plainly complimentary. I had stepped into a world new to me indeed, and novelties were occurring with scarce any time to get breath between them. As to where I should sleep, I had forgotten that problem altogether in my curiosity. What was the Virginian going to do now? I began to know that the quiet of this man was volcanic.

"Will you wash first, sir?"

We were at the door of the eating-house, and he set my valise inside. In my tenderfoot innocence I was looking indoors for the washing arrangements.

"It's out hyeh, seh," he informed me gravely, but with strong Southern accent. Internal mirth seemed often to heighten the local flavor of his speech. There were other times when it had scarce any special accent or fault in grammar.

A trough was to my right, slippery with soapy water; and hanging from a roller above one end of it was a rag of discouraging appearance. The Virginian caught it, and it performed one whirling revolution on its roller. Not a dry or clean inch could be found on it. He took off his hat, and put his head in the door.

"Your towel, ma'am," said he, "has been too popular."

She came out, a pretty woman. Her eyes rested upon him for a moment, then upon me with disfavor, then they returned to his black hair.

"The allowance is one a day," said she, very quietly. "But when folks are particular—" She completed her sentence by removing the old towel and giving a clean one to us.

"Thank you, ma'am," said the cow-puncher.

She looked once more at his black hair, and without any word returned to her guests at supper.

A pail stood in the trough, almost empty; and this he filled for me from a well. There was some soap sliding at large in the trough, but I got my own. And then in a tin basin I removed as many of the stains of travel as I was able. It was not much of a toilet that I made in this first wash-trough of my experience, but it had to suffice, and I took my seat at supper.

Canned stuff it was,—corned beef. And one of my table companions said the truth about it. "When I slung my teeth over that," he remarked, "I thought I was chewing a hammock." We had strange coffee, and condensed milk; and I have never seen more flies. I made no attempt to talk, for no one in this country seemed favorable to me. By reason of something,—my clothes, my hat, my pronunciation, whatever it might be,—I possessed the secret of estranging people at sight. Yet I was doing better than I knew; my strict silence and attention to the corned beef made me in the eyes of the cow-boys at table compare well with the over-talkative commercial travellers.

The Virginian's entrance produced a slight silence. He had done wonders with the wash-trough, and he had somehow brushed his clothes. With all the roughness of his dress, he was now the neatest of us. He nodded to some of the other cow-boys, and began his meal in quiet.

But silence is not the native element of the drummer. An average fish can go a longer time out of water than this breed can live without talking. One of them now looked across the table at the grave, flannel-shirted Virginian; he inspected, and came to the imprudent conclusion that he understood this man.

"Good evening," he said briskly.

"Good evening," said the Virginian.

"Just come to town?" pursued the drummer.

"Just come to town," the Virginian suavely assented.

"Cattle business jumping along?" inquired the drummer.

"Oh, fair." And the Virginian took some more corned beef.

"Gets a move on your appetite, anyway," suggested the drummer.

The Virginian drank some coffee. Presently the pretty women refilled his cup without his asking her.

"Guess I've met you before," the drummer stated next.

The Virginian glanced at him for a brief moment.

"Haven't I, now? Ain't I seen you somewheres? Look at me. You been in Chicago, ain't you? You look at me well. Remember Ikey's, don't you?"

"I don't reckon I do."

"See, now! I knowed you'd been in Chicago. Four or five years ago. Or maybe it's two years. Time's nothing to me. But I never forget a face. Yes, sir. Him and me's met at Ikey's all right." This important point the drummer stated to all of us. We were called to witness how well he had proved old acquaintanceship. "Ain't the world small, though!" he exclaimed complacently. "Meet a man once and you're sure to run on to him again. That's straight. That's no bar-room josh."And the drummer's eye included us all in his confidence. I wondered if he had attained that high perfection when a man believes his own lies.

The Virginian did not seem interested. He placidly attended to his food, while our landlady moved between dining room and kitchen, and the drummer expanded.

"Yes, sir! Ikey's over by the stock-yards, patronized by all cattle-men that know what's what. That's where. Maybe it's three years.

Time never was nothing to me. But faces! Why, I can't quit 'em. Adults or children, male and female; onced I seen 'em I couldn't lose one off my memory, not if you were to pay me bounty, five dollars a face. White men, that is. Can't do nothing with niggers or Chinese. But you're white, all right." The drummer suddenly returned to the Virginian with this high compliment. The cow-puncher had taken out a pipe, and was slowly rubbing it. The compliment seemed to escape his attention, and the drummer went on.

"I can tell a man when he's white, put him at Ikey's or out loose here in the sage-brush." And he rolled a cigar across to the Virginian's plate.

"Selling them?" inquired the Virginian.

"Solid goods, my friend. Havana wrappers, the biggest tobacco proposition for five cents got out yet. Take it, try it, light it, watch it burn. Here." And he held out a bunch of matches.

The Virginian tossed a five-cent piece over to him.

"Oh, no, my friend! Not from you! Not after Ikey's. I don't forget you. See? I knowed your face right away. See? That's straight. I seen you at Chicago all right."

"Maybe you did," said the Virginian. "Sometimes I'm mighty careless what I look at."

"Well, py damn!" now exclaimed the jewelry man, hilariously, "I am ploom disappointed. I vas hoping to sell him somedings myself."

"Not the same here," stated the medicine-man. "He's too healthy for me. I gave him up on sight."

Now it was the medicine-man whose bed the Virginian had in his eye. This was a sensible man, and had talked less than his brothers in the trade. I had little doubt who would end by sleeping in his bed; but how the thing would be done interested me more deeply than ever.

The Virginian looked amiably at his intended victim, and made one or two remarks regarding patent medicines. There must be a good deal of money in them, he supposed, with a live man to manage them. The victim was flattered. No other person at the table had been favored with so much of the tall cow-puncher notice. He responded, and they had a pleasant talk. I did not devine that the Virginian's genius was even then at work, and that all this was part of his satanic strategy. But Steve must have devined it. For while a few of us still sat finishing our supper, the facetious horseman returned from doctoring his horse's hoof put his head into the dining room, took in the way in which the Virginian was engaging his victim in conversation, remarked aloud, "I've lost!" and closed the door again.

"What's he lost?" inquired the medicine-man.

"Oh, you mustn't mind him," drawled the Virginian. "He's one of those box-head jokers goes around openin' and shuttin' doors that-a-way. We call him harmless. Well," he broke off, "reckon I'll go smoke. Not allowed in hyeh?" This last he addressed to the landlady, with especial gentleness. She shook her head, and her eyes followed him as he went out.

Left to myself I meditated for some time upon my lodging for the night, and smoked a cigar for consolation as I walked about. It was not a hotel that we had supped in. Hotel at Medicine Bow there appeared to be none. But connected with the eating-house was that place where, according to Steve, the beds were all taken and there I went to see for myself. Steve had spoken the truth. It was a single apartment containing four or five beds, and nothing else whatever. And when I looked at these beds, my sorrow that I could sleep in none of them grew less. To be alone in one offered no temptation, and as for this courtesy of the counting this doubling up—!

"Well, they have got ahead of us." This was the Virginian standing at my elbow.

I assented.

"They have staked out their claims," he added.

In this public sleeping room they had done what one does to secure a seat in a railroad train. Upon each bed, as notice of occupancy, lay some article of travel or of dress. As we stood there, the two cigar men came in and opened and arranged their valises, and folded and refolded their linen dusters. Then a railroad employee entered and began to go to bed at this hour, before dusk had wholly darkened into night. For him, going to bed meant removing his boots and placing his overalls and waistcoat beneath his pillow. He had no coat. His work began at three in the morning; and even as we still talked he began to snore.

"The man that keeps the store is a friend of mine," said the Virginian; "and you can be pretty near comfortable on his counter. Got any blankets?"

I had no blankets.

"Looking for a bed?" inquired the medicine-man, now arriving.

"Yes, he's looking for a bed," answered the voice of Steve behind him.

"Seems a waste of time," observed the Virginian. He looked thoughtfully from one bed to another. "I didn't know I'd have to lay over here. Well, I have sat up before."

"This one's mine," said the drummer, sitting down on it. "Half's plenty enough room for me."

"You're cert'nly mighty kind," said the cow-puncher. "But I'd not think o'disconveniencing yu'."

"That's nothing. The other half is yours. Turn in right now if you feel like it."

"No. I don't reckon I'll turn in right now. Better keep your bed to yourself."

"See here," urged the drummer, "if I take you I'm safe from drawing some party I might not care so much about. This here sleeping proposition is a lottery."

"Well," said the Virginian (and his hesitation was truly masterly), "if you put it that way—"

"I do put it that way. Why, you're clean! You've had a shave right now. You turn in when you feel inclined, old man! I ain't retiring just yet."

The drummer had struck a slightly false note in these last remarks. He should not have said "old man." Until this I had thought him merely an amiable person who wished to do a favor. But "old man" came in wrong. It had a hateful taint of his profession; the being too soon with everybody, the celluloid good-fellowship that passes for ivory with nine in ten of the city crowd. But not so with the sons of the sagebrush. They live nearer nature, and they know better.

But the Virginian blandly accepted "old man" from his victim; he had a game to play.

"Well, I cert'nly thank yu'," he said. "After a while I'll take advantage of your kind offer."

I was surprised. Possession being nine points of the law, it seemed his very chance to intrench himself in the bed. But the cow-puncher had planned a campaign needing no intrenchments. Moreover, going to bed before nine o'clock upon the first evening in many weeks when a town's resources were open to you, would be a dull proceeding. Our entire company, drummer and all, now walked over to the store, and here my sleeping arrangements were made easily. This store was the cleanest place and the best in Medicine Bow, and would have been a good store anywhere, offering a multitude of things for sale, and kept by a very civil proprietor. He bade me make myself at home, and placed both of his counters at my disposal. Upon the grocery side there stood a cheese too large and strong to sleep near comfortably, and I therefore chose the dry-goods side. Here thick quilts were unrolled for me, to make it soft; and no condition was placed upon me, further than that I should remove my boots, because the quilts were new, and clean, and for sale. So now my rest was assured. Not an anxiety remained in my thoughts. These therefore turned themselves wholly to the other man's bed, and how he was going to lose it.

I think that Steve was more curious even than myself. Time was on the wing. His bet must be decided, and the drinks enjoyed. He stood against the grocery counter, contemplating the Virginian. But it was to me that he spoke. The Virginian, however, listened to every word.

"Your first visit to this country?"

I told him yes.

"How do you like it?"

I expected to like it very much.

"How does the climate strike you?"

I thought the climate was fine.

"Makes a man thirsty though."

This was the sub-current which the Virginian plainly looked for. But he, like Steve, addressed himself to me.

"Yes," he put in, "thirsty while a man's soft yet. You'll harden."

"I guess you'll find it a drier country than you were given to expect," said Steve.

"If your habits have been frequent that way," said the Virginian.

"There's parts of Wyoming," pursued Steve, "where you'll go hours and hours before you'll see a drop of wetness."

"And if yu' keep a-thinkin about it," said the Virginian, "it'll seem like days and days."

Steve, at this stroke, gave up, and clapped him on the shoulder with a joyous chuckle. "You old son-of-a—!" he cried affectionately.

"Drinks are due now," said the Virginian. "My treat, Steve. But I reckon your suspense will have to linger a while yet."

Thus they dropped into direct talk from that speech of the fourth dimension where they had been using me for their telephone.

"Any cyards going to-night?" inquired the Virginian.

"Stud and draw," Steve told him. "Strangers playing."

"I think I'd like to get into a game for a while," said the Southerner. "Strangers, yu' say ?"

And then, before quitting the store, he made his toilet for this little hand at poker. It was a simple preparation. He took his pistol from its holster, examined it, then shoved it between his overalls and his shirt in front, and pulled his waistcoat over it. He might have been combing his hair for all the attention any one paid to this, except myself. Then the two friends went out, and I bethought me of that epithet which Steve again had used to the Virginian as he clapped him on the shoulder. Clearly this wild country spoke a language other than mine—the word here was a term of endearment. Such was my conclusion.

The drummers had finished their dealings with the proprietor, and they were gossiping together in a knot by the door as the Virginian passed out.

"See you later, old man!" This was the medicine-man accosting his prospective bed-fellow.

"Oh, yes," returned the bed-fellow, and was gone.

The medicine-man winked triumphantly at his brethren. "He's all right," he observed, jerking a thumb after the Virginian. "He's easy. You got to know him to work him. That's all."

"Und vat is your point?" inquired the jewelry man.

"Point is—he'll not take any goods off you or me; but he's going to talk up the Killer to any consumptive he runs acrost. I ain't done with him yet. Say" (he now addressed the proprietor), "what's her name?"

"Whose name?"

"Woman runs the eating-house."

"Glen. Mrs. Glen."

"Ain't she new?"

"Been settled here about a month. Husband's a freight conductor."

"Thought I'd not seen her before. She's a goodlooker."

"Hm! Yes. The kind of good looks I'd sooner see in another man's wife than mine."

"So that's the gait, is it?"

"Hm! well, it don't seem to be. She come here with that reputation. But there's been general disappointment."

"Then she ain't lacked suitors any?"

"Lacked! Are you acquainted with cow-boys?"

"And she disappointed 'em? Maybe she likes her husband?"

"Hm! well, how are you to tell about them silent kind?"

"Talking of conductors," began the drummer. And we listened to his anecdote. It was successful with his audience; but when he launched fluently upon a second I strolled out. There was not enough wit in this narrator to relieve his indecency, and I felt shame at having been surprised into laughing with him.

I left that company growing confidential over their leering stories, and I sought the saloon. It was very quiet and orderly. Beer in quart bottles at a dollar I had never met before; but saving its price, I found no complaint to make of it. Through folding doors I passed from the bar proper with its bottles and elk head back to the hall with its various tables. I saw a man sliding cards from a case, and across the table from him another man laying counters down. Near by was a second dealer pulling cards from the bottom of a pack, and opposite him a solemn old rustic piling and changing coins upon the cards which lay already exposed.

But now I heard a voice that drew my eyes to the far corner of the room.

"Why didn't you stay in Arizona?"

Harmless looking words as I write them down here. Yet at the sound of them I noticed the eyes of the others directed to that corner. What answer was given to them I did not hear, nor did I see who spoke. Then came another remark.

"Well, Arizona's no place for amatures."

This time the two card dealers that I stood near began to give a part of their attention to the group that sat in the corner. There was in me a desire to leave this room. So far my hours at Medicine Bow had seemed to glide beneath a sunshine of merriment, of easy-going jocularity. This was suddenly gone, like the wind changing to north in the middle of a warm day. But I stayed, being ashamed to go.

Five or six players sat over in the corner at a round table where counters were piled. Their eyes were close upon their cards, and one seemed to be dealing a card at a time to each, with pauses and betting between. Steve was there and the Virginian; the others were new faces.

"No place for amatures," repeated the voice; and now I saw that it was the dealer's. There was in his countenance the same ugliness that his words conveyed.

"Who's that talkin?"said one of the men near me, in a low voice.

"Trampas."

"What's he?"

"Cow-puncher, bronco-buster, tin-horn, most anything."

"Who's he talkin' at?"

"Think it's the black-headed guy he's talking at."

"That ain't supposed to be safe, is it?"

"Guess we're all goin' to find out in a few minutes."

"Been trouble between 'em?"

"They've not met before. Trampas don't enjoy losin' to a stranger."

"Fello's from Arizona, yu' say?"

"No. Virginia. He's recently back from havin' a look at Arizona. Went down there last year for a change. Works for the Sunk Creek outfit." And then the dealer lowered his voice still further and said something in the other man's ear, causing him to grin. After which both of them looked at me.

There had been silence over in the corner; but now the man Trampas spoke again.

"*And* ten," said he, sliding out some chips from before him. Very strange it was to hear him, how he contrived to make those words a personal taunt. The Virginian was looking at his cards. He might have been deaf.

"*And* twenty," said the next player, easily.

The next threw his cards down.

It was now the Virginian's turn to bet, or leave the game, and he did not speak at once.

Therefore Trampas spoke. "Your bet, you son-of-a—."

The Virginian's pistol came out, and his hand lay on the table, holding it unaimed. And with a voice as gentle as ever, the voice that sounded almost like a caress, but drawling a very little more than usual, so that there was almost a space between each word, he issued his orders to the man Trampas:—

"When you call me that, *smile!*" And he looked at Trampas across the table.

Yes, the voice was gentle. But in my ears it seemed as if somewhere the bell of death was ringing; and silence, like a stroke, fell on the large room. All men present, as if by some magnetic current, had become aware of this crisis. In my ignorance, and the total stoppage of my thoughts, I stood stock-still, and noticed various people crouching, or shifting their positions.

"Sit quiet," said the dealer, scornfully to the man near me. "Can't you see he don't want to push trouble? He has handed Trampas the choice to back down or draw his steel."

Then, with equal suddenness and ease, the room came out of its strangeness. Voices and cards, the click of chips, the puff of tobacco, glasses lifted to drink,—this level of smooth relaxation hinted no more plainly of what lay beneath than does the surface tell the depth of the sea.

For Trampas had made his choice. And that choice was not to "draw his steel." If it was knowledge that he sought, he had found it, and no mistake! We heard no further reference to what he had been pleased to style "amatures." In no company would the black-headed man who had visited Arizona be rated a novice at the cool art of self-preservation.

One doubt remained: what kind of a man was Trampas? A public back-down is an unfinished thing,—for some natures at least. I looked at his face, and thought it sullen, but tricky rather than courageous.

Something had been added to my knowledge also. Once again I had heard applied to the Virginian that epithet which Steve so freely used. The same words, identical to the letter. But this time they had produced a pistol. "When you call me that, *smile!*" So I perceived a new example of the old truth, that the letter means nothing until the spirit gives it life.

Bibliography

Abbott, E.C. and Helena H. Smith. *We Pointed Them North: Recollections of a Cowpuncher,* Norman: University of Oklahoma Press, 1952.

Adams, Andy. *The Log of a Cowboy.* Boston: Houghton Mifflin Company, 1903.

Adams, Ramon. *Come and Get It: The Story of the Old Cowboy Cook.* Norman: University of Oklahoma Press, 1953.

Atherton, Lewis. *The Cattle Kings.* Bloomington, Indiana: Indiana University Press, 1961.

Botkin, B.A. *A Treasury of Western Folklore.* New York: Crown Publishers, 1951.

Branch, Douglas. *The Cowboy and His Interpreters.* New York: Appleton-Century Crofts, Inc.

Cox, James. *The Cattle Industry of Texas and Adjacent Territory.* St. Louis: Stock Growers Association, 1895.

Clay, John. *My Life on the Range.* New York: Antiquarian Press, 1961.

Dale, E.E. *The Range Cattle Industry.* Norman: The University of Oklahoma Press, 1930.

Dary, David. *Cowboy Culture: A Saga of Five Centuries.* Lawrence: University of Kansas Press, 1989.

Devoto, Bernard. *Across the Wide Missouri.* Boston: Houghton Mifflin, 1947.

Dimsdale, Thomas. *The Vigilantes of Montana.* Norman: University of Oklahoma Press, 1972.

Dobie, J. Frank. *A Vaquero of the Brush Country.* Dallas: The Southwest Press, 1929.

—— *The Longhorns.* Austin: University of Texas Press, 1990.

—— *Cow People.* Boston: Little Brown & Co., 1964.

—— *The Mustangs.* Boston: Little Brown & Co., 1952.

Dodge, Richard Irving. *The Hunting Grounds of the Great West.* London: Chatto & Windus, 1877.

Drago, Harry S. *Great American Cattle Trails*. Boston: Bramhall House, 1965.

Drago, Harry S. *Wild, Woolly and Wicked: The History of the Kansas Cow Towns*. New York: Clarkson N. Potter, 1960.

Emmet, Chris. *Shanghai Pierce: A Fair Likeness*. Norman: University of Oklahoma Press, 1953.

Gard, Wayne. *The Chisholm Trail*. Norman: University of Oklahoma Press, 1969.

Gipson, Fred. *Cowhand: The Story of the Working Cowboy*. New York: Harper and Brothers, 1948.

Haley, J. Evetts. *The XIT Ranch of Texas and the Early Days of the Llano Estacado*. Norman: University of Oklahoma Press, 1967.

Harper's Magazine. *The West: A Collection from Harper's Magazine*. New York: Gallery Books, 1990.

Hastings, Frank S. *The Story of the S.M.S. Ranch*. S.M.S. Ranch, 1919.

—— "A Ranchman's Recollections." *The Breeders Gazette*. Chicago, 1921.

Hough, Emerson. *The Story of the Cowboy*. New York: D. Appleton & Co., 1897.

—— *The Passing of the Frontier: A Chronicle of the Old West*. New Haven: Yale University Press, 1918.

Hunter, Marvin. *The Trail Drivers of Texas*. Dallas: The Southwest Press, 1925.

James, W.S. *Cow-Boy Life in Texas or 27 Years a Maverick*. Chicago: M.A. Donohue & Co., 1893.

James, Will. *Cowboys North and South*. New York: Grosset & Dunlap, 1923.

Kennedy, Michael S. *Cowboys and Cattlemen*. New York: Hastings House, 1964.

Linderman, Frank Bird. *Recollections of Charley Russell*. Norman: University of Oklahoma Press, 1963.

MacKay, Malcolm. *Cow Range and Hunting Trail*. New York: G.P. Putnam's Sons, 1925.

McCoy, Joseph G. *Historic Sketches of the Cattle Trade of the West and Southwest*. Glendale, California: Arthur H. Clark Co., 1940.

Osgood, E.S. *The Day of the Cattleman.* Minneapolis: The University of Minnesota Press, 1929.

Patterson, Paul. *Pecos Tales.* Austin: Texas Folklore Society, 1967.

Pelzer, Louis. *The Cattleman's Frontier: A Record of the Trans-Mississippi Cattle Industry, 1850–1890.* New York: Russell and Russell, 1969.

Post, Charles Clement. *The Years A Cowboy.* Chicago: Rhodes & McClure, 1888.

Rhodes, Eugene Manlove. *Good Men and True.* New York: Grosset & Dunlap, 1917.

Rollins, Philip Ashton. *The Cowboy.* New York: Charles Scribner's Sons, 1922.

Roosevelt, Theodore. *Ranch Life and the Hunting Trail.* New York: Century Co., 1888.

Santee, Ross. *Men and Horses.* New York: The Century Co., 1926.

Siringo, Charles A. *A Texas Cowboy, or Fifteen Years on the Hurricane Deck of a Spanish Pony.* Chicago: Umbdenstock and Co., 1885.

Slatta, Richard. *Cowboys of the Americas.* New Haven: Yale University Press, 1990.

Steedman, Charles. *Bucking the Sagebrush.* New York: G.P. Putnam's Sons, 1904.

Stegner, Wallace. *Wolf Willow.* New York: Viking Press, 1962.

Stuart, Granville. *Forty Years on the Frontier.* Glendale, California: Arthur H. Clark Co., 1967.

Von Richthoffen, Walter Baron. *Cattle-Raising on the Plains of North America.* New York: D. Appleton and Company, 1885.

Webb, Walter Prescott. *The Great Plains.* New York: Ginn and Co., 1931.

White, Stewart Edward. *Arizona Nights.* New York: The McClure Co., 1907.

Wister, Owen. *The Virginian.* New York: Macmillan Co., 1902.

anon. *Prose and Poetry of the Live Stock Industry of the United States.* Denver and Kansas City: National Live Stock Historical Association, 1904 and 1905.